SOUTHWELL'S

Jay Whitfield

For Sarah -
Best Wishes
Jay

Published in 2008 by |Youwriteon.com

Published by YouWriteOn.com

Jay Whitfield lives with her husband on a hillside in damp and beautiful West Wales and has been writing for fifteen years.

She also writes seasonal articles about life in rural West Wale for The Countryman magazine. A short story based on the 'ghosts' was also published in the internationally sold 'Scary Shorts for Halloween', Accent Press.

The ghost is 'true' but the story is pure fiction. Acknowledgements to Mark Urban's 'Rifles' and Pamela Horn's 'Life and Labour in Rural England 1760-1850.'

Most of all, thanks to her family, John, Mark and Vivi for their help and support.

CHAPTER ONE

By nine o'clock, with dusk setting in, Mary James was getting anxious.

'Drat the boy,' she muttered, stirring the rabbit stew in the large cooking pot. 'Ben should have been home long since. He's only gone to Banbury market with a cow. Tubbs the carter came back from there an hour ago. If that boy's spent all the money I'll…what can I do? He's twice the size of me. I'll go and look in The Ewe, perhaps he stopped in there? If he's spending my money treating that lot, well I really will clip his ear, in front of everyone.'

The more she muttered and thought of all the possibilities the angrier Mary became.

Ben's father had died the year before and he had had to grow up fast. When Verner became ill, in the space of two months everything changed. The horrible canker in his stomach that could only be appeased by copious amounts of brandy had mercifully killed him quickly. Mary realised immediately that she had to take charge of the farm and keep everything going if she was to have a home and a living for herself and her son.

In the evenings, by candlelight she talked to Verner, listening carefully as he told her of the work that had to be done month by month. Of what to do as the cows came into season and how to help with the calving.

The dairy had been her province and the cows and fieldwork left to the men. Verner had everything in his head. He had never learnt to read and write, growing up and working on the farm since he was a child.

Mary had had some learning at the dame school and could read and write enough to get by. Now as the brandy and laudanum took control of her husband's body, concentrating hard, she hurried to write down as much as she could. Of the wages paid to casual labourers, of prices to bargain for in the market and how much money to save for rent days.

Betty's sale in Banbury cattle market would pay for the thatcher to cover the hayricks. At sixpence a square foot, it would come to two or three pounds. That was what it was like, have something to sell to pay for something else. Ben would have to learn that. There'd be no pocket money for a month if he came back with an empty purse.

In the beginning they made a few mistakes and lost a calf in a bad calving. Mary had realised then how tight money would be and they could not afford many mistakes like that. So when the letter arrived from Mr Southwell asking about lodgings it had seemed like a very good idea. She determined to make him as comfortable as possible. It was no trouble to put a bit extra food in the pot and they would just have to hope he was a decent, respectable sort of man.

Robert Southwell was sitting by his bedroom window watching the bats swooping in and out of the trees. Moths attacked his candle flame and he blew it out. He went to the door, listened and stepped downstairs. Standing at the front door he saw Mary slip her black shawl round her shoulders as she walked across the yard and then hurry down the lane. She was going to the Ewe and Lamb to see if Ben was in there. He smiled ruefully, small as she was, she was quite capable of boxing her son's ears if he deserved it.

As the moon went behind a cloud Mary disappeared from view. Robert turned back thinking to have a tot of rum before bed. Perhaps he would offer Mary some, a thimble full, to see if she liked it. The next time he went to Banbury he would buy some good wine and Madeira for her to try. She might like it.

He went up to his room, shut the window and lit the candle. He took out his journal to record his success (eventually) with the butter making.

"23rd June 1801. Have been here for two months and am very settled. I churned the butter for the first time today. It took a while but the result was satisfactory. Mrs James will sell it in the market at Banbury on Friday."

Weekdays were not quite so busy in the alehouse, beer money had been spent at the weekend and you were lucky if Talbot gave you a pint on the slate. So when Mary put her head round the door the room was quiet. Talbot and Caleb Pound were playing dominoes. Two old men sitting by the fire nursed tankards, making their drinks last as long as possible.

'Has anyone seen Ben?'

'No, not since this morning, I saw him walking the cow along the Banbury road.' Caleb looked up.

Mary sighed. 'Where is he? I'm going to walk up the lane a way. Perhaps he stopped for a rest and fell asleep.' The men nodded and resumed their game with a click of tiles.

'Got you.' Talbot smacked down a tile.

Mary tugged her shawl tighter in the cool air as their voices faded behind her. She was now genuinely worried. This was the first time Ben had been entrusted with a sale on his own. Perhaps he'd been robbed and left for dead? The thought was too awful to contemplate.

Out of the village she entered the darkest part of the road. Trees met in a tunnel overhead with only the occasional gap to let the moonlight through. Rags of clouds blew across the full moon.

A terrific row from Watts' bleating sheep came from behind the hedge. She knew they had been shorn that day and the lambs would have difficulty recognising their mothers without the familiar coat of fleece. With that racket they'd be hearing it in the village she thought, glad of the hard, dry surface to walk on.

She shouted, 'Ben, Ben where are you.' But her voice was lost in the calls of a hundred ewes and lambs. At the end of the trees was dim moonlight, two hundred yards away. Oh Ben where are you? Her steps quickened and she nearly tripped. She was very anxious as she hastened along the Banbury road.

Robert went back downstairs with his drink and dozed in the chair, reluctant to go to bed whilst both Ben and Mary were out. When a log shifted in the fireplace and fell with a scatter of sparks it woke him. It was dark, with only the light from the fire. He stretched and frowned when he looked at his timepiece.

Mary had been gone a long time and Ben was very late, perhaps he'd gone to sleep somewhere, or fallen, drunk into a ditch.

He stood up stretching and yawning and moved to the window. The casement was

open and as he stood enjoying the fresh air he saw a man hurrying up the lane. Moonlight flooded the yard and Robert saw it was Caleb Pound from the village. What did he want?

Robert met Caleb in the doorway. 'What's to do? Where's Mary and Ben?' he asked without giving the big farm worker a moment to get his breath.

Caleb was puffing, rolling his cap in his hands, his face pale under a ruddy tan.

'Oh my, oh dear there's been such a dreadful accident, oh dear, dear me,' he was shocked, his eyes darting about, looking at the things in the kitchen. The pot of rabbit stew hung from the hook, keeping warm. The tasty smell permeated the air and wafted out the door.

'Beg pardon, I was in the Ewe and Lamb,' he gulped, 'Brown, the Byclere's coachman came rushing in.'

Robert started to feel a knot of dread uncoil itself in his head and slither down his spine like a snake waiting to strike.

'Ben?' he whispered.

'She's been killed, Mrs James, that is. It were the offside lead horse from Lord Byclere's coach caught her as she were flitting up the Banbury road. A right terrible knock it were and tossed her onto the stones. She didn't suffer. No, she didn't suffer. It took a few minutes to pull them horses up, a fast canter they were going and when his Lordship picks her up she were gone.'

'Wait here.' Robert commanded. There was only the dim light from the fire in the kitchen and he took down the thick white candle in its pewter holder. Taking a spill to the fire he lit the candle, watching until it burnt steadily. He tossed the spill back into the embers and then strode to the parlour and fetched his best brandy and two glasses. Pouring generous measures he handed one to Caleb who downed it in one.

'Thank'ee, it's a shock isn't it? What a tragedy, such a bonny, tidy little lady.'

Robert tipped his head back and drank, feeling molten fire slide down his throat and hit his chest. No, no he wanted to shout, it's more than that, it's the end of my stupid, stupid dreams. I've only known her for two months but I admire her so much and I hoped she would look kindly on me as a suitor.

His hand was shaking as he tried to concentrate on Caleb. 'Where's Ben in all this?'

'I don't know, he's not been seen.'

Robert refilled Caleb's glass. 'He took a cow to Banbury this morning, early.'

'I know, I saw him on my way to work. He would have been finished by dinner-time. Oh, he's probably drunk somewhere and it'd only take him an hour to walk back. Thing is, they took her to the Ewe and Talbot's laid her up in their spare bedroom. Everyone knows her like so she don't need to be identified and Eve will lay her out.' He sniffed, swaying slightly. 'Joe Armstrong will fix her up with a nice coffin, real pretty like tomorrow.'

Robert shook his head. 'Can they bring her back in the afternoon, later. I'll get the parlour ready?'

Caleb looked at Robert Southwell, the man seemed calm but there was a nervous tic in his cheek and his hands shook.

'I'll tell them and my Marjie can come up and help.' He pushed his glass to the middle of the table anxious to be off. Death was part of their lives but happening like this...well it was a shock. The brandy had gone to his head. He stumbled across the yard anxious for the reassuring presence of his plump wife.

Robert looked down at the table marred by a spilt ring of brandy. On Mary's kitchen table. Hurriedly he fetched a cloth and carefully wiped it. Just as carefully he took the cloth back to the scullery, folded it in four and laid it by her water pail. He walked back into the kitchen and the smell of rabbit stew suddenly nauseated him. With the square of thick, old blanket that she used he took the pot off the hook and ran out to the scullery door. He flung it across the yard and heard a clatter as it hit the stones. He never wanted another rabbit in the house.

He walked back into the kitchen and looked around at all the familiar things. With everything tidy as usual, he went to bed, but left the door unlatched. Ben would turn up with a sore head.

Robert got undressed and put his nightshirt on. He sat by the window, with tears streaming down his face. Nothing seemed to mean anything anymore. If he'd only stopped Mary going at that particular time, she could be alive now. In the few seconds it took to say, what a fine evening or can I help you with the butter in the morning. She would have stopped, spoken and they would still have the possibility of a future together. He sniffed and rubbed at his eyes with a rag. He hadn't cried since he was a small child but he'd never felt like this before. Of course, she might not have cared for him, but she certainly seemed to enjoy his company.

To have the chance of happiness at his age and now it was snatched away. He got into bed and shivered. He must get up at five to get the cows in for milking and help Ben as much as possible.

The healing sleep of exhaustion claimed him and he slept on alone in the house. A golden crescent of moon shone through the window on its way across the heavens. A beam of silver light travelled across the gaily patterned bed cover. A mouse scuttled in the wainscoting, on its nightly foray for food. Full up with rabbit stew, the cat padded softly along the passage, its whiskers twitching as it tracked the mouse. Robert slept, the brandy dulling his mind and shutting the door to dreams and nightmares.

CHAPTER TWO

At five in the morning Robert scrambled into his old clothes and thought longingly of hot coffee to clear his mind groggy with sleep and brandy. He didn't dare stop and hurried down the passage to Ben's room. He knocked and put his head round the door. The bed hadn't been slept in and as usual his clothes were in an untidy heap on the floor. He strode to the window and opened it to rid the room of the smell of stale sweat. He'd give Ben a piece of his mind when he did come home, with his tail between his legs no doubt.

Avoiding the kitchen he hurried to the yard. Splashing his face with cold water woke him up instantly and he cupped his hands and drank.

'Right, first things first, I must get the cows in.' He muttered to himself as he hurried to the small meadow. This was the field the cows used at night. In the day they would go further to different pasture. They took themselves in, well used to the routine. The buckets were in a tidy row from the night before. He fetched water to wipe the udders and received a kick for his pains as he swabbed down Bertha's full pink bag. He realised then that he should have used warm water. He gave her another scoop of oats to keep her busy and ran into the house for the hot kettle hanging on the hook.

The fire was down to embers and he swore, cursing, as he knew he had forgotten to go in and put logs on. He stirred the grey ashes with the metal poker and threw apple logs on, grateful for Mary's routine of always having wood drying by the fireplace. He made a mental note to bring in more wood and also feed the cat.

As he hurried back with the kettle he saw Caleb Pound striding briskly up the lane towards him.

'Mornin, sir.' Caleb was terse.

'Mornin.' Robert equally so, their breath puffed gently in the fresh moist air.

'Calloway, he's Byclere's Steward says to give you a hand, so I'll start with the milking. I had a message five minutes since on my way out.'

'I can't say I won't be grateful. I'm slow, my fingers aren't used to it yet.'

'We'll work together, get them girls sorted and then see what's to do.'

With two of them milking, they were finished by eight o'clock and the buckets taken to the dairy. Caleb took the cows back up the lane to their day pasture. The Dairy Shorthorns had been a bit restless, not caring for different hands and voices. Robert remembered how Mary used to sing to them. He wasn't in the mood for a lullaby so he had talked to them in a low voice. He told them how he would look after them as best he could until he knew what would happen. Caleb was strictly business-like, the cows obviously knew when a professional was at their udders.

Afterwards. the two men sat at the table, shirtsleeves rolled up, with mugs of steaming coffee and plates piled with fried bacon and bread. Caleb sipped noisily and helped himself to more of the precious Demerara sugar. Robert didn't flinch as two huge spoonfuls were tipped in and stirred. He made a mental note to put a teaspoon out next time and then chided himself for meanness.

'So you reckon you'll be all right with the dairy work? Margie can come up later and give you a hand.' Fat dribbled down Caleb's chin and he rubbed it off with his sleeve.

Robert replied slowly, 'I'll start with the cheese turning whilst the milk scalds. I think I'd be glad of a hand with the churning. Surely Ben will be home soon. Has he ever done this before?'

'Stayed away you mean?' Caleb shook his head. 'I haven't heard, but these young lads, they like the drink and the girls.'

As soon as they'd finished both men stood up and took their plates and mugs to the scullery.

Caleb's hobnailed boots rang on the cobbled yard as he walked to the dairy, but Robert had taken a cloth back to Mary's kitchen table and wiped it as clean as he knew she would have done. He took a few seconds to check the state of the kitchen, the kettle of water and the fireplace. It had become important to keep everything as clean and tidy as Mary had done, ship shape Robert told himself grimly.

The cat was fast asleep on her warm spot on the inglenook. Robert frowned, something was missing. Returning from the yard with the cooking pot he filled it with water and left it by the hearth to be cleaned later.

They worked hard outside until after twelve when Caleb asked Robert if he wanted to go down to the Ewe and Lamb for a bite and wet his whistle.

Anxiously Robert rubbed his chin, realising that he hadn't shaved that morning.

'When I've eaten all the bread I'll have to buy some, won't? I. I can't bake. I'm not sure about the soups and stews that Mary made, they were all so tasty.'

He made up his mind. 'I'll have the bread and cheese for now and with Ben home I'll buy bread in and we'll cook some bacon. There's plenty in the larder. Can I pay you for this morning, Caleb?'

'I'm on Byclere's pay, but I'll have a drink with you another day.' He swung round and strode off calling over his shoulder, 'I'll be back at five.'

Surely Ben would be home by then, or they would have heard something.

Robert sat at the kitchen table eating his bread and cheese. He didn't feel like onions and it was dry and tasteless in his mouth but he knew he needed to eat to keep going. The kitchen was so quiet that only the ticking clock in the parlour could be heard. After every single crumb had been cleared and the floor swept he knew he could delay no longer. He must arrange the parlour for Mary's coffin.

With beeswax polish on a rag he polished every inch of furniture until his arm ached. What a lot had happened in the last months he mused remembering how he had fetched up at the farm.

England was under the threat of invasion. Thousands of Napoleon's troops were encamped across the English channel at Bologne and only thirty miles of sea separated England and France: that and predatory Admiral Lord Nelson, poking a cheeky finger at them. The Royal Navy were blockading Toulon and patrolling all along the coast but he had turned his back on the sea.

His Navy service had finished with a sniper's bullet through the side of his shoulder at the Battle of Copenhagen. The Celeste had taken her time to sail back to Portsmouth. He had spent a few days at Haslar Hospital. The conditions were unpleasant, it was overcrowded, smelly and noisy. He knew he had to get out of there so he took a coach to London and booked into a boarding house. The landlady found him a decent, clean woman to be his nurse and change the dressings. Once he felt better he decided to make the journey to Oxfordshire.

He had left Abingdon at dawn, with a cool mist rising up from the fields. Ghostly cows, their bodies concealed in cotton wool mist calmly chewed as they stared after them. The Mail coach didn't run through his destination and for sixpence, a miller's cart had seemed the quickest alternative. Unlike the carter he hadn't had the luxury of a folded flour sack to sit on. But also he wouldn't have the imprint of the Hessian sack across the seat of his breeches, the squares neatly filled in with puffs of flour.

The road was quiet and the carter, who said his name was Geoffrey had told Robert of the scenes earlier.

'I'm on my own now the cart's empty but I had an armed guard to get me into Abingdon,' he grumbled. 'There was a mob in the town square, waiting for the flour. There're all up in arms about the price of wheat and the shortages.'

'I suppose I've been cushioned from all this,' mused Robert. 'I was in Portsmouth in the hospital and then in London and there seemed to be plenty of food there.'

'Aye,' said Geoffrey, 'but you see, the country folks don't want their food sent to the town where they'll pay more money for it. It belongs here, where the corn was grown.'

'I hadn't thought of that before.' Robert never knew the source of the food he had eaten. Even on board ship, counting barrels and sacks he hadn't looked beyond their quantity and quality. That was up to the merchants in the ports.

'We're hungry,' Geoffrey complained. 'Us common folk, it's getting bad. We need a good harvest this year and a mild winter to put us back on track. We've had three bad years, I don't know how you hadn't heard.'

'Well, I've been at sea.'

'I don't mean that I'm actually starving,' explained Geoffrey, 'but my wife and the children, we've had to cut back. I'm in the business so to speak,' he confided. 'I know where I can lay my hands on a sack or two of corn, but when I takes it to the mill, well the miller wants to know where I got it. And then he wants a share, so I end up with only half a sack by the time they've all had their bit.'

'I suppose everyone is affected by this then?'

The carter slowed to negotiate a bridge. 'Everyone,' he said emphatically, 'except the wealthy…and they don't care.'

As they journeyed on through the peaceful rural scene Robert reflected on the changes. He was finished with the Navy, 'on the beach' as they said. He was on his way to a farm with his pension and savings. The Navy Board that were in charge of the Chatham Chest, the fund for injured sailors, had agreed a small pension. Five pence a day was very little and would not have been enough but he had the prize money and the pay that he had saved.

As a purser he had had more than the ordinary seaman's share of prize money. The Captain of Celeste had been a bold, adventurous sort. They had captured three French ships, the last a gun brig in 1797. Robert had bought a new long case clock with his share of that prize money. He hoped that invested wisely, the savings would be enough to see him out. His wound would heal and he would make a new life for himself.

He had never married. Robert had never met anyone he wished to spend his life with. Also, he had never thought it fair to marry a girl, make her pregnant and then leave to go on long voyages. A faithful Navy wife could have a lonely life.

They passed through quiet villages and hamlets and Robert realised that the carter was right. All was not well in the countryside. Women and children working in the fields looked up sullenly as their cart passed. For the first time he wondered if it would have been better to settle by the sea.

An hour later Robert stepped stiffly down from the carter's wagon and stood, swaying with fatigue. His sea chest was dumped unceremoniously on the ground in front of the track that led to Appley Glebe farmhouse. The clock would come on later, delivered by carriage. Various bundles were thrown down to land in the dirt.

'Hup, hup,' shouted the carter and flicked his whip leaving Robert to stand in a cloud of white dust. He looked around. At three o'clock in the afternoon all was quiet and the narrow village street was deserted. He could see a butcher's shop and a forge all built in the local, pale gold Cotswold stone. Behind was the alehouse, with its sign The Ewe and Lamb and a white sheep of the Down breed with a small, skipping lamb. But the paint had cracked and the ewe had lost her ears.

In front was a fifty-yard track with a stone farmhouse placed squarely at the end. Blue smoke drifted from a tall chimney, the thatch was tidy and it looked well cared for. It was all ship-shape he noted satisfactorily. A large barn to the left had huge wooden doors open wide. As he stooped to pick up a bundle a woman stepped from the house and waved to him.

He heard the call, 'Ben...Ben...here. He's here.' It must be Mrs James and he straightened up, smoothing down his grubby coat. A tall young man lolloped steadily behind the woman and together they reached him.

He held out his hand, 'Mrs James?'

'Mr Southwell, how are you? It's good to see you. Have you had a good journey? Let Ben here carry that big chest in.' All said without stopping for a breath. Robert saw a tidy, small lady, with a loud voice, a sweet smile and the merriest brown eyes the colour of shiny chestnuts.

Ben hefted the chest up onto his shoulder easily. Mrs James picked up three of the bundles as if they were feathers and left Robert with two. Feeling shy he followed them to the black front door and up the highly polished wooden staircase.

'Now we'll show you to your room and Ben'll put the chest in there and you can unpack at your convenience. I'll bring up some water for you to wash, if you'd like that is and there'll be a dish of tea for you as soon as the kettle boils, which'll be two shakes of a lamb's tail.

Ben go on you big lummock and let Mr Southwell get his breath. If there's anything else you require you just say. On behalf of us here at Appley Glebe I'll say welcome and we hope's you'll be very happy with us. Now I'll go and put that kettle over.'

All this time she'd been patting the already immaculate bed with its gleaming white pillows and boldly patterned patchwork cover, tweaking a corner here and a fringe there. There was a linen towel placed on a hard Windsor chair.

A small, highly polished oak table was under the window and he walked to it, looking out, hardly able to believe that he was there. The shutters were pushed wide and he breathed in the warm air scented with early honeysuckle. There had been no rain for a month and the land was baking dry.

The view was of fields and the back yard with a washing line and the privy to one side. He wanted nothing more than to fall on the bed and sleep until morning but it was too immaculate, it required a clean nightshirt and a washed body.

CHAPTER THREE

· Using Mary's beeswax polish Robert rubbed the furniture in the parlour until it all gleamed and his arm ached. He turned with a start as a voice spoke.

'My, it looks grand in here, she'd be pleased with this.' Margie Pound waved a podgy arm round the room.

'Do you think so,' he was pathetically glad. 'I'm not used to this, in the Navy we had a servant to do all this sort of work. What else shall I do?'

'Well, we'll just move the table, like this,' she pushed it. 'Then those that want can come in and walk round.'

Hesitantly he asked, 'Do you know what time she's coming back?'

'About one, I think, Joe had a box in stock but it were too big, so he's made a special one. Lovely bit of oak he said it was, and he'll line it, really nice. It's not my business but there'll be money to pay for it?' Her eyebrows lifted, questioning.

'Oh, I'll take care of that.' Robert was firm.

Margie stared at him. He'd only been here two minutes and paying for a funeral! She'd heard of the luxuries of coffee and soap so she supposed he had plenty of money.

Robert cleaned himself up, changed his shirt and breeches and went out to pick flowers for the parlour. He kept an eye on the lane and waited with dread to see the wagon with the coffin that would mean that Mary, his Mary was really, actually dead. He knew she was but couldn't let go of the tiny, tiny thought that it was all a horrible mistake.

They had put a black horse in the shafts. A man Robert didn't know was seated high up driving the borrowed farm cart. Caleb and Joe the Carpenter walked solemnly behind with some of the village women. A blackbird sang sweetly in the hedge and white clouds scudded slowly across in a gentle south westerly breeze. Robert had the silly thought that Mary would have had washing on the line with weather like that. The knowledge that out of modesty she would hide her under garments amongst the shirts and sheets failed to amuse him as it used to.

The coffin was handled with care and placed on the table. The lid was taken off and the pennies removed from her eyes.

'She don't need them no more,' whispered Margie, gently tucking frills in and smoothing down the white linen.

Robert forced himself to look. She was so serene. There were no marks on her face, no lines, nothing. 'Did she hit her head as she fell?'

'Aye, there's a terrible bruise and lump on the back of her head. She fell on a sharp flint. No one's going to survive that.' Joe ran his finger professionally along the smooth oak.

Robert saw the movement and said in an undertone. 'Send me the account, I'll pay for everything.' Joe nodded.

As twilight faded into night, an exhausted Robert sat by Mary. The honeysuckle and wild roses in their china vase smelt sweetly. He had lit candles and they burned strongly with the shutters shut against moths and draughts. Edging closer, he took hold of her hand and ran his thumb along from her wrist to her fingertips.

'Mary there are things to tell you. Ben has gone and enlisted. He wants to be a soldier with Sir Arthur Wellesley and it's my fault. I should never have told him those stories of the fighting and glory. I could see it in his eyes, dreams of red coats and rifles, shiny brass and guns. It'll be nothing but death and a pile of stones in a distant land. I'm sorry Mary, so sorry.' He rubbed his eyes. 'He was seen him in Banbury. The 95th Regiment were there enlisting. They want the country boys who can live off the land and become good shots. He kept the money from selling Betty and your savings money from the china pot have gone. Caleb Pound has been good today helping but I'm not sure what will happen. I'll look after your cows as best I can.'

He drained his beaker of rum and stood looking down at her. She was wearing a small bonnet, edged with lace, her nut brown hair had been brushed loose and streamed down over her shoulders. He took a lock in his fingers and twined it round feeling the silky softness of it. It smelt of the rosewater she always used.

An idea took hold and shaking his head Robert went to the front door and locked it. Going back to the parlour he reached into the coffin and picked her up. She was an unyielding, solid weight and her hair trailed down over his arm. The hem of her nightdress dragged on the floor. The eyes remained shut. Carefully, slowly he made his way upstairs and pushed open the door of her bedroom with his foot. He placed her on the bed.

He sat to unlace his boots and then gingerly lay down beside her. As he shut his mind to the incongruity of it he placed his warm hand over her icy cold one. Robert pulled the quilt over them both, turned on his side to face her and holding her hand sank into a deep dreamless sleep.

He woke with the dawn chorus and lay for a moment feeling strange and slightly disorientated. He was lying on his back, with his clothes on, in a strange bed. The window was open and fresh air touched his nostrils. The dawn sky was pearly grey tinged with pink and cream and memories of yesterday came flooding back. He turned his head and was horrified to see Mary's corpse lying beside him. One arm was placed neatly on her breast and the other next to him was flung out as if in entreaty.

'Oh my God, what have I done?' he muttered distractedly. He sat up and reached for his boots, lacing them quickly. Turning back to the bed he tried to put the arm back but it was locked in rigor mortis. 'Oh dear, I must put her back straight away.'

He scooped her up and hurried downstairs. Placing her in the coffin he tidied her hair, marvelling again at the lustrous beauty of it. He had never seen it loose before as she had always worn a bonnet or had it up in plaits. Using strength he tried to shift the arm across and slowly forced it, bending it at the elbow. It made a strange cracking noise as he gave a tug and his blood ran cold as he realised that he must have broken it. Hurriedly he placed the hands together with a dethorned rose tucked in the fingers and bent and said a final farewell.

As he placed his lips to her cheek he caught the first whiff of corruption. In the heat of summer a body must be buried promptly and the funeral was to be at half past three. The neighbours would be coming in so he must hurry and get as much work done as possible.

Caleb Pound, the tall, brawny farm labourer was like a rock for him. Always there, steady, working calmly and without orders and knowing (more than Robert) what needed to be done. They had shared coffee and honey toast after milking and Caleb had joked holding up his mug, that he could get a taste for it. Whereupon Robert had got up, gone to his coffee jar full with ground beans and handed it to Caleb.

'Please take it, enjoy it, I would have had trouble managing without you.'

Caleb handed it back, him and Margie weren't used to such luxuries. 'Calloway wouldn't have let you manage on your own, knowing you're new to it.'

'Well anyway, can you tell him I could do with you for a few more days until affairs are sorted.'

'Oh yes, there's a note in me pocket for you.' Caleb handed over a sealed missive.

Robert quickly slit the paper. *"I will be over to see you on Friday 26th July at two o'clock. John Calloway, Steward, Byclere Estate."*

He looked at Caleb, 'He's coming to see me on Friday. Right,' he was brisk, clearing the table. 'Let's get the dairy work over and then Margie can tell me what's to be done for the visitors.'

Leaving Caleb to finish in the dairy later he rushed inside, took the bucket of water from the scullery, the kettle from the hearth and hurried upstairs to wash, shave and change.

As he sat by the window scraping off two day's beard he glanced at his smoothly unslept bed and realised that he hadn't straightened Mary's bed from the night before. What if Margie went in there for something?

With his face half lathered, in clean trousers and a bare chest, he ran to the bedroom. Feeling like an intruder he opened the door and saw the patchwork quilt tossed across the bed. As he tugged it neatly in place, a glistening blob of lather fell off his chin onto a red square. He scooped if off in distress and rubbed his fingers over the damp patch. Shaking his head in dismay at his behaviour he hurried back to finish his ablutions.

CHAPTER FOUR

The funeral service passed smoothly and he sang the hymns he'd known from childhood.

Robert kept in the background, he was a newcomer, neither villager nor relative. As he watched from the back of the church yard he remembered his first afternoon at Appley Glebe farm and Mary and Ben.

Ben had dumped his chest on the floor of the bedroom.

'Thank you.'

He got a shy smile from a weather reddened face and a touched forelock of blonde hair.

'Come down, Ben,' floated up and the big lad turned to the door. Robert heard the thud of his boots hitting the wooden stairs. Carefully he sat down and pulled his shoes off. How he longed for a bath. In his stockinged feet he padded over to the chest, unlocked it and found his house shoes. There was a knock and Ben was there again with a bucket of water.

'Mother thought you'd like this.' He poured some in the washbowl on the table and left the bucket on the floor. 'She says ten minutes, and there'll be tea and bread and honey if that's all right until supper.'

'Say thank you, that's excellent.'

He found his wash bag in the leather valise and rinsed his hands and face. Stripping off his shirt he washed his arms and chest and started to feel fresher. Finally he sat on the chair and put his bare feet, one at a time into the cool water. The soap and dust made it scummy but he managed to swish them around in the bucket to avoid putting dirty marks on the pristine white towel..

Mindful of the open window he stripped off his grey cord breeches and white linen underdrawers and rubbed himself over with a rag.

He had always been a clean, fastidious man and was pleased to see that Mrs James obviously kept everything smart as paint.

With fresh clothes from the chest and his hair brushed and tied back with a new black ribbon he stepped out on to the landing to find his way downstairs. He looked round curiously. Three doors opened off from the passage and a tiny door at the end probably went up into the roof. He followed his nose downstairs to the kitchen.

'Come in, come in do,' she was brisk. 'Ben, move that chair. Ben, get some more wood in. Mr Southwell, do sit down.'

He sat at a well scrubbed table in front of a large fireplace. In spite of the warm summer day there was a long log of oak burning. A large cauldron hung from a hook and he caught the waft of savoury steam. A blue and white bowl of steaming tea was placed in front of him. There was a plate of bread and a pottery jar with a spoon. A jug of milk was placed by his tea.

'Now you help yourself. Mrs James watched proudly as her new lodger poured a dab of milk into his tea and took a sip.

'Lovely, Mrs James, just what I've been looking forward to.' It was quite weak but deliciously refreshing. He had a sack of coffee beans in his bag and tomorrow he would show her how he liked it ground up and brewed.

'Now you help yourself to the bread. I made it this morning. That's our own butter churned yesterday and the honey is last years', but none the worse for that. The bees are working hard on this year's crop.' She laughed.

She was all the time whisking around, a wipe here and a flick there. Even the cat was picked up, had its warm patch on the inglenook wiped and got dumped back down again. It looked disgruntled for a minute and then started washing its face.

Robert bit into the crusty bread. There was no plate, so he had helped himself, spread on butter the colour of primroses and drizzled the golden honey over. He was too down to earth to be lyrical about anything but the honey had the most beautiful flavour of summer. He couldn't have named all the flowers that had given their pollen to its delicate taste. How he would enjoy watching the bees at work.

The monotonous shipboard fare of biscuit, salt pork and peas was something to be endured. Food like this was but a dream.

Carefully he wiped his fingers on a rag from his pocket and took hold of the obviously precious bowl. He looked up and caught Mrs James beaming at him.

When the bowl was safely back on the table again he cleared his throat. 'That was delicious. You make excellent bread Mrs James.'

'Thank you, sir, I make it two or three times a week. We're getting low on flour, so we hopes there'll be an early harvest. We could do with a drop of rain now. Ben's a big lad; he needs a lot of filling. Now, if you've finished I'll clear away and perhaps you'd like a sit in the parlour.' The table was cleared in seconds and wiped clean before he'd hardly risen from the chair. What a busy lady she was.

He felt revived and decided to take a step outside and look around. He heard a click of boot nails and saw Ben walking to the corner of the yard. Mrs James came behind him.

'Ben's going to get the cows in to start milking. You can watch from there. He has to start now to get done by supper.' She had on a large white apron and a white bonnet tied under the chin covered her hair. 'I'm in the dairy, starting the butter.'

He followed her to a room at the end of the house. The flagstones felt cool and a net covered window gave a dim light. The walls were whitewashed and stacked with shelves. Round cheeses were placed along. A large, scrubbed table was in the centre. Various pottery bowls were covered with muslin. There was a lingering smell of milk, with the sharper tone of salty cheese.

It was good to stretch his legs and he strolled round and poked his head in the barn. A small cart was parked inside with horse tackle hanging up. A large hay wagon was in the rick yard. He walked through to the door at the other side and saw the cows ambling slowly behind Ben up to the gate. He moved to open it for them and then thought better of it.

'Shall I open this and let them through?' He stood with his hand on the catch wondering if there was a bull anywhere and would it be dangerous?

Ben had a peeled hazel wand and was swishing at flies and slapping cows' rumps. A cloud of gnats hovered.

'Yes, sir if you please, they know where to go.'

Robert watched as they filed through in strict order and moved to an open door at the end of the barn. Ben shut the gate and followed the cows in.

He stood inside and watched as Ben slipped a halter over a cow's neck and rubbed her udder with a damp rag. He pulled a stool underneath him and sat down with his head pressed into the cow's flank. His large fingers were soon busy stripping down the milk, squirting a steaming white jet into the bucket.

'How many cows do you have, Ben?'

'We've got eight and three calves.' He replied proudly. He finished, moved the bucket out of the line of the back hooves and slapped her on the rump.

'Caroline.' He called and Robert watched as another grey and white marled cow detached from the herd and walked in.

'They know their names. What sort are they?'

'Aye, they've all got their place, youngest at the back. 'They're shorthorns, good for the milk.'

'You're very quick,' said Robert.

Ben grinned, I've been milking since I were about ten, it's a knack, it soon comes.'

Robert was fascinated, not that he'd ever thought about the working of a dairy herd before. It was all such a change.

As the three of them sat at the kitchen table later, (he had refused to be on his own in the parlour) he remembered to ask about a local doctor. He felt full to bursting with the most delicious rabbit and bacon stew cooked with onions, stored from last autumn. He mopped up his plate with a herb dumpling and soaked up every drop of the delicious gravy. A jug of ale was placed on the table and they all helped themselves. The table was wiped clean again with just his pewter tankard left and he poured carefully to avoid drips. In spite of the bright evening he decided to go to bed early, his fatigue and the ale had conspired to make him feel very sleepy.

'Is there a doctor locally?' He sipped, relishing the amber brew.

Mrs James stopped and looked at him. 'Doctor Mann is three mile, over beyond Byclere, was it something urgent?'

'I need to get my wound looked over. I still have a dressing on it and I can't manage it myself.'

'Oh bless you, I can do that. I've got the salves and tinctures for most problems. We have to in the country. Doctors cost money.'

'Well if you're sure. I've got bandages for it.'

'When would you like me to do it?'

'Could we leave it until the morning? I'm a bit tired, I think I'll go to bed.'

'Of course, yes, I'll bring up some water for you.'

'No, no please don't.' Robert couldn't face any more washing. He wanted to strip off, don a clean nightshirt and carefully get into bed.

He pulled the shutters half closed and breathed deeply of the cooling air. Birds sang their evening calls and he muttered a brief prayer of thanks for arriving safely at Appley Glebe. His clothes were placed neatly on the chair, the buckled shoes side by side underneath and with a sigh of relief he pulled back the covers. The linen was cool, the pillow felt lumpy and he shook the feathers about a bit. But after years spent sleeping in a hanging cot in a tiny cabin on board ship it was the utmost luxury. He fell asleep in seconds.

He woke with the dawn chorus, feeling vaguely disorientated. There were no bells, no sound of bare feet padding on the deck, no muffled curses and no sound of water slapping against the hull. Just the song birds with their morning calls. As he lay quietly he heard a door opening, a brisk footfall, a latch clicked and Mrs James's voice, 'Ben, get up, it's half past five.'

Robert stretched luxuriously but then felt his wound pull and knew it was overdue for a dressing. He hoped she knew what she was doing. He didn't want to hurt her feelings. They didn't have much in the way of salves and potions on board ship, but their surgeon had been excellent. Robert had the musket ball wrapped up in a handkerchief.

With a feeling of urgency he knew he would have to get dressed quickly and shave later. He needed to relieve himself. He felt shy of using the pretty flowery chamber pot that was placed under the bed, so a trip to the privy was imperative. He could pass from the stairs through the scullery to outside without going through the kitchen. Within minutes he was standing in the little wooden shed, with the door firmly closed.

He had spotted the pump handle by the well the previous night, with a water tank and bucket underneath. Not wishing to contaminate drinking water he pushed the iron handle up and down, until the water gushed. It was icy cold but refreshing on his hands and face. He shook himself free of drops and walked across the cobbled yard back to the kitchen. He had a terrible craving for coffee, his one weakness.

Half an hour later after a lesson in grinding beans and how much to put in the coffee pot, Robert sat at the kitchen table with a thick buttered slice of bread, a large slice of pink ham and his beaker of coffee. He sipped appreciatively. It was extra delicious with the new creamy milk and he insisted Mrs James join him. She refused to sit down with him, but had poured herself a small cup. She had to admit it tasted good.

'It's very expensive in Banbury, we can only buy a small packet of tea and that's over a shilling a quarter pound.' She had brought in some butter to cut up and pack for taking to the market.

'It's my one luxury and something I can't live without. H sat back content to watch her. It was still only half seven in the morning. He had all day to find his bearings and look around. What pleasure!

He insisted on carrying the hot water upstairs to shave with. First of all he took his shirt off and washed with soap, mindful of the lady's sensibilities. He was used to living in a men's world. It was always rough and certainly with no pretensions to comfort, hygiene or smells.

He didn't think it would be seemly for her to be upstairs in his bedroom with him undressed to the waist. so he carried his clean bandage downstairs and sat down at the table.   She was business like with her cool fingers gently taking off the dressing and tracing the length of the wound.   The stitches had been taken out at Greenwich, but the wound was of a depth and length that needed attention.

'I can put some marigold salve on this, that's very good for healing.   It's a little bit red and puffy but it seems to be healing well.'   Mary wiped round the wound with warm water and a clean rag, inhaling his smell of soap, an unheard of luxury in Appley. She had only seen such toiletries when she worked as an under maid for a few years at Byclere House and seen what the gentry used. Mr Southwell must have a lot of money. Coffee and soap!

She wondered if she should charge him more for his lodging, but then he might go elsewhere.   To the Ewe and Lamb and they were quite a rough crowd.

She smoothed the salve on, covered the wound with a clean square and then wound the bandage round.   This involved some ducking and bending.   She was mindful that he was a half naked man, a stranger in her house and she was a widow.   But she was also a farmer now, used to procreation, birth and death.   Much more so since Verner had died.   She deftly tied off the bandage and handed him the shirt.

'Thank you Mrs James, I must pay you, if I'm not paying the doctor.'

'Get on with you, I'm used to injuries, they come here from the village.   I'm nearer and cheaper than the doctor.'

Robert shrugged into his jacket glad that that was done.   He was looking forward to a good walk out in the lanes.   Another day he wanted to go up onto the Oxfordshire downs and he also wanted to see what Ben was doing.   He had decided that he would like to help on the farm, if there was something a real amateur could do.

He kept a journal and after their evening supper he retired to his room, opened wide the shutters and gazed out at the dusk. Long eared bats swooped across snapping up the moths with the background call of the nightingale on the barn roof, singing its heart out.

CHAPTER FIVE

On the afternoon of the funeral he waited by the hedge in the churchyard, the sun hot on his bare head, his hat held loosely in his hands and vowed to keep the grave tidy. Mary's coffin had been placed on top of her husband's and her name would be added on to the James's headstone. It would be a respectable grave if or when Ben came home.

As he walked out of the lych gate he saw a pile of rags by the wall. It moved and a woman's face, pale and haggard looked at him. She cringed from him and he was horrified to see she had a small baby tucked in the crook of her arm.

'Please, sir does you have a penny or two for me?'

Robert felt in his pocket, he had more than that, but then had an idea. 'When the funeral is over, come down that track, wait in the barn and I'll bring you out some food.'

'Oh, thank you, sir. Thank you.' Her eyes were pathetically grateful.

Robert had been introduced to Mary's sister, Dorothy that morning. As the mourners filed into the farmhouse Dorothy and Margie took charge of the funeral tea. Neighbours had brought in food and he had given Margie five shillings to buy extra ale, bread, pies, buns and cakes that were now spread out on the best tablecloth. There was ale for the men and tea or elderflower cordial for the ladies. He had had no hot dinner as there was nothing to cook to make a stew. He had made do with a slice of bread and cheese. Coffee with plenty of sugar had kept him going.

Now he looked at the food and felt sick. What madness had made him sleep with a corpse last night? He sighed, it was his secret and with the coffin under the ground no one would know he had broken Mary's arm when he put her back. He took a plate and two pasties and took them out to the pantry to warm up after milking, when everyone had gone.

He hadn't taken to the Rector. The man smelt strongly of spirits but Robert quietly passed him a guinea for the funeral charge. The gravedigger would get sixpence and the rest would probably go in brandy but he didn't care, it wasn't his business. The sister had no money, it would have been a poor showing without his largesse.

Several people asked him what he was going to do now and if he knew what was going to happen to the farm. He could only tell them that he was seeing Calloway on Friday.

When most of the food had gone he piled scraps and crusts of bread onto a dish and with a jug of milk and an old beaker went out to the barn. The woman was sitting on the side of the cart.

Defensively she said, 'You told us to come.'

'Yes, yes, here, I'm sorry it's only leavings but there's milk as well.'

She grabbed the plate and stuffed pastry flecked with ham into her mouth. Robert watched her.

The baby mewed weakly.

'Can it have milk?' He ventured.

'Yes, I'll make it some pap with a bit of bread.'

'Shall I get you a bowl?'

'All right.' She mumbled.

Robert went back into the house and fetched an old bowl from the scullery. On impulse he asked Margie if there were any old rags or clothes that the woman could have.

'What you doing, Mr Southwell? You don't want to encourage these paupers. On the road they be, you'll never get rid of her.'

'Margie, she's got a baby, it's starving and there's all this food here.'

'Well, Mary had a rag bag over there, cows wipes and things, take a bit of that for the baby, if you must.'

Robert sorted through and found some holey muslin, some patched linen and a threadbare shirt of Bens, very stained but clean. Perhaps the woman could make use of it. He tied it into a bundle and went back to the barn.

The woman was still eating, gnawing at a crust. He gave her the bowl and watched as she broke up a crust and poured milk on top. With a filthy finger she poked it about.

'There's some rags here if you could do with them for the baby and an old shirt if it's any good? Why are you on the road?'

She spoke with her mouth full. 'My man died of the cholera a month ago. The farmer threw us out after the funeral. He had a new cowman coming in straight away. I'm trying to get to my sister in Banbury, she won't want us but I've nowhere else to go. You're the first one to help us. You'd think we'd got the plague the way we've been hounded out of the villages. They don't want us dying on their ground 'cos they'd have to pay for the burying.' She sounded bitter.

'Didn't you have any money?'

'I sold our bits of furniture to buy food, then my bundle of clothes was stolen when we was asleep in a barn. A shilling I've had to pay for a yesterday's loaf. Milk's tuppence a quart and don't go nowhere with Sammy here. I had to keep my best skirt for arriving at Alice's and now...I's got nothing.'

With the spoon she fed the baby who gulped it down greedily.

Robert, who was so fastidious, wrinkled his nose at their unwashed smell, the baby stank.

'Um, shall I bring out a bucket of warm water and you can wash him? This isn't really my place but I'll let you stay the night in here. Keep your head down and in the morning you must go. I'll give you some money for the rest of the journey.'

'Why are you doing this?' she asked suspiciously.

'Charity begins at home. I saw a lot of injured soldiers and sailors making their way along the road. I feel for them too, and no one wants them. There's no jobs for them after all they've given for their country. I'll come out with the water when everyone's gone home.'

Leaving the women to clear up, he slipped out to be by himself in the empty cowshed. Sitting on a pile of wood he rubbed his chin in perplexity, thinking of the future. He didn't want the farm to go to strangers. He wanted to keep it available for Ben when he came home. He had to believe the lad would be all right but reason told him it was more than likely he would be killed and he was tortured by the knowledge it was his fault.

Ben had shyly offered to take Robert along to the Ewe and Lamb one night.

The next evening was a Saturday and Robert was persuaded to go with Ben to the alehouse. He had coins in his pocket, fairly certain, being a newcomer that he was expected to buy a round...or two.

The old alehouse had been squatting at the side of the village street for over two hundred years. The floors were uneven flagstones that had tripped many an unwary tippler. The blackened beams could nearly touch some heads and give headaches to the unwary.

They entered into a fug of pipe smoke and a babble of conversation. A hush descended, Robert was inspected. Of course they knew all about him, everything, as much as Ben had gleaned in the brief time he'd been at Appley Glebe. They knew of the injury, the coffee, the soap and the sea chest with the sword in it and his fondness for washing.

Robert realised that he was expected to buy drinks so he gave a nod to the innkeeper and placed a handful of coins on the bar.

'Thankee's,' were called.

'Good health,' he replied as he sipped his tankard of ale.

Two old codgers moved up for him, guarding their china mugs jealously as he sat on a bench with his back to the wall.

They let him drink half and then one man, his clean smock spotted with ale drips, started the questions. Mr Southwell would be their entertainment for the evening.

'You settled in then?'

'Yes, very nice, it's very comfortable.'

'You'll be here a whiles then?'

'I hope so.'

'And was it the sea you left then?' As if they didn't know.

'Yes, I'm retired now. I shan't go back even if the French fleet come out. Lord Nelson will have to do without me.' This impressed them and heads nodded in agreement. Robert knew perfectly well that there was always another purser glad to get a berth.

'And you've given up travelling?'

'I've seen a lot of countries, been in a lot of ports...all over, and I reckon this is the best so far.'

'Aye, it's a good spot, hard living though.' An old man, a clay pipe in his mouth spoke up, sitting with his back to the fireplace.

'Tell us about them ports you was in.' Ben was perched on the window seat, his head skimming the ceiling with eyes alight with interest.

So Robert told them of the boiling hot sun that poured down its' brazen heat for days on end until the caulking on the deck ran in black streams of tar. Of how the water barrels ran low with green scummy water in the bottom. Of the tropical islands with strange birds and brown and black natives.

There were several women drinking in the room and out of delicacy, although they looked rough and common, he glossed over the partial nudity of the people, particularly the ladies. He remembered vividly that a few flowers did not cover up their private parts.

His voice grew hoarse with talking and smoke and even a replenished tankard couldn't soothe his throat. He looked for Ben and saw him, gazing into space, a dreamy look in his eyes. Another day he would tell them of the blood and injuries, the fighting, the hardship and the easy way men could die. It might be a good idea to mention the diseases sailors and soldiers suffered and the unpleasantness of being treated with mercury after catching syphilis.

They supported each other up the lane,

'Is that ale stronger than I'm used to?' Robert asked, too fuddled to think that Ben wouldn't know what he had been used to. Ben had probably been weaned on it.

Robert saw Ben relieve himself in the hedge and followed suit, thinking a quick sluice under the pump would be all the washing he'd do. With much shushing and muffled whispers they negotiated the front door and crept up the stairs. Ben opened Robert's door, pushed him in and shut it. The young man wasn't drunk on ale but fired with the images of guns and fighting, soldiers and ships of the line. Beautiful dusky women with flowers in their hair and no clothes on would fill his dreams.

The next evening Robert sat at his window letting the night air cool his face flushed with a day of sunshine on the downs. He wrote in his journal:

"June 5th. I have had a good walk up to near Cimpton today and was very lucky to see some silver spotted skipper butterflies. They are so quick darting about, that I quietly eased myself down on the grass and sat watching them, letting them flit from bush to bush. Gorse perfumed the air with its' strange spicy smell, almost like coconut and I felt like it was my own small piece of heaven. I am looking forward to seeing the chalk hill blue butterfly, they say it is a fine sight. It is very dry everywhere, the ground is cracked and the streams are running low."

He read this through, it sounded rather poetical to him, he had always considered himself a very basic down to earth sort, but the peace and tranquillity he'd felt up there on the downs had stayed with him.

CHAPTER SIX

With Caleb's help, they got all the work done over the following days and when Calloway knocked and entered on Friday at two o'clock Robert was proud to know that all was ship shape.

They sat in the parlour. The rum bottle and two poured glasses were ready. Calloway was a pleasant faced man in his early forties, losing his hair, with the remainder tied back. He had on a smart bottle green coat with black breeches as a mark of his status as Steward of Lord Byclere's estate. He sipped appreciatively and placed the glass on the table. He let Robert top it up.

'Now, down to business: I've spoken to Lord Byclere and it seems there are several options. We can take the farm back and find another tenant. We can leave you here and put in a manager, being as you're not experienced enough yet. Or,' he leaned forward. 'You met Mrs Summers at the funeral, Mary's sister, Dorothy?'

Robert nodded.

'Well she has expressed an interest. Like Mary she comes from good farming stock. She could certainly manage the dairy work, if the cows and outside labouring were done. She's a widow. She had to leave the cottage when her ploughman husband died. She's living with her daughter but they've got no room to spare. It would keep it in the family for Ben to come home to. She's a comely enough woman, not such a voice on her as Mary,' he laughed, 'and, plenty of work left in her. Have you any thoughts on this?'

Robert slowly shook his head. 'It's a lot to take in. I'd like to stay here. It's a comfortable billet and,' his face cracked into a tiny smile, 'I enjoy doing the work, it's a complete change from on board ship. But, I'll admit I'm an amateur. It's been grand having Caleb here to help.'

'If Mrs Summers comes here, you would have to leave. It wouldn't be seemly for a bachelor like yourself to live with a widow woman. But...if you married, that would solve the problem.' Calloway was so pleased with the solution he banged his empty glass on the table.

Robert stared at him. Marry Dorothy. The man was mad, but then he realised, Calloway didn't know that Robert had loved Mary.

'Can I have a day to think on it?'

'Come to the estate office on Sunday at twelve o'clock with your answer. Oh, and by the way, I hear you had a pauper through here. I shouldn't encourage them, I know it's hard but the village won't like it.'

'She went off the next day. All the way from Hampshire she'd walked, I only did a little: a scrap of food and a few pence. At least now she'll get to her sister without dying on the way.'

Robert was indignant. It was all very well for Calloway, with his good brick house and a salary of forty pounds a year. The woman had gone off clean, wearing Mary's old wool shawl and winter dress and with a sixpence in her pocket, a loaf and a quarter of cheese. The bucket had been rinsed out and there was no trace of her left in the barn.

After all the chores were finished and he had eaten a simple supper Robert sat alone in Mary's chair by the fire. He was tired and worn out with thinking. To everyone else the idea of marriage to Dorothy Summers was the obvious solution. But could he go through with it? The idea was almost repugnant. He could get lodgings in the village easily enough but he liked the house and whilst he was there he could still feel some contact with Mary. And it would be a job and inheritance for Ben when he came home. After his enjoyable walks up on the downs he had decided that he definitely did not want to go back to sea.

CHAPTER SEVEN

A month later Robert woke up on his wedding morning, still not sure it was the right decision. He had made a visit to Dorothy Summers to talk and offer marriage. This had been accepted with alacrity and the banns called with an almost indecent haste.

To Dorothy, Robert was highly eligible. She had heard from Mary about the cleanliness, the coffee and his generosity in sharing. He also had a pension; she would be set for life. And it got her out of her daughter's tiny, noisy cottage with children and babies everywhere.

He placed some roses on Mary's grave and stood bareheaded in the sunshine, reluctant to speak out loud but wanting to explain why he was marrying her sister. As the church clock struck eleven he walked over to join the future Mrs Southwell and her daughter and son in law by the lych gate. In a new black gown, paid for by Robert, the auburn haired Dorothy was escorted to the church door and into his life. He had to admit she looked rather bonny in her new dress with a matching bonnet and carrying a posy of marguerite daisies

She was quieter than Mary, her voice soft spoken with a country lilt. In any other circumstances Robert would have considered himself fortunate to find such a comely woman at his age. He knew his pension was half the attraction so if the marriage was more business than pleasure then so be it. They would shift together until Ben came home.

The thought of the marriage bed had worried him considerably. How would he feel lying in Mary's bed with another woman? He really didn't know and he was sure Dorothy would expect some lovemaking. So he had ordered good red wine and a sweet sherry from Banbury. With some lemons and oranges, he could make a fine punch, or she might like the sherry wine.

Margie had come in and house swept for him and made the bed up. She had also removed Mary's clothes to Ben's room so that Dorothy could use the closet cupboard. A wedding tea was on the table in the kitchen and so all was ready.

Caleb had offered to milk and finish all the work but Robert was anxious to get out of the house and he made his escape leaving the women chattering in the kitchen. He gave Caleb a rueful smile as the two of them brought the cows in.

'That's a good job done then,' was Caleb's comment walking behind Buttercup.

'What's that then?'

'Your wedding of course, life in the old dog yet, eh,' and he laughed.

'It's all happened so fast I can hardly believe it. Here I am at forty-two and wed for the first time. I never expected it,' liar said a little voice, you hoped to marry Mary. 'I've spoken to Mr Calloway and he's agreed for you to carry on here. When I've learnt the ropes I'll be quicker with the milking but there's still the field work to do. I cannot pay more than nine shillings a week, but there'll be dinner as well.'

'Aye, suits me.' For Caleb it was nearer his cottage and his wife would come in and help Dorothy. That would bring in a shilling a week.

'Dorothy's daughter, Jane is taking the bees home with her. I really don't think I can look after them as well as trying to do all this.' Robert pointed at the cows.

'Does them a good turn, two hives is worth something.' Caleb picked up two buckets.

'A bit of a legacy from her Aunt Mary.' added Robert. As was tradition he had told the bees that Mary had died but it hadn't affected them. He didn't think it would.

That night as Dorothy prepared for bed he sat by the window in his old room and wrote in his journal of the day's events. He kept it brief and finally when he could delay no longer stripped off his clothes. Hastily he scrubbed himself all over with cold water and soap, towelled off and slipped on a clean nightshirt. It made him said to think that it had been washed by Mary. With a glass in his hand he stepped across the passage and tapped on the door.

'Come in...husband.' Dorothy was sitting at Mary's table, hairbrush in hand. 'Would you brush out my hair please, Robert, it's tangled by the wind today.' Her hair was nearly waist length, still richly auburn and as he brushed, letting the silk of it run through his fingers he felt the stirrings of desire. Their eyes met in the mirror and each smiled.

Dorothy relaxed, it had worked. She was as worried as him, knowing men could be brutal but in her marriage in times of stress of which there had been plenty, brushing her hair, her crowning glory had always soothed Jim and brought him back to her arms.

Robert gently took her hand and led her to the high old bed.
Pulling back the sheet and cover he waited until she had settled
herself and then handed her a glass of wine.

'Thank you, are you having one?' she sipped the nicest wine
she had ever tasted. Well, she had never had wine before.

'Yes, mine's here.' He got into bed, easing his nightshirt
discreetly over his hips.

'To us.' she touched his glass and he saluted her.

'To us.' As if by instinct they both put their glasses down at
the same time and he turned to her, 'I haven't been married before
but I have had experience,' a thought struck him, 'and I'm clean and
healthy. I've no diseases to worry you and my wound is healed.'
Resolutely he dismissed thoughts of Mary bending over him, her
gentle hands cleaning his back.

'And I had a good marriage, never enough money mind, but
Jim and I were content, until the bugger went and got himself killed.
So Robert Southwell I'm all yours.' She inhaled his clean smell and
reached to place a kiss on his mouth. Her small hand touched his
warm leg and in minutes they were on fire for each other, with
Robert assuaging a hunger he hadn't known he'd got. His dreams
were of Mary though and her laughing face as she tossed the hay in
June.

They had started haymaking on June 10th. Robert tapped the
glass of his barometer and the needle at high pressure didn't budge.
Ben had screwed his eyes up looking at the sky and wetted his
finger, to test the wind. He seemed satisfied and Mary, having
consulted with her neighbours was also in agreement.

Ben and three others worked as a team, scything through the
grass, walking at an easy pace and Robert watched the swathes fall
to the side. It would be left to wilt, Mary explained, as Robert stood
in the kitchen watching her roll out the pastry. She had a cast iron
box at the side of the hearth in which she baked bread and pies and
she used this with great expertise.

As he moved around the table, avoiding her red faced,
bustling figure he wondered out loud what he could do to help.

She swiped her cheek with a floury hand leaving a white
smear. 'Would you take their drinks down? The sun'll be hot on
them now, and they'll stop for a bite and a mug of cider.'

She loaded up a basket and clamping his summer hat on he
walked out to the hay field.

He could hear them singing as he stepped through the cut lanes of grass. The fresh, green smell of mown herbage was another new experience for him.

'Good on you, sir,' was Matt Tilburn whom Robert had met in the Ewe. He carefully leant his sickle against a tree and sat down in the shade. A good swallow of cider and, smacking his lips he reached for a fat, current bun. The butter oozed out, and he licked it off.

'She makes a tasty bun, does Mary. How do her vittals compare with what's on the ships?'

'They don't really compare,' laughed Robert, 'it was hard tack biscuit, salt pork and peas once we were well away from land and the fresh vegetables were used up. Sometimes the gunroom would kill a pig, or we'd have some of the fowls we took with us. The cook would make a huge suet dumpling on a Sunday.'

Seeing their blank looks he explained, 'the gunroom was where the midshipman and warrant officers lived.'

'You had livestock on board then?'

'Oh yes, chickens, a goat for milk for the captain, a few sheep and a pig or two. They all had names but some of the sailors would get too fond of them. Or the poor creatures would get hit in battle and die or have to be finished off.'

The men gazed at him. They were used to death, but done cleanly, often at prescribed times of the year. No one would slaughter a pig in the summer, it wouldn't keep fresh in the heat.

As they finished their snack they took up whetstones and put an edge on their sickles. Robert noticed that Ben was as expert as the older men. He must have been well taught by his father. They stood up belching, shaking off crumbs and muttering thanks.

The next day Robert was out in the fields from ten in the morning. The hot sun quickly started to dry the green hay. Mary passed him a pitchfork and they walked out together. There were already three other women in the field and two older children. The women all wore sunbonnets with their blouse sleeves rolled to their elbows The men had gone on to cut Tilburn's fields.

Robert watched Mary closely and copied her as she bent, stuck the rake in, twisted and

spun the grass. Dark green turned to lighter and they moved smoothly along the rows. At the headland by the hedge they spun the hay into the field.

'It's thicker by the hedge,' Mary explained, 'and it's in the shade so we toss it into the middle.'

Robert kept moving, concentrating on keeping a rhythm. It wasn't a heavy job, but when he stopped to wipe the sweat from his brow he discovered that his shoulders were aching. Mary saw him flexing and hunching them and came over with a bottle of cider.

'You mustn't do too much and spoil the wound, it's healing too well for that.'

'I'm enjoying it,' and he spoke honestly, 'I can't bake, I'm not sure about mowing, but I think I can do this.'

'You've done a grand job, we'll be paying you.'

'No, I like it out here.' He didn't like to think of the women working so hard and him lounging around. He'd be getting fat with all the good food and no graft to work it off.

They finished the first field by dinnertime and sat in the shade with Mary's bread, cheese and pickled onions. He met Suzey Tilburn and her daughter, ten year old Meg who should have been in school. Caleb's wife, the roly poly Margie Pound was not quite as agile as the younger women but she was still faster than Robert.

In spite of her age and rolling gait the elderly Sally Russell who was wife to Colin, from Tanners farm could turn her swathe with speed and precision. Children came and went, some helping, some hindering, with the youngest rolling about, spoiling the tidy rows.

Robert sat a little way off, feeling stiff in the thighs and shoulders, with calluses coming on the palms of his hands. He listened to their chatter and laughter and had to stop himself from falling asleep. That would never do, they'd be up and working and he'd be the lazy laggard asleep in the hedge!

The other fields were completed by teatime and tiredly they all trooped off to the kitchen at Appley Glebe.

The precious rose painted teapot was brought out and whilst Robert sluiced himself off under the pump the food was put out on the table. There was buttered current scones and new soda bread, sliced and thick with golden butter. With flour costing between five and sixpence a pound no one could afford to make cakes and there was no fruit left from last year to make a pie. A large slice of moist pink ham was washed down with their dish of tea. Mary had boiled an ox tongue, curled up in a saucepan. Glistening with flavoursome jelly, thin, round slices were arranged on a dinner plate.

The children sat outside on the ground, hungrily gobbling down slices of bread with small cubes of cheese. They shared a jug of milk and passed round a small beaker. For all of them it was the reason they had tried to help out.

Robert felt tired in every bone in his body. He watched Mary change her apron ready to go out and fetch in the cows and start milking, until Ben came home and took over. The ladies cleared the table and shushed him away when he offered to help.

'Bless you no, sir,' said Suzey. 'We take our plates home with us and then when it's our turn, Mary will come to us. And you'd be welcome, very welcome, you've done a grand job today.'

Robert felt inordinately pleased at this praise from a woman. He was amazed at how hard they worked. Mrs James didn't stop from morning until dusk. He took a bucket of water upstairs and washed himself down, changing into a clean shirt. He was about to put the dirty, sweaty one out for washing when he thought again. How ever was Mrs James going to have time for washing when she had all the outside work to do and the extra baking. It wouldn't hurt to wear it again tomorrow. That's what Ben did, why spoil a clean shirt when there's one already dirty he would say.

Robert left it on the chair and after looking longingly at the bed went downstairs to see if he could help.

Mrs James was in the cowshed, seated on the stool, crooning quietly to the cow as she moved her fingers up and down, the jet of milk in a constant stream.

He waited until she'd finished. 'Ah humph, ah, is there anything I could do, Mrs James?'

She turned round and smiled and his crusty old bachelor's heart melted like ice in spring.

'Well bless you, oh now let me see. There's butter to churn, the cheeses to turn and the bucket of milk to go into the dairy. Start with the buckets, I'll be out in a minute.' She turned back, pressed her head into the flank and commenced squirting.

Robert carefully took the bucket through to the dairy and looked around. There were round cheeses. swathed in muslin piled up on wooden shelves. A shallow dish had cream in it. He realised he really had no idea of the processes of butter and cheese making and resolved to learn.

An hour later, with Ben home and finishing milking Robert was busily churning butter. That is, he was turning the handle of the churn, a sharp eye being kept on him as Mrs James turned cheeses. He heard the slap of the milk inside and of how it changed sounds as the fat globules came together to form the butter. As she came up beside him he could smell her sweat, but he didn't mind, she'd hardly had a minute to sit for a dish of tea, let alone wash like him.

'Can you hear it, that sound? It's changing...you've made your first butter Mr Southwell.' She smiled up at him and he gazed down into kind, brown eyes. He took off the lid and peered in,

'So I have, is it all right?' He felt so proud of himself.

'Yes, it's perfectly good, we'll take it out and I'll show you what happens next.'

Patiently she took him through the process and sometimes, what looked so easy turned out to be difficult.

'I'm all fingers and thumbs,' he complained as he tried to pat the butter into shape.

She laughed. 'It's practise, I've been doing it a fair few years. We've finished here for now, so we'll go in and get the supper out. I'm sorry it's only a drop of soup, but we can finish Margie's soda bread and cut a slice of ham.'

'And I'll make us some coffee,' he volunteered, not keen to drink ale all the time.

He fell into bed as the moon rose, the argent beams shining through his open window. He was tired out after his day of work in the fields and then in the dairy but he felt marvellous, physically exhausted but mentally rejoicing. He fell asleep with Mrs James's face in his thoughts, her brown eyes twinkling as he added salt to his butter and tasted it. And his surprise that it had really worked as he licked a taste off his finger. He had enjoyed her company so much; he looked forward with great pleasure to the morrow.

After they had put the hay upon tripods to finish drying they went on to the next farm and Robert's hands became used to the work. His face was turning from red to brown and his arms had tanned up to the ends of his shirt-sleeves. Mrs James had checked his wound and was pleased to report that it was nearly healed. The physical exertion had not damaged it in any way. He was getting used to the work and feeling fitter than he had for a long time.

The James family had a large hay wain that was used by everyone round about to bring in their hay. Verner had saved up for five yeas to buy it and it gave them a measure of importance in the village. This was one of Major, the shire horse's busiest times and he would plod back and forth from field to rick yard helped and encouraged by all the workers. In the mornings he rested whilst the hay was forked up into rows. He was owned by Colin Russell of

Tanners Farm and used by all the farms in the area for the heavy work of carting the huge loads.

Appley Glebe was the first farm to bring in their hay followed by Tilburns'. After that it was the turn of Colin Russell. They took it in turns to be first so the order changed every year. They would all hope that the weather would stay dry until the thatcher had been to cover the ricks.

Everyone seemed to know what was happening in all the fields and where labour was required. Robert was surprised to see quite young children working until late in the evening but knew that the pennies they earned were all important to the families.

On the evening of June 18th, Robert, Mrs James and Ben stood in their yard gazing fondly at three fine ricks of hay. They were drinking elderflower cordial to celebrate and Robert looked down at Mrs James, admiring her trim figure.

To divert his mind he asked, 'Will that be enough to see you through the winter?'

'Aye,' said Ben, 'there's a small field of turnips to dig up later and I'll buy in some oats if the price is right.'

'Come Spring we start drying off the cows ready for calving, so they won't be wanting so much feed,' explained Mrs James, 'and I'll have a good store of cheeses to sell so we'll have some money coming in.'

Robert thought of his pay that had been fairly steady over the years and safely banked when he'd been back in Portsmouth or London and compared it to the precarious living of these farmers who had to provide for their animals and their families at the mercy of the weather and market prices. He shivered in the cool evening breeze and decided a warm wash and a beaker of rum would settle him nicely

Over the following days they walked or rode on wagons around the neighbourhood. The hay was turned until it was dry enough for the stalks to crack and then thrown up into conical shapes, to wait for the carter. After misty starts the days developed into sunshine and everyone said how glorious it was and would it last? He met all the neighbours and the farm labourers who worked by the acre. They would start at daybreak and work until dusk. Even the poorest farmer's wife would provide food for them as a matter of pride and he sampled a variety of breads and pasties. But when they came back in the early evening for milking he always made Mrs James and Ben a cup of coffee.

CHAPTER EIGHT

Robert and Dorothy settled down together, learning about each other. She was a good cook and he appreciated the soups and stews that appeared back on the table. He had told her though that he absolutely refused to have a rabbit in the house. She had to abide by this, however many times she was offered a cheap one. Robert was pained to notice that Dorothy was not the quick, tidy housewife that Mary had been. Dust settled on chairs and tables and the crumbs were left from one meal to the next. The cat sat undisturbed in his patch of sunlight.

When Dorothy found the bolt of striped calico she fell on it with joy.

'Where did Mary get this?' she asked holding it up to herself, letting the material fall to the floor in a pool of blue and white stripes.

Robert couldn't tell her he had bought it for Mary and it hurt to see her hands on it but it would be a waste not to use it. 'I expect Mary bought it from the peddlers. Can you sew?'

'Oh yes, I'm a seamstress, I worked at Byclere House before I married. Robert,' she smiled shyly, 'this will be very useful, I think I'm pregnant. At my age! I can make baby clothes and dresses for me.'

Robert stared at her. Why should he be surprised? They were living a very normal married life, even so...

'It'll take a bit of getting used to.' Delight and pride crept over him and her news clinched something he had been thinking about. 'Well that decides it, definitely. We'll get Margie to come in and clean three or four times a week. If you can still work in the dairy and cook, I'll do the outside work. I don't want you tiring yourself.'

She beamed at him, 'I'm fit as a fiddle, but I'd like the help, then I can get on with my sewing.'

The next afternoon, with Dorothy gone to see neighbours Robert left Caleb hoeing in the vegetable garden and strode out for a walk in the lanes. He had discovered a Green Lane, an old drovers' track that had been a Roman road many centuries before. It was rather unkempt and often little better than a footpath but there were a lot of plant species in the verge and hedge. It had turned out to be a shorter way to the downs and knowing that Caleb would bring the cows in and start milking he wanted some time to himself. Seeing Dorothy with the calico had shaken him again and he wanted to think about the day at the fayre as he walked along.

On the evening of June 20th Robert sat in his favourite window seat and wrote in the journal. He had taken the day off and left early for a walk to Ilsley.

"I had a very pleasant walk up to Ilsley across the downs. I found a clump of fragrant orchids, the beautiful pink flowers were nearly hidden and I picked two to bring home, one for Mary and one to draw. She flushed as pink as the flowers when I gave her a small nosegay. 'Mr Southwell what will you do next?' she said. I find myself watching her. She is the busiest, kindest lady I have ever met. I hope we can be friends."

Robert locked his journal away in the sea chest and looked out his clean clothes for the morrow. A fayre was coming to Appley, the annual Midsummer event and everyone was excited. Ben planned to milk extra early so he could spend the day there with his cronies. Robert had quietly given two pence each to all the children who had 'helped' them at hay time and it had been a happy reward to see the joy on their faces.

They were all up at five o'clock the next morning. It was the Summer Solstice and had been a short night anyway. With Robert helping as much as he could, carrying buckets of milk and turning the cheeses, they were able to have their breakfast at half past eight and then change into their best clothes.

Robert was amused to see Ben standing naked in the scullery by a bucket of water as he sloshed a rag over himself. He frowned when Robert offered him soap but when he explained that it made shaving easier Ben's eyes lit up.

'I have the tiny bits left over from Mother's washing,' he said, 'but they keeps dropping out of my fingers.' Robert fetched a cake of his Balsam soap and showed Ben how to lather it. Ben was using his father's blade, honed to a wicked edge. The small mirror was cracked and spotted so Robert went back upstairs and fetched his own.

'Here,' he passed it to Ben, 'this will save you cutting yourself. You can keep the soap but not the mirror.'

Ben's chin was dripping blood onto clean breeches. Robert was smart in black trousers and white shirt with his best dark green jacket. A spotted neckerchief was knotted round his neck. He had washed, brushed and tied back his hair with a clean black ribbon and waited by the front door to escort Mrs James to the fayre.

Mary James came down the stairs in her best summer gown of pale grey. A light summer shawl of silk patterned with daisies and her summer bonnet trimmed with lace completed her elegant outfit.

Her lightly tanned face accentuated her brown eyes. She had changed working boots for buckled shoes and these peeped out from her gown, her trim ankles showing as she stepped down.

Robert turned, saw her and smiled.

She exclaimed. 'Is everything all right? I hope I haven't kept you waiting. I'm not used to dressing up like this. My, you look so smart, Mr Southwell. That jacket is a lovely colour. Have you seen Ben? Where is the lad?'

'Please, call me Robert and Ben has gone. I said I would escort you so he ran off down the lane.'

'He's been looking forward to today. The lads love the fayre, it's a chance to show off to the girls and get drunk. Well, and if I'm to call you Robert then you must use my name. We don't stand on ceremony in the country…we haven't time.'

'You certainly haven't,' agreed Robert, 'Mrs Mary James let me escort you to the fayre.' He gallantly extended his arm and felt himself to be the happiest of men.

'The fayre is in our hay field on the corner,' Mary chatted 'It's the traditional site and I gets a little something for letting it.'

The sun was shining, the blue sky contrasting with the fresh green of the hedges dotted with pink dog roses. Cream and gold sweet honeysuckle climbed and twined amongst the hazel. Robert absorbed the beauty of the day and tucked it into his memory. He wanted to be more interesting. He worried he was a bit of a dry old stick, not used to the company of women.

They heard the music and the shouts and laughter of the children before they reached the gateway. Gaily decorated peddlers and hucksters stalls and tables were set up round the field. The space in the middle was marked out for children's races and trials of strength. The Ewe and Lamb had a tent and benches and stools wobbled on uneven ground. Enterprising village women were selling hot pies and buns. There was something for everyone.

Robert and Mary sauntered along, admiring the trinkets and gewgaws that the peddlers tried to sell, letting them flash brightly in the sun.

'It's rubbish, Mary,' Robert whispered in her ear. He was keeping a lookout for something to buy her, watching if there was anything she showed a special interest in.

They exchanged greetings with their neighbours and watched Ben trying his strength up against a Strong Man. An iron bar was being bent.

Ben rolled up his sleeves. His mother watched as, with sweat dripping off his face and the sinews of his arms straining, he feebly bent the bar. He put it down, disgruntled and watched, fascinated, as the Iron Man (strongest in England) pulled it into a horseshoe shape, held it up to applause and then bent it straight again.

Ben walked across to them. 'I reckon it's a trick.' He was a bit embarrassed to have failed in front of his friends.

'It's his job, Ben,' consoled Robert, 'it's how he makes his living. There's not a lot of brains needed to bend a bar but a lot more for what you do. Shall we wet our throats? I'm getting thirsty. Mary?' He gave her his arm and felt her small hand clasp it.

'I should like one of Margie's pies. It's a long time since breakfast. She's got lamb and rosemary and beef and kidney.'

'That sounds tasty, this is my treat.' Robert held up his hand. 'Have a rest and I'll bring the drinks and pies.'

They sat in the shade of an oak tree, balancing on the stools, sipping cider and munching the warm, savoury pasties. Robert provided a handkerchief as a napkin and watched in amusement as Ben gulped his food down, swigged back the drink and after a noisy burp and muttered thanks loped off.

'He wants to be with the other lads. This is their day off in the year so they all make the most of it. They've come from miles around; even Byclere House lets them have the day off. They wouldn't get much work out of them if they didn't.' She shook out the handkerchief, delicately wiped her lips and sighed with contentment. 'That were lovely and so nice not to have to cook it myself. Thank you, Robert.'

'My pleasure, shall we have a stroll?' He had noticed she gazed admiringly at the stall with materials. Most of it was serviceable homespun and cotton, cords and worsteds but they wandered back there again and he saw her finger a bolt of blue and white striped calico.

'How much would this be, by the yard is it?' The material was soft, the vendor's eyes flicked between the woman and the man. He scented a sale.

'15s.6d. for the bolt, I don't do yardage.'

'Oh.' Mary bit her lip and turned to move away. She walked off to speak to Margie Pound.

'Fourteen shillings, I'll take it,' Robert was firm.

'Oh dear me no, that's best quality calico from India, worked and dyed up in Lancashire. There's a good few dresses in that, or some nice curtains. It's best quality, isn't it?'

Quickly he took out his purse. 'Fourteen and sixpence and I'll take it.' He shook out the coins.

'Go on then, robbery it is. What about some sewing threads, five pence each.'

Robert agreed. 'All right, she can't make a dress without the thread, have you got needles?'

'Have I got needles? Choose, best Sheffield steel at nine pence.' More coins clinked.

It was all wrapped in a brown paper and tied with string and surprisingly heavy. Robert hoisted it onto his shoulder and went in search of Mary. She was talking to some lady friends and he hesitated. Should he give it to her in front of the villagers, would it cause talk and speculation? He decided to go home with it, and whilst there relieve himself of all the cider he'd drunk. Others might use the hedge but it was a short step to their privy. He would surprise her with the parcel later.

At half past three they were back in the kitchen, sitting with a dish of tea. Robert had presented the parcel and received a flurry of,

'Oh no, I can't accept this, oh, Mr Southwell, Robert it's too much, no, no it's much to much.' She was all pink-cheeked confusion.

Calmly he told her, 'My rent is low, you feed me well, do all my laundry, please accept it.'

'I do hope you're suited here, you are a real gentleman.' She held the material up, her finger running over the softness of it, already imagining the dress she'd sew.

He looked at her steadily, his eyes serious, 'I'm very content.' Her rosy cheeks turned rosier and she lowered her eyes and nodded, for once lost for words.

'Now,' Robert was brisk, 'I'll go up and change and get the cows in. I think Ben'll be late, he won't know the time to come back.'

'Yes he will, but it's a convenience not to have a timepiece.'

Robert laughed, feeling light of heart, he would enjoy working with Mary out in the cow shed.

They had finished all the work and were sitting in the glow of a fiery sunset when Ben staggered in. He smelt of beer and his best shirt was torn at the front.

'You been fighting?' His mother knew him well.

He grinned foolishly. 'It was worth it, I couldn't bend that bar but when we played Bull in the field I beat everyone.' He snatched at some buttered bread, cut a hunk of cheese and stumbled out, dribbling crumbs. They heard the clatter of boots work their way up the stairs.

'Don't forget you're taking Betty to market in the morning. Get up at five.' Mary called after him. Quietly she told Robert. 'He'll probably change and go out again. I think he has a fondness for Clarice Pound but he won't get anywhere, she runs rings round the village lads.'

Robert sipped his coffee. 'Can I help in the morning?'

'Well I'd ask Caleb Pound but I think he's busy. I would be grateful.' She whisked cups and plates off the table.

'I'll be up, it's no hardship after all my years at sea. And Mary, thank you for your company today, I really enjoyed it.' He moved quickly to the stairs anxious not to embarrass her or himself by saying anything further.

He was dog tired as he prepared for bed, but his heart was lighter than it had been for years. Mary had smiled kindly on him and they had worked so well together outside. A quick learner she said he was. It would be a while before he could milk a cow as fast as them, but he was learning the names of the cattle and they were getting used to him.

His wound had healed and he could lift buckets with hardly a twinge. As he stood at the open window looking at the familiar sky, he thought how good life was. The stars were diamond bright and he murmured the names of the constellations hoping that perhaps one day soon he would be able to buy Mary a jewel as beautiful.

They were up early. Robert craved hot coffee but there wasn't time so he sluiced his face at the pump, cupped his hands and drank deeply. He went to open the gate for Ben. The cows ambled through the dew wet grass, snorting cool misty breath. Petals of buttercups were stuck to their noses. The sun pushed a pale light through cloud and Robert shivered, wishing he'd put a coat on. Ben as usual had his sleeves rolled up and seemed none the worse for yesterdays' fun.

'Ben, we'll milk Betty first then you can be off. Robert, Mr Southwell says he'll help me. Remember what I tell you now, get the best price you can and come straight back. No dawdling in Banbury and keep the money safe in the purse I gave you. Put that into your breeches pocket. And get yourself some bread and cheese to eat on the way and take a sixpence out to buy pie and peas for your dinner.'

'Yes, mother,' said Ben simply. Robert hid a smile. He knew Ben would do exactly what he liked, as he usually did.

Betty was milked for the last time. She was getting too old for them, not giving enough milk, but would be ideal for a cottager wanting to make a bit of butter and cheese.

'Goodbye, old girl.' Mary patted her rump as she passed and watched the cow swing her way out. She looked to go back in the field, but Ben tugged and picking up a hazel switch gave a tap to point her in the right direction.

Robert spent the whole morning in the dairy as Mary went through the processes of butter and cheese making with him. He sniffed and sampled and gradually the textures and flavours started to form a pattern.

'I'll never get the hang of this.' He grumbled as the butter churn slopped about.

'It'll come, it always does, although they do say butter won't churn for a maid in love.'

Robert said nothing, old country tales meant nought and as for being in love...

He also took over from Mary when the village folk came up for their daily milk sold at a penny a pint. Bringing an assortment of jugs and containers he measured out pints and quarts for them. Very little money was proffered and Mary told him they usually paid on Saturday after the wage owner had received his pay. Sometimes she took rabbits, vegetables or fruit in payment. He also used the market scales to weigh out butter and cheese that they bought in small quantities. With a labourers' wage for most families of about eight shillings a week and butter at nine pence a pound and cheese at one shilling a pound small portions had to be eked out carefully.

They had their dinner of rabbit stew at twelve o'clock as usual and Mary left plenty for Ben. They started milking at five and as they both sat on stools tugging and squeezing, with their heads pressed against warm dappled flanks, Robert asked what time Ben was expected.

'He should be home soon, he can get a ride with a carter, so he'll have a rest. I just hope he's not gone in some alehouse and drunk all the money.'

He's a sensible lad.'

CHAPTER NINE

Robert was up on the downs, puffing a bit after the exertion of the uphill walk. He found his favourite hollow, sheltered from the wind and sat down. A small flask of rum was in his pocket. The sky was heavy with rain, grey clouds were massing from the west so he knew he couldn't sit for too long but he wanted to think about his life, Dorothy and the coming baby and examine it all objectively.

He decided that on the face of it, to an onlooker he had a good life. He was renting a small, neat farm. He had his pension to tide them over hard times, a good wife and soon his own family, a child coming to bless their home. Dorothy he mused, was quite different to Mary in personality.

He spotted a hobby, a type of falcon speeding through the darkening sky, its' scythe shaped wings weaving and twisting as it snapped up insects. He smiled to himself, if Mary had been a robin, then Dorothy would be a tree sparrow. Small, sharp eyed, with the brighter patch on her head. She was proud of her auburn hair and had to be reminded to wear a bonnet for butter and cheese making. Robert would brush it out for her at night, the tresses wavy after being plaited all day.

If he lay awake after their lovemaking Dorothy didn't know, her pregnancy was making her tired and she slept soundly. Robert still thought of Mary, regretting what he considered as his part in her death. The tales of distant countries that Ben had lapped up and the thought that he should have been with her that night still haunted him. He should have been the one to be knocked down by the horses. His death would have made few ripples upon the surface of Appley Glebe.

Robert shivered as he watched a shower of rain sweep across, coming closer. He tossed back a tot, got to his feet and retraced his steps, hurrying to race the shower home. His thoughts had made him gloomy and he stepped into the kitchen of Appley Glebe feeling damp and disgruntled. Caleb had waved to him from the barn and said he was all right. He'd leave everything shipshape. so Robert felt that just for once he would leave him to it.

Shivering, his coat heavy with rain, he walked into the warmth of the kitchen. The fire burned brightly with a fresh log and the kettle was steaming. The table was clean, freshly scrubbed and laid for tea with bread, butter, plum preserve and apple cake. He felt the depression lift and when Dorothy came across and took his coat, fussing over him, he sat down to take his boots off feeling content to be home.

The next time he went to Banbury market in the small cart with butter and cheese piled high behind, he took Dorothy with him. It was a bright, blustery autumn day and with the road dry the cart bowled along at a good pace. For two guineas he had bought a grey Welsh cob. Binnie was heavy enough for light work in the fields but smart enough to pull the cart and he enjoyed the outing as much as his master. Robert wanted Dorothy to see the doctor to make sure she was well and fit for the baby. He was quite prepared to pay for whatever was needed.

Dorothy was enjoying the attention. No one had ever fussed over her before and as for having the doctor for lying-in, well that was unheard of in the villages.

The women were at the mercy of the local midwife whose skills could be good, bad or indifferent. Death in childbirth was common and an accepted hazard. She wanted to buy fine cotton to make nightdresses for the baby and soft wool to make blankets and shawls.

It was just after eight as Robert set up the stall, neatly arranging the dairy products. He was using Mary's individual butter mould with her imprint of an oak tree and the butter had been marked with this. Her regular customers had been shocked to learn of her sudden death and he had to explain whom he was and that he was carrying on as usual. Most of the customers who bought a small amount brought their own dishes and with larger amounts he wrapped the butter or cheese in clean old muslin.

Tiny samples were offered and he enjoyed the good natured banter with the housewives. Dorothy had gone shopping and he was looking forward to having a beefsteak dinner with her in the Red Lion where Binnie was stabled.

By half twelve all was sold and Robert made a mental note to bring more with him next time. He was going every fortnight now the weather was cooler and the butter would keep better. He was still selling the cheese that Mary had made as those that Dorothy had started were immature. They were thinking about expanding their range, perhaps making a different kind of cheddar and after he had cleared up, whilst he waited for his wife he wandered along by the other stalls talking to the vendors. He nibbled crumbly Wensleydale and the salty red Leicester and looked with interest at the Stilton with its' blue veins.

All the different cheeses had been taken for granted on board ship and they had even tried the varieties from other countries. The problem had been keeping it fresh and free from mould, rats and mice. Teeth marks in the cheese had been a common occurrence at meal times. The samples he tasted from these other cheese makers were delicious.

Dorothy's parcels were too heavy to carry, so she left them in the shop for Robert to collect and pay for. She had also called in to the doctor's house as she had promised and been assured that everything was in order. He had agreed to come out for her confinement if he was given enough warning. It would be her fifth baby: two had died in infancy and she had two daughters, so she could expect a fairly speedy delivery. She had spoken to Clarrie Bates, the local midwife and intended to use her services. She wasn't keen on having a man attending to her intimate requirements unless there was a very bad problem. Doctors could be butchers where women and babies were concerned. It was often the case of saving one at the expense of saving the other.

She hurried back to the market place eager to find Robert and get their dinner. Nausea in the mornings meant she had little breakfast. Her coffee and toast was a distant memory.

As they waited for their dinner, they sat in the bow window of the inn with the bottle glass panes shining and watched the passers by. Robert had a tankard of ale and Dorothy sipped a glass of ginger cordial. The warm room was busy with hungry customers and servants carrying trays of china and cutlery. Their beefsteak was cooked in a rich onion gravy. The smell made her stomach rumble, and she giggled, embarrassed, looking to see if anyone had heard. Robert smiled, content for the moment and placed his hand on her stomach.

'And how is he, what did the doctor say?'

'I'm well, the baby's fine and there'is nothing to worry about. Fresh air, good food and I shall be perfectly all right.' She tucked into her mashed swedes and buttered carrots.

'Good, excellent, but I don't think you should come in to town later on, it will be too bumpy on the roads. Have you got everything you want?'

'Yes, thank you.'

'And will it cost more than I have taken this morning?' Robert filled his mouth with succulent beef and wiped gravy off his chin with a large napkin.

'How much did you make today?'

'Two pounds fifteen shillings and tuppence halfpenny.'

She smiled slyly, 'Yes, it is a little more than that,' and touched his hand, 'but I've bought the best quality for our baby, that was what you wanted?'

He nodded. 'Yes, he must have the best of everything.'

'It might be a she, I have had three girls and only one boy.'

'Time for a boy then, but seriously Dorrie, I don't mind. I feel I'm lucky to be a father at my age.' They finished their meal in harmony.

CHAPTER TEN

With Caleb's help Robert prepared for his first winter at the farm. They cut wood to dry for the fire and stacked it in the barn, using Binnie to drag it in for them. Potatoes and carrots were lifted and arranged in clamps to keep through the winter. As the weather turned colder and the days shortened he added a ration of oats to the cows' hay. They discussed the feasibility of growing oats and barley in the next year to avoid buying it in. Robert made a note to discuss it with John Calloway. They would have to plough up a field that was now a cow pasture.

On a cold, frosty Christmas Day they milked early, the better to finish and get back into the warm. Caleb strode back down the lane at eight o'clock, skirting the icy puddles, with a bottle of rum tucked under his arm. Robert had brought their two Christmas geese back from Banbury three days previously. The two wives had plucked and cleaned them together, with feathers drifting round like snowflakes, settling in all corners of the kitchen. With a look of disgust the cat sneezed a wisp of down off her nose. Whilst drinking cups of well-sugared tea they had enjoyed themselves with baby talk.

Christmas day dinner was started with the goose hanging on the spit above the fire. The grease spattered and sizzled into the waiting pan full of onions and potatoes, slowly turning golden brown.

Dorothy was getting large and it was easier for her to sit at the table and peel apples whilst Margie prepared their vegetables.

Apple sauce was piled into a dish on the inglenook ignored by the cat who was more intent on watching the goose. A large pot of turnips and carrots was ready to cook and the Christmas pudding, made in November, was tied up in butter muslin, ready to be boiled again.

Robert came in, muffled up with a wool scarf round his neck and his old Navy dark blue wool coat. He hung them up in the scullery and walked through in his socks. Sitting down by the fireplace, he rubbed his hands and reached for his shoes, nicely warmed by the hot stones.

'The cows are all comfortable in the barn, they've plenty of hay and with luck I shan't have to do so much later. Is the coffee hot? I'll have a tot of rum in it as it's Christmas.' He handled Mary's cup carefully, ever mindful of her pride in them. 'I'll have some toast and dripping this morning as it's so cold. Pass me some bread please.' Silently Dorothy handed a plate with slices of bread. Robert didn't notice her silence and busied himself with the toasting fork. He moved the cat from it's warm place on the inglenook and pushed it away when it tried to lick the bowl of dripping.

'Get off. Have you fed the cat this morning?'

'She's had milk.'

Frowning, he looked at her, she wasn't very cheerful, 'What's up Dorrie? You're very quiet. I've a gift for you later. I got it in Banbury. Would you like it now?'

'No, it's just the baby kicking. I have something for you, we can have them after dinner.'

She hoped he'd like the thick wool jerkin she'd sewn for him, buying the material in Banbury the last time they'd been. It would leave his arms free for working but keep his back warm.

She was subdued because in her curiosity to know if he had bought her a Christmas gift she had rummaged through his things in the other bedroom and found the key of the sea chest.

Very early on in their marriage she had discovered that he kept it locked. She knew Robert was out for several hours.

The key turned easily. The lock had been well rubbed with candle grease and she opened the lid and peered in. There was a sword, some of his Navy clothes and various books. Excited at the sight of a bankbook she opened it, wondering if it would say how much money he had. It was the White Horse Bank of Banbury and the last entry showed a fortune. Two hundred pounds! Another book gave details of bonds held in his name by a London bank. A book with a soft green leather cover had his writing inside. Dorothy had some basic knowledge of her letters and could read and write, with difficulty.

She quashed any feeling of shame as she looked through his obviously private papers and took the book to the table by the window. She sat on the same chair that Robert used. There was no fire in the room so she hitched her shawl round her shoulders and settled comfortably.

It started off with brief notes about his arrival back in May and went on to haymaking time. She could recognise Mary's name. At school one of their lessons had been to write each other's name and she frowned as she counted the frequency of "Marys". Puzzling over the words she suddenly exclaimed.

'Oh my goodness, he loved her. He says he wanted to marry her. Oh my, Oh dear. What shall I do?' Carefully she put the journal back, tucking it down, hoping it looked the same. She locked the chest and replaced the key in the bureau.

She shivered as she went back downstairs to the warm kitchen. She would make herself a cup of tea and think about it. Ten minutes later she sat by the fire in Mary's chair with the blue and white dish and saucer placed carefully on the inglenook.

She spoke to the cat, 'I know he didn't love me when we wed, it was a marriage that suited us both, but we've been lying together and he seems to enjoy it. We've made a baby and he's taught me skills that Jim never knew. I thought we were happy. What shall I do, cat?' Say nothing said a voice in her head, that was his personal diary. These are Robert's secret thoughts. You get along all right and you lack for nothing, don't spoil it. She finished her tea and heaved herself out of the chair. She must prepare some vegetables to go with the lamb for dinner.

She kept her own counsel, but dropped the occasional hint, asking one day why he had never married. He told her how he had been at sea for long periods of time and had never met anyone he wanted to share his life with. He didn't say until he met Mary James. She didn't feel threatened but it made her more determined to feather her own nest. If Robert should die she could be homeless again and that was a most unpleasant prospect.

As she stood by the fire, turning the goose, to change the subject she exclaimed brightly, 'I hope Ben is having a good time, out in that heathen land. Do you think they would know it was Christmas?'

'I'm sure they will, we always did. On board ship the cook would find the ingredients for a large fruit pudding and a pig or sheep would be killed, whatever was left.' Robert lounged in his chair, warmed by an early glass of burgundy, heated with nutmeg, cinnamon and Demerara sugar. The goose was turning a golden brown, his stomach grumbled in anticipation and he got up to stand the saucepan of vegetables on the trivet above the hot embers.

They had heard in early December that so far, Ben was all right and shortly to embark for India to join Sir Arthur Wellesley's army. He had finished his training and was settled. Robert was pleased for him but still felt Ben might have stayed at the farm if he hadn't been there telling yarns. Perhaps Ben had thought that with

Robert at the farm he would provide the muscle power in place of him.

Moodily Robert stared at the glowing embers. He heard Dorothy bustling about laying the table. With a conscious effort he found a smile and heaved himself out of the chair.

'We've a while before dinner, I'll go and find that present.'

They sat at the table, the best plates full with slices of goose smothered in thick gravy. Golden brown onions and potatoes were piled up with a mashed carrot and turnip mixture. Two new fat, white candles burned brightly in the pewter candlesticks to dispel the gloom of a winter day. The old green wine glasses that had been passed down from Verner James's grandfather held a fine hock that Robert had discovered in the wine merchant's shop in Banbury.

Dorrie was wearing her best black silk dress, with a gold chain hanging down. It gleamed like an oriental snake and a pearl, set in gold was suspended from it with a loop. She kept touching it as if to reassure herself that it really existed. She was delighted and had placed its slim black leather case by her plate. Robert was in his shirtsleeves, wearing his new wool jerkin. He had been so pleased with it, exclaiming at the perfect fit and had given her a resounding kiss.

'No one in the village has ever had such a beautiful jewel,' she chattered happily knowing that when she next went to town she would try and find out the value. It must be worth three or four guineas at least. What a start to her nest egg.

She had asked Robert about Mary's small pieces of jewellery but he had said that they must be for Ben to decide upon. Only with official news of his death could they go to her…Mary's next of kin. Dorothy had to be content with that and was wise enough not to press the matter.

A cold hard, frosty January turned into a wet February. It was easier to water the cows as the pump wasn't frozen but there was mud everywhere and he took it into the house. As fast as Margie cleaned the flagstones, more appeared.

In the middle of February he packed the small cart with as much butter and cheese as he could sell. He refused to take Dorothy and after a little sulk she capitulated. He promised to bring her what shopping she needed and, leaving Caleb to finish milking set off for Banbury market a little after six o'clock. It was still dark and the roads were dangerous with huge potholes.

He let Binnie feel his way, trusting to the horse's instincts, taking his time, anxious to get to Banbury without a damaged wheel or a lost shoe from the horse.

It was a raw day in the market square, an icy wind billowed the ladies' skirts about as they scurried from stall to stall. By half past eleven Robert was grateful to have sold out and hurried to clear up and get a hot dinner before he started for home. Binnie was in the stable of the inn having his favourite hot bran mash and Robert left him there whilst he found Dorrie's purchases. He gave way to temptation and bought her a fine wool shawl in soft cream as a compensation for staying at home although he knew she would have done little in his absence. She would have been sitting in Mary's chair, by the fire whilst Margie scrubbed and dusted.

After four o'clock he was blown into the yard by an icy squall and quickly led Binnie into the barn to be rubbed down. Whilst he worked Caleb told him about his daughter, the pert and pretty Clarice or Rissie they fondly called her, fifteen years old and gone to be a maid in a lawyer's house in Oxford.

'I know she's got to go, got to get a job, but we'll miss her, Margie's that upset today.' Caleb was vigorously brushing down the dairy, trying to keep warm. 'I wish she were closer, but she'll be home for Easter, so we're looking forward to that. And she's gone off with a new dress in her box so she's pleased as punch.' He straightened up, tidied the buckets and with a 'Good night, boss,' strode off into the rain falling steadily, flooding gutters and making huge puddles in the yard.

CHAPTER ELEVEN

Robert was more nervous than Dorothy as she neared the time of her confinement. She tried to reassure him, she'd done it all before and much as she wouldn't appreciate the pains, it would soon be over and they'd have their baby.

March was milder and still determined to have the doctor out from Banbury, he timed his journeys to the market so that he knew how long it would take to fetch the doctor and bring him back.

Dorrie had explained to him that babies could come very quick or take quite a while and she was perfectly happy to have the services of Clarrie Bates. If she was good enough for the rest of the village then she was good enough for her. But Robert was unshakeable in his determination to have the best medical attention for his child. Dorothy just took advantage of this preoccupation to acquire all the little luxuries she had never had before.

Spring came in with a sting in its tail. The wind veered to the east and was bitterly cold. Although it was dry the sky turned a sulphurous yellow, tinged with murky grey and Caleb and Robert both thought it looked like snow.

On the night of the 3rd of April Robert and Dorothy sat in front of the fire, with a large apple log burning brightly and the crimson glow of sea coal. The shutters were tightly closed against the howling wind. They had finished their supper and Robert had cleared up, carefully wiping the table over, always conscious of Mary's tidy ways.

Dorothy gasped, 'Oh!' she clutched at her swollen abdomen and looked at him. She had had an aching back all day but kept quiet, not wanting him to fuss.

Robert leapt up, galvanised into action. 'Is it coming? Is the baby coming? I'll ride into Banbury and fetch the doctor. But first we must get you comfortable.'

'Stop fussing, I'll be all right. I don't want you to leave me all that time. It'll take hours and he might not come. Just go and get Clarrie.' She clutched at her stomach and tried to stifle a groan.

He took down the copper warming pan he had bought and quickly filled it with hot ashes He leapt up the stairs, thrust it into the bed and glanced swiftly at the pile of new baby clothes and blankets on the table.

A beautiful oak crib with a bright patchwork cover was waiting, ready to be rocked. He struck a spark with his flint and lit the candles placed on the table. At the door he turned back and looked and sighed apprehensively, hoping everything was in order.

He wished the baby were coming in the daytime, when he could have sent Caleb into Banbury to bring the doctor back. They could have done it in two hours, with fine weather. He leapt back down the stairs like a man half his age and saw Dorothy, her hands pressed to her stomach, was closing her eyes. Her brow furrowed with pain. Quickly he crossed to her, brushed her forehead with his lips and told her,

'Take it steady Dorrie, I'll be as quick as I can.'

Robert pulled his boots on, his thick old coat and a tweed cap that he tied on with a scarf. At the door he looked back,

'Get yourself up to bed soon, I've lit the candles and we'll be back before you know.' He snatched a lantern, lit the candle and tightly closed the glass door.

He opened the door to a white swirling wall of snow.

'Oh my God, a blizzard,' his mouth filled with icy flakes as he spoke and he knew he couldn't possibly get to Banbury for the doctor. Clarrie must come, immediately.

Taking a thick stick from the hallstand he took his bearings from the barns and set off. It was a straight track down to the village. He knew he must keep going. He had been at sea with worse weather but he had never realised how disorientating a snowstorm could be. The snow threw itself at him like a whirling dervish and the cold was numbing. He trudged on, his head down, watching the track, but it became an everlasting expanse of white.

His eyelashes became encrusted with snow and he brushed at them. He tripped and fell down into the ditch and realised he'd gone wrong. Panting, shaken, he got to the end of the lane and saw the cottages with glimmers of light showing through small panes and shutters. Counting doors he stumbled along, his feet finding all the bumps and dips he would avoid in the day.

With an immense feeling of relief he found the cracked and peeling blue door of number seven and banged on it as loudly as he could. The wind was howling like a banshee and he rattled the handle desperately afraid they couldn't hear him.

The door opened, 'What the devil. It's Mr Southwell. Come in.' Clarrie let him into the cluttered, warm and smelly room, which seemed to be filled with children of varying ages and Jo Bates, their father in the only chair.

'It's my wife, Mrs Bates, she's started, but there's a terrible snow storm. I'll never get to Banbury for the doctor, can you come?' He stood, covered in snow and the children, quiet, stared with round eyes.

Jo levered his fat hulk from the chair and ambled to the door. He opened it a crack, peering out. 'It's a terrible night, Clarrie, you can't go out in that; it'd be downright foolhardy. The lass'll doubtless still be heaving and straining in the morning, you go at first light.'

Robert who had taken off his sheepskin mittens, rung his hands in agitation. 'Oh Mrs Bates, can you come back with me, you know it's her fifth, they do say they come quicker. It's a long time until morning.' He looked at them both, seeing the cunning in Bate's face and exhaled a breath. 'I'll make it well worth while, shall we say a guinea?'

'I reckons we'll say two, on a night like this,' the harsh voice, heavy with the smell of beer cut in.

Robert was in no position to argue. 'Two it is, but come now We'll go together.'

He watched Clarrie pick up an old carpetbag and wrap a large shawl around her shoulders and head.

'Have you got a coat?' Robert asked thinking her clothes completely inadequate for a blizzard.

'Take my work coat, woman,' said her husband and Robert shuddered inwardly as she removed the shawl, put on a filthy old coat, tied pieces of twine together and then put her shawl over her head.

'Have you gloves?'

'Gloves. Of course not.' She laughed.

'Here, take these.' He handed her the sheepskin mitts and didn't even look to see what she had on her feet. The children were all barefoot or wearing very holey stockings.

With the lantern in one hand, his stick in the other and Clarrie holding onto his coat they stumbled slowly through the blinding wall of whiteness.

Robert found his bearings from the side wall of the Ewe and Lamb at the end of his lane and tried to concentrate on walking what he thought was a straight line to their house. What were only yards seemed far longer and once Clarrie tugged at him and shook her head pointing to their left. He trusted her and realised he was going off course.

When the barn walls loomed up at them he nearly cried out in relief. Touching the wall with his stick like a blind man he followed it, finding the corner of the house wall. It was a few steps to the door and he opened it, exhausted, sagging with relief. The snow that had piled up on the door fell in after them and he ignored it. He could mop up later.

'Come in the kitchen, Clarrie, we'll get our things off and have a tot, I need it after that.'

The kitchen was empty, he looked at the clock and realised it had taken him over an hour to go that short distance and back. 'We're here Dorothy.' He called up the stairs. 'Are you all right?'

Quite a strong, 'Yes,' floated down the stairs.

Formality returned in the candle lit room. 'Mrs Bates would you like a pair of Dorothy's shoes to wear whilst your boots dry?'

'Call me Clarrie and yes, and I'll borrow that skirt I see hanging up, I'm soaked up to the knees.'

'I'll fetch some water to wash with now,' he told her remembering with a shudder the filthy cottage he'd just been in.

She accepted the soap and towel having been warned by Dorothy of her husband's fastidiousness. It was a very pleasant sensation to plunge her hands in the warm water, lather up the soap and swish her hands clean. Even the towel was soft. What money could buy she reflected and what she could do with two guineas. The glass of rum and hot water was tossed down double quick.

'Right, let's see how mother is doing shall we?'

There was no fireplace in the bedroom. The back wall behind the bed was warm with the heat from the chimney so it was a comfortable room to sleep in. Dorothy, her pale face peering out of her white nightdress was in bed, sitting up, with her new shawl wrapped round her shoulders.

'I'll get hot water,' he muttered clattering back down stairs.

'Aye, it's woman's work now, sir, you can leave us to it.'

Robert sat on through the night. He fed the fire, keeping the kitchen hot, with the door open to let the heat upstairs. Saucepans and kettles were stacked up, full of hot water. He didn't know what else to do.

The howling wind was a background to the patter of feet upstairs, the murmur of hushed voices and occasional groans and cries. Once or twice he dozed, sitting in Mary's chair but it wasn't comfortable and he woke up with a start.

'It's a big baby, Dorothy.' Clarrie had her hands on the swollen mound feeling delicately with work reddened fingers. It's coming well but it's going to take a bit of pushing. What size were your others?'

Dorothy clutched at the rag to mop up the sweat running down her face. She was starting to feel anxious, not quite in a panic but she knew that this one was bigger than her others. She was too old for a difficult childbirth; but it was too late to wish for the Banbury doctor. She must grit her teeth and get through it.

'They were small girls,' she puffed, 'dainty they was, pretty as …ohhh.'

'Easy now.'

Clarrie rubbed her comfrey salve onto the mother, to ease the delicate skin. She would likely be torn with a big head birthing. She hid her unease from the woman lying writhing amongst the tousled sheets. She knew how important this baby was to Robert Southwell.

What should she do if there was the question of saving the child or the mother? Who would he choose? It wouldn't be her decision. She had had difficult births before, breeches, twins and very long labours where the mother was too exhausted to expel the infant.

With Dorothy she could tell the child was coming, but it was large. She was overdue and Clarrie reckoned it was the easy living and good food that hadn't helped. It was at times like these she wished a doctor would coming walking in the door and take over the responsibility.

The clock in the parlour ticked away the minutes and its miniature ship's bell rang out the hours as the night dragged on. Robert looked out the door and saw drifts of snow piling up into weird and fantastic shapes. The blizzard had eased a little, but the snow was still falling, thick and fast. Clarrie would have to stay until they could dig a path through.

As the clock struck half past five he heard Clarrie call, 'Mr Southwell.' He sprinted up the stairs,

'Yes? Yes? What's happening, is it coming?'

A faint mewing cry came from the wrapped up bundle she handed to him. 'He isn't washed yet, she warned. 'It's been very difficult, he's a big lad. Dorothy's had too much rich living these last months.'

'A boy,' he breathed, exultant, 'a son, I have a son.' His face shone with emotion and he pulled back the blanket to disclose a red, blood smeared wrinkled face with two blue eyes gazing directly at him. He felt the most incredible pull of emotion. His son. Belatedly, he thought of his wife and looked down at the bed. Dorothy was lying motionless; her face in the flickering candlelight was a greyish white. She opened her eyes and gave him a tired smile.

'Is he perfect?'

'Oh yes, absolutely perfect. Here I'll put him by you.' Carefully Robert placed the child on the sheet by his mothers's head and she turned and placed her lips against the bundle. Her eyes fluttered and she gasped and groaned.

'The afterbirth's coming, we'll just get this out of the way and you can come back.' Clarrie bustled around, rags and a bowl ready.

Taking this as dismissal again he went back downstairs and thought to take back the brandy and glasses. A nip would restore Dorrie and keep Clarrie awake. At the bedroom door he paused, aghast at the sight that met his eyes.

The blankets were pulled off and Dorothy had her knees pulled up, with a pool of blood spreading across underneath her. Clarrie was vigorously kneading her stomach.

'She's bleeding, I can't stop it.'

'What can I do?' he demanded, horrified. Dorrie's life was slipping away in front of him. Her eyes were sunk in her colourless face . Was she unconscious?

'Get some snow, we'll pack it on her stomach and inside, perhaps the cold would help.'

Robert had seen plenty of horrific sights on the orlop deck of the ships he'd been in. That was the surgeon's work and became a hell of bleeding bodies and limbs after battles. But nothing had prepared him to watch his wife fade away in exsanguinous peace. Dorothy slipped into death as they worked around her. Eventually Robert touched Clarrie's arm,

'It's no good, we've done all we can, she's gone.'

'I'm sorry, sir, I'm really sorry.'

'It's not your fault, she haemorrhaged and there's nothing anyone can do for that.' He looked bleakly at the still figure in their bed. Snow was melting, dripping everywhere. He grabbed another towel and tried to mop it up.

The room was quiet, the baby in the crib was still and Clarrie sat on the chair by the window drying her hands, rubbing unnecessarily. Dorothy was covered over. A pool of pink water soaked into the floorboards. A bucket from the dairy was piled high with sopping wet pink and red towels.

Robert gazed round the room, hardly able to believe what had happened. He had gained a son and lost a wife, all in minutes. His hand strayed to the brandy but he thought no, he must keep a clear head. In an hour or two he must go outside and start milking. He would make some coffee, hot, strong and well sugared, to keep him going.

'Clarrie, will you stay a bit, help me get things organised for,' he thought for a minute, 'for Simon, yes for Simon Benjamin Southwell.'

'Of course I will. We'll have to sort out a wet nurse for him, shall I do that?'

'Please,' he said gratefully. 'I'm going to take him downstairs by the fire, it's warmer and somehow...' his voice tailed off as he looked at his wife. He felt exhausted but he didn't want to leave a newborn baby in the same room as his dead mother. Somehow he must get through the next few days. The snow would cause a lot of problems.

He left the cows until the sky was lightening after seven and groaned at the sight of a huge drift in front of the barn door. Mercifully the yard was clear, swept clean as if by a giant broom.

He stood a moment looking round. There was a massive drift, higher than him across the lane. The snow piled against the back door of the barn was shovelled away in minutes and he quickly stepped in, greeting the cows, as they turned and looked at him. The nearest shuffled nervously, clinking her chain and he realised he'd got his filthy clothes on, his shirt and trousers were spattered with blood and he probably smelt of it.

'I'll be back,' he called. He hurried back into the kitchen and saw the steaming kettle hanging from the hook. He hadn't made his coffee. A pot was made in seconds and while it brewed he changed, grateful for his old working breeches and shirt left on the inglenook to keep warm. The cat had sat on them, they were covered in hairs and briefly he wondered about fleas but decided that was the least of his problems.

He sliced bread, buttered it and poured honey over. With hot coffee inside him, ten minutes later he felt restored. He topped up the pot with hot water, sliced some more bread and called up the stairs to Clarrie,

'Come down, there's food here.' He gently rubbed his finger on Simon's cheek, the child was pink and warm and he felt again the tremendous thrill of fatherhood.

'I'll be down in a minute,' called Clarrie.

Two hours later, as he walked through to the dairy, carefully carrying pails of milk, he heard voices in the lane.

'Hello there,' shouted Caleb over the top of the drift, 'we're digging our way through.'

With the cows munching on hay and the chickens pecking corn in the yard he walked back into the kitchen with an armful of logs for the fire.

Clarrie was sitting by the hearth, the baby in her lap, with a small curved bottle in her hand.

'I'm giving him some of his mother's milk, just a little. He's lucky, she were overdue and with some gentle persuasion I managed to expel some of the first milk. This'll keep him going until later.'

He sat and watched. Simon had been washed and was in soft cotton nightgown, frilled round the neck, with a thick blanket tucked around him. He sucked industriously at the bottle, carefully tipped to allow a drop at a time.

'There,' Clarrie gave him his son, 'you hold him, get to know him.'

He was sitting in Mary's chair, an hour later, still holding his son and fast asleep when Caleb and Jo Bates burst in the door. Full of red faced good humour, they shook snow off their coats and rubbed their hands at the sight of the rum bottle.

'Babby's here then,' boomed Joe, 'a lad or a lass is it?'

Robert gazed at them, bleary eyed. He clutched tighter at the bundle, feeling it slip. 'It's a boy, Simon.'

'The missus upstairs then? Is Clarrie with her?'

'Yes,' and then the full horror of it all hit him. His voice cracking he looked down at the pink shell of a newborn cheek, 'she's dead, Dorrie, she haemorrhaged. We couldn't save her.'

The two men were suitably grave. Caleb swung the kettle across and threw wood onto the fire. He found the tea pot and caddy and measured in two spoonfuls. Fetching bread from the scullery he cut slices, buttered it and made a pile of it on the table. A slab of cheese was cold from the safe and it cracked into crumbs as he cut wedges. Robert watched numbly as the tea was made and beakers fetched out. Caleb fetched a jug of milk and a bowl of sugar. He stirred the tea as he had seen Robert do.

'Clarrie come down for food, Caleb called up the stairs.

'In a moment.'

She went through into the scullery with two buckets of clothes and towels.

'All done, Robert,' she exclaimed brightly, I've laid her out nicely, very pretty she looks too.'

'Thank you Clarrie, you must let me know what I owe you for all this extra work. I'll have to see the Rector later to ask about her burial.'

'Well it's cold enough, perhaps if Joe Carpenter comes up with a coffin later she could go into the parlour. There's no fire in there. It's a mite warm up in that bedroom and you'll want to sleep later. Yes, you go and call on Joe for the coffin later. She said to her husband, 'perhaps Caleb here'll help Robert with the cows and I'll see Fanny Bewick about milk for the young'un. Her Johnny's a year old, ready for weaning and she's milking like a…begging your pardon, she's still got plenty. For a shillun or two she'll be glad to feed Simon.'

Robert sipped at his tea feeling warmth spread through his tired limbs. What good people they all were, how kind and helpful. But one thing he was determined on, he would look after Simon himself. If the lady came and fed him then he would attend to all the personal bits, the cleaning up and changing him. It shouldn't be too hard…should it?

CHAPTER TWELVE

'Wait a minute, just wait a minute.' Robert hurried back downstairs with a nightgown for Simon. The bawling baby was laying on a rug on the kitchen flagstones, his chubby, bare legs waving in the air, fists pummelling away and scarlet in the face. It was half past five in the morning, Robert wanted his coffee, Simon wanted his bottle and the cows needed milking.

Robert had evolved his own system for wrapping up the child's bottom but it still produced a large amount of washing. There were buckets full of rags, napkins, little vests and nightdresses. Where did it all come from? He would have scratched his head in puzzlement if he had had the time. He had quickly discovered that he needed help with looking after the infant. .

'Simon, I'm making my coffee first. I'll drink it while I feed you. Your milk's warming in the bottle so just try and be patient.'

Robert tried to be methodical. Everything ship shape was his motto. He tried to instil this in Margie who cheerfully took on three jobs at once, often leaving little things undone so that he had to run upstairs for binders, or hunt for pins or find Simon's rattle under a chair.

But he didn't complain, well not much, as the kitchen table, Mary's kitchen table was always spotless and they had a hot dinner every day. Fanny Bewick's plentiful breasts provided Simon's milk. She also did all the washing which explained why there were strings strung across the kitchen and scullery, all draped with small clothes and rags. Robert's respect for mothers with large families increased enormously as he found out how difficult it was just coping with one. He had discovered that he couldn't care for the baby and look after the cows at the same time.

'I didn't realise little babies woke up in the night,' he grumbled to Margie, 'it's very wearing, isn't it?'

She was at the kitchen table cutting up butter, 'for a few weeks, yes, then he'll sleep through the night, soon enough. Give him a big feed at ten o'clock and with luck, he won't wake 'til six.'

'It would be a relief.' Eleven in the morning and Robert was nearly asleep at the kitchen table.

A few weeks later, Caleb and Robert were having their breakfast, a big crusty cottage loaf, a slice of cold roast pork and piping hot coffee. Robert had pulled the top knob off and smeared it liberally with butter. Simon was asleep in his box pushed into the corner out of the way. Margie was upstairs, singing loudly, sweeping the floors.

Robert dearly loved keeping written records in books and lists. It had been his life and he sometimes missed the work as a purser in the Navy. Not the life on board ship, the bad weather, the dreadful food and difficult living conditions, just the pleasure of counting stock and making lists.

There were now blackboards in the dairy. Details of cheese started, weights and quantities were all meticulously chalked down in his careful writing. Woe betides anyone who altered anything.

Robert complained. 'They come up for milk at all hours of the day and if I'm not there they help themselves and I don't know how much they take.'

'Well it's always been like that, you're the nearest dairy farm to the village.' Caleb drank and ate at the same time, noisily.'

'I'm going to leave out a gallon in a bucket and that'll be it, if that's gone they'll have to wait for the next milking.'

'They're used to coming up when they can.'

'I know. Well, I'm going to ask if they can come before nine or after six. That way I know how much to use for butter. With Simon to think of now I must run as tight a ship as possible, Caleb. I want to provide for his future.'

Caleb grunted and got up, taking his beaker and plate to the scullery as he had been asked. The bread was put into the crock, the butter in the cold safe and the table wiped clean.

Margie came clattering downstairs, broom in one hand, cloth and polish in the other.

'All done, clean and tidy,' she reported, having nearly said shipshape. 'I'm going home for a bit when Fanny comes, I'll be back for dinner time.'

'I don't want Simon going back to Fanny's house. Will she stay here with him?' Robert didn't think the Bewick's house was clean enough for his son.

'She will; she'll feed him and get some washing out.' Margie filled kettles to warm up from the pails of water Robert brought in from the pump.

Caleb Pound had stayed on, working six days a week and would do a Sunday milking in exchange for his weekly ration of cheese. Dorothy had been the boss in the dairy and Robert had been glad to leave her to supervise whoever had the time to help her.

They all lifted the heavy pails and the vat and picked up information as they worked but it wasn't enough.

With spring calving starting there would be plenty of milk left over for the dairy. Robert had been making small quantities of butter in the winter. He had written down Dorothy's instructions and managed to make a tolerable job of it. With the cold weather it had kept well and he took the surplus to Banbury market twice a month. The cheese that Mary made had long gone and there was not much left from Dorothy's efforts, so they must start again in earnest.

Caleb and Robert had to learn the art of making cheese. Maria Smith, the head Dairy Maid at the Byclere farm taught them the basic processes when she came over three times a week. She left instructions to keep back half the previous evenings' milk and they would then add this to half the next mornings' quantity. Robert would skim off the cream to make butter and then warm the milk gently over the charcoal burner they had installed. It was a trick to know how much rennet to add to get the milk to curdle.

They had finished Mary's supply of dried Lady's Bedstraw which was the natural herbal remedy for rennet so Maria kindly brought over some of the farm rennet extracted from the stomach of a calf. Robert had not realised that making cheese was so complicated but diligently he wrote down notes and instructions and followed everything to the letter. Cleanliness was the guiding rule of his life anyway so the strict hygiene that had to be observed in the dairy didn't faze him.

He took to walking up to the Steward's office at Byclere House to ascertain what John Calloway was ordering the men to do in their fields. He would stride home, his eyes keenly scanning his neighbour's land to see what was happening there and the wayside verges for different plants to add to his collection.

They had borrowed a team of shire horses and ploughed up three acres in April and sown barley to get some feed for the cows in the winter. They would also grow two acres of wheat so that they could have their own bread flour and use the straw for bedding. It had taken Caleb a week of work to plough, harrow and then broadcast the seed. This had meant Robert was flat out looking after the cows and working in the dairy. Margie helped in there as well. By the end of the week he was very tired and fell into bed at nine o'clock, to sleep soundly until Simon woke him.

He wrote in his journal what had been sown, how much weight of seed to the acre and when it germinated. He felt sure that keeping these records would enable him to look back and see how everything followed on.

As Easter drew near Margie was excited at the thought of her daughter, Rissie coming home for three whole days. On the Thursday before good Friday Robert was all set to take butter and cheese to market in Banbury. He was going to bring back Rissie who would have come in from Oxford by the Mail Coach.

With everything organised at home and the cart packed high with butter and the last of Dorothy's cheese he set off soon after seven. Fanny would bring her little girl and stay until he got home. He didn't like leaving Simon all day but knew he had to have some money coming in. He had paid his half yearly rent on Lady Day, March 25th only just managing to scrape together the necessary pounds. Dorothy had spent more than he had realised and now he was thinking ahead to the next Rent day to make sure there was enough cash.

The spring sun warmed them and Binnie trotted briskly, enjoying the trip. Robert worried whether Simon had been picked up if he cried and fed if he was hungry. He knew Margie doted on him but he couldn't help it. Fanny was a good girl, but careless and sometimes she fed him without washing her hands.

With Binnie in the stable tucking into a hot bran mash and talking to other horses Robert got into the swing of the market. He relaxed and enjoyed himself weighing out pounds and ounces, large pieces and small.

'Two ounces, my dear,' to a little old lady he knew lived on her own. 'Three pennies.' he told her, letting her go off with a good three ounces of butter and a finger of cheese for her dinner. He knew that wasn't the way to run a tight ship but he felt sorry for her.

He sold out and cleared the table. The sun had gone in, a fresh cold wind made him shiver and he turned to the inn, looking forward to hot coffee with brandy and a roast dinner. An apple pie with cream would go down well afterwards and then he mustn't forget he was to look out for Rissie.

Binnie was harnessed back into the shafts and Robert walked him slowly back into the street scanning up and down for the prettiest girl he had ever seen. He smiled, involuntarily. Even with his heart still sore from Mary's death he could appreciate the blonde curls and the sensual, swinging walk. Men turned and stared, tugged back into behaviour by their watchful wives. Youths called and whistled. Rissie walked through, even with a pale face, she was lovely.

'Mr Southwell.'

'Hello, Rissie, your mother's been looking forward to seeing you all week.' He saw her hunch into her shawl; her face was almost white with two hectic spots of colour on the cheeks

'Are you well?'

'Yeh, I'll be alright.' In spite of her long sleeved dress, a short jacket and a wool shawl she felt cold and shivery. She longed to lie down in bed. Rissie Pound sat as far from Mr Southwell as she could, hoping the ride would be smooth enough not to start her head banging again. A maniac who had found every bump and pothole in the road had driven the mail coach. She would get her mother to buy one of Clarrie Bates's herbal potions. She'd got to be fit to go back to Oxford on Monday.

CHAPTER THIRTEEN

The sun came out for them, warming their faces and a frisky Binnie bowled them along. A bank of dark grey cloud was edging over from the west and Robert kept a good pace going, to avoid a soaking. The hedges were greening up with young leaves and violets and wild strawberry flowers peeped from hedge banks. There was a delicate perfume of early summer in the air. Robert smiled happy thoughts. Simon was at home, a hot tea would be ready, Caleb would milk and later he would give the baby the bone ship he had bought. He would tell him what all the parts were called and later on when he was big enough he could play with it.

Rissie slid down to the ground outside her cottage, mumbling thanks. The air had whipped colour into her cheeks but she looked dreadful.

'If you've got a cold, Rissie you'd better stay in and let Margie dose you. I'll send up some oranges with Caleb. They'll do you good.' Robert turned to go and had a thought, 'Oh, and I'm sorry, but I'd rather you didn't come up and see Simon, just to be on the safe side.' He clicked to Binnie to move on.

Rissie held on to the doorpost, her head swimming, she'd never felt so bad in her life before. She'd have a drink of water and go to bed. With luck, her mother would have made up her old bed and she'd have a sleep before they came home. As to going up to see Robert's baby, didn't he know she looked after a whole brood every day. The last thing she wanted to see on her precious time off was another one. She wanted to catch up on village gossip and flirt with her old admirers. There had been plenty in Oxford and she'd honed her teasing skills to a fine art. The village youths were callow and dull, she knew how easy they would be to impress

'I'm back, Caleb,'

Smiling broadly, Caleb popped his head round the door of the barn. 'How is she? My we're looking forward to seeing her.'

'I'm sorry to say she looks like she's sickening for a cold, take some oranges home with you.'

Margie came out, carrying Simon, 'There he is, there's your Dada.'

Robert reached for his child, used now to the surge of emotion he felt when he held him. His chin nuzzled against the soft, warm cheek.

'How's he been Margie? Has he been a good boy? Has he had his milk?' Anxiously Robert surveyed his son looking, for any imperfections that had come in the few hours he'd been away. The child was clean, sweet smelling and contented. Robert put him to his shoulder and walked into the house, forgetting all the purchases in the cart.

Margie looked after him with a rueful smile. It had taken quite a while to get the lad clean. She reached into the cart for the parcels. She was dying to see their Rissie.

When Caleb banged his front door shut an hour later Margie put her finger to her lips. 'Shh. She's asleep.'

'Oh.' He whispered loudly, 'I'll take me boots off then.' As quietly as he could he crept into the back room to peer at his daughter. The blanket and sheet were flung off, she'd fallen asleep with her jacket on, her dress was creased and her hair was spread out over the white pillowcase. Her face was pale, her breathing rather rapid.

He frowned. 'She don't look good, Margie. I've brought three oranges home. Can you squeeze them out for her? The juice'll do her good.'

'Give them here; I'll have it ready for her. I've got a nice mutton stew ready for when she wakes. Shall we wait a bit, have it all together?'

Caleb put his boots back on, 'I'll wet my whistle for ten minutes then.'

Margie looked in on Rissie, her heart heavy, disappointed at the anticlimax. She'd so looked forward to a chat and a laugh and hearing all about the family in Oxford.

When Caleb came home an hour later he saw Margie supporting his daughter as she sipped her juice. She'd been put her into a clean nightgown and her hair was brushed.

'Now are you going to have some broth, nice and hot, better than they gave you at that posh house?'

'Ugh, my head hurts, no, no thanks, Mother, perhaps later.' Rissie subsided back against the pillows, her eyes drifting shut again. The incredibly long dark lashes swept her white cheeks and her breathing was worryingly fast.

Quietly Margie left the little room. It was just the two of them then, as usual.

With Simon asleep, Robert got up quickly the next morning and after swinging the kettle across hurried outside. It was Easter weekend and there might be dancing on the village green tonight. Not that he'd be going. Milking was finished, the milk was all in the dairy and still Caleb hadn't turned up. It wasn't like him. As Robert opened the kitchen door he heard the shrill cry of a neglected baby. No Margie, what was going on?

He rushed upstairs, picked up Simon, soothing and hushing him. The baby snuffled and sniffed, not quite ready to forgive. Robert put his hand inside the nightgown and felt the damp.

'Come on, let's feed you and change your clothes.'

Whilst the milk was warming he changed a grumpy child. Warming his milk bottle he told him,

'I'm dying for coffee and honey toast, so hurry up. Where are the Pounds? They should have been here hours ago.' The clock said ten to nine.. Fanny would be coming soon, she could watch Simon whilst Robert finished outside.

Red faced and panting, Fanny pushed open the door, 'Mr Southwell, sorry I's late, I'll get started in a mo. The bad news is you know you brought Rissie home yesterday. Well she's come out in a rash. Margie banged on my door just now, she won't come, she thinks it could be the pox. They think Rissie's brought smallpox home with her from Oxford. She don't want to give it to the bebby.'

Robert looked up in horror, his coffee cup halfway to his lips. 'Smallpox? That's dreadful. I thought she might have a cold, not that, never that.'

'Well, we'll all keep away from them. That's why Caleb hasn't come. I'll have the babe whilst you do the outside work, but I'll have to get back for tea time.'

'Yes all right.' Robert felt terribly anxious, he hadn't had smallpox and he knew how contagious it was. She'd been close to him on the seat of the cart. He'd come home and kissed Simon's face. The thought was too awful to contemplate. He could have infected his baby, his precious child.

'Fanny,' he said slowly, 'Fanny, you'd better go home. Have you had smallpox?'

She looked frightened. 'No, we haven't, none of us has. That's why no one will go near the Pounds.'

'I haven't had it either. But I brought her back from Banbury. Rissie, she…she sat on the seat next to me.'

Fanny backed to the door, reaching for the handle I've got to go, I'm sorry, you'll have to manage…as best you can.' She was gone, running.

Robert ran his hand through his hair and looked at Simon, propped up in his box. Baby bright blue eyes gazed steadily back.

'What can I do, Simon? How can I help us? I'm on my own until I know we're clear, no one will come near us now. You'll have to come out with me to the barn. I'd better send word to Calloway the steward in case I fall ill. Perhaps the cows could go somewhere else?'

He put some rum in his coffee and stirred it in with plenty of Demerara sugar. He must think and plan what to do. He must cover all eventualities. What, God forbid would happen to Simon if he died? Who would look after him?

He must speak to Calloway. He would write a note for the Bank in Banbury so that the steward could, if necessary take out some money. And he must write to the Share Factor in London for the shares to be released to Simon's guardian. John Calloway had agreed to be Simon's godfather and his godmother was Margie, who might die. He had no living relatives of his own and Ben might never come home.

With Simon wrapped up against a chilly wind, Robert walked to the end of the lane. He waited to see someone, anyone. No one had come for their usual milk and he wanted to ask if they would take a message to Calloway. When he saw Clarrie Bates leave her cottage, walk to the Pounds and place a bottle by the door he called.

'Clarrie, stay there, can you hear me?'

'Yes.' Even from that distance she backed away, pressing into her front door.

'Will you take a message to Calloway for me please? Ask him to meet me in the long meadow tomorrow at nine o'clock. I'll keep well back tell him. I must make arrangements. Oh, also, I'll leave a small churn of milk down here, can you make sure the Pounds get some and anyone else who needs it.'

'I will.'

Clasping the baby, Robert hurried back home. With the extra milk he would set on more cheese, but first he must feed his baby. Without Fanny's milk Simon would have to have cows' milk. Robert pondered. There was a beef stew to warm from yesterday. He would have a bowlful at dinnertime and try Simon with some gravy.

He mashed warm gravy and vegetables into a little piece of soft bread and the child lapped it up. Robert had no idea about weaning babies but thought that if he filled up with food Simon would need less milk. Robert breathed a sigh of relief at his idea.

The next job was to wash out some of the rags and nightgowns and put them on the line above the fire to dry overnight. It was getting dark by the time Robert had finished all the chores and he was exhausted. He made himself wipe over the kitchen table and take the cloth outside and then slumped into the chair. Simon was upstairs in his cradle, warm and fed.

He had squeezed the juice of two oranges into his rum in the hope it would prevent the smallpox. He felt a bit light headed and then realised that he was hungry. He had had nothing since the bowl of stew at dinnertime. With some bread, cheese and pickled onions inside him he felt better for his supper and climbed wearily up to bed.

There was a bowl of cold water in the bedroom left from washing Simon so he scrubbed his hands with soap, washed his face and undressed. He blew out the candle and climbed into a cold bed. The shutters were closed against the night air and the room was warm. H fell asleep muttering a fervent prayer for God to look after them all.

Robert woke at five o'clock as usual and gingerly turned his head, no headache, no fever, he was all right...so far. It was dark with the shutters closed so he lit a candle, opened the shutters a crack and saw the beginning of a chilly, grey day. Simon stirred, he too looked normal, nicely pink and sleepy.

Hurriedly Robert changed the wet rags and carried him downstairs. The baby clothes were on the inglenook to keep warm. He put him in his box and gave him a bone rattle to chew on whilst he warmed milk and made coffee. Robert had decided that he would look after himself properly and must have a hot drink before he went out. Simon would be bundled up and the box taken out to the cow shed. He could watch the cows.

With Simon asleep, wrapped in a blanket and tucked into a hollow in the hedge, Robert stood at the near end of Long Meadow watching for Calloway. As the steward opened the gate Robert shouted,

'Stop there. I've been in contact with smallpox. If I fall ill will you take the cows in?'

'Yes.'

'If I die will you look after Simon? There's money in the bank in Banbury and I've left a letter in the sea chest instructing the shares to be put in trust for him. Will you do that?'

'Of course, but I do hope you'll be all right. Was it the Pound girl? There's been talk of smallpox in Oxford. They've been isolated. Don't forget it takes about two weeks to come out.'

'I brought Rissie home from Banbury, next to me on the cart. She didn't look well then.'

'You'll be all right, Robert, drink plenty of rum. Are you managing on your own?'

'Just about. Your wife will look after Simon if I die, won't she?'

'Like our own, don't worry. Now, you'd better take him out of the cold wind.'

With a wave they parted and Robert began two weeks of isolation and mental torment as he checked himself and Simon for signs of fever.

He took the cows out to their pasture and cleaned out the cow shed, leaving everything ready for the evening milking. He left the churn of milk at the end of the lane for the villagers. Would they risk using it? How superstitious were they? Surely the disease wouldn't travel in the milk or on the container? He had read in the London paper of a physician called Edward Jenner who was using the scabs from a cow with cowpox to inoculate people against smallpox.

Dr Jenner had noticed that milkmaids rarely caught smallpox. They seemed to acquire immunity from their cows. As Robert thought about it a tiny seed of hope uncurled inside his chest and he wished fervently that he would be all right. He had to admit realistically that he hadn't been around cows for very long.

He would have to wait and see and pray. He wished he'd taken more notice Dr Jenner's report. Caleb had been with cows all his working life, perhaps he would escape? He must ask Calloway what he knew about it.

He would also try and find out how the Pounds were and if they needed anything. As he ate his morning toast and honey he suddenly thought of all the people in the mail coach whom Rissie had sat with. And the family in Oxford, where she worked, surely they must have known smallpox was rife? She had walked through

Banbury High Street. How many people had she infected on her way?

He cleared up and fed Simon and went outside. There was something white halfway down the track and he hurried to investigate. A grubby cloth concealed a still warm loaf of bread. What a heavenly smell, what joy. It was enough for two or three days. A note was with it, crudely written, "*Yu wont starv.*" Who could write in the village? Not many.

He called out, 'Thank you, thank you for the bread. I've left the milk here for you, I don't know if you'll want it.' The village would look after him. He had eggs, cheese, a side of bacon, and potatoes. He wouldn't go hungry.

He spent the rest of his day until milking time bringing in wood for the fire and working in the dairy. In between checking on Simon who was starting to miss the attention he had received from Margie and Fanny. Robert didn't know whether it was a good idea to keep taking him in and out of the house but he didn't like to leave him grizzling on his own. As he tried to hurry through the late milking with Simon crying in his blanket, propped up in a pile of hay he had an idea from his shipboard days.

He found a hessian sack, made a hole at each corner and threaded twine through. Attaching each end to a low beam he made a hammock. He placed Simon carefully in the middle and gently rocked it, watching to see if he would fall out. The baby stopped sobbing and smiled, his eyes looking up. Robert also looked up and saw the cobwebs blowing in the breeze from the open door. He breathed a sigh of relief as Simon quietened.

The cows didn't like the squalling noise and Betsy had already kicked the bucket of milk over. Fortunately it was only half full. With renewed vigour Robert got down to milking and started to sing them some of the sea shanties he had heard on board ship as the sailors turned the capstan to haul up the anchor. In a somewhat cracked voice he chose the inappropriate tune,

'Haul lads haul, the weather's fair today, heave boys heave, our sweethearts we do leave.'

When he collected the empty churn later, there was a dish by the side of it with three hot sausages and fried onions piled up. His mouth watered with the smell and he carefully carried it back to keep warm by the fire. He would fry some bacon to go with it. Tomorrow he would put cheese out with the milk. He couldn't let the village go without its' weekly ration.

That night he spent five minutes with his journal

"April 30th, 1802 The days fly by. I worry about Rissie and the Pounds but Simon and myself are free from the smallpox, so far. I pray that we will escape it. The village people are giving me food, they have little to spare so I am very grateful."

He spent hours in the dairy every day making cheese and butter with the surplus milk. After ten days he checked himself thoroughly and although he felt very tired he had to admit he was fit and well, with no sign of the dreaded fever coming on and Simon was the same, thank God.

The previous evening, as he put the churn out he saw Talbot, from the Ewe and called out,

'How are the Pounds?'

'Rissie's very bad, sir. Covered with the pustules she is, not long now, they reckon.'

'I'm so sorry, I wish there was something I could do.'

'Ain't nothing, sir. In God's hands she is. Are you all right?'

'Yes, I'm managing and no sign of fever, thank God.'

'Aye, thank God it is.' And he turned and went into his outhouse.

Poor Margie. She was nursing Rissie day and night and was certain to catch it in such close proximity. Robert knew she loved her daughter and would never leave her. What of Caleb? He was shut up close with them. Robert had had a shouted conversation with him over the hedge one evening. Caleb had taken to going out in the night, when everyone was in bed. He told Robert he needed the fresh air. He was still well and prayed for Rissie to be saved.

Robert saw the black ribbon on the door the next day. From his vantage point half way down the track, as he reached for the warm loaf, he saw the door open and Caleb speak to the rector, standing some paces away. So Rissie had died. He felt so sad for the Pounds. How they had loved her, a bright and beautiful young woman, full of life and fun.

Now he had Simon it all meant a lot more to him, he had a child of his own, to lose or keep, God willing.

The next evening he sat in his chair by a good fire, sipping some hot blackcurrant cordial laced with rum. Seeing Rissie buried had brought back the sadness of Mary's burial. At least they won't have to have an inquest he thought.

The inquest for Mary had been held in Banbury at the courthouse. It was taken by Mr Marriot-Kemp a local Justice. Lord Byclere did not attend and all the evidence was given by Brown the coachman. He described in simple terms how they were galloping down the Banbury road out past Appley when his right lead horse stumbled and nearly fell. He wasn't sure if it had hit something but he pulled them up smartly and got off to check the horses.

When he turned back he saw a body lying on the side of the lane. He ran down to it, calling to his Lordship as he passed the coach. Lord Byclere brought the lantern and together they approached the body and saw that it was of a middle-aged lady.

Brown recognised her as Mary James of Appley Glebe. His lordship felt her neck and confirmed there was no pulse.

'This is a bad business, Brown,' said the coroner.

'It were an accident, Sir, I didn't see her.'

'Was it very dark?'

'Aye, sir, pitch black down there among the trees.'

Marriot-Kemp knew from previous testimony that the lady had been looking for her son and that the newly shorn sheep were making a lot of noise.

'I conclude,' he intoned, 'it was an unfortunate accident; circumstances conspired to create a scene whereby this could have happened. I shall notify this as an accidental death.'

The inquest was over and the crowd dispersed. Robert left the courtroom to get on with his life with Dorothy.

CHAPTER FOURTEEN

Rissie was buried in the churchyard late in the evening. Caleb carried her, wrapped in her shroud and placed her in the coffin. Between them, Robert, the Rector and himself they got it into the hastily prepared hole. Margie, wrapped in a black shawl, her face ravaged by grief, stood back and watched the Rector hastily mumble the words of the funeral service.

'Our daughter Clarice Margaret...' was uttered with unseemly haste. Robert and Caleb threw the earth in, working from opposite sides, anxious to keep away from each other. As the earth thudded down on the plain deal Caleb started to unburden himself.

'Her face would have been terribly disfigured. She would have hated that. She was so proud of her beauty. I suppose we made her vain always telling her she was the prettiest in the village.'

Margie had vanished, unable to watch her daughter being so unceremoniously buried.

'There was something I did when she were a nipper. I'm not proud of it.' Caleb rested on his shovel, panting. He wiped the sweat from his brow with his sleeve and left a dirt trail. The candle in the lamp flickered in the breeze and the night stayed very dark. Cloud covered the moon and stars.

'Go on.' Robert gave himself a minute.

'A fayre came to the village, she were five or six, she wanted a ribbon, a red ribbon but I had no money. You know, the hucksters stalls, lots of people milling round, so I took advantage. Rissie had her ribbon and that's the only time I've stolen anything. Funny thing is, the next year when the fayre came round again, I'd saved a little bit. She had a blue ribbon then and the man said to me, "That'll be tuppence to you, Caleb Pound." He'd known. I felt that ashamed. I gave him thruppence, that's the interest I said. He winked at me and gave the child a sweetmeat. What are we going to do without her?' he finished piteously.

Caleb had been very close to the infection for ten days, perhaps in four days or so he would be the next victim to start a fever.

It was Margie who succumbed, inevitably so. As Robert thankfully came out of quarantine Caleb began the awful task of nursing his wife. Robert had told him to put a handkerchief over his face when he was near her and wash thoroughly every day with the soap he had given him. He placed great faith in his balsam soap. With that and some clean fresh air every day the two men hoped the smallpox would be defeated.

The butter had piled up and Robert knew he had to go to Banbury to sell as much as possible.

'Would you stay here until I get back, Fanny? I can't manage Simon when I'm in the market and it's busy.'

Fanny was up to her elbows in dirty water, trying to catch up on the washing. Fortunately it was a sunny, windy day and she was filling every inch of the washing line. Even the bushes had Simon's rags draped over them.

She smiled at him, showing the toothless gaps in her gums, 'We'll manage, he can watch me working, I might have to bring my youngest with me though.' Seeing Robert's face fall she reassured him, 'It's alright, she's clean, or she will be.'

Robert felt a bit embarrassed. 'Sorry, Fanny, but you know what I'm like.'

'I knows, Shipshape, I knows.' She hid a grin, plunging red hands back into hot water.

He loaded up the cart the night before, got up even earlier the next morning and surprised the cows with such an early start. In consequence they were slow to move and he had to contain his impatience with them.

'You know the time don't you, Buttercup, it's stupid of me to try and get you out of your routine I could have had an extra half an hour in bed. I'll know in future.'

A languid gaze from heavily fringed eyes surveyed him and her tail whisked as he held on to the bucket.

With Simon in her arms Fanny waved him off at seven thirty. A toddler with a crust in her hand clutched at her skirts.

Binnie briskly trotted, his tail swishing, his ears pricked. It would be a pleasant ride in the summer sun. Robert breathed the mild air, appreciating the freedom after being cooped up in the farm for nearly three weeks. He was worried about Caleb, he couldn't manage on his own for much longer, especially with all the summer work to come. He would have to look for someone else. He didn't intend to tell them in Banbury that he had been so close to the smallpox but he would drop a hint to find out if there had been any other cases.

Robert's regular customers were pleased to see him. To the few that asked he just said they had had a bit of trouble and no one was interested enough to pursue it, thankfully. As he sat eating his dinner later, enjoying a roast fowl with greens and forcemeat stuffing he spoke casually to his fellow diner.

'I hear there's smallpox in Oxford, I do hope it don't come here.'

His neighbour gulped up a spoonful of dark brown beef gravy and then carefully wiped his plate with bread. Filling his mouth he masticated slowly. Robert watched out of the corner of his eye, pushing his tankard out of range of flying crumbs.

Finally, 'There has been some here, must have come with the coach. Two deaths and a few got the pox on their faces, badly scarred they'll be but alive.' He swallowed his ale in one, stood up pushed his chair back and belched in a satisfied manner. 'I ain't got time for Bakewell pie, my nephew's being buried at four.' At Robert's alarmed look he hastened to add, 'it's alright it's not the pox. It were cholera.'

Robert shifted uneasily in his chair. He had nearly finished his dinner, he pushed the plate away, he didn't want anymore. Cholera. He didn't think it was contagious like smallpox, but how did it travel? Simon was so precious and vulnerable. He walked to the bar and placed coins on top.

'Thank you, Sir.' John the barman picked them up.

'That man over there told me there's cholera about.'

'Oh it's down by the river, those hovels in the Rows. No need to worry.'

'I've got a little son now, I don't want to take anything back with me.'

'Oh I shouldn't trouble your head, it's for poor people, very poor.' He turned away, 'Yes sir, what's your pleasure?' There was a burst of raucous laughter as Robert went out of the door.

Two days later Fanny told him the grim news that Margie's eyes were affected.

'All blurry they are.' She was peeling potatoes with the sharp knife whirling round creating a spiral of peel. 'Caleb reckons, well he's at his wit's end, Shipshape, what's he going to do with her. She won't be able to work; it's dangerous to leave her. She's had a fall already. I told him he's got to make it easy for her, put things to hand and she'll learn, like my old Granny did. Blind as a bat she were, but sharp as a pin. Used her stick a lot, from what I remember. On our bottoms sometimes.' She grinned. 'It's not my business but if he can leave her settled in the chair, with the fire safe, he can come up here for milking and pop back odd times through the day. She may come good, we all hope so. I like her, she's always got a smile.'

She removed the peel that had fallen on Simon's lap and was halfway to his mouth. He started to grizzle and she gave him a finger of dry bread. Robert watched his son make a face and then slowly put it in his mouth and suck on it.

His cheek was red. Fanny had said he had probably started teething and to expect trouble, sleepless nights, runny noses and a grumpy baby. She was all for putting a drop of rum or brandy in his milk. Robert hoped she didn't do that when he was outside, so she could have peace and quiet to get the work done.

Caleb came back a week later. Robert wrote in his journal that night.

"Caleb Pound has come back to work, but with reduced hours. He comes early to milk, leaving Margie in bed and then goes back after breakfast to get her up. We do a mornings' work and have dinner and he goes back to give Margie hers. She is nearly blind, it is so sad. On a fine day she can sit outside and passing neighbours look to her needs. He helps with evening milking and then goes back to get their supper. It is hard for him but I must have the work done. I think I shall have to look for someone else as well. Summer is coming and there is a lot of work with the hay just to start. Oh yes, Simon is cutting his first tooth. Quite early apparently. He's a bright child with a happy smile."

CHAPTER FIFTEEN

On Whitsun Day, May 15th, he went to the Banbury hiring fair to try and find a cowman. He was surprised to see Tom Farthing from Appley village standing amongst the labourers.

Robert looked at the ruddy face, with the black eyes peering out over the chubby cheeks. Tom was dressed in his cleanest, finest smock for the day and was known to be a good stockman.

'What are you doing here? I thought you worked for Harrison at Lower End.'

Tom knuckled his fist at Robert who was liked in the village. 'I bin laid off, he's selling the farm and retiring, the new owner don't want me.'

'I'll pay you nine shillings a week to come in and milk the cows at six o'clock in the morning and five o'clock in the afternoon. There'll be fieldwork and well, anything that needs doing. You get the usual perks, milk, cheese and a dinner.'

They spat on their hands and shook, sealing the bargain. Tom walked back to Appley village gloriously happy. He had landed the best employer in the neighbourhood. He could pay his rent to the Byclere estate and live frugally but sensibly.

Within the week they had settled into a satisfactory routine and took it in turns, one cleaning out and one milking. Tom was strong in muscle and calm in demeanour and the cows liked him. Caleb came in after breakfast and took on the fieldwork, using Binnie to harrow the hay fields. He enlarged the vegetable garden so that more potatoes and green vegetables could be grown, with the possibility of selling the surplus. Caleb built a small chicken house complete with nest boxes and Robert brought a dozen hens back from Banbury one day. Simon could now have a fresh boiled egg for his dinner.

With Fanny busy with the washing and cleaning he paid a shilling a week to Susan, sister in law of Clarrie Bates who provided a rota of children to keep an eye on and later, as he grew, to play with Simon. He didn't like the idea of a five year old watching over his son, they seemed to lack concentration. Very often he would come in to find Simon on his own, on the floor bawling as he scrabbled about on the flagstones whilst the baby sitter had wandered off to play with the cat.

Robert complained, 'Susan, the children are too young, they should be in school.'

'I know, sir, but they has to earn their keep, they can take it in turns.'

'No, no,' he said hastily, 'they must have their education.'

An ancient crone was then produced, her grandmother, who sat in the chair all day by the fireplace and was too stiff to bend and pick up Simon. At eleven o'clock in the morning he discovered that she had found his brandy bottle and was dribbling into one of his best glasses. Simon was in his box, grumpy with hunger.

By dinnertime Robert had had enough. He knew he would have to find a housekeeper, someone to do the washing, look after Simon and cook for them. Susan was consulted and frowned at the loss of her potential income.

'I want someone steady now, Susan,' he told her sternly, 'no one young, flighty, inattentive or too old to work.'

'I'll look around for you, sir, leave it with me,' she wheedled anxious to keep in contact with his money.

For the next three days Robert took the baby out to the cowshed and sat him in a corner. Simon chuckled and cooed and seemed happy. At eight months old he was drinking cows milk and eating mashed up food from Robert's plate. Simon liked the hard biscuits he brought back from Oxford and he gave the child one whenever he cried. Simon now had two teeth, red cheeks and a runny nose.

Helen Canning sat in Robert's parlour two days later waiting for him to come in. She smoothed down her skirt, tugged at her hat, and hoped she looked older than sixteen. They had heard about Mr Southwell and his baby and been very pleased to have the message from her Aunt Susan to come over from Byclere. She heard footsteps and stood nervously. This job was the alternative to being an under nursemaid at Byclere House and that was absolutely her last choice.

She saw a middle-aged man step into the room, with a baby boy sitting on his hip. He had a shock of rather unkempt thick grey hair tied back at the nape, piercing blue eyes and was in clean breeches and a white shirt.

Robert placed the child on the rag rug and gave him a toy boat and some small wooden people.

Turning, his gave his attention to the...girl in front of him. She was a chit, too young, and he frowned.

Helen's heart sank as she watched his grim face.

'Er.. Miss Canning is it? Susan sent you. I did explain that I need someone a little older, more mature. I'm sorry, I'll pay your way here.' Robert had firmly decided on someone over thirty, a widow or spinster who would be sensible, calm and could tackle absolutely anything.

'Sir, please hear me out.' Helen turned her anxious blue eyes on him. She smiled down at Simon and prepared to argue, persuade or beg if need be.

'I knows you were hoping for someone a bit older, but Susan's wracked her brains and there ain't anyone round here, that's free like. I'm the second oldest in my family, I've got seven brothers and sisters. I've been looking after babies since I could toddle myself.' A slight exaggeration here, but she thought it sounded good. 'Me Mum's been dead this two year and I've been cooking, cleaning, washing for a whole houseful. Now my Dad's married again and she don't want me there, 'cept as a slave.' she added bitterly. 'I love children and I can sew and cook. Give us a try, if I'm wrong then I'll stay until you can find someone more suitable.' She thought that was a brilliant suggestion and waited anxiously.

Robert looked at her, she seemed clean and tidy, but spoke with an Oxfordshire accent. He didn't want Simon growing up with all his aitches gone like the rest of the village. He rubbed his chin with fingers that smelled of milk and the sharp flavour of cheese.

'Would you work in the dairy?'

'Oh yes and I can bottle plums and make preserves.'

'Hmm all right, a months' trial, we'll see how Master Simon and Appley Glebe take to you. Have you got your box with you?'

She shook her head, 'I can send, it can come with the carter. Shall I start now? It's dinner time, shall I get you both some dinner?' She was so happy she felt like dancing. He had forgotten to mention her wages, she would ask him later.

Robert hadn't forgotten to talk about the girl's wages but wasn't sure how much to offer. Susan would tell him, but it might come out on the high side. He would start low and see how much she could do.

It seemed that Helen could do anything and what she didn't know she learnt quickly. To be mistress of this farmhouse because that was how she liked to see herself at sixteen, was a job in paradise.

Robert Southwell only ever smiled at Simon, and then his face would soften indulgently, otherwise he maintained a strictly master/servant relationship. But he was pleased with her. Simon had never looked so clean and well cared for. Helen sang to him and played games on the floor. After he was in his cot at night she sat by the light of several candles and mended their clothes.

Helen had at first thought of him as an old man but as she got used to seeing him work about the farm and dairy she realised how fit he was and that he was not really as old as she had thought. He was still like a grandfather to her but she started to see him in a different light.

In a way her age was a relief to Robert. She was nothing like Mary or Dorothy and didn't remind him of them. In spite of plain, white bonnets and voluminous aprons she still looked like a young girl but he was too taken up with the farm and Simon to think of her as a young woman with a woman's body.

"April 5th 1803.

This will be a short entry. Just to say Simon is doing well, he is a year old today and the time has flown. He is crawling around and tries to follow me to the barn. We have to watch him like a hawk, he can pull himself up to put his little fingers in to all sorts of mischief. The farm is doing well, I could sell double my butter and cheese but that would mean more cows and we do not have enough food for them through the winter months.

Helen Canning has turned out to be suitable and a hard worker. It is the anniversary of Dorothy's death and I took spring flowers to the churchyard. I still think of Mary at nights, I think that if it had meant her staying alive I would not have asked her to wed. Never would I have wanted her to die in childbirth like her sister. I have so many regrets. I earnestly pray that Ben will come home safely and take over the farm".

Helen settled down and revelled in her work. Robert had no idea of what hours she should do and was content to let her go out once or twice a week in the evenings whilst he stayed and kept an eye on Simon. Never had a child been so well tended. He seemed to favour his father in looks which made him doubly precious and it was Tom Farthing who told him one day that he was spoiling the child.

'Spare the rod and spoil the child is very true.' Tom, nodding wisely was bent over the broom sweeping up the bucket of milk that the two-year old Simon had just knocked over. 'Let the little varmints get away with it now and they'll lead you a merry dance later, you mark my words.'

Robert had seen enough beatings on board ship to last a lifetime; the idea of even taking a cane to Simon was repugnant.

'Do we indulge the child too much?' he asked Helen one evening when they were churning butter.

She pushed a damp lock of hair back under her bonnet and straightened from turning the handle of the churn. 'He's an only child, stands to reason he'll get more attention than a brood like we had at home.' She didn't add that Robert having money also helped.

'But is he going to be ruined? I want him to grow up steady and kind and respectful.'

'I'm sure he will, he's got a good example to follow.' she cocked an eye at him, he still treated her in an impersonal way.

'I'm going to send him to school when he's five, he must learn his ABC and counting and later on arithmetic and history and Latin.'

'Would you like him to go to sea like you did?' she asked curiously.

He actually grinned, and shook his head, bending down to pick up a bucket. 'If there's no war on there's no navy and it's a hard life for a youngster. He might like to stay here and work on the farm.' His eyes swept round the dairy. 'When you've done that you can wash the floor down.' Was ordered in his usual terse way.

She grimaced behind his back, now she wouldn't be able to get out so early to meet one of the village lads.

CHAPTER SIXTEEN

Simon was a charming child, able to get his own way, but sweetly so. In 1805 with Napoleon raging across Europe, the life at Appley Glebe was contented. Robert took his son out on long rambles in the summer months once haymaking was finished. They picked flowers and grasses to bring home and draw. Simon rolled about on the soft down land fescue grasses, chewing on a stalk of salad burnet. He liked the flavour, and would mix it with his bread and cheese at dinnertime.

Robert had a telescope, brought from the Celeste and with this they watched the kestrels hovering and then plummeting to earth to pounce on an unfortunate rabbit or even a tiny vole. The shriek of the birds was at odds with the pure blue of the sky and the soft warm wind that always blew across the downs.

Simon liked the songs of the skylarks and linnets and tried to whistle. When he told Tom at milking time about this, pursing up his lips and making a puffing sound, Tom laughed and brought forth a perfect bird song. In spite of a mouth full of terrible teeth that were full of gaps and brown molars.

Simon listened entranced, sitting on a bucket, trying and trying to copy him.

As Tom washed out the last of the buckets he relented on the red-faced child and squatted down beside him.

'Now watch closely,' he instructed, 'follow my lips.'

Together they pursed their lips. 'Think of that little bird, Simon, what sound does he make, does it warble?' Tom warbled, 'Does it trill?' Tom trilled.

Simon puffed out, exasperated, 'You're showing off, Tom.'

'All right, now breathe in, deep breaths, and jiggle your lower lip, like so.'

Simon peered up at him in the fading light and wobbled his lip, 'I'll never do it.'

'Yes you will, try again.'

They tried, and suddenly the melody came, a little unsteady, rather short but, it was a whistle.

Simon whooped, 'I've done it, I can whistle, I'm going to tell Father.'

He ran out, tripping over his feet and picking himself up. He cast a beaming smile back at Tom, who he loved dearly, especially his face which was like a fruity bun with the twinkling eyes set deep like shiny currents.

Robert was in the dairy weighing out slabs of butter to take to Banbury market the following day.

'Bed time, Simon,' he said when he saw him.

'Yes, father but listen I can whistle now.' He tried again puffing and spluttering and then remembered that little brown bird with his sweet song. Slowly and carefully he tried again.

Robert wiped his hands on a rag and watched his son concentrate. His heart was bursting with love for him. Simon was his very reason for living, the meaning of his existence and the light of his life. And when he got older he would have to part with him, to send him away to school. He pushed thoughts of that to the back of his mind.

The wobbly whistle finished and the child stood grinning from ear to ear. His light brown hair streaked with sunshine was untidy and decorated with scraps of grass. He was in breeches that were too small. He was growing so fast and tomorrow they would sell the butter and go to buy more clothes.

'Right, lad, bed time, there's milk and buttered buns on the table and then you have a good wash, I'll see you after.' Helen had gone to see Susan about preserving blackcurrants and it did not occur to Robert that his son might need help with his ablutions.

He found himself whistling as he scrubbed down the dairy table. He was content, luckier than most in the country with his pension and the money he had put by barely touched. Because he was able to keep the farm in good shape, with cows that milked well he was making a reasonable living. They had ricks of new June hay in the yard and a field of barley growing nicely, to thresh for winter feed for the cows.

Susan and Helen were sitting in Susan's yard, with a basket of blackcurrants between them. Their hands deftly stripped off stalks, whilst their mouths talked non-stop.

'He don't even see me as a person,' complained Helen.

'Have you tried taking off your bonnet and brushing your hair, men like long hair like yours,' suggested Susan.

'Yes,' she was exasperated, 'he said, put your bonnet on Helen, we don't want hairs in the butter.'

'Have you tried showing an ankle?'

'I sit on the floor and play with Simon, my skirt comes up a little, what does he do?'

Susan shook her head, popped a current in her mouth and grimaced at the sourness.

'He pulled it tidy for me, you'll get cold on the floor, Helen he said.'

'Do you want a potion?' Susan said carefully.

Helen shook her head, 'I don't know. What if it went wrong, I don't want to make him ill, not yet anyway. You see, Susan, if I could get him to marry me, he's an old man and he wouldn't last long. Think of all that money I'd have and the farm, I'd be wealthy. Then I could pick and choose.'

Her aunt stared at her, her face at thirty lined with work and worry, the idea of wealth unimaginable in her hard life.

'You are serious then, you'd marry Mr Southwell.'

'Yes... yes. I know it's rented, but Mary James was a widow, she ran the farm.'

'With Ben, don't forget, and he might come home from the wars, don't forget that.'

'Well I could marry him then.'

'Helen I think you're too young to know what you do want.'

The girl's eyes were hard and bright, 'Oh yes I do, Aunt Susan, I don't want to end up like you, ten children and worn out, like a dried plum.'

'Helen!'

'Sorry, Aunt, but I want to have nice dresses, a maid to do my work and coffee in the morning and wine at night. Wine, Aunt, not ale.'

'There.' Helen dropped the last of the sprigs of currents into the basket. 'You'd better tell me what happens next, quickly mind, I'm meeting someone.'

Susan sighed. 'Stew them in a little water; you can make jelly with this lot. You're going to be trouble I'm thinking Helen Canning, and I think Mr Southwell's too wrapped up in that boy of his to notice you.'

'He's going to school when he's eight, to Banbury probably, he'll be glad of my company then.'

She picked up her bonnet, shaking back her lustrous, silvery fair hair. With her long lashes and bright blue eyes she was beautiful.

Robert had noticed her but resolutely put all carnal thoughts out of his head.

'She's young enough to be your daughter,' he muttered to himself as she slipped past him in the dairy. He realised that marriage to a young girl like Helen would be a different kettle of fish to his time with Dorothy. Their short marriage had been pleasant, he had tried to hide his grief for Mary and fortunately, with a busy life Dorothy had not noticed. She had enjoyed the treats and comforts he bought her and shown her gratitude in their marriage bed.

The pleasure they enjoyed had been a surprise to him. They had been relative strangers at the beginning but necessity had made them bold and the lust he felt had surprised him. His initial shyness had soon evaporated with her encouragement. The tricks he had learnt from various ladies at the ports he had visited had intrigued Dorothy.

As he strode back into the house to see his son up to bed he smiled to himself, his genuine sorrow for Dorothy had faded, but he did not want another wife. Mary had been his true love; he did not want to be encumbered with a slip of a girl. Simon regarded Helen as his mother. There were plenty of 'Aunties' around but it was Helen who soothed his cuts and bruises.

CHAPTER SEVENTEEN

All through 1805 Robert had followed Lord Nelson's progress as the great admiral tracked the French fleet from one end of the Mediterranean round into the Bay of Biscay and up towards France. Every time anyone went into Banbury they brought home a news sheet knowing that Shipshape would read it to them. When Robert took the butter and cheese into the market he always had his dinner at the Red Lion and tried to glean as much information as possible. Banbury was a long way from London and the Channel ports and news took a few days to arrive, depending upon the frequency of the mail coach.

Autumn was giving them pleasantly crisp days, the nights were drawing in and Robert was busy amassing a huge pile of cut timber for the winter months. Sometimes when he came back from Banbury he also brought a sack of sea coal and the precious fuel was stacked up in the outhouse to keep dry.

In the middle of October there were rumours that Admiral Nelson had sighted the French Admiral Villeneuve. The whole village was vexed with the frustration of not knowing what, if anything was happening. Shipshape had told them, knowing Nelson as he did (by hearsay) that he wanted to go in for the kill and annihilate the French completely.

There was a strangely subdued atmosphere in the Ewe and Lamb in the evening. They supped their ale, smoked their pipes and talked quietly. There was a comfort in being together and solace to know the wife and children were safe at home. It was as if England was holding its' breath before fighting for her life.

Suddenly on the 24th October, sitting quietly in the inn they all heard Tubbs the carter shouting, yelling at the top of his voice.

'He's dead, Nell's dead. They won the battle and lost the admiral.'

Everyone crowded out of the Ewe. It was past eight o'clock. Tubbs swayed on his bench on the wagon. He had had a drink at every village he had stopped at from Banbury through to Appley. Robert had taken to spending his evenings at the inn. Helen had to stay in the house, so Susan or Clarrie walked over to her, leaving their youngest in the charge of the oldest.

'What's happened, Tubbs? Here, let's help you down, get you in here and have a drink.'

'Had a drink, Hazlebury, Bimp..Bampton and all along the road.'

'Well, Talbot can make you some tea and food. Tell us what's happened.'

'All I know is…three days ago there was a big battle by a place called…? Traffalger.'

Robert frowned, thinking, 'I think you mean Trafalgar, go on.'

'That's about it. They're bringing his body up to London. It were a terrible fight with the French and the Spanish. And then a storm came up and knocked them about more.'

'So it's true, Nelson has died. Our Admiral.'

Tubbs greedily bit into the hunk of buttered bread that Talbot slapped in front of him. A slab of Robert's cheese had bite marks from a mouse in the inn pantry but the portly carter ignored them. He slurped on a pot of steaming tea and belched.

Tom Farthing was there, Caleb Pound and Armitage the Carpenter, Charley White the blacksmith, the Bates brothers, Ned, Joe and George were there with other Byclere estate workers. They watched Tubbs eating and then Charley said, strangely subdued for such a big, bellowing man,

'It were a victory for us then, definitely?'

'I said so, didn't I?'

'I wonder what the losses were,' said Robert ruminatively, 'how many ships and men did we lose?' How many did the French lose? I wish I were closer to the Channel ports at times like this. That telegraph they have now sends news across country so fast, rather than the days it used to take. I wonder if the Celeste was in the battle, I expect so.' He drained his tankard. 'I don't think there's anything more to learn tonight so I'll go home. Can you milk in the morning, Tom?'

'Sure I will, Shipshape, I'll be to my bed, it's fair knocked the stuffing out of me. I thought Lord Nelson, well I hoped he'd live…a long time. He's had his share of injuries, losing an eye and an arm.' Tom stamped out, followed soon after by the others, all grieving for England's hero.

Two days later, on the Sunday, Robert sat outside the inn with Appley village residents in front of him, from the youngest to the oldest. All had been to church. There had been a victory peal of bells and then the death knell had been rung for Lord Nelson. Appleys' bells were repeated across the vales of Oxfordshire and the whole country. Great Britain reverberated to the sound of ding dong and clang clang, from the majestic peal of the cathedrals to the humble resonance of the small country churches.

Prayers were said for those lost in the battle and a speedy recovery for all the injured.

Now they all eyed him impatiently as he spread a broadsheet entitled *"Victory"* across his lap. This had come from Calloway via Lord Byclere, sent down from London. Robert cleared his throat meaningfully, not unaware of the drama of the occasion. Armitage took it as a hint for a drink and a tankard was placed on the stone wall by the side of him. He looked up,

'Thank you, Joe.' And had a swallow.

'Get on with it.' Someone muttered.

"On 21ˢᵗ October, in the year of Our Lord, 1805, off Cape Trafalgar off the southwest coast of Spain there was a battle between Admiral Lord Nelson with the British fleet and the combined fleets of France and Spain under Admirals Villeneuve and Gravina. They had forty-three ships including their frigates and the British had just thirty three ships including six frigates. During the course of the fighting seventeen French and Spanish ships were captured and one sunk and some 7,000 casualties inflicted.

This was without the loss of a single British ship but British casualties numbered 450 killed and 1200 wounded. This included Nelson who was mortally wounded by a sniper's bullet. At the start of battle the message "England expects every man will do his duty" was signalled from the Victory, Nelson's flagship and every British sailor was a hero that day.

Lord Nelson and the British Fleet have rid the seas of the threat of Napoleon. It has dealt the enemy a mortal blow."'

Robert paused to quaff some ale and let the information sink in. Everyone was quiet, children fidgeted and were hushed and those with drinks and pipes, drank and puffed. Robert thought perhaps he ought to make a comment.

'Well it seems as though we can breathe easier now. Napoleon Bonaparte can't come across the Channel to us. His army might be in Europe but they need ships and...by my reckoning they only have about sixteen ships left. That's not enough to mount an invasion.'

'Well I feel for that Lady Hamilton, she may be Nelson's fancy piece but she's lost him so sudden like.'

'They'll have a big funeral for him?'

'Oh yes, it'll be St Paul's Cathedral no doubt. The whole of the City of London will turn out for him.' Robert was certain of that. 'I wonder how the old Celeste did? Normally frigates don't fight in battles. They would be smashed to pieces with one broadside but I understand that at Trafalgar Nelson ordered everything into battle. I expect my old friend Matthew Mason, the surgeon on board had a dreadful days' work.'

'Don't,' said Susan Bates shuddering. 'I can't bear to think of all those poor men groaning and moaning in agony and then they gets tossed around in a storm.' She walked away, clutching the hand of a small child, more for her comfort than the little boy.

In 1806 Appley was fortunate to have a village school that was funded partly by the Byclere estate and partly by the Church. Robert had visited the school and spoken to James Noble the schoolmaster to find out exactly what his son might learn.

Simon already knew his ABC and could count to twenty. Although Robert had done no navigation on board ship he knew the names of stars and constellations and Simon had also learnt these. James Noble saw a bright child in front of him, better dressed than most of the others and already in advance of his years.

He explained carefully to the father that it would not be possible to give too much attention to one child. There were forty two children in school and only one assistant teacher. Simon must learn to sit quiet and watch the others, only speak when spoken to and curb his natural ebullience. In truth he was a chatterbox with a constant why this and why that. At home he was indulged. Robert would stop and explain everything and Helen was also happier to sit with him and draw than wash and polish.

Helen had given up her ambition to become Mrs Southwell. Robert had told her he would not marry again.

On Simon's fourth birthday, he had remarked casually,

'You know Simon's mother died four years ago now this day. I'll not marry again, I think I'm too old and there's the lad to consider.' He stamped out of the room, his face strangely emotional and she watched him go, dismay written all over her.

'So now you know,' Helen told herself, 'you've wasted your time here my girl.' But what was the alternative? Nursemaid at Byclere House...no thank you. Lord and Lady Byclere were aristocrats and very casual with the feelings of their staff. She knew from other members of the family who worked for them that nursemaids came and went frequently. She was earning four shillings a week which was good money, especially as she had board and lodgings as well. She saved a little, who knew what might turn up.

Robert rattled pails and stabbed at mucky straw, feeling lonely and bereft. Mary still stayed with him in his thoughts. Did he keep the pain alive thinking of her so much? He didn't know. He had the miniature painting of her that had been done by the fayre artist that fateful Midsummer Eve and he took it out and looked at it occasionally. There she was, a solemn but pretty face, framed by her bonnet and the lace collar of her gown just showing. It was a sorrowful secret, nestling in his heart like a small canker.

They knew that Ben had been alive six months ago, hearing from a fellow soldier in his regiment who had come home injured. Ben was now a corporal in the rifle brigade and well thought of. Robert had been very interested to know that Ben had been in Denmark at Copenhagen encouraging the Danes to surrender to Sir Arthur Wellesley.

Robert had been at the Battle of Copenhagen with Lord Nelson in 1801 but they had seen little of the land then. Ben should be home to take up the reins of the farm Robert decided, before he got himself killed.

"September 1st 1807

Simon started at the village school today.   He ran out of the door this morning.   He was so excited he could hardly eat his bread and honey breakfast.

He came back at dinner- time for more food.   He had given his lunch to 'a very hungry little girl.'   I hadn't the heart to chastise him, I am sure there is more than one hungry child in that school,   I cannot feed them all.   He has chattered non-stop about the lessons and what he did.

We missed his company today."

Simon's schooldays were a mixed blessing. He became bored with his lessons, having raced through the work he was set. This gave him opportunities to annoy his neighbours. He spent time frequently in the corner on a stool, but had discovered that he could see out of the window and watch the village forge.

James Noble was aware of this, but hadn't the heart to change the position of the stool to a blank corner, with plain walls. He knew that Simon had absorbed all he could teach to his age group, but to put him up with the older children would be to make him more different than he was already.

Simon's father was the wealthiest in the village He always had clean clothes, a clean face and a good breakfast inside him. He would share his lunch with whichever hungry child came to him and his sunny nature belied any envy. His pranks caused laughter and admiration. Robert couldn't bear to smack him but Mr Noble had no such sentimentality. Simon was only mortified when he had to pull down his breeches in front of the girls.

CHAPTER EIGHTEEN

In the early Spring of 1808 he was standing on his stool, gazing out of the window as usual when he spied a soldier marching down the road, in a green uniform with a rifle at his shoulder.

'Sir, sir,' he begged, 'sir please look, there's a soldier.' His voice squeaked with six year old excitement.

The children rushed to the window, with Mr Noble looking over their heads. James Noble knew who it was.

'It's Benjamin James come home from the wars,' he announced, 'to your farm, Simon.'

Simon had heard of the mysterious Ben, who had left so suddenly before he was born. He had acquired a certain glamour, which did not diminish with the reality.

'Is he going to my house?' He asked, 'can I go home? Please sir, please.'

'Have you done your work, Simon?' Mr Noble asked sternly.

'Yes, sir, all of it.' He leapt to his desk and produced his slate.

It was scanned, the classroom held it's breath; with luck they could all troop down to Appley Glebe later and stare at the soldier. They might even be allowed to touch the gun.

James Noble smiled, he was not a hard man. 'Go on then, and we shall want to hear all about a soldier's life in school tomorrow.'

With inherent courtesy Simon bowed to the schoolmaster. 'Thank you, sir.' He walked to the door and opened it to slip through quietly. The whole school heard the hoorays and hurrahs as he ran and skipped across the schoolyard.

Ben James was sitting in the parlour at Appley Glebe. He had barely remembered Robert Southwell and had listened in silence to Robert's account of the years past. Ben knew his mother had died. He heard from other soldiers in the regiment, but living a life that suited him, he had given little thought to the farm or what was happening there.

Helen was filled with excitement. She hadn't known the tall, bronzed stranger, with a scar down his cheek and had been prepared to send him away. She disappeared upstairs to tidy her hair and put on her best, frilled apron.

Robert came out of the dairy wiping his hands on a cloth and saw Ben standing in the yard looking round.

He exclaimed in delight, 'Ben, it's Ben James isn't it.' Hands were wrung and faces scrutinised.

Helen watched from the doorway and decided her future husband stood before her.

At that moment Simon came pelting along the lane calling 'Father, father...there's a soldier coming...oh.' His mouth was round with astonishment.

Close up Ben was taller and broader than before. He was a magnificent sight, with black pantaloons and a green jacket with black facings. His hat, or shakoe with it's cockade and a green plume was on the table. There was a sword in a scabbard slung negligently around his hips and a rifle, now leaning against the house wall. A knapsack sat on the ground.

'And who are you?' enquired the deep voice still with it's Oxfordshire burr.

'He's my son, Simon,' said Robert proudly, 'who should be in school. I married your aunt Dorothy, sadly she left us.'

'Sir let me come to see the soldier, Father,' piped up Simon.

Ben grinned down at his nephew. 'Well you can carry my baggage, young Simon.'

Simon dearly wanted to carry the rifle, but contented himself with trying to lift the pack. The adults watched with amusement as he struggled until Helen stepped forward and took one strap,

'I'll give you a hand, Master Simon, we'll do it together, you're not as strong as this here soldier,' and she gave Ben an arch look.

'Oh, Helen Canning, our housekeeper,' introduced Robert, 'she'll make up a bed and find some victuals for us.'

Helen contrived to walk ahead of them, swaying gracefully, a trim ankle showing as she put one foot on the bottom step. As she reached the bend in the stairs she looked down. Ben was standing, looking up at her laughing and he winked at her.

Helen resolved...it was marriage or nothing,

Ben James made a silent bet with himself, a guinea I have her by Saturday.

With coins jingling in his pocket Ben James was a popular customer at the Ewe and Lamb. It seemed that everyone wanted to meet him and hear his tales of far off lands. After his training under Colonel Coote-Manningham he had taken ship to India and was with Sir Arthur Wellesley at Assaye.

Ben looked at them indulgently as he laid out coins. They were a simple lot he decided, choosing to forget that the Appley life had been his before he enlisted.

He had come back to the village to scout for more soldiers, having been told by his major that Sir Arthur Wellesley wanted more sniper rifles. So as Ben was slapping his money down on the scrubbed wooden table he was scanning the village lads for likely recruits. With his tales of elephants as big as houses and fierce tigers that got fiercer with the telling, they were all enthralled.

Helen slipped into the back of the room to watch. She saw the ease with which he parted with the coins. The uniform jacket was open revealing a white shirted broad chest with hair crinkling at the neck. A pale scar on his cheek added to his attraction. The keen blue eyes, used to scanning open country for enemy soldiers and wild animals had crinkle lines at their corners. His moustache was trimmed to long drooping points and he made the local young men seem very callow.

That evening, as she took a candle up to her room, she heard the outside door open and close. She knew Robert had gone to bed earlier and Simon was now sleeping in a small room of his own. Helen had the room next to it and Ben had been put in the spare room, with a bed fitted in amongst old chests and chairs with three legs.

Ben sprang lightly up the stairs. Helen put a finger to her lips to quieten him, pointing to Simon's door. Which is your room mouthed Ben pointing to the doors. Helen reached for the handle of the door and saw the brown hand fastened over hers. A breath of brandy floated by her nose and her neck was touched with feather light lips. Her breathing stopped for a second, she stood still, excitement pulsing through. It would be so easy to let him have his way with her. It would be exciting to be made love to by this handsome soldier. He was so strong and virile. But no, she could be left with a fatherless brat, unmarried and unwanted and Robert would throw her out as a slut. She stiffened as his hand caressed her back, from her neck to the base of her spine.

'No,' she whispered, as firmly as she could manage with her breath coming in pants, 'no, Mr Southwell's next door.'

'We'll go outside then,' he murmured, his lips on her hair as he removed her bonnet.

'No,' she moved aside, 'no, I daren't.'

They both heard a movement from Simon's room and his door opened.

'Helen, I'm thirsty can I have a drink. Ooh Ben, can I see your rifle please?'

'Not now Simon, in the morning, I'm going to bed, good night lad.'

'Good night, sir.' Simon padded back to bed, his night-gown trailing on the floor, several sizes too large. Not bought for him to grow into, but because his father did not know what size to get.

Helen closed her door and sagged back against it with relief. Her body knew it's frustration but as she calmed down she determined that for Ben James it was marriage or nothing.

Ben relaxed on the feather mattress. It was softer than he'd known for many a year. Soft like a woman's body he thought drowsily. I'll try again tomorrow. She'll give in, I can see she wants me.

As Ben wove his spell in the evenings down at the Ewe and Lamb, so he tried to pull in his fish at Appley Glebe. Helen was keen he could tell, she would flirt and coyly flutter her lashes at him as they churned butter together. Giggling merrily she would let him chase her across the meadow, but a kiss was all that was permitted.

Ben had three more days of his furlough left. There were five young men keen to march back with him to barracks and he had had to impress on them the need for secrecy. The village needed strong young men to work, to marry and father children. An army life was no good to anyone, the soldier's pay rarely found its' way home.

Ben had been given an ample purse to recruit with. He had erred on the generous side when asked how much he would require by his major and had spent little at the Ewe. He would keep it for later. Give a few shillings to the families of the recruits. He could see how very poor some of them were. The money would get them through next winter…if they didn't drink it all first!

Now he just had the problem of the pretty Miss Canning. Ben accepted that she wasn't going to give in to him. Ever the opportunist which was why he was such a successful soldier, he had taken a young Lucy Bates round the back of the hay rick. They snuggled into a secluded corner and he showed her his battle scars, the ones that didn't get an airing.

His lust was slaked, but Helen had caught his imagination. She was obviously competent, a good housekeeper and would probably make a good wife. He noted with interest how Robert treated her. As a friend, but distant and cool, there was obviously nothing going on there.

Ben wondered why she had never married, she was twenty two, old to be unwed in the village.

'I'm going back to barracks tomorrow, I don't know when I'll be back, it depends on orders,' he told her next day. They were standing by the hedge looking at Robert's cows. 'When I come back next we could get married.' He was casual, but his hand clenched on a branch was tense.

What an unromantic proposal thought Helen, disappointed. She had wanted him to get down on one knee and flourish his hat.

'I don't know that I want to be a soldier's wife,' she replied coolly, 'what happens? Do I have to live in barracks? Are they big smelly places full of noisy soldiers?'

Ben had to confess they were. 'A bit,' he muttered, 'but there are some married quarters. I'm a corporal and hoping for promotion, so I'd have a good room, quite a nice one.'

'Not as nice as here.' said Helen, wondering how she could still live at Appley but receive his pay.

'You could stay here and I'll come back as often as I could, I'd have a reason to,' he said eagerly, 'and I'll send home my pay to you. You could save it for us to start a home when I get out.'

'When will you leave the army, Ben? Don't you want to come home and farm here?'

'I don't know as I want to be a farmer. I'll have a look around when the war's finished, when Boney's trounced out of Europe. The Little Emperor is a slippery fellow. Sir Arthur Wellesley, Old Nosey we call him, says he's a tricky chap to catch. It would be good to think of you here, waiting for me,' he said softly, lifting her hand to his lips 'Give me a reason to come home quicker,' he murmured huskily.

'I'll be Mrs Helen James,' she said pertly.

'You will my dear, you will.' He smiled down at her, content. She was tested, he didn't think she was easy, she would be safe to leave whilst he was away.

Helen smiled, satisfied. She had got what she wanted and she could keep her meetings with Mark Calloway a secret, from Robert and her husband. She would have her wages from Robert even after Simon went to school. He would still need her and if Ben sent his pay home, then she could live like a lady.

Robert expressed satisfaction at their news the following morning. He still hoped Ben would want to come back to the farm but could tell from the eagerness with which he packed his bag that he was anxious to get on his way again. Robert worked on alone in the dairy.

'Helen has disappeared with Ben. It doesn't take much imagination to know what they're getting up to.' he remarked to Tom who came in to help.

'She's a hard headed young lady that one.' Tom was brushing down. 'She's got what she wants now, I reckon.'

Robert stared at him. 'You saw it coming, did you?'

'Well she were after you for a long time but you're still carrying a light for that wife of yours, so she gave up.'

'She was after me. I'm old enough to be her grandfather.'

'You're old enough to wed, Robert Southwell, that's all that matters, and you've money, to boot.'

'My money? Helen was after my money.' This threw a completely different complexion on things.

'It helps. Her family's got nought, if she married you, she could wait, her'd be a rich widow.'

He nodded his head wisely.

Robert was bemused at this information, and something clicked into his mind. They still thought he was grieving for Dorothy, well he would let that be, it wouldn't harm.

'I don't want someone like that, wanting trinkets and fol de rols all the time. If it suits her to wed Ben and be a soldier's wife then good luck to her. If she wants to go, then it's with my blessing. I'll find someone else to look after us.'

'She don't want to go, sir.'

'How do you know all this, Tom?' said Robert laughing.

'I keep my ears open and my Missus is Susan Bates's sister.'

'Oh.' was eloquence in the still evening air, as cows swished their tails against flies and ruminated on their evening grass. Swallows swooped low, catching midges and blackbirds squabbled noisily as they made their way back to their nests.

Ben left early the next day. He turned round and waved at the figure up at the window and Helen fluttered a handkerchief. Robert up early for milking saw him stride off up the track whistling a marching tune. With his rifle to his shoulder, his pack on his back and a special piece of parchment carefully folded and tucked inside.

Ben had arranged a rendezvous for his recruits, some two miles out of the village. He was pleased to see that word had spread and several more than his original five were waiting for him. The lure of the uniform and their very own rifle had proved too much for two Bates brothers and Tom's eighteen year old son George.

Ben gave them a lecture about discipline and drunkenness and then told them they would make a smart pace. Anyone who couldn't keep up was left behind. This was hard on the village lads who had barely a decent pair of boots between them.

At a morning stop, he had collected five more young men, and was halfway to Reading. He bought bread, cheese and ale and let them rest. He was indifferent to the tears of the mothers and the rage of the fathers as they discovered their sons had left to be soldiers.

Ben had been recruiting before, this was easy, doing it like this. And they were quality, raw but keen and would soon lick into shape before they left for the next campaign. They would spend a few days in barracks and then on for intensive training at Shorncliffe in Kent under Colonel Coote Manningham.

Helen had a guinea in her pocket from Ben and intended to buy herself a very pretty dress for when he next came home. Ben had promised her, on bended knee that if she would get the banns called in the meantime, then as soon as he was next home, they could have the marriage ceremony.

Mrs Benjamin James, she liked the sound of that very much and a husband who was away a lot, even better. She could pursue other interests. Ben probably has other women she thought, so surely I'm entitled to satisfy my needs. Mark Calloway is under my spell, he's young, comely, lusty and, completely manageable. She smiled smugly, he's besotted with me. I can wind him round my little finger.

Simon came in from school and found her looking in her clothes box.

'Are you going away?' He asked anxiously.

'No, dear, I'm getting married, but I shan't be leaving here. I'm going to Banbury to buy some new clothes soon. I'll get you some toy soldiers while I'm there…shall I?'

'Yes, Helen, ooh yes please. With rifles like Uncle Ben, and feathers in their hats.'

'We'll see.' She ruffled his hair before he could duck away, 'now run and see your father, I'm busy.'

Robert was in the pigsty, a converted store shed. He had started his pig keeping by purchasing two runts at a shilling each from a nearby farmer. They were small and squealing. Simon squatted down by them stroking their wriggling silky bodies. They were still clean and pink.

'Do they have names, Father, could we give them names?'

'One is for bacon, and one is for pork,' said Robert with no sentimentality at all.

'We can't call them that!' was Simon's shriek. 'I shall call them...Trotter and Snout.'

'Trotter and Snout,' laughed Tom, he still didn't know his son had gone off with Ben. 'What sort of a name is that? We call ours apple sauce and sage and onion.'

'I shall call mine Trotter and Snout,' said Simon with dignity. 'What do they eat, Father?'

'They can have milk for the moment, they're still young'uns. Then it can be some scraps, and barley and apples in the autumn.'

'Helen's getting married, will she leave us?'

'She says not, Simon, but if she does, we'll find someone else to look after us.'

'In school, sir said how many boys want to be soldiers and we all put our hands up. It's for the glory of the country, isn't it?' he said uncertainly.

'It's an easy way to get yourself killed, lad, but nothing will deter them if they want to go.'

Robert knew of Ben's seduction of the young men. He had seen evidence of the press gangs when he was in the navy. This village out in the middle of England knew little of such happenings and was sheltered from the Navy who plundered men from seaside ports and villages . He had several families to visit, how would they react to a few shillings compensation? He would confess that although he hadn't known of Ben's intentions he was not surprised. The country needed prime soldiers, every village must give. The road to Reading barracks would echo to the sound of marching feet. Handkerchiefs would flutter at windows and fatherless babies would be born nine months hence.

The piglets arrival took away Simon's sadness at Ben's departure. He had touched the rifle, had picked it up and staggered under it's weight. He heard footsteps and carefully placed it down again. He looked up guiltily as his father came into the parlour.

Robert smiled at his son. 'Shall we look at it together?' he said gently, picking up the Baker rifle easily.

They both sat down and looked at where the bullet would go and how the powder was pressed in to cause a spark. There were notches on the butt. Simon fingered them.

'Do you think that's how many men he's killed?' he whispered, awe-struck.

'I shouldn't think so, but we'll ask.'

'Perhaps it's the number of tigers, in Inndya.'

'Perhaps.' Robert knew of the enhancement of the stories. He had done a little of it himself when he came to Appley. And look what happened he admonished himself, Ben went and enlisted and Mary was killed looking for him.

'Bed time,' he spoke gruffly and propelled the child in the direction of the stairs.

The next morning Robert was up with the dawn chorus getting an early start.

It was a gruff, 'mornin',' from Tom that caused him to look up from where his head was tucked into the warm side of Belle as his fingers squeezed and pulled in rhythm.

'Morning, Tom.' he responded carefully, a quick look informing him of Tom's mood.

'You knew of it?'

'Has George gone with Ben?'

'You know damned well he has. His mother hasn't stopped wailing all night, along with others.'

'I'm sorry. Ben didn't tell me but I'm not surprised. Short of locking them up, they're grown men, Tom, they make their own minds up.'

Tom was pacing up and down. Belle turned her head nervously and Buttercup waiting in line snorted anxiously.

'Why's he have to go and get hisself killed out in some foreign parts. And they're all heathens,' he raged, why couldn't he stay in the village, where he's needed? Glory, damned bloody glory and that Wellesley. I heard down the Ewe, it was Sir Arthur Wellesley says this and Sir Arthur Wellesley says that. As if Ben James was one of the magical inner circle. Waving his rifle about. If he wants a gun, we'll get a gun. I know he can't shoot on Byclere's land but he could go up on the downs.'

Robert had never before heard such a long speech from the usually taciturn Tom. He sighed, stood up, carefully picking up the bucket away from Belle's back hoof and slapped her on the rump, her signal to walk out.

'Buttercup,' and the next cow moved into the parlour. 'Tom, get cracking, there's nothing you can do. He'd be mortified if you went after him and ordered him home. He wouldn't settle once he's got the notion in his head. Ben'll look after him; it's not in their interests to get them killed. The army needs good shots like George and the others. You see, he'll be home before you know it, and the glamour will be out of his system after two weeks in barracks.'

'You think so?'

'Yes,' he said impatiently, 'now, start on the separating. You're too upset to milk, the cows know there's something wrong. They can sense it, they'll hold back their milk. Take the pans and your worries to the dairy.'

'Oh aye.' Tom picked up the earthenware bowls and stamped out, outrage ringing through his hob nail boots on the stone floor.

Robert finished Buttercup and slid his hand down her warm rump, enjoying the softness of her skin.

'I hope he comes back, old girl. Tom'll be fit for nothing here. That boy's an only child, but you got to let them go. Like we'll have to do with Simon.' The cow turned her head, her breath warm and smelling of cud, the grass and the meadow flowers she'd been eating in the dawn.

'Go on,' he told her briskly, 'Belinda,' was called and another moved in. Robert settled down to get finished before having breakfast with Simon at eight o'clock.

Tom poked his head round the door again, Oh by the bye, Beauty's bulling again. You need a new bull Robert, that old Shorthorn ain't up to it.'

'I know, Gideon's too old. I've spoken to Agent Calloway, we're going over Britwell way to look at a Jersey bull, to share like. So once it comes, Gid can be killed for the butcher.'

Belinda mooed and swished her tail, her rump was smacked and she moved on.

'Barbara.' A cow with the distinctive marled black and white markings and reddish face moved in, delicate hooves tripping lightly on the stone floor.

'My beauty,' murmured Robert in her ear, 'we're going to get you a fine young Jersey bull.'

She snorted, licking his face with a rasping tongue leaving a trail of white saliva tinged with green. Robert smiled and wiped a sleeve on his cheek, then bent to milking his favourite Shorthorn cow.

That evening he sat by the open window, bathed in moonlight and a warm summer breeze.

"1808 July 4th.

Ben James came home briefly. I am sorry to say he came to enlist some young men for Sir Arthur Wellesley's Rifle Brigade for the Peninsular war that is going on in Portugal.

He also captured Helen Canning our housekeeper whilst he was here and they will wed when he next comes on leave.

Gideon the Shorthorn bull will go soon. We are to share a fine young Jersey bull with the Byclere estate. This should improve the richness of the milk.

Simon is in school, he is too forward and talks too much but I am proud of him.

June 23rd was Midsummer Eve this year and there was the usual fayre in the village. It was the anniversary of Mary's death and as I sat in the parlour I thought I saw herby the fire, in her grey gown. There was the faintest smell of her rabbit stew with herbs, like she used to make. How I wish she would walk in that door. She'd be so happy to know Ben has come home safe. If it is Mary's spirit that I see then I shall definitely never marry again."

Helen wanted to go into Banbury for her wedding fancies. He had the suspicion there would be little concentration on their affairs at home now. Perhaps he should get another housekeeper? But Simon loved her and they were used to her and she ran the house well. And he could feel easier knowing she was Ben's fiancé.

Helen had an aunt living at Otwell just outside Banbury. Two days later she rode in with Robert on the cart. As she slipped off the wagon he pressed a guinea into her hand,

'For you to get yourself something nice and with the change buy some soldiers for Simon.' he gave him a huge smile, but her eyes were already looking to the shops lining the street.

He sighed as he started to lead the horse round to the inn. How he would have enjoyed bringing Mary in. They would have sold the butter and cheese together and then gone off for a pie for their dinner and perhaps buy some ribbons or something for the farm. Doing it all in harmony, how happy they would have been.

Dismissing himself as a sentimental old fool Robert concentrated on getting his butter and cheese unloaded.

He had his usual pitch and always used Mary's butter mould with the imprint of the oak tree. For his regular customers he was happy to weigh out large and small amounts. Everything was carefully wrapped. He used a fresh dock leaf for the small pieces, but larger amounts were enclosed in clean muslin. This was what he had used to strain the whey, the liquid off the cheese and they were carefully washed to use again.

His customers appreciated the high standards and courteous service they received and he was soon sold out. He would have to get home for Simon coming out from school as Helen wasn't coming back for two days. Caleb and Tom were around the farm but he always had the fierce desire to be there when Simon came running up the track and into the yard.

He cleaned off the stall and took his bowls back to the wagon. It was still only just gone eleven, too early for dinner and he decided to look out for some breeches for Simon. There was a haberdashers stall also selling made up smocks and breeches for country folk. He looked at them in bewilderment, not knowing what size to get. They seemed so large. He scratched his head and fingered the cloth. Thick wool flannel for winter? And some serviceable corduroy for the summer? What was best? The stall woman looked old enough to be sensible, he would ask for advice. In the end he went home with three pairs: two of cord and one of warm flannel, being assured they would wear well.

Helen came home with the carter two days later. Mysterious parcels were whisked away to her room and Simon waited impatiently for his soldiers. Finally he stood outside her room hopping on one foot, calling,

'Helen, can I come in, have you my soldiers?' He wanted them to have green uniforms like Uncle Ben's. He had collected up small chicken feathers from the yard to decorate them with and tiny sticks to make swords.

'Not now, Simon, I'm busy,' there was a rustling sound.

'Please, Helen.' He tried the door handle and it opened but stuck.

'Simon, later, do as you're told, you naughty boy,' but it was too late. He pushed his head round the door and seen her in her new lace under drawers and white camisole top.

'How dare you,' and she threw a small parcel at his retreating face. It hit him on the side of his head, surprisingly heavy and he squeaked,

'Ow!' The parcel fell in the doorway and snatching it up he ran to his room rubbing the side of his head.

Helen walked to the door and pushed the chair against it again. Wretched child, she fumed. But she forgot her anger at the sight of the froth of white lace on the bed. She would be a very beautiful bride for Ben James on their wedding night. The nightgown was so beautiful. She had half a mind to wear it later. Her dress had been chosen and would be made for her. A seamstress in Banbury had taken her measurements and she would go in again with Robert to collect it. Oh yes, she would have the finest gown in the village, almost to compare with the Bycleres up at the House. She smiled complacently, holding up an impractical satin slipper. Everything was working out nicely.

Simon undid his parcel, carefully saving the string.

'Oh.' he stared at a pile of little green men. He picked one up. It held a rifle to its shoulder, and had a small peaked cap on. He had told everyone he was having soldiers like his uncle. Helen had got the wrong hats. Sadly, he stood them on his clothes chest. Grudgingly he had to admit they were quite good. One was kneeling, one was lying down, and one was running with his rifle held across his arms. They were quite lifelike. Almost in spite of himself he began to play. The pile of twigs was arranged in a heap and hid a skirmisher. Eagerly he put two men behind his window shutter. He hurried to his box to get his other soldiers and with them out, played on, oblivious to shouted calls to come down.

He was making a popping, whistling sound of bullets flying when he heard the door open and Helen put her head round.

'Is it safe to come in?' she laughed

'Helen, they've got the wrong hats.' He killed a light infantry officer with one bullet. 'Bang!' The soldier collapsed to the ground with his feet in the air.

'Ben told me that most of the time they wear what they call forage caps like your soldiers. They can't always get the shakoes with the cockade like Ben had. I think our lot are going out to Spain and Portugal when they're trained. He says they call recruits Johnny Raws. Now, pack it all up and help me get the dinner.'

'When's he coming home?' Simon clattered down the stairs ahead of her.

'I don't know, I hope it will be soon and we can get married before he goes away.'

The note came three months later. *"I will bee ome zoon. Ben James."* The name was written beautifully in copperplate script, the spelling was quaint.

It had been left by the son of a cousin of a brother whose older brother was in the brigade.

Helen looked at it and turned to Robert, 'I didn't think Ben could write,'

'He can't but before he left I wrote his name on a piece of paper and he took it with him, so he could copy it.'

'I wish he said when,' she was petulant, how could she get ready if she didn't know the actual day.

'Perhaps he'll write again, or just turn up and give you a surprise?' Robert noted her irritation. Miss Canning liked to have everything her way.

'Huh,' she walked off with the note, already planning her wedding day.

Ben came home on a Sunday afternoon when they were sitting quietly, after their dinner. The door opened and a huge, green shadow filled the light.

Ben,' squealed Helen rushing to him.

'Uncle Ben.' shouted Simon drinking in the sight of the dusty green uniform. Were the dark streaks down the sleeve enemy blood?

'Hello, all,' Ben, his arm round Helen, gave her a smacking great kiss with a grubby, unshaven face, placed his pack by the wall and unstrapped his sword.

'I've got five days leave, is that time enough to get married?' he grinned.

CHAPTER NINETEEN

Helen was very glad that she had had the time to prepare and on 19th November she became Mrs Benjamin James.

It was a still, cold day with sullen grey clouds, but the church was warm with the packed village of Appley to fill its pews. Ben made a fine figure in his green Corporal's uniform. His sword gleamed, polished by Simon and his boots, with Robert's spit and polish, shone like mirrors.

Helen was beautiful in her cream empire line silk dress, trimmed with silk rosebuds and cream swansdown that floated and rippled. A dainty hat, tip tilted on her piled up silver hair was decorated with pink ribbons. She had been assured that it was the latest design from London, come from Paris. She was secretly thrilled to have achieved her ambitions so easily. Ben was putty in her elegant, mitten clad hands.

In his best, new green corduroy breeches Simon stood with Robert. They had been run off their feet getting everything ready. The barn floor had been cleaned and trestles laid out, ready for all the guests. Bowls, dishes, plates covered every inch, it was a feast for a king and all paid for by Ben.

Helen's parents were dead and only a few of her family would come. Robert was paying for the ale and punch to drink the toasts. Tom had agreed to stay home and keep an eye on it.

The bell pealed as the happy couple came out of church. There were no rose petals to throw in November, so they were showered with barley. Little children had to be restrained from too vigorous throwing. Laughing, Ben picked up his wife and ran with her to the waiting wagon.

Robert's horse, Binnie had been up since six, patiently standing whilst he was curry combed, brushed and then decorated with ribbons. They did this for Helen. A nasty squall of rain would have ruined her dainty slippers.

'But why, father?' complained Simon later, watching as Robert packed a bag with his night-gown and hair brush.

'We're leaving the bridal couple to ...be here on their own tonight.'

'Will Helen have a baby now she's married?'

'I don't know, I expect so, eventually.'

'I don't want her to die, like my mother did. I want her here with us.' Simon ran to catch up as Robert walked briskly up the lane to the Ewe and Lamb and their bed for the night.

'Not everyone dies when they have a baby. Look at all the mothers in the village.' said Robert reasonably. Simon had grown up with the daily sight of animal's copulating but he was very hazy about how mothers and fathers achieved their children.

'I asked Uncle Ben not to give Helen a baby and he said, he said why not.'

Robert was trying not to laugh, 'And what did you say?'

'I told him I don't want Helen to die. She could have a baby from the village if she wants, Susan Bates is always having them.'

'What did he say to that?'

'He laughed and said it was all a matter of luck.'

Robert opened the door of the Ewe and stood aside for Simon. It was quiet, most of the villagers were still in the barn enjoying the food and drink.

Eva Talbot hurried to greet them.

'Come in, come in, is it Simon's bed time now?'

'Yes, Mrs Talbot, show him up please. I'll just have a small brandy before I go.'

As the evening wore on the dancers got sweatier, noisy and tipsy. Ben and Helen had danced together and danced with the other guests. Their faces were flushed and he drank his thirst away.

As Helen danced with Mark Calloway she whispered in his ear. 'This won't change nothing. Ben'll be gone soon.'

She also had no desire for a baby and as they got ready for bed explained to Ben why.

'I don't want to be left alone to bring up a child, not knowing when or if it's father is going to come home. I'm not even sure I'd be able to stay here.'

They were in the big bedroom with Mary James's large double bed before them. A rare fire blazed in the fireplace. Ben watched Helen as she brushed a gleaming waterfall of silver over pale shoulders that glowed rosily in the firelight. She was too beautiful to be a virgin. He hesitated to ask, he didn't want to break the mood of pleasurable anticipation.

'Turn your back,' she teased.

'Why?''

'I want to surprise you.' Helen slipped the beautiful white lace nightgown over her shoulders. Standing up she let the frilled hem swish to the floor. The neckline was low, it was not a gown to keep warm in.

'Now...husband.' she smiled. She was as aware as he was of the question of virginity and had decided to ignore it. If he asked she would make up some story.

Ben looked, drinking in the sight of his wife with her pleased, cat like smile. Her breasts peeped out provocatively.

'You're beautiful Helen James and the nightgown is lovely, but I'd rather see what's underneath.'

He held out his arms and she came to him.

'You know how to prevent it then? A baby.' he asked quietly.

'Well, how to make it less likely. Let's wait a bit Ben, 'til we knows each other better and you're going to be home more.'

He pushed the lace over her breasts and bent his head. He was mesmerised, enthralled and would have agreed to anything.

The noise and goings on in the barn and the busy atmosphere in the house had awakened the spirit of Mary James. A wraith of mist hovered, uncertainly in the kitchen beside the fire. With a swirl of a grey she disappeared. back through the wall.

Robert slipped into bed beside Simon. His son had his thumb in his mouth and was fast asleep, a warm small body which he had to resist the impulse to cuddle up to. He thought wistfully of Ben and Helen in Mary's bed and of the nights he had spent there with Dorothy. Of the firelight and the quiet talking, of the pleasure of their coupling and the pain when he allowed himself to think of Mary. He closed his eyes and wished the couple a long and happy marriage.

"November 20th 1808

Ben and Helen were married yesterday. Susan Bates was very drunk, there'll be another baby there I suspect. It was a happy day though and the wedding breakfast became a rowdy good natured night, with all the food and drinks gone by eleven.

Simon is very worried about Helen dying in childbirth., I am not sure what forthright comment he is going to make to them today. He was a smart little boy yesterday, I was proud of him."

The business of the farm started as usual at six o'clock the next morning. Ben was used to getting up early and unused to a soft comfortable bed like theirs and an even softer more comfortable wife. He turned his head and looked at her. Helen was asleep, her shell pink rounded shoulder showing bare above the sheet. Desire surged through him and he ran a finger lightly down her back to her warm, firm buttocks. From there it was only inches to ignite a fire of mutual passion and as she lay in his arms afterwards, listening to the sounds of cows lowing and Robert's voice calling names she smiled sleepily, content to let Ben do what he would with her.

Simon went straight to school from his bed in the Ewe and Lamb. Mrs Talbot had given him a bread and milk breakfast and he didn't see Helen again until he went home at four o'clock. He looked at her suspiciously. She seemed to be very pink cheeked and laughed gaily at everything Uncle Ben said. He was sitting in Father's chair with his legs outstretched to the fire. Simon hopped from one foot to the other anxious to ask what was on his mind.

'Will Helen be having a baby soon, Uncle Ben?'

Helen and Ben both turned to look at him. Helen thought of that morning when she hadn't been quite so prepared.

Ben rubbed his chin, newly shaved in anticipation of more enjoyment that night.

'Simon no one knows that soon, it do take more than five minutes to grow a baby.' Then Ben realised that the seven year old child did not know about gestation times. For him a lady suddenly had a large tummy and days later a baby was there. There was no nine month interval in between.

Helen took pity on Simon. 'We thought we'd wait a bit until Ben can come home and be a proper father, instead of going off to play at soldiers,' she finished slyly.

Her husband playfully smacked her bottom and she whipped round quickly and tugged his moustache. To Simon it seemed as though he was forgotten, so he took himself into the scullery and found some milk and buns to eat for his tea. He had set up a whole army across his bedroom floor and intended to defeat Napoleon so much that Boney would never again be able to raise a single soldier.

He wanted Ben to play with him, but one look told him they were oblivious to anyone but themselves. Helen was sitting on Ben's lap in Father's chair and they were kissing...again. Simon snorted in disgust and tramped up the stairs.

It was dark by five o'clock, and when Robert came in the house was quiet. The fire was made up and he stood listening. Quietly he mounted the stairs and heard Simon's voice, 'bang, shoot, bang, pop pop.. oweeee...' He smiled at the dying soldier noises and turned the handle.

Simon looked up with a grin, 'Father I'm beating Boney, they're nearly all dead.'

'We've got a beefsteak pie, are you coming down for your dinner?'

'What about Uncle Ben and Helen, will they come?'

'I'll tell them, but they might be busy.'

'I'll ask,' and Simon ran to the bedroom door and banged on it. 'Uncle Ben and Helen, do you want beef pie? It's dinner time.'

Robert chuckled to himself, all was quiet but he was quite sure that whatever had been going on had been spoiled by Simon shouting.

In the bedroom Ben groaned,. 'Don't stop woman.' Helen had turned out to be a very quick learner in the art of pleasing a husband and seemed to have natural skills.

But she lifted her head, 'I'd better go down to get the dinner out, it is my job.'

'They'll manage, just for today, do that again, he purred. She sat astride him and her long hair covered them both.

Robert saw little of Ben except at meal times. He liked to go down to the Ewe in the evenings and would roll in late and lurch straight up to bed. Helen went up earlier, to change into her beautiful night-gown. The brandy at the Ewe seemed to have more pull on him than the charms of her body and his initial delight and tenderness in her had not lasted. She realised that he was probably missing the camaraderie of his fellow soldiers.

Some nights he would fall asleep on the bed, with his clothes on and she could undress him roughly without him waking. She was disappointed, but was careful to hide it and in the morning he would turn to her like a contrite little boy and beg her forgiveness for his behaviour.

He was waved off with few regrets. Helen had extracted the remaining shillings from his pocket. Robert had received little help from him on the farm and his large fist had broken one of Simon's soldiers.

'Perhaps life can get back to normal now, Helen,' Robert observed the next morning.

'I hope so.' She gathered up plates, anxious to get her chores done and meet Mark later in the Byclere stables.

Robert had finished the work by ten and wanted to go over to talk to Calloway about rams. Appley Glebe now had twelve sheep; all downland ewes and he hoped to borrow a ram.

The pig called Trotter was a girl, a gilt and they had decided to keep her and breed. Snout had been despatched one day by Sam Jackson the pig sticking man whilst Simon was at school. He had become very fond of the pigs and argued fiercely for their reprieve.

'We can't keep Snout, he's a boy,' said Robert hoping Simon would be sensible.

'Why not, Father,' a thought struck him, 'we need a man pig for her to have babies, he could be the one.'

'No. his father shook his mop of whitening hair. 'We can't keep one boar just for that, we haven't the room, or the feed for the winter.' They only grew enough barley for the cows and an acre of turnips for the cattle and sheep.

'I'll ask Agent Calloway if we can use the Byclere boar. It's a very good one, then Trotter can have babies.'

'For you to sell,' grumbled Simon.

'That's farming lad, yes.'

So now he had to decide whether to take Trotter to the boar, by walking her over there, or have the boar brought over to Appley.

An hour later he sat in John's office with a warm beaker of hot toddy in his hand. A log fire crackled in the grate and the warmth dried the old off his coat. Outside a hoar frost covered the yard, with no sun to dry it off. Mark Calloway passed the window and waved to him.

'Mark's doing well for himself now,' Robert remarked. 'Head groom at twenty five...is it?'

'Aye, I'm getting near retirement, I wish he'd follow me but he loves the horses.' the Steward sipped noisily at his steaming drink.

'Right, now about our young gilt, which is best do you think?'

'Well, he's three years old our Percy, and a bit strong sometimes. He'd be a handful to walk to Appley and just for one, what say you your gilt comes here. I'll keep her till she comes on heat, he does the business and then you can collect her.'

'Being a bit of a pet, she is quite quiet.'

'If you could get her in a wagon it would save her trotters, but that wouldn't be easy,' John chuckled at the thought of lifting a pig that size up into a wagon.

'I'll walk her slowly, Simon can help at the weekend. Now that's settled, what about the ram?'

'You want us to do all your farming for you, is that it?' said John sarcastically.

'You've used our bull in the past. Twelve ewes wouldn't be much for your Southdown ram.'

'It should be soon, I'll have Shepherd Giles bring it over, he can go in a wagon. Now that's decided, have you heard from Ben?

Robert shook his head. 'No, I don't expect to.'

They chatted for another half an hour then Robert drained his glass and stood up stretching. He winced slightly as he pulled his coat on. The cold was getting in his bones and his shoulder ached from his wound. It was always worse when there was frost. This chilly weather dug deep into his bones. He would ask Susan Bates for some salve to rub in.

As he crossed the yard, his boots ringing on the slippery, whitened cobbles, he looked across at the stables. Horses' heads poked out over the doors. He caught the flash of a green cape whisking round a doorway, but it was the hem of red and white that puzzled him. Helen had a dress that colour, the maids in the house all wore blue or grey. What was she doing here and by the stable loft?

As he reached the gate and turned back to shut it, Mark Calloway came out of the loft doorway, shrugging on a jacket. Robert watched him stop and look both ways and then turn to speak to someone hovering inside. Robert didn't want to see anymore. If Helen was going with young Calloway and so soon after her marriage it would only cause trouble. There were few secrets in a place like Byclere and certainly not in the village. Everyone knew everyone else's business, almost before they knew it themselves.

He walked home deep in thought. Should he say something to Helen? She would probably deny it, but he didn't like to think of young Mark's chances if Ben found out. The soldier was taller, broader and tougher. Helen was playing with fire.

She came in the door as he was eating his bread and cheese lunch. Her cheeks were pink, from the cold he presumed and she was her usual calm self. But as she moved past him to go upstairs he saw the wisps of hay on the hem of her green woollen cape The fashionable cape that was part of her trousseau, a gift from her husband.

'How was Susan?' he enquired quietly.

'Oh she's all right, expecting her tenth, she's hardly a minute to herself.'

He laid the small pot of salve on the table, Helen's eyes widened as she recognised Susan's handiwork.

'She was kind enough to put this up for me, some comfrey salve for my shoulder. She didn't say you'd been in.'

'I just popped in there a minute ago.'

'After you got back from Byclere, Helen?'

'No, no, what would I be doing there?' she stood at the bottom of the stairs twisting her blue bonnet ribbon round and round.

He saw her agitation and knew she was lying. 'Playing with fire, that's what you're doing. Your new husband barely gone and you go up in the loft with Mark Calloway. Ben'd kill him and after that he'd leave his mark on you. Don't do it Helen, you're married now.'

Her bravado faded and her voice deflated. 'I do love him, Robert.'

'Helen he's got a wife and four children, he's not for you. Why didn't you marry him when you had the chance?'

'He was only an under groom then, I want better than that. I don't want to end up like Susan with all those children, I want to enjoy myself.'

'Marrying a soldier means you stay faithful whatever and however often he comes home. It's like a navy wife, some of them don't see their husbands for years on end, but they still remain true to their vows,' he told her sternly.

Would you tell him?' she was sulky.

'No, but if you keep this up there'll be no place for you here. You know Simon can't keep a secret, and he's all eyes and ears.'

She sighed and nodded and left, trailing her hat ribbons on the floor.

"December 25th 1808

Today has passed with a reasonable measure of success. We have played games here in the evenings, even simple ones like Hunt the Slipper have passed the time for us. Simon gave us guessing games and I made a hot rum punch with lemons.

Next September Simon will start in the Church School in Banbury. I have been in to ensure a place for him. He will be a weekly boarder and I will find a suitable lodging for him with a kindly woman.

It has been a good year for the farm, the weather was kind and the cows are healthy.

With our own lamb and pork I think we shall have sufficient for ourselves and some to sell."

CHAPTER TWENTY

The wet winter of 1809 turned into a dry spring. June was showery, teasing, never enough days to cut and make the hay. In the middle of July the weather finally came good for them.

With the rush of haymaking and then harvest the beginning of September came round too quickly for Robert. He had been assured by James Noble, their schoolmaster at Appley that Simon was well up to standard and in fact his arithmetic was above average. They had gone in to school in July to find out what type of clothes he was expected to wear and if there was anything special to buy. Armed with a list they hunted through the shops in Banbury.

Robert had to rely a good deal on the common sense of lady shopkeepers in order to buy the right sizes of everything. He did not want his son to be a laughing stock by wearing the wrong clothes.

It was a subdued Simon and proud but anxious father who set out at six o'clock on the Monday of September 9th to start his schooling. When he saw Simon start to sway and his eyes begin to close he pulled his son into the crook of his arm and tucked the blanket round him. The child slept until the outskirts of Banbury. He was oblivious to the morning birdsong and the sun touching the dew drenched cobwebs festooned on hawthorn hedges. Diamonds sparkled on ripening blackberries and sloe berries tucked up in the prickly blackthorn.

Simon would stay in the week with Mrs Green of Key Street and come home on a Friday afternoon with the Appley carter.

Robert had debated whether Simon should use his old sea chest for his clothes but had decided it was a bit big and old fashioned. Accordingly, Joe Armstrong, made him a new box with a handle. His initials were engraved on the side. Simon had tucked a few soldiers in amongst his clothes, together with some keepsakes from home. Tom had whittled him a bird, carved in cherry wood. It was polished and smooth and a comforting thing to stroke when you were anxious.

They decided he would go direct to Mrs Green's house and walk to school from there.

'Are you sure?' asked Robert.

'Yes, father, I'll go in on my own, I've been going to school for three years now.'

Robert nodded. He was pleased with his son's independence. After all, he had seen eight year olds come into a ship in the Navy. They would come on board either a trembling child or full of excitement and bravado. And nearly all reduced to a quivering jelly within days by sea-sickness and homesickness.

Recommended by the schoolmaster, the middle aged widow, Mrs Green seemed kindly and competent. She was comfortably plump with a broad beam and hips that swayed under her serviceable grey skirt. Her apron was as white as her day bonnet. With a smile she ushered Simon into her cottage. Robert watched the small figure disappear through the black front door, surprised by the lump in his throat and the pang in his heart.

If Helen thought her life would be easier with Simon away she was disagreeably surprised. With the Autumn flush of grass the cows were milking well and she spent all her days in the dairy, churning butter and making and turning cheeses.

Caleb was despatched to the vegetable garden to lift potatoes and these were put into a clamp to store for the winter. The same was done for carrots and two piles of sandy soil full of vegetables were left tidily by the yard. Golden onions were strung up with twine and hung from the kitchen ceiling and Helen was sent out blackberry and elderberry picking in the early evening. Robert resolved to make her too busy to think of dallying with Mark Calloway or anyone else!

He decided to make an extra trip into Banbury on the first Friday of Simon's school week. The cart was packed with all the extra butter that Helen had made and cheese that was maturing nicely. Robert looked forward to seeing his son again. He had missed his bright eyes and eager chatter and even Tom had commented that he missed the young'un around the place.

After a successful market he took his money into Brownlaws' Bank. He would need extra now to pay for Simon's schooling and it would be convenient when he had to pay a term in advance.

He fetched Binnie from the inn and headed for school. It was after three, Simon would be surprised. He was expecting to go home with Tubbs the Carter after four o'clock.

Robert stopped at the Widow Green to tell her he was taking Simon home but it was really to find out how Simon had been in the week.

'He's been fine, a bonny lad, full of chat once he got over his shyness with me. The cat's had kittens, so that helped and he's given them names. Though I shan't be keeping them,' she added. 'To be honest, Mr Southwell, it was a pity he was here, or I'd have drowned them but I'll find homes for them later and Simon has chosen the black one to take home.'

'Has he,' said Robert irritated. 'We have enough at Appley but I daresay one more won't harm,'

'That's what the boy said,' she beamed at him.

'Well thank you, Mrs Green, we'll see you Monday morning then.'

Robert couldn't park the trap near the school. It was a narrow lane and already crowded. Accordingly he stopped round the corner, looped the reins round a tree branch and left Binnie, patiently waiting. There was a flint stone wall, as high as his head surrounding the school yard and as he walked quietly along to the gate he heard voices.

A young, shrill voice was taunting, 'Southwell, Southwell, Simple Simon Southwell, farmers boy,...moo, hiss, honk honk,' There was boyish laughter from others, but no reply from his son. Rage built up in Robert's head, they were bullying Simon, he had seen enough of that in the Navy.

As he walked round the gate he saw Simon with his back to the wall and his three tormentors in front of him.

'Is Farmer Southwell coming for his precious calf, or is it a little lamb?' They were obviously older than Simon, well spoken and well dressed in a grubby, end of the week fashion.

Simon had his head down. He looked like he was either going to charge at them like a raging bull or burst into tears.

They didn't notice Robert until he was behind them. Simon looked up and drew in a breath sharply.

'Fa...' he began.

'Hello, Simon, introduce me to your friends will you?'

Simon stared at him mute. He had been teased and tormented all week by these boys and he was seriously thinking how he could avoid coming back next week.

'Your name?' Robert snapped with an echo of past naval discipline. He fixed the boys with his eyes daring them to move.

'Harry Chevenor Sir, the Hon...honourable.'

'And...' Robert looked at the others.

'Rupert Lansing.'

'Josiah Marriot-Kent.'

'Well, well,' said Robert reflectively, 'Harry Chevenor, Harry Chevenor..' he rolled the name round his tongue reflectively whilst the ten year old cringed.

'We were only funning sir, nothing much to bother him.'

'Are you the son of Lord Clembourne of Astonbury, there's Chevenors there?'

'Yes, yes, sir,' said Harry grateful to be known.

'And you were accusing Simon of being a farmer's son.

'No harm meant, Sir,' Harry tried to regain his aristocratic bravado, 'all the new ones get it.'

'Well, as I remember right, your father breeds pigs, Oxford Sandy and Blacks. I saw them at the County Show this year. I went with Byclere, we talked about boars and breeding. Your father's very keen on his pigs. And of course, Byclere had a good Oxford down ram off him.'

Harry pulled and twisted at the cap in his hand.

'So I reckon that makes him as much of a farmer as me, don't you?' he started softly, dangerously and spat the final words.

'Sir.' agreed Harry.

'And as for you two,' Robert looked contemptuously at Lansing and Marriot-Kent. 'If you can find nothing better to do than tease the new boys then I'm sure your housemaster can find you some extra school work. What shall it be, extra Latin declension or fifty spellings to learn?'

'We're sorry sir, it weren't our fault.'

'Lansing?' mused Robert, looking hard at the owner of the name. 'There was an Edward Lansing on board my last ship, the Celeste, any relation?'

'My cousin, Sir.' said the boy anxiously.

'Yes, well he was a bright child when he wasn't bawling or being sea sick. And I had to teach him basic arithmetic before he could even start on simple navigation. Simon knew more at five than he did at nine.'

'Yes, sssir,' he stuttered.

'Oh...Go away,' said Robert, 'come on Simon, let's go home.' He strode off, leaving Simon to run along behind.

They got into the trap without a word, although first Simon had given Binnie a hug and buried his face in her warm neck. It had been his first real experience of the cruelty of children and he was close to tears.

It had been a nice and nasty sort of week with him discovering a keen interest in the lessons and trying to find somewhere to be inconspicuous at meal times. There were other new boys but they all came from the town and knew each other. He had gone from being a big fish in a small pond to a very small tiddler in a large pool.

He quickly discovered that he wasn't supposed to be a know-all and answer the questions. He wasn't sure quite where he fitted in.

Simon broke the silence as Binnie clip clopped along the flinty road, 'Do I have to go back there next week, Father?'

'Was it all bad?'

'Noo...Mrs Green's got kittens. I said we'd have the black one, it would be company for our Sooty.'

'So how many cats would we have then?'

'Um, six or seven?' ventured Simon. 'But there's plenty of milk at the moment...you said so.'

'Yes, for butter and cheese, for selling, not to give to cats.'

'He can have mine, the milk I would have drunk in the week if I'd been at home,' said his son with unarguable logic. Robert laughed and ruffled the child's hair, he smelt of chalk and that certain school smell and his clothes were grubby and creased. Helen could clean them up for Monday.

They arrived back to a hug from Helen and a beaming smile from Tom. Caleb had left early to look after Margie before it got too dark. Robert produced the new fork he had bought for Cal to weed round the leeks and a parcel he had collected for Helen.

They were a happy family all sitting round the dinner table, tucking into a large pork pie, all golden pastry and tasty aroma and fresh dug potatoes and carrots cooked with mint.

'So, Simon,' said Helen her mouth full of pie, 'do you get food as good as this at that Widow lady's house?'

Simon chewed for a minute and told them, 'we had rabbit pie, not as nice as yours, Helen.'

She smiled and said, 'I've got secret ingredients Simon.'

'And,' he continued, 'beefsteak and turnips and spotted dick pudding and one night a friend came to dinner.'

'What sort of a friend, Simon?'

'Mrs Green's gentleman friend. His name was Carl um...don't know. He said call me Uncle Carl. We had a game of pennies on a board, before I went to bed.'

Robert looked askance at Simon. Was the Widow Green as respectable as she was supposed to be? He would have to make enquiries if there was any goings on there.

The weekend flew by for them all at Appley Glebe. Simon left early again on Monday feeling ambivalent about his new life. He discovered that in the space of five days a different boys gang had been formed in the village of which he had no part.

New friendships had been struck and somehow in this loose melding of children Simon lost his place. At the village green on Saturday morning he stood on the fringe in clean clothes, full of egg, toast and coffee and watched ragged children fight a mock battle. They asked him if he wanted to be Boney but he declined, not wishing to be on the losing side...as it would be. Then he wished he'd said yes. It would have been better than being a spectator with seven year old Lucy Talbot hanging round.

She was the daughter from the Ewe and Lamb and fell in love with Simon at six years old. Age had not diminished the feelings and she was a silent shadow, everywhere he went.

But the two of them could not have stemmed the advance of nine well armed children, so he sat and watched and whittled a stick, hoping he looked indifferent.

"September 15th 1810

Simon has started school in Banbury, I hope he settles. It is quiet without him but he must have some more learning if he is to have a good start in life. I hope he will go to the university in Oxford, but that is a long time ahead.

The crops are coming in, we have plenty of apples this year, I shall make some cider. Trotter the sow had eight piglets, all plump and with the distinct markings of the Sandy and Black breed. Tom says they make his mouth water, just looking at them. We could kill one for Christmas if it's big enough. Before Simon comes home for the holiday. As you can imagine, they all have names, although they seem very similar to me. Simon swears they are all different characters. He seems to spend more time here on the farm than out with the village children."

Simon had settled in at school, but he had lost that bright effervescence that made him such a charmer. Somehow in conforming to the rules and regulations of the school it had dulled his personality a little.

Ben didn't come home again until a surprise visit in November 1810. He walked into a farmhouse that was totally deserted. He dumped his kitbag on the chair, placed his cap on the table and strode to the fireplace, stretching his hands to the blaze. He swung the kettle across and looked for the tea caddy. Ten minutes later, with a steaming cup in his hand he walked across to the dairy. An open door revealed Robert in his usual apron sampling a cheese, a knife in his hand, an O of surprise on his mouth.

'Ben good to see you.'

'Well you're here, but where's Simon and where's my wife?'

'Simon is in school in Banbury, he's doing well there.' Robert thought desperately, where was Helen? He'd thought she was in the house.

'She must be over at Susan's, I believe there's another baby on the way there.'

'I'll stroll over and then call at the Ewe, I'll see you later.' He put his cup down and leaving a ring of tea on the scrubbed table stamped out, his boots ringing on the stones and before Robert could argue.

'Oh dear,' he muttered, 'where is she? I hope she's not over with young Calloway.'

They met in the lane. Helen was hurrying back knowing that Robert wanted his dinner. Her cheeks were flushed and her lips slightly swollen.

Ben saw his wife coming towards him and broke into a run, 'Helen.'

'Ben what are you doing home?' What was he going to think, would be suspect anything? She felt very guilty.

'That's a nice welcome,' he teased, 'I was coming to find you.'

'I was over at Susan's she's expecting again, it's due any minute.'

'Then why do you smell of hay?' he nuzzled the top of her head as he embraced her and hurried her back to the farmhouse.

'I've been making a hay palliasse for her bed for the lying in.'

'A hay palliasse?' He said incredulously. 'What for?'

'It goes on the bed, they're short of linen, Ben, not like us. It can be burnt afterwards.'

'Oh I see, well, talking of sheets.' He pulled her with him onto the stairs.

'Not now,' she hissed, embarrassed, 'it's Robert's dinner time.'

'He won't mind getting his own for once, he knows I'm back. Come on, I've been looking forward to this since last Sunday when I knew I was coming home. It's been a long time for a strong man like me to go without.'

Outside their bedroom door he picked her up. 'Are you ready, Mrs James. You look a bit hot and bothered. Lets make the most of our time before Simon comes home.'

Helen was in a panic, she hadn't had time to prepare and Ben was hustling her onto the bed, tugging at her shawl. With a quick twirl she whisked herself out of his arms and ran to pull the curtain.

'Miss Modesty is it?' He mocked.

'It's still daylight,' she insisted, watching as he sat on the bed pulling off his boots.

'Here let me,' and she tugged and as the boot came off she fell backwards, her skirt in the air and her legs in their white stockings, flying out.

Ben laughed, but it died on his lips as he saw her sitting on the floor, her silver hair spread out over her shoulders and her breasts heaving with exertion.

'You're beautiful, wife, do you know that?' He held out his hands to pull her up and onto his lap and gently, using one hand started to untie the laces at the back of her dress.

'My, you've hay everywhere, isn't it a bit tickly,' he murmured, kissing her shoulder.

She felt him freeze as his eyes looked over her shoulder at the cloak dropped carelessly on the floor. Apart from wisps of hay she saw the white hairs. Long, white, coarse horse hairs, they could be nothing else. And Robert had the chestnut, Binnie. Determined to amuse him she reached up and nibbled his ear and missed the speculative look on his face.

Robert sat at the kitchen table eating a solitary pork pie, a mug of ale at his elbow. He heard them go upstairs and knew he'd not see them again until they got hungry.

Much later Helen came down for some water to wash with but she had a horrible suspicion it would be too late. Ben had kept her with him. They'd made love more than once. She'd tried coaxing to stop him, but, his face grim, his eyes hard, he told her,

'I want a son, Helen, one to carry on the James name. A man needs a son. And he needs to know that it's his.' And he rolled her over and imprisoned her with his strong legs.

As she washed she thanked God that he said nothing about the horse hairs on the cloak. If he knew about Mark Calloway...she shuddered to think what vengeance he would wreak. If she became pregnant the affair would have to stop anyway as she got bigger. Perhaps it was for the best.

In the space of time it took Ben to see those horse hairs he stopped trusting his wife. He knew he would get nothing but lies from her. He decided to do some quiet investigation of his own and when he found out who it was, as he would, he would ensure the man would cuckold nobody else. He would use the surveillance skills he had learned in the Army. With patience and the judicious use of coin he knew he could find out who Helen had been straying with. Hay and horse-hair narrowed the field considerably.

And knowing of Helen's talent for avoiding conception, he would ensure she was left in no doubt that her husband would be the only man to make her pregnant.

Two nights later, with Ben at the Ewe and Lamb and Robert sitting in the parlour poring over his flower drawings Helen dared to steal out and meet her lover.

She was desperate to warn Mark. Ben had been much as usual, demanding of her at night and in the early morning and watching her in the dairy and round about the house. But he had been smiling and joking, telling stories about the Army and she had started to relax.

Robert had mentioned to her quietly that afternoon in the dairy that Ben was asking questions.

'Don't play the innocent with me, Helen, he suspects you have a lover.'

She had stared at him, her eyes fearful, slowly and carefully placing the bowl of milk on the table. 'Do you think he knows who?'

'Not yet, but he soon will.'

'I must warn him, Robert, he must go away,' she said wildly, 'Ben would kill him.'

'I think not,' said Robert drily, 'but he will certainly leave his mark on Calloway. Enough to put him off other men's wives...for life.'

'Oh no…no.'

'Oh yes, Helen, and you know it. Ben's changed, he's learnt stealth and cunning.' Robert left her there, trembling with fear.

'Where is he tonight?' they were in the stable again..

'Down the Ewe buying drinks, you must go away until he goes back to barracks. He's dangerous, Mark, he'll kill you.'

'He wouldn't dare, besides he's no proof.' Mark was full of bravado. At twenty-five, promoted to head groom at Byclere House he felt he had achieved sufficient importance to make him immune to minor problems. He started to push Helen back onto the pile of hay in the loft,

'Come on one more time, until he goes back.' She lost her balance and fell and laughing triumphantly Mark fell on top of her.

'So it's proof is it?' Said a well known voice. 'It looks like I have it.'

In the gloom of the hay loft Ben was standing with a lantern, massive shadows dancing and flickering off the white washed walls. He hung the lantern on a hook hanging from a beam.

'We don't want to start a fire,' he remarked conversationally. Two pale faces looked up at him, identical in their terror.

Quickly Helen jumped up, tidying her skirt in one movement. Ben watched Calloway jump to his feet and look around for a weapon. There was a pitchfork in the corner.

Watching his face the guilty pair missed his hand reach for a knife and only saw the flash as it arced towards Calloway's arm. The blade pieced his coat and he shrieked.

'Murderer.'

'Oh no, you're not worth swinging for.'

'He's been forcing me, Ben, he won't leave me alone,' Helen tried to cling to Ben's arm but he shrugged her off.

'No one forced you to come here tonight, my dear, I thought you were home by our fireside.'

'I was, I was. I had a message.'

Calloway was sidling along the wall in the shadows and with a quick flick Ben threw another knife, this time catching the man's breeches.

'Stay there,' was the command. 'So you're saying…wife, that you've been forced. That all these months when I've been away and sending my pay home this Calloway has been at you like one of his stallions.'

'Yes, yes,' she said eagerly, desperate to shelve the blame.

'She's been after me for months, won't leave me alone. I've got a wife and children at home, I don't want none of this.' Calloway muttered, his eyes on Ben's face.

'I know what to do with him,' he spat contemptuously in Calloway's direction, 'but I don't know what I'll do with you...yet, go home, wait.' He pushed her firmly, propelling her out of the door.

'Don't... don't hurt him Ben he's not worth it, you'll get into trouble with the Army.'

She was breathless, sobbing, terrified and desperate to get home. They heard her boots clatter across the cobbles as she fled.

'Now,' he spoke softly, another knife in his hand, a stiletto acquired in Portugal. There was a rustling in the hay, red eyes looked out from the corner and a rat rushed across the stone floor. With a shriek Calloway leapt for the door and was adroitly overbalanced with the tip of Ben's boot. He fell heavily to the ground and tried to cover his face with his hands.

Whimpering, he cried. 'There's nothing in it, Ben, we was just talking, she likes to tell us all about you.'

'About me.' Ben exclaimed in disbelief, 'you talk about the absent husband when you're pawing at my wife.' He looked at Calloway in disgust. He curled up, trying to protect himself.

Ben stared at him dispassionately, thinking. The lantern flared in a draft, giant shadows played out across the walls and silence enveloped them in a black cloak. Still he played with the knife, it's blade glinting in the light.

'We learn how to interrogate in the army. My division, we're ones that go off on our own, for days at an end, hunting our own food, talking to villages, capturing prisoners. Sometimes they live, sometimes they die.'

Calloway gave a sob and looking round desperately started to shuffle along on his bottom nearer the door. He was stopped with a boot placed on his stomach. Pressure was applied and he gasped.

'I won't castrate you, though God knows you deserve it,' as he talked and Calloway watched his face, Ben dropped the knife and Calloway screamed. The blade had pierced his breeches, catching his skin. Dripping blood showed red through the dirty cloth.

'You've killed me,' Calloway sobbed, 'I'll die.'

'It's barely a nick,' snorted Ben, 'I've had worse, far worse in battle, but it should be a reminder, every time you get it out, that if you look at my wife again, you'll lose the whole lot. Your fucking days are over.'

Calloway scrambled to his feet, his hands clutched to his groin. Doubled up, he ran out as best he could, whimpering and muttering. Ben picked up his knives, wiped them on clean hay and reached up for the lantern. What was he going to do with Helen? Teach her a lesson. Beat her? He'd let her stew for a bit. He'd have a drink at the Ewe, there was still time if he hurried.

Helen sat up in bed with a clean nightgown on. The fire crackled, the warm glow lit up the room and made her look even more beautiful. Her long, silvery hair shone with vigorous brushing and her skin was a pearly gleam. Her full breasts peeped out from their lace and ribbons and would have tempted any red-blooded man. Ben's nightshirt was on the chair by the fire, warming for him and now she sat waiting nervously.

She decided, she mustn't play the coquette. She had better be the penitent wife. She must say how she missed him, how she was a poor, weak female, flattered by the admiring glances from a good looking man. Yes, she must say how she had missed him. What did he expect if he went off for months at a time?

'No, I don't think that's a good idea either.' She mumbled to herself. 'If I just say sorry, in a little girl voice, that might work. I bet he's unfaithful to me,' she muttered, whipping up some anger, 'I bet he goes with any common whore he can get.'

She sat leaning against the pillows, her knees bent up to her chin. The house was quiet, Robert had gone to bed when she came in. He had warned her, she could expect no sympathy there. He slept like the dead, working hard all day and getting up so early. But if Ben made a scene and starting shouting, she could hush him with the excuse of waking Robert.

As she sat quietly waiting, she started to doze and slipped down into the bed. Sleep overwhelmed her.

Ben had had enough drink to fire his temper but not damp his lust. Quietly he opened the front door and took his boots off. Mounting the stairs in his stockinged feet he avoided the creaky tread and walked noiselessly along to their room. He opened the door and took in the scene. The glowing fire was burning down, the room was warm, the shutters closed. It was too hot for him so he strode over and pulled open a shutter letting in the cold night air.

For a minute he breathed in deeply, calming himself. He was no longer the callow youth who would impulsively rush off in any direction. He had learnt to use his brains, act quickly and stealthily, always to his advantage.

With barely a rustle of cotton and wool he stripped quickly.

Naked, his muscular body gleaming with the sweat from his run back from Byclere stables he pulled back the bedclothes and twitched Helen's night-gown up over her head, imprisoning her in its folds.

She gave a muffled shriek, and he laughed.

'It's only me, your husband. Now...after what happened earlier, I don't feel like looking at you, you've been a whore, I'll treat you like one.'

The coupling was accomplished quickly and efficiently. At first she lay quiescent under him, refusing to participate in any way, but as he moved within her she responded, unwillingly and then excited by his rough handling she pulled him down, her nails raking his back.

'Harlot,' he cried, 'no man could rape you.'

Twice more in the night he took her, until in the morning as they lay awake, looking at each other warily she climbed on top of him, sliding across his damp body, feeling his muscles and sinews.

'Remember this...husband,' she spat manoeuvring him into her, 'when you're using your whores at the barracks, you remember that you have a wife at home.' Her hair hung over them, unbrushed and wild. It covered his face as she bent her sharp teeth to his chest and throat.

Helen accepted her pregnancy grudgingly. Ben returned to barracks and promptly forgot about her as he trained his riflemen to be ready for Lord Wellington's next campaign in Portugal.

Her stomach swelled and it became difficult to bend over the racks of cheese and the table with its mound of butter waiting to be patted. Helen insisted that she have more help in the house and dairy.

A Bates girl was produced. Nell, at fourteen was very pleased. After leaving school at ten she had been out in the fields for four years, earning a pittance. Robert insisted that Helen train her and the small, plain Nell, with her long brown plaits was as quick as a Bates was expected to be.

Simon continued to come home at weekends and seemed to have settled down in school. He had changed though, the sunny child with the quick smile was gone, replaced by a boy who lazed around, content to watch and let others do the work.

On a Sunday morning Robert was trying to get the dairy work finished when Simon sauntered in at ten o'clock.

'Give me a hand please, Simon. Would you turn the cheese this morning?'

'Father,' he whined, 'do I have to? My chums at school don't have to work, they have servants and farm workers. Tell Nell.'

'It's Nell's day off and yes, I would like you to, please. It's not onerous.'

With a sigh, Simon started turning over the cheeses. Robert ignored him and put his mood down to mixing with his Banbury chums.

They missed his chatter around the dairy but if he was going to be like that then it would be better if he stayed in the house.

Nell was still overawed and pathetically anxious to please. Simon would tease her telling her he had let the cat into the dairy and it was in the cream dish. She would fly off with a shriek expecting trouble and discover that all was quiet but she daren't complain to Mr Southwell of his son's tricks.

They heard that Ben was in Portugal and Robert wrote in his journal:

"April 28th. Easter was late this year but have planted the potatoes on Good Friday as is usual and the tradition. Am trying to persuade the village folk to grow them. We have three rows each of Ashleaf Kidney and White Elephant. These last ones are ugly things but grow large so are useful to eke out the turnips, carrots and cabbage. Am not giving any more away though, we need all our produce here.

I am sure that Ben is active out in the countryside of Portugal. We saw in the Times that in March Marshall Andrea Massema withdrew towards Santarem. Wellington has been harrying them on the flank and rear of the French army."

In June, as the hay was drying on a rather cloudy day Simon came home with a news sheet.

That evening, at the Ewe and Lamb Robert sat outside, on the wall and read to them of the latest campaign.

"On the 3rd May, 1811 the two armies of Lord Wellington and the French met outside the town of Fuentes de Onoro. It was a hard and savage battle in which Crauford's Light Division performed a brilliantly executed service in rescuing the shattered battalion of the 7th division from what seemed at the time to be almost certain defeat."

Robert looked round at the faces and took a draught of his ale. 'I should think that was a hot, very hot battle. The French are a brave bunch, I know that, they'll fight on but our British boys, there's none like them.'

'Well, I hope Ben's come through safe,' said Charley, Blacksmith, 'he's a big target.'

'Oh I expect he's out in the hills somewhere with the Rifles, ambushing supply wagons, mopping up stragglers.'

'What's a straggler?' piped up one child.

'A soldier who gets caught hanging behind. Ben's a skirmisher or sniper. They go out in front of the red coats and with the longer range of their rifles they try and pick off the captains, generals, the leaders of the Frenchies. They work in pairs, he told me. One crouches down, rests the rifle on his knee and picks off one of the enemy. His mate stands behind and covers him and then also shoots. It's very effective on a small scale. Ben told me all about it. Wellington thinks highly of the 95th .' He drained his tankard after all that and put it on the wall.

Helen's son was born in August 1811 after a noisy labour as she shrieked and screamed up in the big bedroom. Clarrie and Susan Bates looked after her, raising their eyebrows at all the fuss.

'She won't make so much noise after the fifth,' commented Susan.

From the start Bayley Verner, named after a captain friend of Ben's and his grandfather, was an easy child. This did not make him loved the more by Helen who was content to leave Nell to look after him. Coming from a family of countless children Nell was only too happy to take charge of the infant. Unlike her home there was no lack of money to buy clothes and linen for the babe. Ben had left instructions for the child's name, which would be his choice for a boy and Helen's for a girl.

Accordingly in the father's absence Robert arranged for a baptism at the beginning of November. It was a very cold, early winter, a hard frost held the land in an icy grip and all water had to be carried in pails as the pump had frozen up. They kept the stream flowing by the yard but it was hard work all day fetching water for the cows and the house.

Robert employed Kenny Bates, at eighteen a strong young man to cut wood for the fires from the fallen ash tree in Thrumstone field. He had been put on short time on the Estate as there was less field work in the winter.

The kitchen was kept warm for the baby and Helen turned the parlour into a temporary bedroom for her and Bayley to save coming down in the night. Robert's bedroom was above the kitchen and the wall behind his bed was always warm from the chimney behind it.

When Simon went back after the New Year holiday he elected to stay in school all week until Easter. He complained of the baby crying and the fuss it had caused and said he would either stay in his lodgings or visit friends at weekends. Robert agreed, distressed that his son didn't seem to want to come home, but half glad that they wouldn't have his petulant complaints.

When he'd lugged the fifth pail of water across the icy cobbles one morning, Tom said to Robert as they passed each other,

'What if we lights a fire under the pump, gets it going and then wraps hay and straw around it? It would be a sight easier than this fetching and carrying business.'

They were warm with working, but their breath was misty puffs in the freezing air. Mufflers were wound round their necks and they had crude leather mittens on their hands. Raw skin touching icy water quickly became chapped and sore.

'All right, we'll give it a try.' Robert tilted his head to look at a sheet metal grey sky. 'This weather's not going to change for a few days yet, you finish the watering and I'll get some sticks.'

Half and an hour later they were warming their hands round the little fire. Robert built up a neat pile of logs to keep it hot and they left it to do its job.

The kitchen made a cosy scene with a long branch of ash smouldering in the large fireplace, Helen laid out bowls of oatmeal porridge and the baby lay in his box by the fire. The men stamped their feet to bring life back to frozen toes and held their hands round mugs of hot coffee.

No matter what it cost, which was considerably more than tea, Robert preferred to have coffee and always shared his meals with whoever was working for him. They carefully stirred a small spoonful of molasses into their porridge, relishing the strong sweetness. Tom slurped his coffee noisily and then banged the pot down,

'I'll go and check if the pump's working yet, you stay there, Boss. Put my porridge by the fire, Helen please,' he stomped out, the door banging shut behind him. The room was quiet, just the clock ticked and they heard his nailed boots strike the cobbles. Suddenly they heard a yell and a shout,

'Robert, Robert.'

Robert dropped his bowl and spoon on the table and rushed to the door. Helen grabbed her shawl and flew to the window in time to see Robert bending over Tom, stretched out on the ground. Quickly she changed her house shoes for boots, knotted the shawl in front, and slipped out the door, trying to cause as little draught as possible. They bent over Tom who was groaning.

'It's my leg, I think it's broken, ohh, I reckon it is, Boss.' His face was white and already his teeth were chattering.

Robert looked up; there was a drip of water coming from the pump. The fire was working.

'Right,' he took command, 'Helen run to the Ewe, carefully now, see if there's anyone there who can help us carry him in. We'll need a door or a piece or wood from the carpenter. Tom, you're near to the fire. Can I drag you across to be close to it, until we get you in. You'll catch your death lying on this ground.'

'I'll pull myself over there. Groaning with pain he dragged himself closer to the little fire.

Robert ran back with a coat for him and a bucket of logs to keep the fire hot.

'Tom, I'll go and get some hay, you can lie on it and then when the pump's freed itself I'll cover it with the hay and finish off with the old coat. When the others come we'll get you in the house and see what the damage is.'

Tom nodded his head gloomily, no work meant no pay. They'd starve in this cold weather. They needed wood to keep warm and hot food. His missus wasn't working, there wasn't any work for her. No one could afford to have their washing done and that was her only skill.

They had no savings for a rainy day. Having his meals at Southwell's farm was a tremendous help for them and Robert paid him fairly. He was lucky, ten shillings a week and a can of milk at

night. He shivered in spite of the warmth of the fire and felt the thud
of boots stamping the ground. He looked up to see gaitered legs, an
assortment of old coats, capes and scarves and two whiskery, pink
faces gazing down anxiously.

'What you done, Tom?' was the reedy voice from Joe,
carpenter and coffin maker. 'What you doing down there? Waiting
for me?' He laughed shrilly at his own joke.

'He'll be ready for you if we don't get him out of this cold.
Come on, roll him onto the plank.' Robert snapped alarmed at
Tom's face, turning greyly white, with the lips edging blue.

Stoic, Tom clamped his tooth stumps together to avoid crying
out as he was pushed and rolled onto the plank. They hoisted him
up and slowly and carefully edged across the yard. Robert looked
back in time to see the pump gush water and put out the fire in a
hissing splutter of smoke and sparks.

Helen hovered anxiously, as they propped him in the big
chair.

'I'm just wrapping up the pump,' called Robert as he went
back outside. It was a pity to waste all their work and without Tom
it was going to be difficult.

Out of decorum and to save Tom's blushes Helen went into
the parlour with Bayley whilst they pulled Tom's breeches down to
examine his leg. Robert could see a fracture above the ankle, the
bone showing broken and sharp against the skin. Tom was sipping
scalding hot coffee laced with brandy to warm him up.

'Is it bad, boss?'

'Well...I've seen worse. What we'll do,' he decided, 'we'll
bind it up tight with a stick. ry and get it straight and see if the
doctor'll come out.'

'Aw no, I can't afford the doctor, not with no wages coming
in. You do it, Robert, I trust you.'

Robert stood up, 'I'm not sure I'll get it back straight, I might
make it more painful.'

Tom closed his eyes and sighed, colour was returning to his
face in hectic spots. 'You do it, it couldn't get more painful.'

Nell said in a small voice, 'It might be a good idea to put the
bandages on damp and cold, to help the swelling. That's what
Mother does,' she told them as they swivelled round, gazing at her.

Joe, in his capacity of carpenter had taken an off cut of wood
and whittled it to size and shape to fit into the shin. Robert tried to
warm his hands at the fire before he touched Tom's leg.

Suddenly he thought of the Navy and his visits to the surgeon's deck. He remembered the smell of rum and the leather wedge the men bit on. He looked round, wood might splinter and then his eyes alighted on their leather gauntlets, slung down on the inglenook. They were certainly smelly, but better than a bitten tongue.

With the bottle of brandy in one hand and the gauntlet in the other he approached Tom.

'I want you to drink deeply of this and then bite on the mitt, while I try and get your leg straight. Nell, while I do this I want you to go home and get a draught for the pain, take three pence.'

Yes, sir, yes,' she snatched up her cloak, pulled up the hood and ran to the door. 'I'll be back as quick as I can.' Sometimes the money from her mother's herbal remedies was the only reason they didn't starve and she knew three pence would buy a meaty bone and some turnips to make a soup.

Caleb pulled a heavy stool into the kitchen, folded a blanket to put on top and placed the offending leg on it. Robert rubbed his hands together, and bent to his task. Feeling gently he tried to discover if the end was splintered or if it was a clean break.

'I think it's a clean break, thank goodness,' he murmured and carefully pushed the protruding bone in. Tom's groan was muffled by the leather and Robert ignored him, concentrating on his task. He didn't expect a click, but suddenly the bones seem to fit together.

'Ah,' he held out a hand, 'Joe, the splint, Helen, the strips.' She was back, assisting having ripped an old linen petticoat into strips. These were damped with cold water and whilst Robert held the splint, Joe wound the linen tightly round the leg from knee to ankle. He then placed the other splint against the break and more strips were wound around.

Tom was lying back, his face a ghastly pale colour, his eyes closed, the gauntlet hung limply from his mouth resting against his chin.

Robert looked up. 'He's passed out, let's finish the job.' He tied off the last bandage and gently eased down the breeches. A warm sock was pushed onto the foot and the leg gently placed on the stool. A blanket was tucked round Tom and Robert stood back, surveying him, glad to ease the backache caused by bending over.

'Thanks, boys.' He poured small glasses of brandy and shyly they took them, standing looking awkward now the crisis was over.

Robert saw his breakfast bowl of porridge half eaten on the hearth and realized that it was nearly dinnertime and he was starving.

'I must finish off,' he muttered, 'get me some dinner ready please, Helen.'

Already he was thinking ahead, planning. Without Tom he would have to do all the morning milking. Caleb could come for the evening and if necessary bring Margie and sit her by the fire to wait with Helen. Kenny would come earlier and bring plenty of wood in and fetch water. He must also send word to Tom's son who had enlisted with Ben. George must send some money home to keep them going until Tom was fit again.

Nell came back in with another small figure in a worn and patched grey cloak. Elizabeth Farthing had been a very pretty girl who enslaved Tom's heart from the first moment he set eyes on her. Unfortunately, as the pretty girl aged, common sense had not replaced it and she was fluttery and useless. As she saw her husband lying back in the chair with his face a pasty white and his eyes closed she let out a small scream and rushed to his side.

'Tom, Tom, what's happened? What are we going to do?'

He opened his eyes, bleak despair in them, 'We'll have to manage Lizzy, George'll have to help us out.'

'Oh, oh,' she moaned and her hood fell back to reveal long straggly grey hair.

Robert eyed her with distaste. If Mary had lived she wouldn't have whinged and wailed, she would have been calm and sensible, he knew. Now he took charge.

'I think it's best he stays here the night, Mrs Farthing and tomorrow we'll get some help to get him home. I'll supply you with potatoes and carrots, milk and cheese, so you won't starve. And I'll get a letter off to George, see if he can't send home some of that pay he's been earning.'

'Aw thank you, Mr Southwell, thank you,' she took his hand in her own, clammily cold, limp grip.

Later that evening they sat in front of the fire which hissed and spluttered with damp wood nursing tankards of hot rum, blackcurrant cordial and lemon juice. Tom relished the peace and quiet of an evening away from his silly wife. He pushed thoughts of tomorrow resolutely away. He calculated they had enough money to pay a months' rent and Robert wouldn't let them starve. He had no idea how often or when the Army paid its soldiers but prayed that George would be able to send money home. A few shillin's would help he mused.

Robert gazed at the stones above the inglenook willing Mary to come. Sometimes he thought he saw a wisp of smoke, other times he could almost swear to the sight of a flick of a grey gown. How he longed for her to be there. They would share the work of the farm and like today, all the problems would be halved. They would have sat there, growing old together and then climbed the stairs to sleep in the big old bed, pushed up by the warm wall.

As he stared he hardly dared to breathe. She was there. Her face, pale with it's halo of bonnet, her long white apron, and the grey dress. She looked straight through him, with never a sign of recognition and then turned and passed into the stone at the back of the fireplace. The fire flared up.

Tom raised his head, from sunken on his chest and commented, 'You've got a draught pulling the fire up the chimney.'

Robert stood, briskly clearing tankards and plates, anxious to keep his secret safe.

'I know, now I'm off to bed, there's a chamber pot for you in the night, tomorrow we'll get you home. Will you be alright?'

'Aw, I can't do that.' Tom was distressed.

'One night can't be helped and you mustn't put any weight on that leg or you'll undo all my good work.'

'I know, Boss, I can't thank you enough.'

'No need, there were plenty of long days you worked on, with no complaint and no extra pay. I'll not let you down now. Your job's here for you when you're better. I'll miss you,' he harrumphed, not used to expressing such emotion and quietly left the room.

CHAPTER TWENTY ONE

It was still bitterly cold at half past six the next morning, pitch black with a late moon and the stars closing down for the night.

He was pleased to see a trickle of water from the pump and had the idea of bringing a hot brand from the fire and warming it up again.

The barn, although cold inside, with the bodies of the cows and the sow in the corner, was still appreciably warmer than outside. Robert warmed his hands on Belinda's side before he touched her udder. His cold fingers on the warm pink bag would have made her jump and kick. They could lose a pail of milk like that.

He'd brought out a kettle of hot water and rinsed his rag in that prior to sitting down at her side. As his fingers teased and pulled rhythmically she delicately nibbled up the oats he had placed in her manger. A large pink tongue searched out every one and as Robert finished she turned her head, a last oat stuck to her nose. He laughed and affectionately slapped her rump.

'Good girl, Bel, I'll hay and water you as soon as I can.'

At seven o'clock as he carried a pail of water carefully across the yard, Nell and Kenny appeared, wrapped up tight against the cold. Always in other people cast offs. Nell was wearing Helen's boots, too large but that didn't matter as she also had a pair of Robert's socks, carefully darned to give long life.

Kenny had on his woodsman's outfit, an old tweed coat, a sheepskin waistcoat, grey cord breeches and boots laced up high.

'We've come in early, Mr Southwell. Me and Kenny now that Tom's laid up. We'll help with the cows and feed the pigs and sheep before I goes into the house. Kenny here'll clean out before he gets the wood in.'

Robert, relieved agreed. 'All right, I'll see you straight for the extra hours, until Tom's on his feet again.'

Nell was a deft milker. Robert watched as she quickly stripped teats, talking quietly to the cows and, he was pleased to see, keeping everything tidy and shipshape.

They worked like Trojans and Helen had the sense to fry a huge platter of bacon and eggs for them when they trudged wearily into the house after nine. A large pot of coffee stood on the hearth, with a mound of buttered bread by it The butter oozed it's golden path down across the plate.

As Nell made as if to serve them, Robert brusquely ordered her to sit at the table.

'Helen's had the warm job, you stay there, she can serve.'

'I've been up in the night, twice, with the baby,' Helen complained, 'and I came in here and put more wood on the fire.'

'Well thank you for that,' Robert had his mouth full, golden egg yolk trickled down his chin, 'I still say you've got the easy work today.'

After dinnertime Joe and Charley White came to help Tom back to his cottage. Against the weedy Joe, Charley was a giant. On the coldest days he wore his leather jerkin open to the chest. His muscles gleamed and glistened with sweat from pumping air for the forge fire.

He could have carried Tom easily but out of respect for Tom's feelings they supported him between them. Joe had made him a crutch with a leftover plank from Mrs Smith's coffin, he told him gleefully. Before they set off he trimmed it to fit under Tom's armpit.

Tom was standing on his good leg. His face blanched as, with the gentlest knock pain shot up the broken leg. The brandy had worn off, unfortunately. Slowly they set off, Robert watching from the doorway. He'd take a bacon hock and some vegetables round to their cottage that evening.

Nell and Kenny had never eaten so well, since they had worked at the farm. It was good plain fare, but ample and Nell had to repress the urge to take half of hers home for her brothers and sisters who would be glad to have bread and milk. She realised that she needed the energy. Helen had her running around in the house and she helped in the dairy after tea. The days were very short, they must accomplish as much as possible in what day light there was.

Robert's shoulder ached and he remembered that with all the to do the previous day with Tom he had forgotten to rub some salve in. He shrugged into his old sheepskin coat wearily wishing that Ben was here to give his strength to the work.

The whole country was heartily glad when the cold weather broke. A watery sun broke through at mid day and icicles dripped and plinked cold drops off the roof.. Dangerous patches of grey ice lurked round the cobbles to catch the unwary.

Nell had a fall but was so well wrapped up that she was cushioned by all her skirts and shawls and bounced up to sit, legs akimbo on the wet stones.

'Oive had a fall.' She lapsed into a broad village dialect.

'Stupid little heifer, said her brother unhelpfully.

'Are you all right?' asked Robert more helpfully.

'Thank you yes, but no thanks to him.' And she tossed her head in her brother's direction as he laughed and disappeared into the wood shed.

It was raw but the biting chill had gone. The fields looked blasted as though nothing lived and the trees and hedges had a desiccated look. Bold robins emerged from barn roofs and pecked at the scattering of oats that Nell threw for them. Breakfast crumbs were scattered for the hens.

Once or twice a week after supper Helen would ask if Robert would mind Bayley whilst she visited Susan Bates.

'Just to step out for a spot of fresh air.' Helen would say, wearing her second best cloak and warm grey flannel skirt. The evenings were getting lighter and she would hurry in breathless and pink cheeked as the evening stars came out and the moon rose. Robert was sure she was meeting Calloway again but said nothing until one evening she was extra late coming home.

He was genuinely worried, thinking she could have been attacked and he didn't want to leave Bayley alone. Nell had gone home two hours previously and the baby was crying. He picked him up and hushed him against his shoulder. Briefly he rested his chin against the downy dark hair. The blue eyes gazed at him, the crying stopped but he could feel the tell tale dampness.

He looked around the room for baby clothes and linen, he had changed Simon's rags frequently so he knew what to do. As he put the child down he was relieved to hear the door open and close and the sound of Helen's footsteps.

'Thank goodness, Bayley's wet and hungry. I can change him but I can't feed him.'

He handed the child to Helen.

'Yes you can.' She said cheekily.

'Can what?'

'Feed him.'

'How?'

'He's having cows' milk now, mine has dried up.'

'Oh, I'm so sorry, Helen.' Robert was genuinely distressed. He'd always understood that a mother's milk was the most important food a baby could have until it was weaned.

Helen had done it to please her lover.

Mark had complained about his wife's breasts always leaking milk. 'Like a bloody cow she be,' had been the unkind comment she'd heard. At that Helen determined to regain her pre pregnancy figure and weaning Bayley became a priority. Robert realised he'd been sidetracked and decided to interfere.

'You're playing with fire again. You're meeting Calloway, aren't you?'

She glared at him, pulling Bayley's clothes off roughly.

'Aren't you, Helen?'

She sighed, 'I can't give him up and when I say no he's on to me. Helen he says, my girl, my lover, I knows you want me, or it.' She blushed and Robert looked sceptical at the false attack of modesty.

'Well Ben's marked him once, he won't be so lenient again, you could end up thrown out of the village.'

'But my home is here...isn't it?'

'While I'm here, but I won't live forever and you'll long outlast me. This is Ben's inheritance. I feel I'm keeping it for him and Simon, if he wants it. Although I don't think he's a farmer.'

She folded up Bayley's clothes and reached for his nightgown. His legs waved in the air and the plump rounded buttocks were red with soreness. He grizzled unhappily.

'Helen, that child needs salve, get some lanolin from the medicine box. He's a good little boy, don't you love him?'

'I'm not sure whose he is.'

Robert stared at her. You've been going with someone else, another man.' His voice was incredulous.

'Just the once, in Banbury. I won't do it again, I know it was stupid.'

Robert was heartily glad that Simon was away in school. 'You're a slut.'

'No, no, it's just temptation.' She looked defiantly at him. A handsome stranger on a large horse had accosted her in a back street in Banbury and offered her a half guinea for a tumble in the back room of the Red Lion. Who would be fool enough to turn that down?

He'd ridden her as magnificently as he rode his black stallion, with her skirts in the air and her head pillowed on a parcel of shirts for her husband.

As she looked at Robert from under her eyelashes she had the grace to feel ashamed. But only a little, that money had bought lace and ribbons and Special Lady's Rose Water, for the complexion. She was now the best dressed woman in the village and she intended to stay that way.

Aunt Susan had said she was a whore first and a housekeeper second. 'It's alright for you, Susan', she replied, 'your man is in your bed every night. When's mine coming home?'

Bayley continued to thrive in a household of elderly men and a flighty mother. Robert, Tom and Caleb all doted on him and once he could walk he was toddling everywhere. They all kept an eye on him.

Helen was supposedly busy in the house but all too often Nell had cooked the dinner and washed the clothes. Robert became increasingly annoyed with Helen but didn't want to risk losing Bayley if she went off in a huff or moved away. He didn't think she could get another job with a child in tow. She didn't get any money from Ben. No one knew what happened to that. She had asked Robert for extra towards Bayley's clothes but he had looked at her sceptically.

'Helen, for heaven's sake. I already feed you both. Nell does most of your work and all the dairy, what are you doing all day? You have three shillings a week: you only want to spend it on gee gaws and lotions. With the price of wheat going up and down and flour costing so much sometimes I certainly cannot spare anything else. You can cut down Simon's old clothes for him.'

There was still a trickle of destitute folk coming through the village. The Enclosure Acts had badly affected the rural people. Landowners had fenced in common and waste land which meant that villagers had to walk round these, on the roads. There were no short cuts for estate workers and they could not graze their cows or fatten geese as they used to. The geese provided feathers, quills and money for Christmas. If they were desperate they sold the geese and bought a cheaper joint of beef or pork.

Landowners liked to grumble about the poor condition of some of the villager's cows as an excuse for taking away their independence.

The village of Appley was part of the Byclere Estate but Robert had bought the farm earlier, whilst he still had the money.

Lord Byclere was a reasonable, though often absent owner and his workers had security as long as they were honest and worked hard.

There was always the problem though of what to do with the family when a farm worker died and the cottage was needed for his replacement.

This was what had usually happened to the poor who passed through. Robert always gave them bread and soup and a few pence to take with them.

Helen sniffed one day, 'Huh, you know they'll spend it on drink.'

He stared, exasperated. 'If they do, they'll go hungry. I've done my Christian best.'

Sometimes Robert felt beset by the problem of providing the wages for them all, eleven year old Simon's school fees and expenses and maintaining the repairs on the farm.

He didn't have to find the rent anymore but he also had to pay the annual tithe and poor law rates. This varied from year to year but last year it had been five shillings in the pound and he had had to save hard. He had not bought himself any new clothes, except boots for work, for three years. He could not think of any other way of economising apart from getting rid of Helen and Bayley. By rights she was Ben's responsibility but perhaps Ben felt, knowing his wife as he did that if she took a lover then he could support her.

But Mark Calloway, had his own wife and family, Helen was an easy diversion for him.

CHAPTER TWENTY TWO

In July 1812 they heard via a soldier who came back to a nearby village that the British Army had marched to Salamanca. The French had withdrawn but left strong garrisons in the town fort. A week later they had surrendered and Robert could imagine how the British would have poured into the town, drinking, whoring and looting what they could.

Whilst part of the French Grand Armeé was so ignominiously routed by Wellington, who was now an earl, Napoleon, with the bulk of his army had invaded Russia.

When the village eventually heard about the French being so far away Charley was heard to say loudly, 'well, if they're that far away, they can't be bothering us here. How far is it, Shipshape? A fair way I should think.'

Robert was having a rare evening in the Ewe enjoying his ale. 'Russia is...oh well...many thousands of miles, I'm not sure. Don't forget, Charley that the French are still in Spain, enough of them to give Wellington a merry dance around.'

'Oh, yes, I suppose so. But they wouldn't come here, would they?'

'I doubt it, I don't think they've built up the Navy enough. Napoleon likes this rampaging through Europe. Britain is just a flea on his backside to annoy him.'

The harvest of 1813 was one of the best for some years. There had been weeks of gloriously hot weather and the winter wheat ripened well. Robert had even managed to plough up and sow five acres of oats to feed the cows in the winter. Everyone was very pleased with all this bounty but they had the problem of where to put the grain. Once the Byclere Estate harvest had been brought in and threshed some of the Irish labourers came over to the village looking for work.

In two weeks of hard work they had part of the barn filled with threshed oats and one end piled up with the straw. The wheat was taken in a grain cart, borrowed from Byclere, to the mill and ground into flour. This was now in sacks but had to be kept dry and away from rodents. Caleb invented a type of staddle stone. This was shaped like a mushroom. They were normally placed on a base outside for the barley, wheat or oats to be piled up on. This kept it safe from rats and mice. Robert used the stones from outside and laid wood across them to support the large sacks. There were always two or three cats living in the barn and he fed them with a dish of milk and some scraps every day to encourage them to hunt.

With such a bountiful harvest everywhere, the price of flour dropped but Robert managed to exchange two cows for some sacks of flour from a farm where the farmer had died and the wife could not manage the cows.

Tom's son George who had enlisted in Ben's 95th Rifles had been injured at the capture of Badajoz in 1812. Wellington and his army had captured the fortress of Ciudad Rodrigo, pouncing as the French moved into winter quarters. Moving south quickly he had besieged the fort of Badajoz for a month. In one dreadful, bloody night they had taken it. The British dead and dying had been piled up under the walls and the French also had heavy losses.

Tom and Elizabeth were overjoyed to have him home but he was a wreck, his spirit more broken than his arm. His hearing was damaged by the noise of cannon fire. The recoil from a cannon had broken his arm in three places. Ironically he had only just jumped in to take the place of a friend who had been killed. He thought he knew what he was doing but he was a sniper, not a gunner and he paid the price.

George was now partially deaf and seemed content to sit on their doorstep all day and watch the village go by.

Tom had given him weeks to mend but was dreading the thought of having to feed him through the winter. He had his five pence a day army pension but that seemed to go in ale. He couldn't begrudge his son his drink of an evening. But, it was a tight fit now. The milk and vegetables from Robert were a godsend but a large, grown man like George seemed to eat so much and the injury hadn't affected his appetite.

Tom decided to go and ask Agent Calloway on the Estate if there was any work suitable for an ex-soldier with a gammy arm. There might be some gardening or something in the house? Southwell's farm couldn't take on anyone else: he didn't even ask Robert, there was no point.

CHAPTER TWENTY THREE

Since Simon had been staying at school, Violet Bates, Susan's sister in law and widowed at forty, had been visiting Robert at three o'clock on a Sunday. They would enjoy a cup of coffee and a chat together.

Violet hadn't quite skipped down the church path to Ned's funeral but his loss had been the biggest blessing of her life. He had drunk their money away until they were nearly homeless, hit her regularly and caused her to miscarry their three babies. Beatings and malnutrition had not been the ideal start for an infant's life.

To find Ned dead one frosty morning stretched out on their doorstep had not been a surprise. He had looked rather white, tinged with blue and she had checked carefully that there was no sign of life. If there had been the tiniest flicker she would have left him there longer to finish the job.

Befriending Robert Southwell had been a surprise and a pleasure. She had never before met a man who was courteous, clean and so quiet and dignified. She was a seamstress and he had asked her to make himself and Simon some new shirts. One Sunday afternoon she walked over to tell him that the shirts would be ready later in the week.

She knocked and walked in and surprised him in the bath in front of the fire. He was modestly covered with water and to Violet, used to Ned's grossness, a man's body was not a thing of beauty.

'I'm so sorry, Mr Southwell,' she'd stammered, embarrassed, ready to back out but also admiring his muscular back and intrigued by the white line of his scar across the shoulder.

'Mrs Bates?' He'd turned in the water. What a nice chest he had she noted, what a fine figure for a man of his age. She backed to the door, letting in a draught.

'I'll, I'll come back later.'

'No, wait a moment, I won't be long.'

'I'll wait outside then.' And she shut the door behind her, leaning against the wall, smiling.

Five minutes later, when Robert opened the door Violet was sitting on the bench by the dairy door.

'Please, come in.'

She followed him back in and watched as he emptied the bath with pails, back and forth to the yard. Finally he lugged the old hipbath out and stood it against the wall to dry.

'There, sorry to keep you waiting, shall we have some tea?

'That would be very nice, but I only came to tell you that the shirts won't be ready until Friday.'

'That's fine and you must tell me how much I owe you.'

'There's no hurry for that.'

They enjoyed their drink and chatted pleasantly. Robert even walked with her to the end of the lane.

When Violet came back with the shirts the following Sunday Robert was waiting for her. He had had his bath and put a clean shirt on.

She had made two for him and two for Simon.

'Do you want to try one on? Just to make sure, I can always alter it.'

'Oh, well, just quickly shall I?' He pulled his shirt over his head and reached for the new one.

'Oh, I'm sorry Mrs Bates, I was forgetting myself. I got so used to the lack of privacy on board ship.'

She waved it away. 'Don't you worry yourself about a bit of modesty. I was married to a Bates. That was an education in itself. Now, let's have a look at the shirt.'

He turned round and showed her and she pronounced herself satisfied with the fit.

'Are you happy with it, Mr Southwell?'

'Call me Robert, and yes, it's very comfortable, plenty of room in the arms.'

'There, that's good, any time you want anything else you just let me know. I'm at Byclere House in the week but there's time at weekends and summer evenings. I sew for Lady Byclere you know. She sends the children's clothes down from London for me to mend and sometimes some lovely materials to make new dresses for the girls.'

The next Sunday he took some money over to her cottage to pay her and was asked in. It was clean and tidy with a small fire in the hearth. A faint smell of dinner was in the air but she left the door open and invited him to sit down whilst she made a cup of tea.

They chatted pleasantly for an hour and he left. As he walked back down the lane he thought what a very nice lady she was, dignified but homely. Marrying into the Bates family had not coarsened her like Susan, her sister-in-law.

What with one thing and another they seemed to meet up nearly every Sunday afternoon. Robert became fonder of her and wondered if she would let him kiss her. He knew he was old for that sort of thing and not very bold in the art of wooing.

It happened suddenly and unexpectedly one day as they were strolling down the lane. He was carrying a parcel of sheets that Violet had mended and she was carrying a cake she had baked for him. They heard someone shout and turned to see who it was. Her foot caught in a pot-hole and she fell.

'Oh what a shame, look.' She had dropped the cake and was kneeling on the road where she had tripped over.

'Violet, here I'll help you up, are you all right?'

He put his parcel on the ground and his arms around her to lift her. She showed him her grazed hands.

'Oh dear,' he looked at them, 'let's go in and wash them and put some salve on. Violet...? '

She swayed, 'I feel a bit wobbly.'

'Here.' He pulled her to him to support her and tucked her head under his chin. After a minute she looked at him and reached up and pecked a kiss on his cheek.

He blushed, happily. 'What's that for?'

'Looking after me, I feel silly now.'

'No, are you hurt anywhere else?'

'I think my knees are sore.'

'Let's go home and wash them.'

With his arm around her they walked slowly up to the farm. He left her with a bowl of warm water and some rags whilst he went back and collected the sheets and cake that had split in half. He placed the bits on top of the parcel and left the crumbs on the road for the birds.

When he went back into the kitchen she was dabbing at her hands. She showed him the grazes and he fetched the marigold salve.

Gently he rubbed some in to soothe them. 'Now let's have a cup of tea, you're still pale.'

'I feel better now, thank you.'

'Have you hurt your knees?' He handed her a cup of tea.

'No, thank goodness, my skirts saved me.'

Robert had noticed how trim and neat she was with a clean brown skirt and white blouse that had pretty buttons and some sort of pleating down the front. Her shawl was a soft fawn colour and her boots were polished. Her light brown hair was tucked in under her bonnet and her hazel eyes normally sparkled. Now, she still looked somewhat pale after her shock.

Robert wished he'd got a settle, so that they could sit by the fire together and he could put his arm round her. He could hardly ask her to sit on his lap in Mary's chair as Dorothy used to do in the early days of their marriage.

Later, he gave her his arm as they walked back to her cottage. He saw her in and made sure the fire was burning well.

'Thank you, Robert.' She smiled up at him.

Emboldened he clasped her to him. 'Send a Bates child if you want anything.' He murmured and put his lips to hers. After a second she returned the pressure and they clung together.

'Oh I'm sorry, Violet.'

'What for,' she laughed, 'I've been wanting to do that for weeks.'

He beamed at her, So have I.'

What had started with a fall and a kiss, after a few weeks led to some very pleasant times in the bedroom.

Helen knew of Violet's visits, but they were widow and widower, it was nothing to be ashamed of and provided them both with pleasure and enjoyment. A relief from the never ending daily toil.

On Sunday afternoons she walked over to Fanny Bewick's cottage with Bayley. He could see Fanny's children and Helen would show her the latest bit of lace or fancy trinket. She left Bayley there and quickly walked over to the old hut in the wood that Mark Calloway had found.

CHAPTER TWENTY FOUR

With the occasional Times Newspaper that came into the village, several weeks old but still very interesting, they were able to keep track of Wellington and the army's progress in Portugal and Spain.

In May 1813, as the French withdrew across the River Douro, Wellington's men, including Ben's 95th Rifles, marched into Spain. They continued up northwards and ended up in St Jean de Luz just inside the border of France. The Spanish troops engaged with the French and bravely defeated Marshal Soult.

After the ignominy of the invasion the Spanish wreaked vengeance upon any French they came across.

Sergeant Ben James came home in the autumn.

'It's just a brief visit.' He told them as a very beautifully dressed Helen served up their supper that evening. It looked somewhat inappropriate dishing up pork and roast onions with frothy lace at her wrists and a plunging neckline to her blouse. As the gravy splashed she hurriedly tied an apron round herself.

Ben contented himself with observing her flirtatious glances and enjoying the secret he carried in his pocket. Bayley had been bundled off to bed, protesting bitterly to Nell, but she had stayed with him and sung a song.

'At last.'

They were alone, the shutters pulled halfway across to let in some air but keep the moths out. Ben had dressed to the minimum after his bath and now he lolled on the bed, his shirt open to the waist, watching as she carefully brushed out her hair. He got up and started to untie the ribbons at the back of her chemise. Her shoulders, silky pale in the candlelight needed a kiss and his lips licked across. He felt her shiver and his excitement grew. He was in his prime and had a beautiful woman, all his own to bed for the next few days until he took ship back to northern Spain.

He'd brought her a reward for good behaviour but she must please him, better than any Spanish or Portuguese girl he'd used. Some of them had been very passionate, with a fiery spirit, Helen must come up to scratch.

Helen knew that he wanted to get her pregnant and accepted the probability philosophically. She had not see Mark Calloway for some time, mainly because he had been moved to another estate ten miles away which was too far to walk to.

'You've been spending money on trinkets then.' He saw all the scraps of lace and bottles of rose water and lavender oil. He was lying back, his head raised on the pillow and his chest lightly speckled with sweat. His wife ran her fingers lightly down the scar that ran from right nipple to ribcage.

'I've saved quite a lot, Ben, you do like me to look nice, don't you?'

'You don't need no fancy fripperies with a body like yours,' his fingers were calloused on her soft skin but she liked the roughness. He reached for his shirt, tossed down by the bed.

'Here, try this on.' He tipped a glittering jewel out and she snatched it up.

'Ooh.. For me! It's beautiful.' Helen gazed at the ring, a large ruby set into a gold claw setting. She ran her finger lightly over the stone, facetted, glowing and cold. The gold felt soft and warm.

'Put it on, see which finger it fits.' He encouraged. He watched her face, the expression of triumphant greed as she licked her lips and knew he wouldn't tell her where it had come from. He'd save that for the right opportunity.

'Where did you get it?' she admired it on the middle finger of her right hand, holding her fingers up, letting it catch the candle light. She would unquestionably be the wealthiest wife in the whole area and almost as good as Lady Byclere. I bet she hasn't got a ring like this, she thought.

'I bought it off a woman in St. Jean du Luz,' he lied easily, 'she needed money for food, after the soldiers had left.

'Where's St Jean d...?' Helen watched the ring that seemed to glow in the moonlight streaming through the window.

'It's on the border of France and Spain. So what do I get as a thank you?'

'What would you like?' They both laughed, knowing and she pushed back the covers and climbed on top of him.

The ring was allowed it's five minutes of admiration the next morning at breakfast until Robert decided to call a halt and get some work done.

'Be a shame to lose that in the washing bowl or the cheese vat, Helen.' He remarked cryptically.

'Yes, yes I must hide it upstairs,' and she plonked a slice of bread in front of Bayley and clattered up the stairs. He looked at his breakfast in dismay.

'No honey,' he cried.

'Come here,' Robert buttered the bread, smeared golden runny honey on the slice and cut it into fingers. Bayley banged his mug on the table.

'Coffee?'

'Please, Uncle Robert.'

'Is Mamma coming back?'

Robert sighed, handing the child his mug of milky coffee. 'Yes, but I daresay she'll be going to the village later.'

'She won't want me,' said the child knowingly, 'can I stay with you please?'

'Of course and Nell.' How did Bayley know his mother was more interested in clothes and trinkets than her son? He was still very much in awe of his father, too young to be dazzled by the glamour of the uniform and rifle. He tended to cling to Robert who had the patience to talk to him in the cow shed and dairy.

Robert and Tom were finishing milking that evening after six as Ben stood in the doorway, leaning casually against the wall.

'You're in my light.'

'Oh, sorry.'

'That's a beautiful ring, how did you pay for it? Money...or something else?'

Robert straightened up, a pail of milk in each hand and gave Barbara's rear a wide berth, her tail could flick out and catch a face quicker than a bee sting. He gave Ben a keen look.

'I paid for it.' Ben sounded surly.

'With flattened regimental jacket buttons? I know what the Army gets up to.' Robert watched Ben's face and saw the denial chase across.

Ben shrugged. 'Everyone was doing it. I would have been stupid to miss the chance to get something like that. The Spanish were very pleased to see us. Saviours from the French we were.'

'An undisciplined rabble I heard. I read it in the paper. Our sailors got drunk and had fights in port but on board ship they are disciplined and trained to work as a team.'

'Well, with all that wine flowing everywhere it was impossible to stop them, even some of the captains and sergeants were drunk.'

'Here, make yourself useful.' Robert hand Ben a besom to sweep the flagstones. 'Is it cursed? Did she call you Inglese Diablo before or after you raped her?'

'What do you think I am?' Ben shouted and shook the bundle of birch twigs at Robert.

'Human…and a soldier in a foreign country.' Said Robert cynically.

'Well I didn't need to force her and she was glad to get off so lightly.'

Robert said nothing, giving Ben a long look, he didn't believe him.

Helen decided that she would walk into the Ewe and Lamb that night on the arm of her suitably washed and shaved husband. Casually she would hold her hand out, admiring her nails and the ring would catch the light and sparkle. It will dazzle all those ignorant dolts she told herself with satisfaction. I'm the queen amongst them. I'll show them. I just hope no one mentions Mark, he couldn't buy me a jewel like this…ever.

Ben was greeted with hearty friendliness that evening with all the regulars hoping for free mugs of ale. Helen's best dimity dress and curled up hair were a stark contrast to the rough and often smelly working clothes of the few women present. She had to look around to find herself a chair to sit on. Stools and benches were the order of the day.

Perching on the end of a bench she carefully arranged her skirt, aware of rings of beer on the tables and dirty sawdust on the floor. The place stank of ale and pipe smoke and was not really suitable for a lady such as herself. She must get Ben to take her into Banbury; a coaching inn would be more suitable.

'I'll have a glass of Madeira, Ben,' she called, waving her hand to attract his attention. The ring flashed but no one saw it. She tried again, saw Susan come in and waved to her. Susan Bates, pregnant again, waddled over to the bench and plumped herself on it, holding the table as it tipped alarmingly.

'Really, Susan be careful,' said Helen pettishly, 'I've my best dress on.'

'What for, Helen? 'Tis the Ewe, we're not grand here.'

'I am, Susan, I am, look,' and the ring was held forth and admired.

Susan looked at it knowing it was as much out of her reach as the moon.

'It's beautiful, Helen, I think I'll send Bates to be a soldier. It would give my belly a rest and he could bring me some jewels like that. Here, Ben,' she called, 'what age is it for the Army, is Bates too old?'

Ben laughed, 'No one's too old, I could train him up.'

Nat Bates heard, 'You wouldn't catch me going out to those foreign lands, I likes it here. I likes my own hearth and my own bed,'

Everyone laughed, knowing the number of children produced in that little upstairs room.

CHAPTER TWENTY FIVE

As they got to the shortest day in December, 1813, Helen knew for certain she was pregnant again. Ben had only stayed three days and gone off very early in the morning. Robert gave up on Ben's help. There was too much going on in the borderland between Spain and France apparently and Ben had orders to get back to his regiment.

Simon spent much of his time in Banbury or visiting friends. After his early battles he was accepted into their select group, partly because of his ability to whistle. He had never forgotten his lessons with Tom and was useful as a lookout when the others got in late in the evenings.

On Sunday nights they had to be back in school by eight o'clock or risk a caning. Simon was bribed to be punctual and let the others in. Owls were to be heard hoot hooting from the college roofs and the occasional nightingale. This was Simon's successful idea and these antics lasted for several months until the masters found out and the whole gang of them were publicly caned.

Simon came home for Christmas, glad of the plentiful food that Robert had bought in from Banbury. It was a full kitchen as they all sat down to Christmas day dinner. Nell was scarlet in the face, having spent hours by the fire, turning a large goose on a spit. The fat dripped and sizzled, filling the kitchen with blue smoke, causing their eyes to water. A large cauldron with bacon was also boiling and she decided to tip the potatoes into this to cook. A pan of kale and turnips stood on the inglenook ready to cook at the last minute.

Two days previously Robert had made a huge suet dumpling, stuffed with raisins, tied up in muslin and boiled for hours over the fire.

After plentiful helpings of the goose and bacon they all sat around the table sipping their drinks. Ale for the men, wine for Helen and Nell and watered wine for Simon, much to his disgust.

'I can drink wine, you know, Father,' he protested.

'Well I hope you don't at school.'

Simon opened his mouth but then thought it more prudent to keep silent. The older boys brought in bottles and charged the younger ones for a drink. He had had all sorts of drinks, some of it rather rough.

As Robert passed round the dish of cream to go with their helpings of fruit dumpling he remarked, 'This is like the boiled baby we had on board ship.'

There was a momentary pause in the lifting of spoons to half open mouths. A sudden hush, Simon had cream dripping down his chin.

Bayley, sitting up to the table on a cushion heard 'the boiled baby' and, eyes wide asked for everyone., 'Uncle Robert. Did you really eat babies?'

Robert grinned, helping himself to honey to drizzle over his portion sitting steaming lusciously in his bowl.

'I suppose, when the cook made it and it was all wrapped up, the shape looked a bit like a baby all swaddled up. Sometimes they put plum preserve in, if they had any, that's nice with an egg custard. We never had cream on board ship, except perhaps for the first day or two in or out of port. A big suet dumpling was a good filler of men's stomachs, Bayley, like it is here.'

Helped by Nell, Bayley managed to eat his pudding tidily and was allowed to get up when the others had finished.

'If you're a good boy, you can come and play with my soldiers.' Simon was ready to be bored and had decided that a two year old was better than nothing.

Bayley's face transfused with happiness. 'Soldiers, play soldiers.'

'You can be Marshall Soult,' offered Simon graciously.

'Marshall Soo, ooh yes please.' Bayley's little legs followed Simon upstairs, climbing the steps on his hands and knees, scrambling as best he could. Simon didn't wait for him.

The adults watched in tolerant amusement.

Tom lit his long stemmed pipe. 'He don't know he's goin' to get a lickin', he's goin' to be the Frenchy for the day.'

'I'm just pleased to have Simon back home, I do miss him.'

'He's certainly growing up.' Caleb poured port into small glasses and passed one to Helen. She was sitting back like a lady letting Nell do all the work. She took the glass and let the ruby on her finger glow through the vermilion liquid. For a fleeting second or two she thought she saw a face in the jewel. A woman's mouth open in a shriek, the eyes wide and staring, but as she frowned and looked again there was nothing. She sipped the warming port and shivered feeling a cold, creepy feeling on her face and neck and put a hand to her neck to tug her silk fichu higher.

The neckline of her dress was rather low for a winter day but she had heard in Banbury that fashionable ladies did not wear shawls, they were for the common classes. The white silk trimmed with lace and tucked into her décolletage had been Robert's Christmas present to her.

The room was hot from the fire, an old oak branch had been burning since day break and was now down to grey smouldering ash but the heat in the stones round the fireplace was awesome and Nell had placed clothes to dry on the inglenook.

'You all right, Helen?' Tom had seen Helen shiver.

'Just a sudden…draught.'

'I'll get you a shawl.' Volunteered Nell and ran upstairs. Tom raised his eyebrow to Robert and then saw he was asleep, snoring in his chair.

Helen was finding her pregnancy trying. Sickness still bothered her in the mornings and she made that the excuse to do as little as possible.

Robert felt quite exasperated with her sometimes. If it hadn't been for Bayley's delightful presence he would have thought seriously about telling Helen to make her home somewhere else. He had cut her weekly wage to two shillings. Feeding so many people cost too much.

On a warm evening in the middle of May 1814 Robert sat on the wall outside the Ewe and Lamb and read to the assembled villagers from a penny broadsheet he had purchased in Banbury after the market had finished.

'There's been quite a lot going on,' he told them, stopping for a good swig of ale.

He scanned it first. 'It says that The Treat of Chaumont was signed at the beginning of March. Russia, Austria, Prussia and Britain have undertaken, not to negotiate separate peace agreements but to continue the fight against Napoleon until he is overthrown." Finished for good, that is.

Apparently, if we cannot put enough soldiers into the field with the others, which I am sure we won't be able to do, then we have to put a large sum of money into the coffers of the Allies. Goodness knows how the Government will be able to afford that when Wellington and his army are down near Toulouse somewhere.'

Tom Farthing rubbed his chin thoughtfully, 'It don't sound good, Shipshape, either way, do it?'

'No, Tom,' replied Robert simply, 'trouble is, so much can change and we don't hear about it for weeks and weeks. There could be a battle happening right now, Ben James could be anywhere.'

'He might be dead,' piped up a Bates child.

'Hush,' said Susan, 'don't say such a thing.'

At the end of June, the hay was being mown in Whiteacres, with Robert, Tom and Caleb all in a line with Matt Tilburn and his sons Jed and Joshua. A panting Bayley came running over. He jumped, as best he could the swathes of hay and landed in front of Nell who had just brought out their dinner pies.

'Mother says, she says, can you come, she's got a nasty pain and she's cryin'.'

Nell put the basket under a tree and called out to Robert. 'Your dinner's here, I think Helen's started, I'd better go.'

Tom waved to her and she picked up the hem of her skirt and hurried across the field, giving up all thoughts of her dinner and a pleasant sit down under the trees away from Helen's peevish demands.

Nell had been trying to do several jobs at once. Keep the kitchen stocked with food, watch the cream in the dairy and even do a turn in the field. She liked being out in the sweet air, pulling the hay into the middle from under the hedges and at the corners where the grass was thicker. The sun warmed her face and as she wielded a pitchfork and listened to the good natured banter it got her away from Helen.

'Run home, Bayley, tell Helen I'm coming.' As he hopped about on his stocky legs in front of her.

'I haven't had my dinner, Nell.'

'I'll give you something in a minute, off you go.'

He grinned, trusting Nell.

Helen had brushed him off with a snappish, 'not now,' when he'd asked for his mutton pasty. It was only because he couldn't reach the shelf himself.

Marion Faith was born in the early hours. She was a big baby and very obviously Ben's child. With her fair wisp of hair and red, square shaped face she was the image of him. A message was sent to the barracks in Kent to be sent on to wherever Sergeant James was.

A reasonable hay harvest was brought in, not a huge crop, but enough to see them through the winter. Robert had bought two more Shorthorns and now had twelve which was plenty for three very middle aged men to milk and tend.

With Helen getting over the birth and looking after Marion who was, thank goodness an easy baby, Nell was run off her feet. She got Bayley to run errands for her, even going to the shop for them. He ran upstairs and down, fetching and carrying for Helen. As long as he had his dinner with the men, eating a small pie or his bread and butter, he was happy.

In July they received news that back on Easter Sunday, 10th April that year there had been a big battle at Toulouse. Wellington had 49,000 men and fifty guns and the French under Marshall Soult paraded 42,000 soldiers. In one of the fiercest battles of the war, on the night of April 11th the French withdrew to Carcassone.

Robert had read all this on a page out of the Times newspaper that Calloway had sent over from Byclere, knowing they would be interested.

The momentous news was that Napoleon had abdicated.

Wellington had pushed through to Paris and was made a Duke at the beginning of May.

'So the British are in Paris, eh, Boss.' Tom puffed on his pipe in the Ewe and Lamb.

'It seems like it, but we don't know for how long, or really what's going on.'

'Well, I hope Ben comes through and gets home to see the baby.'

'So do I, Tom, so do I.' Robert agreed heartily. He also hoped that Ben would be home soon and somehow get his family a home of their own. The baby seemed to have taken over the house. Robert had had to be firm with Helen.

'Nell has her own work,' he told her, 'I pay you to get the meals, it doesn't take all day to feed a baby.'

'Well…' began Helen, knowing full well that if she was very unlucky Ben might be killed and if Robert threw her out she'd be stuck with two children and nowhere to go. Her parents had died, she didn't see her brother and sisters so she had few options.

CHAPTER TWENTY SIX

Christmas 1814 was a quiet one for the folk at Appley Glebe farm. Simon had gone to stay with a school friend. Robert agreed to this jus to keep the peace. He knew they were a household of old men apart from Helen, Bayley and the baby and Simon would have been most displeased to put up with her. He had come home at half term in October and complained about her crying and all the small dresses and baby things left everywhere.

So Robert had met him in Banbury the week before school finished and over dinner at the Red Lion had given him two guineas so that he could 'keep his end up' as Simon put it.

'You'll have a hard job keeping up with your wealthy friends.' Observed Robert, tucking into his boiled mutton and onions. He was hungry after a morning in the market. .

Simon had a mouthful of potato. 'You'd be surprised, Father, Lancing is always moaning his parents don't give him enough.'

'Perhaps they know he won't spend it wisely.' Robert was sick of all the carping comments about how little Simon had.

'We have to have a bit of fun. It's all work, every day, in school.'

'That's the idea, Simon, for you to learn the knowledge that will enable you to make your way in the world. Have you any idea what you want to do later?'

Simon screwed up his nose, thinking. 'Not really, some chaps will go into the Army, like their Fathers, you were in the Navy, weren't you?'

'Yes, but as a Purser, I didn't go in to fight.'

'It was more a clerical job?'

'You could say so.' Robert said drily, thinking of all the work involved in maintaining supplies for a large ship and the crew.

They parted on pleasant terms and Robert went off to buy extras for their Christmas dinner.

Ben surprised them all in a whirlwind visit on Christmas Eve and whisked Helen and the children off to see a distant cousin over in Highclere. Fortunately the weather was fine, even warm for the time of year as he had hired a trap. As Helen bundled clothes into bags he shared a cup of coffee laced with rum with Robert and Tom.

They looked at Ben, lounging at the table in his green uniform. He had aged, he looked tough, used to giving commands and being obeyed.

'So, what's next for you, Ben?' asked Tom, slurping his coffee.

'Back to Faversham to collect some more recruits. We've lost some the last two years, done quite a lot of fighting and it's said there might be something coming up soon. With Napoleon on the island of Elba we can't help thinking anything could happen if he escaped.'

'Do you think he might?' Tom was shocked.

'He's a slippery customer. He's still got a lot of friends in France.'

'They should have shot him, while they had the chance.'

'Or put him overboard,' laughed Robert.

'How can he come home so much?' asked Tom later.

'I suppose it's because he's trusted not to desert and he's in with the colonel at Shorncliffe. They've lost a lot of men, what with death and injuries, even Johnny Raws are better than nothing.'

'Hmm…' Tom stamped off.

So Nell cooked their dinner and Robert shared a goose with Caleb, Margie, Tom and Elizabeth.

Nell had bought a large capon and cooked it in the baker's oven for her family. With some of Robert's potatoes, onions and a huge cabbage, the Bates's sat down to a feast. Children sat on the floor with piled up bowls and spoons and ate until their eyes popped. There was enough left for a big fry up in the evening and with the carcass she would make them a soup that would last for at least two days.

She didn't have the time to make an extra pudding but took a dish of cream from the dairy and some currenty biscuits that she'd baked on a hot griddle.

Elizabeth Farthing had made the pudding for their dinner. Robert agreed that she had a light touch and with fat raisins and chopped apple it was moist and delicious. They had some cream with that but waited to let their dinner go down a bit so it was not until three o'clock that their bowls were scraped clean.

'Thank you, Elizabeth,' Caleb picked up their bowls, 'that was real tasty. I could do with a sleep now but I reckon I'll go out and bring the cows in and start milking. Let's get finished early whilst it's light and then I'll go home and have a sleep before we have our game of cards tonight.'

'I'll wash up,' Elizabeth surprised them, 'whilst you are outside. Shall I cut some bread for your tea, Robert?'

'I shan't want tea, thank you, but we can have it later with the ham.'

'It'll be nice to have a game of cards, for a change.' Caleb drained his tea and stood up. 'Right, boss, I'll get the cows in.'

He went out whistling, his boots clattering across the yard. The cows were out for the day in the meadow by the barn. There was not much grass in there for them but it made less muck in the parlour and they enjoyed the fresh air on a pleasant day. There were even a few midges about as the sun started to drop lower in the sky. High clouds trailed pearly white and a robin sang in the hedge.

As the first cow ambled her way in Robert and Tom were ready with their stools and buckets.

'Come on, Coral.'

'Come here, Catherine.'

They both got down to the job of pulling and squeezing the teats as Caleb started to load up the hay racks for the night.

By seven o'clock, having worked off their dinners they were all back in the house sitting round the table in the kitchen with a glass of hot toddy in front of them.

Elizabeth laid out buttered bread, sliced ham and onion pickle. There was a steaming saucepan of beef broth and bowls put to warm on the inglenook.

She was enjoying herself. The company was pleasant. With Tom spending so much of his time here at the farm she was on her own most of the day. Her neighbours were all busy people and if they weren't they gossiped amongst themselves. She often felt like an outsider even though she had been born in Appley.

Robert lit the extra fat, white candles he had bought in Banbury and they had a good light to play Chase the Ace and Penny Jacks. Mellow with warmth, food and drinks they laughed and joked, slapped cards down and spent farthings, halfpennies and pennies with gay abandon.

By ten o'clock Robert felt his eyes starting to close with sheer tiredness. He'd been up since five o'clock and the day was catching up with him.

'Right, that were a grand evening, Robert, thank you, I'll look in on the cows on the way out.'

'Will you, Tom?'

'And I'll milk in the morning, you have a lie in, boss.'

'I can't do that.'

'Well try, make the most of the peace and quiet.'

Robert gave him a tired smile. 'Thanks, Cal, I miss Bayley but I must say I enjoy it without the baby crying and all the...' he waved his arms. There was still some small dresses hanging on the rack, 'things everywhere.'

Elizabeth and Margie had cleared up everything. He put a log at the back of the fire, hoping it would keep in all night and blew out all the candles except one.

With this, he made his weary way upstairs, undressed, pulled on his nightgown and fell asleep as soon as his head touched the pillow. His clothes were dumped on the chair and he hadn't washed his face. A bright full moon passed across his unshuttered window, the air cooled but warm in his bed, Robert slept on.

On the 27th December Ben drove the trap back into the yard in a flurry of sleety wind. Bayley jumped down and rushed in yelling, 'Uncle Robert, Uncle Robert.'

'Hello,' he smiled at him, 'had a good time?'

'Yes, I've got soldiers and a top. What you doing?'

'Having my dinner, do you want some?'

'Please.' Bayley would have sat down there and then but his mother coming in, made him pause.

'Bayley, go and bring some bags in.' Helen told him, sharply. She put Marion down on the floor and untied her cape. 'It's getting colder, Robert.'

Ben was piled up with bags and a blanket. 'This is damp,' he said dumping the blanket on the chair. 'I'm getting off in a minute, this sleet could change to snow. I must get back to barracks.'

Robert finished his stew and took the bowl outside. Nell was in the dairy making cheese, Tom was down in the Fayre field clearing a ditch that had flooded and Caleb was spreading muck out in Whiteacres field. They said they would come in when they finished. With the sky a sullen, heavy grey they wanted to get the outside jobs done in case the snow came.

Ten minutes later Ben was hurrying down the lane. With his knapsack on his back he had an old sack over his shoulders and his shako clamped firmly on his head. Helen had made him some sheepskin mittens as he had complained of cold hands.

The kitchen settled down again. Helen was upstairs, Bayley sat on the inglenook with his bowl of stew and Robert found himself feeding Marion. She sat on his lap and greedily opened her mouth to take spoonfuls of warm, chopped beef and carrots.

'Please may I see Nell?' Bayley asked.

'Take your bowl out and put your coat on.' Instructed Robert.

Bayley grinned and dashed through to the scullery. Clatter, clatter and then the bang of the back door.

'Right, Marion, have you had enough?' Robert wiped her mouth with a rag and put her back on the floor. 'Helen,' he called, 'come and change Marion.'

'In a minute,' floated down.

Robert raised his eyebrows in exasperation as the door opened and Tom stamped in.

'Phew, it's cold out there, but that's done now. The ditch is running so if we gets flood or snow melt it'll be alright.'

'Good, come and have some stew.'

'Don't mind if I do.' said Tom, ladling himself out a bowl. He warmed his hands on the bowl first and then sat down. As he helped himself to bread he commented, with a jerk of his head, 'They're back then.'

'Yes, Ben's gone, Bayley's in the dairy and Helen's upstairs.'

'And the baby's on the floor.' Said Tom drily.

'Yes.' Robert walked to his chair and sat down, rather heavily.

'What's up, Boss?' Tom knew him, rather too well.

'I think Ben knows there's going to be some action. The Iron Duke wants to sort out Bonaparte once and for all. They'll throw everything, or rather, everyone into the fight.

He's asked me to look after Helen and the children if he doesn't come home.'

'That sounds serious.'

Robert frowned, 'how can I cope with them all? Bayley's no trouble and he's growing up, he's a help, but the baby...and Helen. She's always wanting fripperies and...things.'

'Let's wait and see, shall we, Boss? It might not come to that and we'll all help. Nell's a good lass.'

'She'll go off and get married.'

Tom harrumphed. 'Hmm, let's see, I'm going out to fill up the hay. Cal'll be in for his dinner soon.'

CHAPTER TWENTY SEVEN

The cows got through their spring calving with few problems, the grass grew with just the right amount of sunshine and rain and the farm ticked over nicely. Robert's only real problem was that as the evenings opened out in early March, Helen announced that she was pregnant again. He realised that it must have been a Christmas baby. Ben was still keeping his wife on a maternal leash. They were all too busy to be sympathetic to the morning sickness so she learned that she had to get on with the work. Marion was left to crawl around the floor and then as she hauled herself up, totter and then fall on the cold flagstones. Helen put some little leather slippers on her feet and the child scuttled around as best she could after Bayley.

They had heard nothing from Ben but in the week after the 18th June news started to filter through of the great battle that had taken place. The country was jubilant and church bells pealed across the land. The great Duke of Wellington had beaten Bonaparte. He was finished. With Blucher's help, the Iron Duke had a victory that meant the country could now sleep easily at night. Gone was the fear of a French invasion. All that business of counting carts and wagons in 1803 to evacuate people from the coastal regions was forgotten.

On the morning of the 22nd June a Bates child ran up to the farmhouse with a broadsheet in it's grubby hand.
'Please, Mr Southwell, will you read us the news?'
'I have to finish my work, Clara, I'll be over later. All right?' He turned back to washing down the parlour and had a sudden thought, 'Clara, ask Mr Noble to read it to you.'
'Yes, sir, thank you, sir.'

Robert was very worried about Ben. He looked at the newspapers with dread, knowing he was very unlikely to see soldier's names in it, but aware they might mention the actual destruction of a whole regiment. He knew this could happen. From the little he had heard so far it sounded like it had been a close run battle and both armies had had a bad mauling. A lot of men had been killed and injured. He knew, Ben would be lucky to come home alive.

After he finished he felt the need to go into the church and as he was making his way towards the door he suddenly realised it was midsummer, Mary's time. The time when she would appear most strongly to him. He must take some flowers to her grave and Dorothy's grave, he mustn't forget his wife.

He knelt in a pew, grateful for the peace and silence. The smell of beeswax polish filled the air and a bee droned, hitting itself against a window. What a contrast, he thought, this quiet backwater of rural England to the battlefield in Belgium. There would be piles of dead and injured, horses and men. The cannons would be on their sides, or the wheels stuck, in thick, glutinous mud. All weapons of destruction.

He prayed quietly, 'Please God bring Ben home safely to us. Thank you for the great victory at Waterloo that has saved our country. Please take into your tender care all the dear souls of the brave soldiers who gave their lives. Treat kindly all those who are injured and bring them back to us. Amen. And, please make sure that Bonaparte never escapes again. Thank you.'

He stayed awhile, kneeling on a blue hassock embroidered with red and white roses. Slowly, a sense of healing peace restored calm to his mind. He would shoulder any burdens that came along. It was his knees that caused him to grimace as he stood, feeling the stiffness of his advancing years.

The children would be company for him as he grew older. After this new baby there would not be anymore, unless Helen married again. In which case she would move away. That was the problem. Robert loved Bayley like his own. If Helen left she would take the boy with her. The child had a natural affinity with all the animals from the largest horse to the smallest bantam. Robert would never have uttered the thought out loud but he was obviously the child of Mark Calloway. He wasn't like Ben in character or physique.

He slowed his steps as he neared the back door.

Helen was shouting at Bayley and the child was crying bitterly. This happened every day now and upset him. He hurried in.

'What's the matter?'

'That,' spat Helen, 'monster has made a noise and woken Marion, just as I got her to sleep. He's a nuisance.'

'He's four years old, Helen, it's natural he wants to play and make a noise, why can't the baby be upstairs?'

'Because then I'd have to be up and down stairs to her.'

Robert forbore to say the exercise would do her good. Pregnancy had just increased an already curvaceous woman into a very plump mother.

'Come on Bayley, you and me, we'll go and check for eggs. Bring your basket.'

The boy rubbed his sleeve over his damp cheeks and ran for his egg basket. Robert held out his hand and the two went out the door, Bayley already chatting again.

Helen watched them go and saw Nell coming in with a huge basket of washing.

'Make me some tea, Nell.'

'I haven't time, Helen, it would be nice if you made us a cup, for a change.'

Helen's ill temper was put down to her concern for her husband and allowance was made. She took full advantage, but what she really wanted to know was what would happen if she were a widow. Would there be any money or a pension? Even she hadn't the effrontery to put a value on Ben's death.

CHAPTER TWENTY EIGHT

Two weeks later, still with no news, they were disturbed at dinner time by a small Bates child hurling itself through the door yelling, 'Ben James is coming home. Ben James is coming home.'

They all stood amazed. Robert, with a big smile on his face called the child over. Not knowing his name he handed him a penny and asked, 'when? What's happening?'

'I don't know.' Was the wail.

Helen grabbed the child and went to shake him. 'When's he coming, brat?'

'No one said.' He shook himself free. He was Arthur Bates and living in that household gave you a tough start. He wouldn't take no swipes from Helen James.

'Who told you?' asked Robert.

'My sister, Sally, had it from a man at the house.'

'Right,' Robert had the picture, 'Sally works at Byclere and a deliveryman told her. Yes?'

The child nodded, sniffing. His nose dripped onto Nell's clean flagstones. Helen flinched back.

'When was this? Today or yesterday?'

'This morning, she sent a messidge.'

'So, he might not be far now away now. Let's see if we can make a welcome for him. Does the school know?'

'Yes sir, Mr Noble's showing us how to make flags.'

'Right, you run back now, he'll be here soon enough. Now Helen, do we have enough food and wine. I'll check the brandy first. Shall we put out a welcome sign, Bayley?'

'For my father? Is he coming home a soldier?'

'Yes, let's find an old sheet and paint on it, "WELCOME HOME SERGEANT JAMES.'

'I'll draw him a rifle and some banging noises.' Bayley rushed to the parlour for some of Robert's precious paper.

Helen ran upstairs to change her dress and brush her hair.

A lookout had been posted at the beginning of the village street. Instructed to watch out for a marching soldier, thought to be in full, green uniform, plumes waving and rifle shining or riding a smart horse, he ignored the cart trundling towards him in a cloud of dust. It was only as it passed that he saw the body slumped amongst the sacks. He craned his neck, jumping up and down. Suddenly he realised who it was. The figure in dirty green, with a bandage on it's head was Ben James. He turned and pelted down the track, arriving seconds before the horse turned the bend.

'He's coming,' he gasped, 'he's in the cart.'

The school children, all thirty three of them were lined up on either side of the village street, paper flags in sticky fingers, all primed to shout, "Hurrah, Three Cheers for Sergeant James." Old folk and young mothers stood at cottage doors.

As James Noble, the Schoolmaster saw the cart with the slumped figure he realised his mistake.

'Oh my God, he's injured.' He put up his hand to silence the children but they mistook it for the signal and as the cart passed by they all called out, 'Hurrah, Hurrah, Hurrah for Sergeant James.'

A pale face, the eyes deadened in pain looked up briefly. The chattering villagers fell silent as the cart turned into Southwell's lane. James Noble ushered the chastened children back into school.

The welcome party stood in the doorway, smiles on faces. A very old sheet was nailed between the two downstairs windows. "WELCOME HOME BRAVE SOLDIER" was in black paint, their only colour.

As they saw the cart come up the track, a stranger holding the reins their smiles faded. Where was their handsome, marching hero? Where the tall, straight, sun burnt soldier of before with the proud cockade and the rifle? Was this hunched shape, slumped in a heap, their Ben?

Robert ran forward to take the horses' head as the carter pulled up.

'That be two shillun's you owe us, I brought him all the way from Wallingford. Thought he was going to die in my wagon, I did.' He grumbled.

'Bayley, fetch my purse.'

Robert handed over the money. 'Thank you for your help.' he said courteously.

The man sniffed and stood, looking meaningfully at the open door of the kitchen. He threw the soldier's knapsack on the ground.

Robert ignored him and went to the tailgate, sliding out the pins. The back dropped down and he held out his hand to Ben. Slowly, the wounded man pushed himself to the edge of the cart and Robert gasped as he saw the damp stain at the top of the thigh. The filthy green trousers were streaked with dried blood. Gingerly, Ben swung over the side and let himself down. Tom and Robert took an arm each and supported him. They could smell the filth of unwashed clothes and the slightly sweet odour of putrefaction.

'Easy does it, Ben. Easy does it,' instructed Robert. He was surprisingly heavy and they both felt the weight of him as he sagged into them. They almost carried him into the kitchen and let him fall into Robert's chair. His eyes closed in a colourless face.

Robert took command and pulled over a stool. 'Helen, get him some clothes to warm. No, it had better be a nightshirt. Put that to warm and when Cal and Tom bring a bed down you can make it up. He'll not get upstairs with this leg. Tom, we could do with your crutch that Joe made for you when you broke your leg. Have you still got it?'

Tom, red faced with the exertion of bringing down the base of the bed and mattress grunted. 'Oh, aye, do you want it now?'

'Yes, when we've cleaned him up, we'll put him in the parlour. He needs sleep.'

'Nell, get some mead from the Ewe please.'

Helen cut both legs of the trousers off as high as she could. He wouldn't be wanting them again anyway. Robert poured hot water into a pail, sprinkled precious salt in and dipped in a rag. Seating himself by Ben he gritted his teeth against the smell of suppuration. Carefully he washed all round, as high as he could into the groin and down the legs. Tom took his boots off and placed the feet on a cloth. Filthy water ran down.

Helen hovered, offering the beaker to Ben's mouth. He slurped it up greedily, thirsty from lack of water.

Nell came back from the inn and Robert poured the mead into a clean bowl.

'This is going to hurt, Ben. It will clean it out but it's going to be painful. Do you want something to bite on?'

Ben shook his head. 'Used to it.' he muttered.

'Hmm, I wonder,' murmured Robert as he took the rag and soaked it in the sweet honey liquid. As he swabbed into the wound Ben screamed once and slumped back.

Robert hesitated but after a quick look, 'he's fainted. Tom hold him. Oh, he's gone.

Helen, support him if you can.'

Robert carried on, trying to clean out the wound. He thought it might be a sword cut, a slash down, deeper at the bottom than the top. He cleaned away all the muck and ooze, putting the used rags in an old bowl to burn later. It was a very nasty infection and might lead to gangrene. The stitches had barely pulled the skin together and he made a decision.

'Look, Helen, I'm going to take the stitches out. It's a bad job and it needs re-doing properly. I'll clean right into the wound at the same time.' He frowned, 'Put some socks on him, will you?' Ben's feet were white with cold.

'I'll cut these stitches and sew it up as best I can, or we can send for the doctor. He might not come until tomorrow so what shall it be? You're his wife.'

'You do what's best, Robert.' She had seen him stitch up cows and horses at various times, she had confidence in him. Besides the doctor cost money and it looked like Ben had come home penniless.

Robert sighed, 'All right. I'll need my needle and thread and more hot water and wax.'

Ben was muttering as he came round again. He looked down at his legs and mumbled, 'Oh, oh it's bad.'

'Sh, sh,' Helen put her arm around him, holding him. She had never seen a leg like it. What if he had to have it off? What would he do?

Robert was thinking out loud. 'I think we'd better get him into bed and do it there, then if he faints again he'll be lying down. He can go to sleep then. I'll just tie a rag round it and then we'll get you up. First let's get this jacket and shirt off.'

As Robert supported him Helen pulled the jacket off, touching it with fastidious fingers and wrinkling her nose at the smell. The shirt was worse, streaked with sweat and the grey of gunpowder. Holding it with two fingers, arm outstretched she carried them outside and dropped them into a pail of water. Nell could scrub them. Robert was washing Ben as she came back. There was another wound on his arm, but although it was a livid red it looked as if it was healing.

Carefully, Robert washed all around and wiped it with mead to make sure it would heal. The alcohol stung and a string of oaths filled the room.

'It was your mother told me about using mead for serious injuries. I'm sorry but it had to be done. Helen fetch his nightshirt and we'll put it over his head. Then I'll take a look at what's under that bandage round his head.'

Carefully he untied the knot and tried to peel off the dirty neckerchief. It was stuck with dirt and blood at the hairline so he soaked the rag in water and swabbed it. After a minute it peeled away, but there was little to see.

'I can't see much here, Ben. Did you have a bad knock?'

'Umm, I think I was out for hours.'

'Well you don't need a dressing, is it 'cos it hurts?'

Ben had learnt not to nod or shake his head, so he grunted, 'Yeh.'

Tom was waiting with the crutch.

'Stand up, Ben and hold onto me. Tom'll give you the crutch to support you under your good arm. We'll get you into the parlour, the bed's ready. All right?'

It took them five minutes to walk the few yards to the parlour and get Ben onto the bed.

He sat on the edge and Robert gently lifted his legs up. He could see the man was exhausted, at the end of his tether. It was obvious he had eaten little since the battle. His rib cage was sharply defined as they slid the nightshirt over. He would need careful nursing and luck to get this wound healed. It was only his strong constitution that had helped him to survive so long.

Helen placed an old towel over the pillow to protect it from the filthy hair.

Robert untied the temporary bandage and stared at the gaping split in the man's leg. The skin at the sides was puffy and dark red. Irregular stitches had been put in like a broken down ladder and the wound gaped between them. If this wasn't stitched up properly, eventually the wound would heal leaving a wide slit of raw flesh, if it didn't degenerate into total infection and then gangrene.

The sickly sweet infection was now overlaid by the honeyed smell of the mead. Robert gazed at it trying to make up his mind. He had never attempted anything quite so difficult before. It was one thing stitching up a cow, or even a dog, if it didn't mend it could be killed, but that wouldn't do for Ben Could the doctor do any better? No one had a great deal of faith in Dr Newton, who had to come three miles from Hazlebury Martin anyway.

Robert wished he had one of the ship's surgeons near, Mathew Mason for one. He had done a fine job on his shoulder after Copenhagen. It had healed well.

Robert thought aloud, anxiously he told her, 'it's a big responsibility, Helen. Ben's not going to go soldiering again, is he? He's going to have to work at something. If he's got a gammy leg, what can he do? He won't be fit for farm work, not the very physical jobs'

'Let's get him through this first, Robert, shall we?' she answered sensibly.

'Aye, I'll do my best.' As long as Ben could get down to the Ewe and Lamb he would be satisfied.

Ben watched him, his eyes very blue in his chalky face. The brandy had put hectic spots of colour in his cheeks, his leg, head and arm throbbed but he felt safe for the first time since the battle. It was a colossal relief to be home. He wanted to go to sleep and wake up with the pain in his head and leg gone.

The dressing station outside Waterloo had been a morass of mud, the tents filled with hurrying figures and groaning men. On the second day a doctor had come and stitched the wound, wrapping it up in a strip of sheeting. No attempt was made to clean it. He was given a swig of brandy for the pain. He made himself walk to a wagon and climbed onto it to be taken to the ship. A burly sailor lifted him into a hammock and he had passed out, oblivion claiming him for most of the voyage. The sailor had shared his rum ration with him. That and some hard tack biscuits that he had nibbled on.

They had been taken to Haslar Hospital outside Portsmouth but it was nearly unbearable. He was dropped onto a filthy palliasse, given water and thin soup and handled roughly by the orderly.

A doctor came round and untied the bandage. He sniffed it and said, 'Hmm. Orderly cover this up again, with a clean dressing.'

Grim determination kept him going and after three days in the hospital, with more men coming in all the time and dead ones removed he had known it was leave or die. He paid an orderly to bring a trolley to the door and was pushed down to the coaching square. Another soldier, from the Essex regiment had got him up into the coach in Portsmouth. When the other passengers protested he had told them that Ben was a wounded hero, they would answer to him if they had complaints.

That journey would be in his nightmares for years to come. The coach jolted with every pot hole and the hostility of the passengers was nothing to him normally but in his weakened state he felt vulnerable.

He watched Helen bring in the thread and needles. The catgut bought in Banbury was curled up like long worms in the hot water. The wax melted in the glass jar by the kitchen fire.

'Helen, open the window. It's too hot in here. Ben, are you sure you want me to do this. I'm not a surgeon. I don't want to make it worse.'

'If you'd seen the conditions in the hospital where they took us wounded and the way we were treated, I'd say that whatever you can do will be better.'

'Yes, but shall I fetch Dr Newton? He's probably doing stitching like this all the time.'

'When he's not drunk,' said Helen waspishly, 'what if he doesn't come until tomorrow or the next day even?'

'You're sure, Ben...Helen?' turning to her.

'Yes.' They were both emphatic.

'All right, I'll try. You'd better have more brandy, Ben and bite on some cloth because it will be bad this time. I want to use plenty of mead to keep it clean and try and pull the inside muscle together. Are you ready?'

Tom held his shoulders down. Ben screamed once and then his head fell to the side. Helen stood by him, tears streaming down her face. She could hardly bear to watch as Robert worked over the thigh. First he took out the old stitches. It was a disgusting mess. He swabbed the whole area in mead trying to clean out every little bit of debris. Helen tore strips off an old petticoat and handed them to him as he dropped filthy rags into a pail.

'Now,' he looked at his hands and shuddered, 'I'll wash these before I start stitching. Get rid of the mucky stuff, Helen. Burn it all.'

Nell had filled the two kettles and the water was hot. He scrubbed his hands in the scullery and folded his sleeves up to his elbows.

Robert was completely absorbed as he ran the catgut through the wax then slid it through the mead to help it pull through easier. He wasn't sure if he should do two stitches, one in the muscle and one in the skin. Then he reasoned that if the skin healed first he couldn't take the stitches out from inside.

He straightened once, easing his back. Of course the bed was lower than the table used for operations on board ship.

'Ah, I've just remembered something. Tom can you find me some good long pieces of straw. I need to put a drain in this, I've seen them doing it.' He remembered the way the surgeon dressed the sailors' wounds. How a straw was inserted to keep it drained. He had nearly forgotten.

Sweat dripped from Robert's brow. He was lost in concentration of the leg in front of him. He studied the flesh and muscle, the anatomy of it all and tied the stitches up as tightly as possible. It was criminal the way it had been left but he tried to put this to one side as he tied the knots and used his knife to cut off each thread.

As he tied the last knot and straightened up he discovered his back had a terrible crick in it. A pain shot up from the base of his spine and he winced.

'Helen, be a love and get me some brandy please.'

Tom put Ben's arms tidily by his side and seeing the strain on Robert's face reached for the clean, white bandages that were strips from sheeting. He smothered the wound in the marigold salve that Nell had brought and then deftly wound the strips around the thigh, pulling it together tightly, working quickly as Ben stirred and groaned.

'All finished, lad,' Tom told him as he pulled up the sheet and blankets, 'Robert's done a grand job, you can sleep now.'

They had forgotten to wash his face, but Helen planted a kiss on the bloodless lips, smoothed the hair off his forehead and tucked a warm stone bottle by his feet.

Nell brought in a beaker, 'Here, can he drink this? It's warm milk with a draught to give him a good sleep.'

Tom lifted Ben up a little and Helen held the drink to his mouth. He drank it down and collapsed back onto the pillow. Sighing briefly he relaxed into the soft warmth of the feather bed and sank into sleep.

Nell watched from the doorway, 'Susan's made him a powerful draught, it'll give him a chance to get over that.'

Robert was sitting in his chair by the fire, nursing a beaker of coffee liberally laced with brandy. He felt rather shocked now it was over.

'I hope I've done the right thing,' he repeated again. 'we'd better get the doctor.'

'What can he do that you haven't,' said Tom reasonably, 'you fixed my leg good enough.'

'You still limp, Tom.'

'I would have anyway, I've no complaints, a bit of rheumaticks in it, but that's my age.'

Well, we'll see how he goes for a day or two. If he gets a fever I'll ask Susan if she's got anything else to try. What do you think, Helen? You're his wife.'

'You did a good job, Robert, I'm grateful and Ben's tough, he's had injuries before, he's got over several wounds.'

'But nothing as bad as this,' Robert drained his coffee, 'I'd better get on.'

'No, boss, Cal is back and we'll do the milking together. Nell will be in the dairy. Just for once, have a rest. That effort's taken it out of you, hasn't it?'

Robert managed a weak smile, 'I think it has, is supper ready soon, Helen?'

Their dinnertime had been and gone, the brandy and coffee made him feel light headed and he'd had nothing since breakfast.

'Here you are,' she placed a dish of roast lamb and potatoes in gravy in front of him. The steam wafted up and made his stomach rumble. He went to sleep by the fire afterwards and only woke up when Bayley came home.

'Where's father, Uncle?'

'In bed, in the parlour, having a sleep. He'll be better soon. He's got a bad place on his leg.'

The child wound himself around his legs and Robert picking him up, sniffed. He smelt of urine and wood smoke.

'Bayley, are you dirty?' Robert held him back, looking the boy up and down, feeling damp on his breeches.

'No, Uncle. But it's ever so dirty at the Bates's,' he lowered his voice, whispering in Robert's ear, 'there's puddles...you know...on the floor.'

Robert was suitably shocked, 'You'd better go and change, wash properly first mind.' He propelled the boy in the direction of the scullery, as he had treated Simon, expecting the child to take care of himself.

'How's Ben?' he asked Helen, coming through from the parlour.

'A bit restless, is he starting a fever? He's a bit hot now.'

'We'll have to take it in turns to watch him, sponge him down if he gets too hot. Can you do that?'

'I'll have to, but Nell will have to look after Marion.'

'Nell's outside, she's got enough to do. Perhaps Violet will come, she could sew by his bedside.'

'Huh.' Sniffed Helen.

Ben woke as twilight deepened into dusk. The shutters were open and the cool evening air freshened the room. The scent of stocks and Robert's white climbing rose that he had secretly planted in memory of Mary perfumed the air naturally. If he didn't move he was comfortable but he needed to relieve himself and felt too weak to get out of bed.

'Helen, Robert?' He whispered.

'I'm here.' She bent over him.

'I'm sorry for this, I might not be much good anymore, I wish I'd died.' His eyes beseeched her for reassurance. He knew his wife too well. There was no deep love between them.

Helen stifled all unworthy thoughts and reached for his hand, 'Get better first, it's nothing much, you had worse in Spain.'

'No, my leg, it's bad.'

'Robert's done a good job, wait and see.'

'Can he come? I need to...I'll need a hand.'

They sat him on the edge of the bed with a bottle. Afterwards he leaned back against the pillows, exhausted, his face a sickly white, a sheen of moisture on his face.

'Can I have water?'

The clear, clean spring water from the yard pump soothed his dry throat and he vowed to himself that he would never go soldiering again, even if he got the opportunity.

Helen fed him potato mashed into gravy. He managed a few mouthfuls and some warm milk with rum and then his eyelids slid shut and his head slipped to one side. He slept as one insensible.

In the early hours as dawn claimed the night sky, Robert looked in on him. Ben was thrashing about, the bedclothes were in disarray and he was drenched in sweat.

'It's started, he must have had a fever before, I'd better get Helen.' He rung out the cloth in cold water and wiped the face and down into the chest. Ben shuddered. Swiftly Robert dried him off and pulling the nightshirt sleeves up, he wiped his arms. He decided to leave Helen to sleep. She could take the day shift whilst he was outside. They could all take turns whilst the fever broke.

CHAPTER TWENTY NINE

Southwell's farmhouse lived through the Battle of Waterloo over the next three days as Ben slipped into delirium.

Susan sent herbal draughts for him and they seemed to help a bit but again and again he cried, 'Michael, Michael, Glyn...shoot, shoot damn you, they're coming for us. They've seen us.'

He would sob. 'Pain, pain, help me, don't leave me.'

As they worked over him, pouring mead into the wound and tying the leg up again he would lapse back into unconsciousness.

'He must have had a bad knock on the head, Boss,' remarked Tom, 'he's probably got concussion. He just needs time to heal.'

They both felt exhausted. The vigils through the day and night and keeping up with the outside work took their toll. Robert felt his age more and more and Tom, limping everywhere was younger but less fit. Caleb did most of the milking and then was out in the fields getting ready for haymaking. Nell was everywhere at once; Robert truly felt that he could not have managed without her: whereas Helen was a bit of a mixed blessing.

She seemed to disappear upstairs with the baby and not come down for hours. How long did it take to feed and clean a baby? As he sat by Ben's bedside, wiping down the glistening brow Robert thought wistfully of Mary. How she would have been so calm and sensible, a bit noisy perhaps but so useful. He thought on that he really meant that she was practical and always cheerful. She would have looked after her son devotedly, as a mother should.

Violet came in when she could, to take a turn at the bedside. She was very busy at Byclere House sewing for a forthcoming wedding and by the time she had walked the two miles home in the evening she was tired. Robert insisted she have some supper with them and would take his food in to sit with Violet and Ben.

'Sh...' he soothed, as Ben tossed from side to side, 'hush,' he wiped saliva from the corner of the soldier's mouth. He was having nightmares. Robert knew, the sound of cannon fire, the whine and boom of the balls roaring overhead, the flames and the screams of men and horses would be in his mind for a long time. The passing years would soften the edges, but the demons would come back...again and again.

Robert had read in The Times newspaper about the battle. Of how on the 17th June, Ben's 95th Rifles had covered the rear of Wellington's army as it fell back towards Brussels and taken up position on the Mont Saint Jean Ridge. The Prussian, Blücher had been mauled by the French who were out in massive numbers.

On the 18th June, the day of the Battle at Waterloo, the French with over eighty cannon fired the first shot. The Rifles were skirmishing with the French Voltigeurs but were chased back to the Ridge. The French Cavalry, the crack Cuirassiers attacked and over ran the Hanoverian Legion who had defended the farmhouse of La Haye Sainte. They were run down without mercy and the powerful horses with their sabre waving riders charged after the British, some of whom were the Rifles with Ben amongst them.

The British Cavalry charged and the French were pushed back, losing two Eagles to our horsemen. This was a massive blow to the confidence of the French but even so with their superior numbers it was a very close run battle. At six o'clock in the evening the French mounted a huge infantry attack and the battle raged on but with the assistance of Blücher on Wellington's left Bonaparte was forced to admit defeat especially after his own Imperial Guard were routed.

Robert tried to explain to Bayley how it had all happened but it was impossible to convey the deafening noise of the cannons, the thick pall of smoke from the gunpowder and the terror of the foot soldiers as they were run down by the huge horses of the French Cavalry.

When they heard that Bonaparte had abdicated the whole village turned out to celebrate and tried to drink The Ewe and Lamb dry. Children danced in the street and the mothers heaved a sigh of relief that the spectre of Boney was no longer a threat to their families. For more than eighteen years Britain had lived with the threat of invasion, real or imagined and the sense of relief was tangible.

Bayley had acquired Simon's old soldiers, the broken and chipped ones and he brought them into the bedroom whilst Robert was sitting with Ben. Quietly he put them in position amongst chair legs and tables and as his Uncle hushed him with a finger to his lips, Bayley systematically killed off his soldiers, leaving the Greenjackets alive and well. Robert was amused, it lightened the atmosphere in the room.

It was a week before Ben was able to get out of bed and sit in a chair. They had used a bucket and an old bottle for his bodily functions and it had taken the combined strength of Robert and Caleb to lift and steady him as he relieved himself. It proved too much for Tom to try and help with his gammy leg. He didn't want to aggravate it anymore than Robert wished to risk Tom being unable to work.

Caleb came into the house four times a day, in the early morning, late evening and when he could fit it in. He still did as much outside work as he could manage but Margie was more dependant on him. She walked with a stick, tapping the furniture, but refused to make an effort to learn how to cope better. She would wait for Caleb to come home and make them some dinner, but very often he would bring in one of Clarrie's hot potato and mutton pies.

Caleb was struggling to work as many hours as he could with Robert just to pay the rent and live. He didn't mind the struggles in the parlour at the farm as he knew Ben would be on his feet again soon.

Joe Armitage had come in and measured Ben up for an arm crutch and the length of oak, sanded to a silky finish was duly delivered. Ben sat by the window, enjoying the warm breeze, feeling his stomach settle after his breakfast porridge. His beaker of coffee was to hand and for the first time since the battle he knew he would not only survive, but get better.

They had looked at his leg that morning. Five pairs of eyes had stood round the bed. Tom, Caleb, Helen, Robert and somehow Bayley had sidled in and watched as Robert eased off the dressing. New pink flesh was puckering around the stitches and it was the unanimous decision to remove them. He wasn't looking forward to it.

'Well seasoned it is,' Joe cackled in his reedy voice, 'smooth as a baby's bottom, the best bit of oak I've had for a long time. I'm going to save the rest for you. They were saying you were at death's door for nigh on a week,' he laughed shrilly, 'I likes to be ready for a customer.' He loved his jokes, but no one else appreciated them.

Ben smiled. In spite of the impending removal, he was going to be up and walking later. No one could stop him.

Two hours later, his brow covered with a film of sweat, he lay back against the pillows. There had been a lot of stitches and Robert had been meticulous in removing every single fragment. In his stronger condition he had had to hold on tightly to the sides of the bed to avoid moving but he couldn't help his leg jump as he felt the stitches pull out. The leg was now bandaged again with a new straw in to keep the fluid draining out, but everyone had agreed how well it looked. It was a horrible, ugly scar but a healing one and the only person to see it would be his wife.

With his crutch tucked under his armpit and holding onto Caleb's arm, Ben walked into the kitchen later. There was no one there to see his triumph.

'Hmph, where are they?'

'Robert and Tom are with Betty, she's calving soon. Helen has gone to the baker with Bayley and Nell is in the dairy. Marion is, I don't know.' Shrugged Caleb. 'Will you be alright if you sits in Robert's chair by the fire? I've got to get in an hours hoeing before dinner time.'

Ben carefully sat down, easing his leg out. 'You go, I'll wait for them to come in' He wanted a drink but didn't dare try and get one for himself. A tankard full of good ale would do him more good than anything, especially milk. He must get Bayley to fetch and carry for him, the boy must be useful. And in a day or two he would get down to the Ewe and Lamb.

He was an injured hero. That should be worth weeks of free ale as he regaled them with all the gory details of the Battles of Quatre Bras and Waterloo. They were simple country bumpkins, they would probably think he knew the famous Duke himself.

Well, he had seen him, riding his great horse, Copenhagen. The man was everywhere and had nearly got himself captured, he had ridden so close to the front line

Ben looked round the cosy, well scrubbed kitchen and decided that it would be a very comfortable billet for the time being. He had served his country well, it owed him now. Robert was obviously doing very nicely with the farm. He would rest for quite a while before he decided what he wanted to do, although it wouldn't be farming. He would have to go back to the barracks to ask about a pension. He'd probably get five pence a day and that would keep him in beer. And, with this leg no one would expect him to work. He knew hay time was nearly upon them, they were just waiting for the barometer to rise before cutting commenced. He certainly wasn't fit for any of that. Perhaps he could manage to take out a basket of food to the hayfield, with Bayley to help him.

The barometer was hanging from a nail on the wall above the table in the parlour. As Robert tapped it every morning Bayley would climb from the chair onto the table and crane his head to watch the needle move. He loved the faces, the golden sun with a huge smiling mouth where it said SUNNY: the pale round face with a down turned mouth for CLOUDY and the oval face with a thunderous expression and water drops dripping off his nose for RAIN.

On the Friday morning the needle was stuck in SUNNY. Robert turned to Bayley and smiled. 'Hay time, Bayley, are you ready?'

The boy grinned from ear to ear. Joe, Carpenter had made him his own small hay rake and he was desperate to use it. The decision to start cutting had actually been taken the night before in the Ewe. Robert was third in turn that year. They would go to Tanners first, then Park Hall and hopefully be at Southwell's by Tuesday.

'You can't come into the mowing field, Bayley. The men work fast, you might get hurt.'

Robert put up his hand as Bayley's lips quivered, 'No, once the tedding starts, then you'll be busy from dawn to dusk. You'll be fed up with it, you wait and see.'

'But Uncle Ribott,' in his distress Bayley sometimes mixed up words, 'I'll be good, I'll stay by the edge, I pomiss.' Two tears rolled down his cheeks, he felt the rejection keenly.

Robert controlled his impatience and knelt down, feeling his knees creak.

'Bayley, you're too precious. A farm's a dangerous place for a little'un, you want to grow up big and strong like your Father...don't you?'

'S'pose so.'

'Even...' Robert changed his mind, 'your father's in the dairy with Nell, churning butter. How about helping him? Perhaps Nell would let you put the stamps on the pats. Tidily mind.'

'All right.' Bayley was grudgingly persuaded. In fact he loved Nell who was far more patient than his mother.

Helen was in the kitchen making pasties. With a hot fire to heat the oven at the side she had a red face and a crotchety mood. Marion, who was teething and grizzly had been dumped in her box outside the back door. The doors and window were open and flies buzzed busily around the large bowl of meat, onion and potato mixture. She cut out circles of pastry with a small plate, spooned mixture into the middle, wetted the edges, pressed another circle on top and placed it on a tray.

It was endless work, providing enough food for the men and she would have complained but she knew she had it easy at other times of the year. She got Nell to do as much of her work as she possibly could.

She ignored Marion, who cried herself to sleep and wiping a floury hand across her face marched across with another row of pasties. There were also current buns to make. Robert brought the fruit home from Banbury specially so she had no excuse not to bake them. Sliced in half with a generous smear of butter they filled up hungry men..

Susan Bates had agreed to make her a large spice cake and Helen had taken over the eggs, flour, butter, sugar and spices the previous evening. Robert would probably refuse to eat it if he knew it had been cooked in a Bates cottage, unless it was his precious Violet's, of course.

Ben dragged a chair to the dairy and sat, turning the handle of the butter churn. Even he had realised that there was a lot to do and had offered. Nell accepted gladly and nimbly reached up to the shelves to turn the cheeses. Ben quickly discovered that he could watch Nell's ankles and still turn the handle.

She had a trim figure, rather a plain face and her glossy brown hair was bundled under the obligatory white bonnet but Ben thought she was worth a try when his leg was stronger. Helen had told him that she didn't want any more children and that they'd have to slow down on the lovemaking. Well, he was only thirty years of age, still in his prime, a man needed plenty of comforts so he might have to look around.

When the butter started to slop and bump in the churn he knew it was about ready so he called Nell to check.

'Lovely, Ben, thank you.'

Dragging his chair with him he went from the cool dairy, blinking into the bright sunshine. A wailing noise came from the box, with a white bonneted head bobbing about.

He hurried as best he could and placed the chair at the side of his daughter. He knew he was not firm enough on his legs to pick her up, so balancing with his crutch he sat down, leant over and picked her up. Sitting her on his lap he looked at her. He hadn't really taken much notice of Marion up to then. He saw the blue eyes in the red face, the wisps of blonder hair escaping from under the frilled cap and the arms pummelling the air.

For the first time he felt the stirring of parental affection. He tickled her little hand with his index finger, which emphasised how thin it was and of how much weight he'd lost in the weeks past. She closed her fist round it with surprising strength.

'That's the ticket.' He pulled up the frilled dress and gingerly touched her nether regions. It was damp and he said indignantly.

'asn't anyone the time to look after you? Where's your mother?'

He felt the pillow she'd been lying on and that too was damp. He picked it up and found it was a straw filled pillowcase lying on top of a piece of old drabbet. There were specks of moisture pooling on the oiled cloth underneath which was probably cut off an old waterproof cloak of Roberts. The damp patch in the box had the smell of ammonia that reminded him of army barracks and unwashed bodies.

'Nell, Helen.' He called.

Nell poked her head round the door. 'Be with you in a minute, sir,' and disappeared.

'What do you want?' Helen stood in the doorway, an impressively large apron tied around her middle.

'This baby's wet, Helen. How long as she been like this?'

She stared at him. Ben, Ben taking an interest, it was unheard of. 'I'm too busy, I'll bring you a clean rag and her milk and you can feed her.'

A few minutes later he gazed bemused at the pile of white linen he was supposed to do something with. The sun beat down on them and he felt the heat, even in his shirtsleeves. The baby couldn't be comfortable could she?

Shifting so that his shadow fell across Marion he pulled the dress and petticoat up round her waist and fumbled with the knots. It fell off in a soggy heap and revealed a small pink and red bottom. Using a clean piece he patted her dry and supporting her with his arm, tilted her legs in the air, jiggling them, making her laugh. He grinned down at her, amused at the easy entertainment.

A shadow fell over him and Nell stood there smiling. 'Shall I help?' He watched as she deftly wound a strip around the child's buttocks and tucked it in at the top.

'What about this box, Nell? It's damp and smells.'

'I'll get a clean case and more straw but it would be better to let it air. If you can give her some milk, I'll take her into the house. It's hot out here for her.' Efficiently Nell removed all the smelly linen and returned with a little bottle filled with warm milk.

'She doesn't have mother's milk then?' He hadn't even noticed that Helen wasn't breastfeeding.

'She's weaning, she has food as well now.'

'Oh, I see.' He didn't really. He just assumed you kept breast feeding them until they were eating food like theirs. For the first time he realised just how much he'd missed of his children's early lives.

Bayley was still almost a stranger and shy of him, clinging to Robert as much as he could. Helen treated Marion like a doll, when it suited her but it was Nell who rocked her when she cried. He watched the small, rose pink lips sucking greedily, the milk disappearing with a final gurgle and sat her up on his lap, wondering what happened next. It was women's work, he'd done enough for one day.

'Nell,' he yelled, 'Nell, come and get her.' He wanted to stretch his legs and get them to take him as far as the Ewe to have a nice cool draught of ale. Then he would come home and have a sleep in the parlour.

Nell's good nature was tried to the limit. With three men working in the hay fields she had all the dairy work to do as well as keeping on top of the washing and probably cleaning up the kitchen after Helen's baking marathon. She knew how Robert liked everything clean and tidy, still shipshape as ever and she dropped into her bed at night worn out with all the hard work.

She loved Bayley, tolerated Marion and respected Robert and did it all for them. Helen she regarded as a lazy slut and she was wary of Ben. She had noticed his eyes following her. She was a Bates, brought up in a rough, coarse household and she knew from an early age where babies came from. Letting Ben James have a quick tumble would be the ruin of her. Her father would foist her off on the first man who would take her. He had been saying lately how she was old enough to wed but much as they needed her bed space in the tiny cottage bursting with children, he also wanted the coins she brought home on a Saturday.

Nat Bates didn't know that Robert was keeping her nest egg for her. Knowing how avaricious Bates was Robert had suggested he give Nell four shillings a week to take home and put one in the box. Locked into the sea chest Nell felt her future was secure and if one day a decent man came along she would have a dowry, some money to put towards a home.

But she didn't want to antagonise Helen, who could be spiteful, so she scooped up Marion, kissed her button nose and hurried into the house with her.

Ben got up, easing his leg and stretched carefully. He felt a bit hungry and ambled into the kitchen. He regarded his wife warily, she looked harassed. The table was coved with uncooked pale and golden brown pasties. His mouth watered at the savoury smells and the steam coming from the little vents cut at the tops of the pies. She wouldn't miss one.

'Leave that alone,' Helen snapped, 'go and get yourself some bread and cheese. Oh no.' she ran to the oven box and grabbed the thick cloth. Pulling out a tray she muttered, 'thank goodness,' as she saw the dozen pasties were no more than a dark golden brown. A minute more and they would have burnt. 'If you can't be useful in here get out of my way,' she grumbled to his hastily retreating figure.

He carefully closed the door, which meant she had to open it again to let some air in. Helen watched him limp quickly down the track heading for the Ewe. She frowned, once they'd got haymaking over they must have a talk and decide what Ben was going to do. He must have work of some sort and his leg was mending nicely. He had been after her body last night and she had pushed him away.

'I'm tired, Ben, I've been in a hot kitchen all day, Marion's teething and got me up in the night and what have you done? Sat in the chair, supped ale in the Ewe and eaten half the food I cooked for tomorrow.' She turned on her side, seething with indignation, not placated by the muttered apology.

It wasn't until she felt him settle down beside and a whispered, 'Night, love,' that she relaxed into sleep. Marion was sleeping soundly in her cot, helped by the addition of a few drops of brandy in her bed time milk.

CHAPTER THIRTY

The village decided that Robert Southwell and Violet Bates were courting. The youngsters thought it either hilarious or disgusting but Robert and Violet knew better. After the hay had been carried in and was snug and tight in the ricks in the yard, it was tidily thatched against the winter weather. Robert had the time to meet Violet on her way home from Byclere House. He had had his supper and was glad o get some peace and quiet in the country lanes. With Ben ensconced in his chair in the kitchen, Bayley playing on the floor and Helen and Nell bustling around, the house was crowded and noisy.

Violet's talents as a seamstress were highly valued by Lady Byclere's housekeeper and she had her dinner and tea in the kitchen with the house staff. As she strolled home on summer evenings, her arm tucked into Robert's, she looked forward to a glass of something special that he provided.

Violet's cottage was tiny, clean and tidy and the two chairs almost filled the kitchen. On August evenings Robert relaxed, content to nurse a beaker of rum, aware of how tired he was after the exertion of haymaking and the strain of nursing Ben.

They sat side by side in her doorway, looking out to the village, receiving the comments of Violet's relations as they passed to the Ewe or came home from work. They had no intention of marrying.

Violet enjoyed her work and was careful to avoid eye strain, the bane of a seamstress's life. She wanted to carry on for many years and had a savings box full of sixpences and shillings that she was saving for her old age.

Robert had promised to take it in to the Bank in Banbury and open an account in her name. If the other Bates's in the row knew of her small hoard they would have been after borrowing and it would have run through their fingers like sand.

She had been a Templeton from over Highclere way before she married Bates. Her father had died from typhoid fever and her mother was left destitute so she had had to marry quickly to find them a home. Fortunately Jane Templeton did not live long enough to see her daughter suffer the beatings from the brutish husband. Robert understood her desire for independence.

From the gossip she gleaned and the snippets overheard she had the suspicion he had been in love with Mary James. He had said, categorically, after Dorothy died that he would not marry again. He didn't want anyone, young or old. Violet was a quiet soul who let a body rest in peace after a day's work and their arrangement suited them both.

One evening, as they watched the sun go down in a blaze of scarlet glory she saw his brow furrowed, he was tapping his beaker, chewing his lip.

'What's on your mind?'

He looked at her, unsurprised at her perception. 'Ben's leg is all but healed now and he shows no sign of looking for work. Or even talking about it and he's got no interest in the farm.'

'More interest in the Ewe, I reckon.'

'I know, he drinks his pension away. I don't want to appear uncharitable but I'm keeping Ben, Helen and the children and I'm paying her. I can't do it indefinitely.'

'Where would he go?'

He sighed, 'I don't know. I love Bayley, he's such an asset now, running errands and helping, I realise now, much more than Simon ever was. At the moment Ben couldn't keep a family, not on five pence a day.'

'Has he got any savings or anything to sell?'

Robert shrugged, 'I don't know, he didn't come home with any. There's Helen's ruby ring, they could sell that.'

'It's not work though, is it? Talbot at the Ewe is getting old: perhaps Ben could take over there? There's plenty of room for the children and Helen could flaunt herself behind the bar. She'd have to work harder than she does now.' This made her smile but her tone was acerbic, she thought Robert was taken advantage of.

'I suppose I could spare a few pounds to set him up, just the once.'

'It would be a gamble, Robert. You might never see it again and he'll drink himself sozzled with all that ale on tap.'

'He could pay me back later. If he does drink himself to ruin...well, I couldn't stop him. He might make a go of it, if it's what he wants. He misses the company of army life, it's too quiet here at the farm. And if they are there, it's close enough for Bayley to be in and out with me. I'd like that and so would he.'

'You've made your mind up?'

He nodded. 'I'll have a quiet word with Talbot, see how the wind blows and then speak to Ben.'

'You don't want Nell living in?'

'No, no need. She comes early and stays late, it suits us, well me anyway and it wouldn't be right, a young girl living with an old man.'

'Not so old.' S   he gave him an arch look.

He blushed, thinking of their Sunday afternoons and grinned at her.

+

It was all arranged far quicker than even Robert anticipated. Talbot had been almost prescient when Robert called in with him later on in the week.

They sat in the back room as befitted a business discussion. The alehouse keeper was suffering from rheumatics and the effects of his trade. His mottled, red veined cheeks and bleary eyes were the result of too much sampling. It was his standard joke that he had to try every barrel.

'Well, I'd better try it first.' Was said morning, noon and night. Hefting barrels from the outhouse had stooped his back and damaged his bones. He wanted to go and live with his daughter, hoping she would look after him in his old age. He needed the money to pay his way and keep him in sups. There had been no one in the village who could afford to take over the Ewe until Ben came home. It had been a disappointment when the gossip hinted he was penniless.

Robert was sitting with a beaker of ale. 'So you see Talbot, Ben don't like the farming life now and this could be a solution. But how much would you want for the stock?'

'And the goodwill, Shipshape, don't forget that, that's worth a lot. I got,' he breathed expansively, whooshing out his fumey breath, 'well, hundreds of customers.'

Robert doubted that, but let it slip. 'I suppose so, but what would be a fair sum, give us a figure. I've not a lot of experience in these matters.' He knew he'd make sure a proper inventory was made before Talbot left, that was one skill he did have.

Talbot hoped to benefit from Shipshape's ignorance. 'I reckon thirty pound would see me right.'

'Too much, Talbot, say ten and I'll have a look down the cellar first, shall I?'

The old man was prepared to come down a little in price but not happy to show the contents of his meagre cellar. There was little call for fine wine in Appley. The occasional passing traveller would demand something better but they would probably avoid the old alehouse anyway.

He lit a lantern and shuffled to the cellar door. 'Here you take it, have a look, I'm not going down there unless I have to. My knees can't take them steps.'

There was no hand rail, just worn steps leading into darkness. The air was dank and Robert shivered. There were a few wooden shelves, leaning at angles, with dusty, dark bottles stacked up. Blowing off dust he peered at a label. Faded ink revealed a claret. There was no date on the scrap of parchment tied on with twine. He looked along the shelf estimating the number of bottles. If they had aged well they could be worth a considerable sum but he wouldn't tell Talbot that. There was no call for that quality in Appley but they could be sold in Banbury and cheaper madeira and sherry wine purchased. Robert had learnt enough from the extensive quantities of wine the Captains took on board to know a good vintage when he saw one.

He climbed back up the stairs putting on a suitably grave face. 'I can see why you haven't sold any, Talbot. Let's see how many barrels of ale and cider you have out the back.'

Together they counted and Robert estimated their retail value. He turned to Talbot, 'I thinks ten should see us right.'

'Twenty pounds, with the goodwill.'

'Fifteen, my final offer.' Robert drained his beaker and put his cap on.

'Done.' They shook hands.

At the door Robert turned, 'I'll have to speak to Ben first, I don't want him to think I'm running his life for him.'

Robert took cheese and butter into Banbury market next day and took the opportunity to call into the bank to withdraw the money. It was a sizeable dent into his savings but he consoled himself with the thought that he wouldn't be paying Helen or feeding Ben's family anymore.

He let Binnie trot home briskly. Flies were bothering him and Robert flicked the whip around his pricked ears to stop them settling. In the hot afternoon air they both looked forward to a cool drink as they clattered and rumbled along the dusty lane.

He turned into a deserted yard after four o'clock. He walked Binnie into his stable and took the harness off. He rubbed him down, gave him a bucket of oats and smoothed his hand along the broad back.

Robert chuckled, 'You're getting old, we'll have to put you out to grass and get a youngster in to train.' He drew a fresh pail of water from the pump and left it by the horse's head. Then he splashed the dust off his face and drank from his cupped hand.

Feeling pleasantly satisfied with his day he walked into the kitchen. He would enjoy a cup of tea and a buttered bun before milking. Immediately he sensed a strained atmosphere. There was no sign of Bayley and he thought the boy must be in disgrace upstairs.

Nell was in the scullery with her back turned, Ben looked sulky, sitting by the fire. Helen was standing at the table with a flat iron, pressing creases out of Marion's little dresses. She banged the heavy iron down hard onto the thin cotton dimity.

'Is the tea on, Helen?' he enquired mildly, 'I'm parched. It was a dusty drive back from town.'

'In a minute, I'm busy…whilst this is hot.'

Robert raised his eyebrows. There was too much of this lately, as if she'd forgotten he was paying her two shillings a week to look after him. He swung the kettle over, threw a log onto the fire and surveyed Ben. The lazy man had even let the fire die into ashes.

'What's been going on? Where's Bayley?'

They all started talking at once.

'She's got to go, that slut,' pointing her hand at Nell, 'that drab is throwing herself at my husband, giving him ideas. I'd have thrown her out but she says she won't go without seeing you. I'm the housekeeper here.'

Robert sat down heavily at the table and knew this was going to take the wisdom of Solomon.

'Ben, what's your side of it?'

Ben muttered, 'It were just a bit of fun, there ain't nothing to do round here, just a bit of teasing it were.'

'Nell, come in, come in, it's all right. I'll sort this out. Helen,' he spoke firmly, 'I want some tea made please.'

She saw his face and realised it was an order.

'Nell, what happened?'

'Mr James, sir,' she started crying, her face crumpling, 'he put his arm round me, squeezing my,' she couldn't say the word and pointed to her rather full breasts, 'and then he pinched my…' her face reddened with shame. 'He says he'll see me right if I let him, you know.'

'I know.' .said Robert grimly.

Nell was wringing her fawn work apron between her hands. 'I'm a good girl, Sir, I wants to get married one day, I don't want a baby out of wedlock.'

Robert's tea was pushed across, splashing onto the table. He took his time, sipping slowly but he had made up his mind two days ago. This was the perfect excuse, but he didn't want them leaving with bad feeling between them so he ignored their lazy ways.

'She'll have to go, there's plenty more where she came from, though how I'll ever have time to train one up I don't know.' Helen buttered a bun for herself and then realised that Robert couldn't reach the plate that was convenient for Ben.

'Nell, you can go home now.' At her alarmed face and her,

'But sir.' He raised his hand.

'It's all right, this will all be straightened out. I'll expect you at seven o'clock sharp in the morning, as usual. Now, I've got family business to discuss. Oh, ask Tom if he will milk tonight, please.'

Nell took off her apron and hung it on the peg in the scullery. It would probably have dirty marks on it in the morning where Ben or Helen couldn't be bothered to find the towel. She had been in terror of losing her job. The thought of leaving had been dreadful but if Shipshape said to come in at seven then that was what she would do. She trusted and respected him.

She hurried outside and saw Tom going to fetch the cows in. 'Boss says for you to milk tonight.'

'All right, lass, tired is he? I know he's back from market.'

'They're having a talk, there's been a bit of bother and I'm to go home early.'

'You haven't lost your job?'

'He says to come in at seven as usual. Oh, Tom, I hope it's all right, I love it here.'

Tom gave her a keen look but didn't want to embarrass the maid by asking if Ben James had been up to his old tricks. He knew the girl would work her fingers to the bone to keep her job and Helen Canning that was, would exploit her. As for Ben, there was no reason now why he couldn't bring in an armful of logs or a few pails of water. Waited on hand and foot he was.

'Robert's a fair man, lass, he'll do what's right. Now, I must get on.'

In the kitchen Helen had put the flat iron down on the inglenook to cool. The cat would have to watch its paws itself she thought spitefully. The pile of baby dresses was taking up a corner of the table. Robert looked at them meaningfully. With a thin mouth and exasperated sigh Helen snatched them up and marched upstairs.

'Now, Ben, we must have a word or two, this can't go on.'

'I didn't mean anything, the girl's too full of herself, plain as a pikestaff she is and only a Bates.'

Robert felt the need to control his temper. 'That Bates as you so rudely put it is a damm good worker. I don't want to argue or have any bad feeling but I think it's time you had your own roof. The family's growing, you need a job and I know you don't like the farming.'

Ben was sulky. 'It's just that after soldiering it's all bit tame, a bit quiet here and I've been getting over a very nasty wound.'

'I won't deny that, but I think it's time.'

'What can I do? I'll have to ask Byclere if there's any jobs up on the estate and hope a cottage goes with it.'

'I was thinking of The Ewe and Lamb.'

'How do I do that?'

'I'll lend you the money to buy you in, give Talbot the money for the stock and goodwill. It would give you and Helen a hand and I think you'd like the inn trade.'

'How much do you think that would be?'

'Well I'd have a word with Talbot, but I think it would be worth about fifteen pounds.'

Ben stirred a log with his booted foot, making a show of reluctance. 'I suppose it could work, but what about some cash to see us through. It needs quite a bit of work in there. Talbot has let it go.'

'I can't pay anymore, you'll have to sell some of Helen's jewellery unless you have something you've brought back from Spain you haven't told us about. You've got to look after yourself and your family now, you've got your army pension.'

Ben snorted derisively. 'That's barely three shillings a week.'

'Well, if you're living at the Ewe you'll have ale on tap, that's a saving.'

'That's drinking the profits.'

'Talk it over with Helen.'

'She'll do what she's told.'

'I'll see Talbot in the morning and I'll have no more teasing Nell. She's a good worker.'

'I'll go down the Ewe and sort out a date with him tonight.' Ben lumbered to his feet. He liked to make it look as if he still favoured his injured leg. It was galling to know he couldn't play the wounded hero anymore. But, it had all worked out very nicely. Helen could lord it over a maid that he would choose and there'd be a bit on the side in that direction if he were careful.

He hadn't said whether he had any money or not because he had no cash but he did have a jewelled cross that he had acquired after the storming of Ciudad Rodrigo in January, 1812. That had been a very hard affair. The French had dug themselves well in and Lord Wellington wanted them out.

The cold nearly froze their hands to their rifles. Facing death, he'd been lucky to escape with a flesh wound, so that by the time they'd got into the town most of them felt they were due some reward.

He wasn't the only one but he'd had the commonsense to grab something small. The stupid senorita had tried to hide but he'd found her in a cupboard and after he'd helped himself to her body he'd pocketed the cross and chain she wore.

The trouble was that Way the Jeweller wouldn't take it. Ben knew they were diamonds, it was worth a lot but the wretched man had taken one look and said he didn't like the history of it. As if he knew what had happened. The pawnbroker would only give him a guinea and that wasn't worth bothering with so Ben was stuck with it unless he took it up to London.

If he did a trip like that they'd all be wondering what he was getting up to. He could say he was meeting old comrades. He'd thought it all out but if Southwell was prepared to stump up for the Ewe then he'd let him. He'd pay him back some other day.

It was all sorted out within the week. Ben went to see Calloway who agreed without demur that he could take over the tenancy of The Ewe and Lamb.

Calloway hoped that Robert would carry on until Bayley James was old enough to take over. It didn't look like the son, Simon, away at his fancy school would be going into farming.

The house was so quiet he could hear the mice running in the wainscoting at night. The clock in the parlour was tick tocking louder than ever and Robert wondered if he would be lonely, but he had company until seven.

Very often Tom and Caleb would both sit at the table and share some bread and cheese with him. Margie waited for Caleb but he had asked a Bates child to go in and light a candle for her. With this dim light and a beaker of tea and buttered bread she could sit by the fire. Caleb found it increasingly difficult to look after her and keep his job. He couldn't bear the thought of not working and sometimes felt almost ashamed that he wasn't kinder to his wife. It wasn't her fault she had been nearly blinded with the smallpox, but she made so little effort to help herself and without his money they would starve.

Tom stayed because his empty headed wife Elizabeth irritated him. Whilst George had been coming home for his supper she had prepared a meal but their son was courting a maid from the House and had his supper in the kitchen there.

Instead of cooking meat and potatoes and leaving it by the hearth to keep warm Elizabeth would flutter around at the last minute asking him what he wanted. As if there was a choice? He didn't want to be eating his meal at nine o'clock when it was bedtime.

So they all shared Nell's hot dinner at twelve o'clock and ate buns, bread, cheese and preserves for tea and supper. Robert didn't mind feeding them, they often stayed late to finish a job and never asked for extra pay

As autumn evenings drew in Violet had to leave work earlier. Robert couldn't go to meet her and sometimes strolled over to her cottage. He avoided the Ewe, Ben was making a success of it. He was a popular innkeeper and Helen had started to let the spare rooms to passing travellers.

At the beginning of October, Robert sat on the other side of Violet's fireplace having brought wood in for her. He tossed a log on and as sparks flew he was surprised to see her looking anxious.

'Is there trouble up at the House? You look worried.'

She gave him a small smile. 'No, nothing like that, it's good in a way but it will mean changes.'

'How so?'

'Lady Byclere is going up to the Town House for the winter soon.'

'She always does, for the Season.'

'Yes, but she wants me to go with her. My talents as a seamstress will be useful. She thinks I could learn to make the fashions and see what's up to the minute with the dressmaking.'

His heart had shrivelled into a small, cold ball. Violet was going, leaving him. 'When would this be?'

'A week.'

The words fell into silence and she looked at him anxiously. Friends they were, always had been and always would be. He had made such a difference to her life, showing her that men could be kind and courteous lovers.

'I shall miss you and our little chats. Our friendship means a lot to me, Robert but this is too good an opportunity to miss. I can learn new skills, perhaps earn more money and I can save that. And, I should like to see London,' she said wistfully, 'they say it's so busy, all those throngs of people and carriages and big houses.'

'Yes, it is that, but not safe for a lady like you. Promise me you'll take someone with you when you step out.'

'Oh nothing will happen to me. What could happen to a plain county bumpkin like me?'

'Pickpockets, thieves, all sorts,' he said gruffly, 'I'll miss you Violet, but I'll wish you well and a great success with the dresses.'

'Robert, I may be busy now helping pack up and I must leave this cottage tidy. Oh, by the way Nell is going to have it. She's thrilled to be moving out of that overcrowded hovel and she'll be able to keep all her wages, after paying the rent.'

Robert looked at her, it was all decided, everything orderly and shipshape. She had bloomed in the last few months without the shadow of Ned Bates hanging over her. She had blossomed into an attractive, middle aged lady with a happy smile. He wondered if she would have stayed if he had suggested marriage but it was too late now.

'Well. I'd better be off, you'll be busy.' He stood up, his shoulders drooping.

Violet could read his face, she touched his arm. 'This is a chance for me but I'll come back. I don't think I'll be here on Sunday so would you like to stay here tonight? I'm sure the once won't harm my reputation.' She leant and blew out the candles on the table and then led him to the bed in the back room. With the door open they could undress in the light from the fire.

The following Friday he left Caleb milking and at eight o'clock Robert and Nell set off to walk the two miles to Byclere House to watch the entourage of carriages, horses, servants and Lady Byclere and her youngest children leave for London.

It was a perfect October morning with the sun drying the dew off the cobwebs in the hawthorn hedge. Robins and blackbirds sang their goodbyes to summer.

Blackberries hung, ripened to dark purple by the sunshine. They picked the choicest end fruit in the clusters as they walked along and Nell lamented that she hadn't brought a basket to take home enough for a pie.

The Byclere carriage with the crest on the gleaming mahogany door waited at the front entrance, a groom at the horses' heads. Robert and Nell took the side path and hurried round to the stable yard. Here all was bustle and activity as two more carriages and a wagon were loaded up. Everyone had been pressed into service. Even gardener George Farthing, looking nervous, was walking a horse round and round the perimeter. A liveried groom fitted the traces onto the carriage horses.

Robert looked at Nell, 'It's a grand sight, isn't it?'

She turned a shining face up to him, 'All these people, in their smart clothes and look at George, holding that huge horse.' She continued to watch the gardener and Robert saw the look. She's younger than him, he reflected and it looks like she's got a fancy for him. I thought he was courting one of the maids here.

'Thank you for coming to see us off.' Violet was pink cheeked with excitement. In her second best dress she looked as smart as a newly painted ship in Robert's eyes. 'I think we're ready to go. Her Ladyship has been up since nearly eight o'clock and the children are running everywhere. I'll get someone to write a letter to tell you how I am. If you write to me I'm sure Mrs Greaves will read it me. As housekeeper she's better eddicated than me.' She ran out of breath, laughed and saw Robert trying to smile. 'We'll be back in the spring, it'll soon pass.'

'Just you watch out for all those bad types in London. Make sure you take company when you go out.'

'I expect I'll be in the carriage with Mrs Greaves or her Ladyship. They don't have much more than a butler and under-housekeeper in London normally so it's going to be a big change for all of us.'

A shouted, 'Violet Bates,' echoed across the yard.

Robert bent his head, kissed her lips and then watched her fly across the yard, her shoes tapping on the cobbles.

With Nell at his side they waved to everyone, handkerchiefs fluttered and the men shook their hats in the air. Whips cracked and the horses strained forward easing into their harness.

They would rest the horses at the posting inn in Wallingford at luncheon time. Her Ladyship would have a cold collation picnic whilst the servants ate a hot dinner at the back of the inn. This was the routine and they would be in London in three days barring accidents to carriage wheels and lame horses.

It was only ten o'clock but the sun felt pleasantly hot on his face as they walked back to Appley. He felt restless.

'Nell, shall we take the trap and drive into Banbury? I need a few things and you might want to buy something for the cottage.'

She grinned, 'I'd love to, sir, oh yes. I'd like to get a new sheet, mine are older than old, all in holes, sir. Violet's left her linen but she might want it when she gets back. And a new pillycase and if there's enough, a little saucepan for my soup at night. But, sir, I'm only in my working clothes.'

'You're clean and tidy, like you always are. Tom can harness Binnie and while he does that we'll get some of your money out of the chest. Do you know how much you should have?'

'Oh no, sir. I can't count beyond thirty.'

'Let's see, you'd be surprised how it mounts up. You know really, Nell we should put it in the Bank to gain interest, like mine does.'

'Oh no, sir, I like the thought of it up there, all shiny and waiting for me.'

As they walked into the kitchen Robert told Nell to put Tom and Caleb's dinner ready for them and he ran upstairs to change his breeches and find the money.

Five minutes later he sat down heavily on the chair, feeling faint, wiping his kerchief over his sweating face. He leant over and opened the window wide. He heard Nell's boots clattering up the stairs. Honest, hardworking, completely trustworthy and trusting Nell for whom a trip to Banbury was such a special treat.

'Oh, sir, all that money.' Her eyes shone.

He cleared his throat, 'Nell, be a good lass and fetch me coffee whilst I count this.'

When she came back the gleaming piles of coins were counted out in pounds. She had worked for him for six years. He had put a shilling a week in the chest apart from Christmas and fayre time when she kept the coins to spend on her family. By Robert's reckoning that should come to something like fifteen pounds. A fortune for a country girl like Nell but one she had slaved for. She had been Helen's skivvy all that time. There were only ten shiny, silver piles.

He cleared his throat, he had to tell her. The coffee was hot and he scalded his mouth in inattention. 'Nell, someone has taken some of your money. Don't alarm yourself, I'll make it up.' If it's the last thing I do, he thought grimly. Ben or Helen James, you're greedy, unprincipled thieves. It must be one of you.

'Sir?' Nell sat down and looked at the money. She absently took a coin and tapped it on the wooden table. It made a nice, comforting sound.

'I'm so sorry, Nell, so sorry. I think we can guess who might be the thief. I shall count this properly and then tonight I'll work out exactly how much should be here. After that I'll make good the deficit.'

'But, sir, excuse me for saying, you shouldn't have to use your money, after all you've already paid me.'

'Don't worry, Nell, I won't.' He knew how to get it back.

'Now, how much money should you like to take to spend, two pounds?' He made a note on a paper and put it back into the chest. The money was scooped up and tipped into a soft chamois bag.

'Do you think that's an awful lot?'

'No, my dear, you've worked for that. Come...Binnie is ready and the sun is shining.' He felt a sudden revulsion for the farmhouse. He couldn't wait to get away.

Robert put all thoughts of the confrontation he would have that evening out of his mind and set out to enjoy the drive to Banbury. After he stabled Binnie he agreed with Nell to meet at half past one to have a late dinner at the Red Lion. Then he went to the Bank to check his account although he knew to the nearest farthing what it should be.

If Helen was the thief then her husband was responsible for her. He was determined to extract the money from Ben somehow. He would have to be as clever as them, or cleverer.

After their roast pork dinner followed by a plum pie and cream custard they went back to Arkell, the Draper to fetch Nell's purchases. She discovered it was much cheaper to buy the material and sew the sheets herself. Twenty yards of a soft white calico with the thread had come to one pound and three pence. She bought three brightly coloured remnants to make neckerchiefs for the men in her life.

Some sweetmeats for Bayley were two pennies and she treated herself to three pence worth of liquorice. For the firs time in her life she had felt a little bit special, not just the maid of all work, the plain and drab skivvy but a woman in her own right. She had Robert to thank for that.

They bowled home along the dry country lanes with dust billowing out behind them. The sun was still warm on their faces and the smell of ripe blackberries fragrant to their noses. Each was lost in their own thoughts and Binnie trotted at his usual pace content to wait for his comfortable stable.

He left Caleb and Tom to do all the milking and evening dairy work. Robert cut himself a chunk of bread and wedge of his own Cheddar Cheese brought in that morning. He went in the parlour and poured a tot of his best Navy rum and then sat at the table and thought about Helen and Ben. Of all he had done for them, of the money he had paid out over the years and the little he had had in return.

At seven thirty he went upstairs to get his jacket, brushed his hair and tied on a clean ribbon. He splashed his face with cold water and strode down the track, steeling himself for a confrontation.

CHAPTER THIRTY ONE

'Hello stranger.' Was the cry as he strode in through the open door of the Ewe and Lamb. It was quite busy for a Tuesday evening and he wondered how much was on the slate. Ben was behind the bar about to lift a foaming, frothy tankard to his lips.

'Robert, what a pleasure, to what do we owe the honour? What shall it be? I've just started a barrel of this excellent ale.'

'A tankard of that would be good.'

'Ah making up for lost time eh, Shipshape?' Called Charley White, his greasy leather gherkin barely covering his massive chest. There was laughter.

Robert managed a smile. 'Your health, gentlemen.' He placed it back on the table, licking his lips. The froth was like a white moustache on his upper lip. 'Where's Helen?'

'Putting the littl'un to bed, she'll be done then.'

'And Bayley, where's he?'

'In the back, in the kitchen.'

Working hard no doubt, thought Robert grimly, but he kept a jovial expression on his face.

'Well you've done a tidy job in here Ben, it's looking better, the walls are clean looking with the whitewash and what's this? A new table?'

Ben preened, 'We've worked hard, Robert, it was a mess. Talbot had let it go but I'm going to make a success of this.'

'And a lot of money.' was a comment from Joe.

'That too definitely.'

Helen swept in, bows in her hair and her skirt sweeping the sawdust on the floor. The pungent scent she used was at odds with the earthy smells of the men.

She smiled and called, 'good evening, everyone.' Then she saw Robert and her smile faltered but pasting it on, she exclaimed in her best hostess voice, 'Robert how nice to see you.'

'He grunted, 'Helen, how are the children?'

'Fine thank you. Marion's teething but I'm managing as best I can.'

She made it sound as if she was doing all the work but he knew better. Sukey was the skivvy here as Nell had been at the farmhouse. But he let it go.

As Ben pushed a tankard across the counter to Charley, Robert spotted a flash of gold on his middle finger.

'Another ring, Ben, let's have a look.'

Ben held out his hand demonstrating a gold band, wider at the top and engraved with a cross. A diamond was set into the apex of the cross section.

Robert gave him a quizzical look, 'more spoils of war?'

'I had it fair and square, he was grateful.'

The stupid bugger thought I'd spare his life, but I took the ring and slit his throat with my stiletto. Ben justified his action with the idea that if he hadn't done it another soldier would and it might have been more brutal.

'Who was that, Ben, a Spanish Count or a parish priest?'

'Don't remember.' An old fool of a priest trying to slam his door in our faces.

Robert put on what little charm he possessed. 'Why Helen you're looking lovely, inn keeping suits you.' He watched her swallow the compliment. 'And you have that beautiful ring on. May I see it? I hardly had a chance when Ben gave it to you before. It's certainly lovely.' Robert held it up to the light and pretended to examine it. 'Do you know, I think it should be valued properly and then you would know how much it was worth. If it was sold why the money could be used to pay back a debt or even money that has been borrowed.'

With these final words he looked keenly at Ben, pocketed the ring, supped his ale and got up.

Helen shrieked, 'you've got my ring, give it back. I don't want it valued.'

Ben had gone pale and snapped, 'leave it, Helen.'

'Why, why should I?'

Robert turned at the door. Their actions had confirmed that Ben was the thief. 'Come and see me tomorrow night at seven o'clock, Ben.' He left with the sound of Helen's voice yelling and a particularly vicious 'shut it' from Ben.

He wasn't sure how valuable the ring was worth but if it was worth less than £20.00 then Ben must make up the difference. As he strode back up the lane he dearly wished Violet had been there to talk to. He didn't feel like going to Banbury again and Binnie would look askance at two trips in succession.

He would take it to the goldsmith to sell. He had no compunction about doing this, he knew Ben had stolen the ring and there was 'blood' on it. He had seen a brief glimpse of that face in it again. A tormented soul with her mouth open in a scream. It was probably cursed.

He left early the next morning as mist rolled in, the sun was barely up and the air damp and chilly. Binnie was asleep and had to be cheered up with a bucket of warm mash.

A little after nine o'clock he was tying up the reins outside Richard Way's neat, bow fronted locksmith and goldsmiths' shop.

'How can I be of service, Mr Southwell?' He was as smart and trim as his shop, elderly with pince nez glasses on the end of his nose.

Robert produced the ring. 'I should like to sell this, Mr Way.'

'Ah,' was eloquent. 'Mrs James brought this in some time ago for a valuation.'

'They wish to sell it to buy furniture, you know they have the inn in Appley.'

'Yes, I had heard told.'

It was fortunate that Robert's reputation was one of absolute honesty and integrity. No one had ever had cause to doubt his motives or words. It suddenly occurred to him that Way might wonder why Helen hadn't come in herself, knowing she loved a trip.

'She's busy today, the children...you know.'

'Ah yes, little ones...and the inn.' He had an eye glass pushed into his right eye socket.

'It's very unusual, polished in the cabochon style, a truly rare corundum. Of course, it's twenty one carats with this claw setting, quite worn though. From Portugal... or Spain I believe. Strange,' he mused, 'sometimes one thinks one can almost see a face in it and not a pleasant one.'

'I wouldn't know.'

'I'm not sure of a market for it, Mr Southwell, I think twenty guineas would be fair. How say you?' he regarded Robert quizzically.

'You're the expert, Mr Way, I should think they will both be happy with that.'

'I shall have to go to the bank, where will you be?'

'I'll be down at the Red Lion, I'll wait there.'

They shook hands and Way let Robert out with a ting of the door bell.

The deed was done. As Robert slumped down onto the hard seat of the cart, letting Binnie have his head to trot along at his own pace he mused on the way his life had turned out. He was fifty six years of age, working a seven day week, out from seven in the morning until seven at night. And what for?

'What's it all for Binnie? Simon's at school, but he's not interested in the farm. He just wants to know how much money I can send him. Ben is probably going to drink himself to death. I'd never have put him down as a thief, not at home like that. It just shows, you can't trust anyone. Well I know Nell isn't family but he must know I'd make it up to her.

I hope I'll be able to leave the farm to Bayley, he's the only one who shows any sense. I love that child like my own. But then if I leave it all to Bayley what will Simon have? He's the son and heir. It's a problem. I'll have to alter my Will. Perhaps I'll leave it for a while and see how things turn out. But I'm lonely, I miss them, even Helen. There's no life in the house now. But I couldn't trust them again, not after taking Nell's money.

What am I going to say to Ben tonight? He'll bluster and swear but I'm sure it's him, Helen was too surprised and he tried to shut her up. He owes me the money I lent him for the Ewe, I didn't think I'd ever get that back. I'll keep most of it, if he wants he can get a copy made. I bet he's got other stolen jewels. That gold ring he was wearing...there was a cross engraved on it. Was it looted from a church? That's sacrilege.' He sighed heavily and turned his attention to the road.

Fortified with a tot of rum he waited for Ben. The evenings were getting cooler, so he threw an elm log onto the fire and stirred it with the long poker. Sparks flew up and flames illuminated the tidy room. Then he lit two candles, placing the pewter candlesticks on the table. He wanted a good light to see Ben's face. He hadn't long to wait.

The door burst open and the large frame of Ben James filled the doorway as he ducked his head to come in.

Robert pushed the rum and small beaker across the table. The man's breath smelt of ale and his shirt was stained. Ben sat heavily, pulling the bottle towards him.

'So, what's this all about Robert? Where's Helen's ring? I've had the devil of a job keeping her quiet today.'

Watching him steadily Robert replied, 'when I went to the chest to take out Nell's money I discovered some of it was gone. I've checked it carefully, there was ten pounds missing.'

'What's that to do with us? Tom or Caleb could have taken it...anytime. Even someone from the village, everyone knows about your sea chest.'

'Yes, but they don't know where the key is. I'd trust Tom with my last shilling and Caleb would cut off his hand rather than steal a potato. So it had to be you or Helen and as she seems very surprised by all this I'm thinking it's you.'

'You're accusing me of stealing?' Ben thumped the beaker down hard on the table and stood up, red faced, his whole demeanour one of outrage.

'I thought perhaps you just wanted to borrow it and you'd pay it back,' replied Robert quietly.

'I've got money, I don't need to steal.'

'I didn't say steal, after all that would be a matter for the authorities, wouldn't it? The Justice of the Peace in Banbury would know who lived in the house and who knew where I kept the key.'

'Yes well, I'll ask Helen if she knows anything, she's always wanting something new.'

'Helen has been well paid over the years. Good Lord she'd have taken the sheets off the beds to take with her if I hadn't stopped her, but she's never been a thief. She could easily have pilfered odd coins from the cash jar but to say fair to her, she's been honest like that. You were the one who helped himself to the odd shilling from the jar, since you came home.'

At Ben's protest he put his hand up, 'I don't mind that, you'd had a hard time, but I do mind you taking someone else's hard earned money. Nell's worked like a slave for us, that's her nest egg, I want to make good the money.'

'It seems like you've made up your mind. Ben helped himself to more rum, 80 per cent proof, tossed it back and coughed. The diamond in the ring winked in the candlelight.

'How will you pay the money back?'

'Why should I, you've no proof.'

'I hoped you'd show a shred of decency. Those campaigns in Spain and Portugal have brutalised you. Is that your last word?'

'Thanks for the rum, I'll have the ring and get back. It's busy in the evenings now, a lot livelier with me in charge.'

Robert slid a golden guinea across the table.

'Here, what's this?' Ben shouted and waved his fist belligerently as Robert, 'what have you done?'

Robert sat, watching him calmly. 'I've sold the ring and taken out what you owe Nell and some of what you owe me. You can have a guinea. There's a receipt in there. Get a copy made or buy her something flashy. Or you can go into Banbury and buy it back. Now, we're all fair and square.'

'You!' Ben shouted shaking his fist. Robert drew himself up to his full five foot ten inches, he was a lot shorter than Ben and many years older.

'Yes? You're worried about how you are going to explain it to Helen?'

'No, she'll do what she's told.' He suddenly seemed to deflate. 'It were never a lucky ring anyway.' He laughed mirthlessly, 'you were right, there's a curse on it. We raped her, this Portuguese woman. One had the cross on a chain, I had the ring and Lenny, he's dead now, he took the buckles off her shoes. After he killed her. Sometimes I think there's a face in it, it's horrible, the mouth opens like it's screaming. Someone else is welcome to it. I'll get her another bauble, as long as it's big and sparkly she'll be happy.'

'You've got a lot on your conscience, I hope you can live with it, now...get out.

The door slammed, the fire flared in the draught, smoke billowed out and Robert sat with his head in his hands, dejected and shaken. He looked up and saw Mary watching him, gazing through him, but clearer than for a long time.

'Mary,' he whispered, 'just stay a while, I'm sorry about your son, I'm sorry I had to do that.'

He willed her to come closer. Smiling, he held out his hand.

'Please come closer. Stay a while, keep me company. Was it Ben shouting that made you come tonight? He can't help being like that. All those years in the army have changed him, he's hard now and I'm sure he drinks too much. It was his choice, he loved the army life. I'm glad the war is over, he can stay here and settle down. He won't come back to the farm but I'm going to carry on as long as I can and hope Bayley takes over. Have you seen Bayley? Would you mind if he wasn't actually Ben's child. He might be Calloway's son. Perhaps Helen went with other men, I don't know. I don't think I want to, either.'

Robert saw her fade a little, turn to the hearth and reach for something. She was becoming translucent, he willed her to stay. 'I'm sorry, am I talking too much?'

She looked straight through him, he knew she didn't see him, she couldn't see him and as he watched she slowly disappeared. The faintest whisp of grey dissolved into the stone at the side of the hearth. The fire flared up, flames licked hungrily at the log, then as if appeased the wood crackled and ash fell onto the hearth.

Robert sat staring into the fireplace. There was no trace of his ghost. But, when he wrinkled his nose there was the tiny whiff of savoury cooking. Was it Mary's rabbit stew? The thought occurred to him that an onlooker might say he was mad…talking to a ghost. It had been a comfort though and he tidied the room feeling lighter in heart.

A few weeks later he had a letter from Violet, delivered from Byclere House, carried down by one of the servants who came back regularly. Carefully he opened the seal. He was sitting upstairs in his bedroom, by the window as he didn't want to be disturbed by anyone. He flattened the thick parchment that had the Byclere crest at the top.

"Dear Robert. I hope this finds you as well as it leaves me. Mrs Greaves has kindly agreed to pen this for me. We are all settled nicely here in London. The lady's fashions are elegant and some are quite daring. The shops have everything in them you could wish for. I have bought some fine blue alpaca to make myself a winter cape. I miss you all but I'm keeping busy. Please write if you have time. My affectionate regards to you and everyone from Violet Bates, your friend."

He could picture Mrs Greaves sitting, writing at her housekeeper's desk, her rather grim face serious with concentration. There were a few spelling mistakes and he felt it made her more human. Violet would have been fussing, asking if she should say this or that. She sounded happy and he was pleased. He would write a reply. That would keep him busy in the evenings. But it mustn't be too long or too personal as someone, probably Mrs Greaves would have to read it to her. He got the key from under his mattress, opened the chest and carefully placed the letter with Simon's early letters from school.

Seeing Simon's letters reminded him that he would be coming home for half term in a few weeks. This was something to look forward to and he might bring a friend with him. Robert thought he'd put his farm work on one side for once and devote more time to entertaining Simon. The lad was growing up fast, he was thirteen and in a few years he would be gone.

It was the week before the half term holiday and the house was in disarray.

'I'll be running out of polish, Shipshape.' Nell had her hair pushed up into an old dairy cap. She had a clean but ancient apron tied round her slim middle and her sleeves were rolled up past her elbows. 'There's not a single cobweb in the house now,' she was definite. 'I've scrubbed and polished 'til me arms ache. The bedding's had a blow on the line and there's not a lot more I can do.'

She went to the coffee pot, keeping warm on the inglenook and helped herself. 'Ah, that's better.' She bit into a buttered scone and pushed the plate across to Robert. 'You've got the dairy up to the minute, I've got the house clean and sparkling and tomorrer you'll take the cart and fetch the provisions and master Simon.'

'You've worked like a Trojan, Nell, I'm grateful. I don't suppose he'll notice but we know it's done, don't we?' Robert slurped his coffee. He was bone tired. He'd done Nell's work in the dairy to enable her to concentrate on the house and he thought he might have overdone it.

'I'll have a bit of a rest after this. I'll be able to spend time with him Perhaps we can go for walks like we used to,' his eyes brightened, 'I'm really looking forward to seeing him.'

Nell risked a question, they had got on much more friendly terms in the last year or so. 'Are you missing Aunt Violet?'

Robert nodded, his voice rueful. 'Yes, but it's my fault, perhaps I should have asked her to marry me.'

Nell was definite, 'She wouldn't have, not after Uncle Ned. She was really excited to be going to London, it's an opportunity for her. I'm sorry you miss her but…well, she'll be back in the Spring, probably with lots of new dresses. Perhaps then I'll be able to have one of her old ones.'

'I hope so, Nell, I hope so. I'm up early so I'm going to bed soon. Tom and Caleb are milking in the morning, I'll be off before seven so I'll say good night.'

Nell had her old cloak round her, a dark grey, patched affair given by Helen. 'Goodnight, sir, I hopes master Simon appreciates what we've done.' But she knew from experience that he wouldn't even notice. He was a lad she reflected, her boots striking the flinty cobbles. He'd be more interested in the local girls and if those snooty friends of his were around then it was a case of lock up your daughters.

By eleven o'clock the next day Robert had sold all his butter and cheese and as quick as he could packed away everything on the cart. The next job was the grocers and then the wine merchant. He spent all his cash from the market buying in fine wine and some luxury items. Apples and hazel nuts were available at home but he bought in almonds, oranges and lemons. He knew Simon liked biscuits so he added a pound of Bath Olivers to his grocery list. Extra tea and coffee made him a very good customer at Mr Chalmers, the Grocer and Purveyor of Provisions. A large smoked gammon joint was now at the bottom of the sack of victuals as Robert turned Binnie's head out from the inn yard, into the main street.

The school was a short walk from the centre of town and it was nearing four o'clock.

Robert's usually solemn face had a broad smile. He had rinsed his hands and face at the inn, combed and retied his hair and brushed down his coat.

'Simon, it's good to see you, let's take your box. Binnie's round the corner waiting for us.'

'Well actually, father, I won't be coming home today.'

'Oh no, why not?'

'Hugh wants me to go home with him for a day or two, then I'll be over for the rest of the hols. I did promise him. I know you're always busy, I thought you'd be glad I'd got myself something to do.'

Robert swallowed, disappointment clutching at his heart. 'I've got everything especially nice for you and I'm up to date with the work so we can spend time together.'

'We still can, I'll only be over Byclere house but Hugh wants me to well, be with him.'

'Yes but the family is in London. I know, Violet is up there.'

Simon scuffed his shoe, looking a trifle impatient. 'His father is coming home for a few days, clay pigeon shooting, we can go out with him. Hugh wants me there, he says they're all the old cronies otherwise.'

'You haven't got a gun.'

'I can borrow one, look I'll have to go, there's the Byclere carriage. We'll be over in the week to see you.'

'We?!'

'Oh yes, Lansing's coming as well.'

A groom walked over, dressed in Byclere livery. 'Do you have a box, Sir?'

'That one.' Simon pointed imperiously and turned to follow the groom. 'Goodbye, Father.'

Robert watched as his son climbed into the carriage. Another lad climbed in and there was laughter as the groom struggled with a very large chest. No one offered to help and the three young faces turned into the carriage, intent on themselves. Robert stood and watched the carriage trot smartly out of the school yard.

'Come on Binnie, let's go home. I hope this food will keep. He don't mean to be thoughtless, he just doesn't realise how much work has been done the last few days. We'll have to be good and ready when he does come home. And make the most of his time with us. But if another lad is coming I'm sure they won't want to go for country walks. Perhaps we can play cards in the evening.' But his heart was heavy as he slipped the reins off the post.

The weather seemed to echo his mood as he rode home. October rain lashed spitefully onto his best coat and he had to drape an old sack over his knees to keep them dry. The sky had darkened, the wind increased round to the north east and he arrived back into the yard feeling chilled and miserable.

Tom took one look at his face and clamped his mouth shut apart from a brief, 'I'll put the hoss away and me and Cal will milk.'

'No it's all right, Tom, I'll get changed and come out. I might as well. Simon's mixing with the nobs, he's gone to the Bycleres' for a few days, he'll be home next week.' He got his hands under the large sack of provisions and pulled it up off the cart. 'I'll get this lot put away and then I'll be out.'

'All right, boss.' Tom walked back into the dairy. Caleb was getting buckets of oats and barley mix ready for the cows when they came in. They had a small scoopfull now the days were getting shorter, it helped to keep them in milk. 'The lad's not here, Cal, he's gone off to Byclere. Boss looks a bit done in.'

'Aye, he'll be that disappointed, him and Nell have worked hard. Trouble is the lad's growing up, he'll want to be with his friends. They don't want to know their old Dads...and Mums,' he added as an afterthought. His eyes darkened with pain as he remembered how keen their Rissie had been to go off to work and how she had thought it would be so exciting. But she had brought the smallpox home and died of it. They would never get over her death and Margie with her poor eyesight was a shadow of her former self. Yes, children were a pleasure and a pain.

'At least your George is home again,' he remarked to Tom as they walked the cows in from their meadow.

'Aye, but he's a miserable sod. That girl he was courting, she went off to London as under maid. It seemed his feelings didn't count at all. He'll get over it, but what with his gammy arm and being deaf in one ear, he's not much of a catch. He do seem to get on with Nell though. I've seen them chatting, quiet like, a few times. Now she would make anyone a good wife.'

Tom grunted and saw Robert come in the door, 'Everything under control, Boss.'

'Thanks lads, if we all milk we'll be done quicker. I think I might go down the Ewe tonight, for a bit of company.'

'Good idea, boss, we'll join you later, won't we, Tom.' Caleb nudged him,

'Oh aye, yes, yes we will.'

CHAPTER THIRTY TWO

On Sunday morning Robert shaved, changed into a clean shirt, put on his best coat and walked over to Byclere. He thought he'd have a chat with Calloway and if he did happen to see Simon, well that would be a bonus.

After a heavy dew it was a fine early winter morning and a pleasure to stride along the lane. A weak sun took the chill off and fluffy white clouds were scudding along in a light south westerly. The blackberries were over but the sloes were plentiful and he thought he'd like to make some sloe gin. He'd get a pint of spirits from Ben, prick the sloes with a pin and then leave them to soak in the gin. He had had it once and it was a very rich, potent drink, nice and warming on a cold night.

He turned into the stable yard. All was quiet as his boots clattered across to the office. Calloway came to the door.

'Well good morning, Robert, how are you?'

'Fine, John, I just thought I'd look you up, as it's such a nice morning.'

Calloway looked at him searchingly, he guessed why he'd really come. It wasn't like Robert to be nervous.

'The lads all went off at seven o'clock. Lord Byclere gives them an early start when he's out shooting for the day. They looked a bit shocked but it'll do them good. High spirited they are.'

'Have they been behaving themselves?'

'One or two pranks, nothing that can't be sorted.'

'What sort of pranks?' Robert said sharply.

'Only horse play. Lansing slid down the banisters and ended up in the hall, but he frightened a maid who dropped a tray she was carrying. Cleaning silver they were. Made such a clatter the under butler came running and fell over the clean pots. On the hard floor it was, he broke his wrist.'

'Oh no, how bad of them.'

'Simon was hurtling down after Lansing, and landed on top of him. It was all a bit of a meleè. Nothing that couldn't be sorted though.'

Robert shook his head in dismay. 'I'd better see his Lordship and apologise.'

'Oh he's got them under control, don't worry.' Calloway chuckled. 'On Friday evening they went into the Library and drank a decanter of his Lordship's best claret. They must have taken fright because they then substituted it for an inferior one. When his Lordship took a glass later he was bellowing for the butler to find out what rubbish he was drinking.'

Robert had his head in his hands, shaking it in dismay.

'It all came out, there's no secrets in a big house like that. Anyway the next morning the three of them had thick heads and sore ears from his Lordship's hand. He made them work in the stables for Saturday morning and today they are helping with the clay pigeon shoot. He told them they aren't mature enough to be trusted with their own gun.'

'I'll call up tomorrow and see him and take Simon back with me.'

'Yes and have Lansing. Hugh's been told he has to spend the rest of the week in the Estate Office with me. He's the heir, he has to start learning the ropes. And I'll stand no nonsense from him. I'm Mr Calloway and I expect respect.'

Robert looked around the office appreciating the orderly lines of account books on shelves, the oak desk gleaming with polish and the shallow wooden box of quills with a knife to trim them. John had everything shipshape, even the window that looked out onto the yard was clean. The Steward missed nothing that went on.

'There's no discipline anymore. I don't know why I send Simon to that expensive school. It's supposed to be the next best to Oxford in the county but I'm not sure I like the way he's turning out.'

'They're alright, Robert, just high spirited with plenty of energy. You wouldn't want a milksop would you?'

Robert grinned, 'I take your point. Well I'd better get home.' He got up to go. 'Oh by the way, I think our Nell is courting George Farthing. He's a good chap isn't he? A bit dour, but he's well thought of here?'

'One of the best gardeners we've got. Gets on with it quiet like. He doesn't like to be startled on his deaf side. You mustn't creep up on him. The war certainly gave him problems. He told me the other day he prefers plants, they don't kick like a horse and argue like a woman. I had to agree with him. He's a good steady man, Nell Bates could do worse.'

'I'll be over at ten o'clock with the cart to collect the boys and their boxes. I'd better think of some jobs for them, to keep them from mischief.'

'Yes well, best of luck then.' Calloway pulled his boots on, 'I'm off up to the four acre field to see how the ploughing's getting on.'

It was unfortunate that the next day started with drizzle. The two lads sitting on the seat up behind Binnie looked damp and pale with tiredness. Simon was yawning, his handsome face sulky whilst Rupert Lansing, huddling under Robert's old boat cloak looked thoroughly disagreeable. Their holiday had not turned out to be the lark they planned. They looked forward to the next few days without enthusiasm, expecting to be bored with the simple life.

They jumped down in the yard and started to move towards the house door.

'Aren't you forgetting something?' Robert said firmly, his voice carrying.

'What?' was from Simon.

'Pardon?' was Rupert slightly more politely.

'Come and unharness Binnie, give him a rub down as he's wet and then carry your boxes in.'

'Tom can do it, or Caleb,' said Simon carelessly, 'they're staff.' He said to Rupert who hadn't been to the farm before.

'No, they have their own work, this is yours. You can lift your boxes together, two of you should be able to manage it, if you can't, I'll help. When you've done that and taken them upstairs we'll have an early dinner. You both look fagged out.'

'He got us up at seven o'clock this morning, said we had to pack our own boxes. The man that does it broke his wrist. I would have thought a maid could have helped.' Simon was petulant.

Robert was appalled, what did this boy sound like? 'Who is he? Lord Byclere? I think you outstayed your welcome there. What would your father say about your behaviour, Rupert?'

Rupert was wiping Binnie with a soft cloth. He took a brush and started to work over the old horse's back. He discovered he enjoyed it. The stable was warm, there was a pleasant smell of hay and he felt more relaxed with Robert. Lord Byclere tended to huff and puff, shouting at them and generally causing tension.

He answered slowly, 'my father's dead sir, my mother would be cross, I hope she doesn't hear of it.'

'She won't from me, but I want you both to behave yourselves whilst you're here. Respect my men, the farm and mostly Nell. I don't want you ordering her or them about. If you want anything you ask me or do it yourselves. Simon, Rupert, do you understand?'

Yes, father.'

'Yes, sir.'

'Good. Simon hang up the cloth to dry, Rupert leave the brushes tidy and we'll go in. Who's got the heaviest box?'

'I have.' Simon picked up one end.

'Right, you boys take that, I'll bring Rupert's.'

Nell had left a side of lamb on the spit above the fire. It was roasted to succulent perfection. There were potatoes ready to mash and a dish of carrots baked with mint and butter. The big table was laid with six places. Robert insisted that Caleb and Tom eat their dinner with them. The boys fetched glasses from the parlour and Simon was despatched down to the Ewe to buy a jug of cider. He came back looking more animated.

'I've got something to tell you,' he whispered to his friend as they busied themselves with the glasses, 'later.'

Simon was used to the farm labourers eating at his dinner table. He disapproved but his father simply told him they were his friends.

Rupert hid his amazement that two yokels in their smocks, their faces damp with water and their hair brushed tidily back, actually sat down at the table with them. Furthermore they talked. They certainly didn't know their place but as he was a guest and Simon hadn't said anything he held his tongue.

Robert stood at the end and carved thick slices of juicy lamb onto the best blue and white plates. Nell served out vegetables and gave each plate an onion, roasted golden in the fat. Everyone was hungry and the boys both had healthy appetites. It was good plain food but Simon and Rupert both discovered how delicious the home grown dinner was.

'Is this the lamb with the broken leg, Shipshape?' Caleb stopped masticating and speared a carrot on his fork.

'Yes, you wouldn't know though, would you? These are all our own vegetables, mostly Caleb's work.'

'I enjoys working the veggies and they tastes good. You've done us a grand dinner, Nell.'

Nell blushed, she was used to the company of the two men but not the young lads and the visitor was definitely rather superior. 'Thank you Caleb. Who would like some more?'

Plates were passed and Caleb remarked, 'This lamb we're eating broke his leg jumping off the bank down by the river, when he was a little'un, Master Rupert. Boss here, he splints it up with a stick and the lamb mends, good as new.'

Rupert had his mouth full and didn't respond.

'What are you planning on doing with yourself, Master Rupert, when you leave school?' Tom slurped his cider and wiped his mouth on his sleeve.

Rupert was a handsome boy, at fourteen older than Simon. His dark eyes shone with enthusiasm. He ignored the eating habits at the table and replied, 'I should like to be a soldier, like my father.'

'Oh that's interesting. Was he at Waterloo? What regiment, Rupert?'

'The first Foot Guards...er Tom. He was a Colonel, he died at Waterloo.'

'We're all sorry, lad,' Robert surveyed the boy who was putting on a brave face. 'Would you like to go into the Ewe and Lamb? Ben James, Simon's uncle is landlord there and he was injured at Waterloo. He's pulled through that but he does love talking about the battle. He likes to tell you how many French soldiers he shot with that rifle of his. Would it upset you? Hearing about it?'

'I should like that. My mother doesn't like to talk about it but I should like to hear more.'

'Well it were a very close run thing by all accounts.' Tom remarked, 'They do say if it hadn't been for Blücher coming in late on the second day at Waterloo old Nosey could have lost the battle.'

'Well the French had more troops than us.' Rupert was anxious to defend the British, 'and more cannon.'

'The British did an admirable job, considering some of the Dutch were deserting.'

'We're the best army.' Rupert wiped his plate clean.

'Well then, this evening we'll have a stroll down there. Simon clear the plates please, there's baked apples and cream now.'

Nell had a large shallow dish with six Bramley cooking apples swimming in syrup. Their green skins had burst and the creamy flesh was golden brown with Demerara sugar. Tom fetched a brown pottery bowl of cream from the scullery.

'Here we are,' he placed it in the middle of the table, 'set this myself this morning. Lovely clotted cream, better than anything you get in Banbury, I warrant.'

'Very nice, er...Tom.' Rupert felt obliged to say something. Simon scowled at him as if to say don't encourage them.

Ten minutes later they all scraped back their chairs. Rupert hesitated, not sure if he was supposed to do anything.

'We're going upstairs, Father, we have some school work to prepare.'

'Oh yes, what's that?'

Simon ground his teeth, he wasn't supposed to ask that. He thought quickly. 'Some Latin verbs and Rupert's to do some work for the history master.'

'Oh all right then, come down later, try and have a bit of fresh air.'

Robert watched the boys escape upstairs.

'At last, now you know why I don't want to come home. Fresh air.' Simon flopped on the bed, keeping his boots on. Brown polish smeared on the shiny white counterpane, washed so assiduously by Nell the previous week.

'I think they're all right, genuine sorts.' Lansing had sat to take his boots off. He placed them neatly by the chair and lay on his bed. 'I'm having a bit of a kip, I'd like to go down the alehouse tonight.'

'That's what I was going to tell you,' said Simon eagerly, 'there's a really pretty wench there, only fourteen, and I reckon keen as mustard. Shall we try our luck?'

Rupert was asleep. Simon lay back against the pillows and thought of Sukey Armitage. Pert breasts the size of small apples straining against her bodice. Her hips swayed and her cheeky smile promised untold pleasures. He fell asleep, completely forgetting that he should have got a book out, just to confirm the impression of school work.

Robert put his head round the door at five o'clock just before he went out to help Tom. He pursed his lips, not at all surprised to see them fast asleep and not a book in sight. Why can't he be honest with me he thought as he trod as quietly as he could down the wooden staircase. Am I an ogre that he cannot be straight with me? Is it so awful here that he only comes home as a last resort? His mood was sober as he carried pails into the milking parlour.

'I don't suppose the lads want to come out and watch or give us a hand.' Tom remarked as he led Cara into a stall.

'They're fast asleep, Tom, I left them to it.' Both men worked in companionable silence with only the sounds of the cows huffing and snorting, shuffling their feet and rattling their neck chains as they gobbled up a scattering of oats in their feed trough. It soothed Robert and when he went back into the house later he was able to greet them pleasantly.

'Would you like some bread and cheese before you go down the Lamb?'

'Thank you, sir,' piped up Rupert, 'yes I am...' but Simon interrupted.

'We'll get something down there, I'm sure Uncle Ben will give us food.'

'I wouldn't be too sure, Helen will probably charge you and you may have to pay for your drinks.'

'But I'm family.' Simon was outraged.

'Yes, you might get the first one free, but Ben likes to drink the profits, not give them away.'

'Oh well, I see. In that case, I'd better have some money.'

'Your allowance was paid at the end of the month.' Robert reminded him.

'Oh that's all gone,' he said carelessly, 'have you got any, Lansing?'

Rupert demonstrated his empty breeches pockets, containing fluff and two small coins. He shrugged helplessly.

'Can you advance us some, Father, until the next month?'

'Yes, but then you'll be short next month.'

'Then I'll have to go without, won't I.' Simon replied testily.

Robert handed him half a guinea, 'That's for both of you, to last the whole week. I'll deduct it from the next allowance.'

'I suppose it'll do, I want to keep my end up.'

'Anyway, go easy on the strong beer and Ben doesn't have much in the way of good wine so stick to a light cider or small ale.'

'We will.' promised Lansing edging out of the door.

'I'll be over later when I've had a wash.' Robert promised.

The Ewe and Lamb had been tidied up by Ben. The sawdust on the floor was swept regularly by Sukey and another table and bench had been fitted in. There was even a pot of geraniums just outside the door, placed there by Helen who thought it lent tone. The doors and windows had been freshly painted black and the inside walls were newly whitewashed.

The joke amongst the regulars was that prices would be going up to pay for it all. Ben and Helen hoped to attract passing travellers. There were few coaches that went through, but one or two of the higher servants from the Byclere estate had put their noses in and they were an improvement on the village folk.

When Simon and Rupert stepped into the room that evening there was a hush and then talk resumed.

'Evenin', Master Simon. Evenin'.' Charley White held a tankard and raised his massive fist in greeting.

'Simon, it's good to see you and who's your friend.' Ben came round the bar counter and shook Simon's hand.

'Rupert Lansing, sir.' Rupert spoke firmly, impressed by the size of Ben.

'Now, what'll you have, what's Robert said you can drink?'

'A glass of ale please,' Simon spoke quickly, 'and one for Lansing.'

'Ah, Helen,' he called loudly, 'fetch two glasses for ale.'

Helen was in the back kitchen and thought there must be quality come in to want glasses. Quickly she tucked a wisp of hair behind her ear, smoothed down her skirts and fetched the glasses. Entering with a smile she saw the two young lads. She didn't need to make a fuss over Simon but the other lad, although untidily dressed had the look of quality about him. The easy assurance of wealth and breeding.

'So who de we have here? Simon where's your manners, introduce us to your friend.'

'Rupert Lansing, I think he's an Honourable, but I don't know what,' he said ungraciously.

Lansing held out his hand to Helen, 'Charmed Mrs James, quite charmed.'

Helen was flattered and Sukey, watching from the doorway was very impressed. The young man was wearing toff's clothes and she decided she'd get to know him better...a lot better. Simon was still too young and she had known him from schooldays.

The two young men sipped their ale carefully, not sure of the taste or potency. Rupert licked the froth off his upper lip and cleared his throat.

'Is it to your taste?'

'Yes, thank you, sir. Mr Southwell says you were at Waterloo.'

'Aye lad, well Quatre Bras, it were on the first day and then Waterloo. I won't deny it were tough. Do you want to hear about it? It's not pleasant.'

'Please sir, yes, my father was there.'

'Well,' Ben sighed, scratched his chin and gazed reflectively at his beer pot. 'Me and the lads were tucked behind some trees. Not a lot of shelter. Rifle brigade I was. Sharpshooters we were, trying to pick off the enemy, always aim for the captains and majors, shoot a marshal or two if you're lucky.

Anyway, a few Cuirassiers, that's French cavalry, came riding towards us. It still gives me nightmares, don't it Helen? Nothing seemed to stop them, a great horse comes flying along, this huge Frenchie leans over and slashes with his sword.'

The inn was quiet, listening, Rupert gazed at Ben's face.

'I hit out with my rifle, trying to get my knife out of the holder in my trousers. I've got a stiletto, I...acquired it in Spain. It has it's uses. He missed me, I was standing up, ready to throw the knife in his back when there was another great dammed horse looming over me. I saw his face, all red and sweaty as he leaned out the saddle, slashing. It caught me on the leg, up on the thigh, but I didn't feel a thing. No, sir, I heard a shot and Glyn at my side fired. The Frenchie falls out of the saddle and the horse gallops off. I walked over and gave him the coo de grase.'

'Coup de grace.' Corrected Rupert.

'Yes, that, it were only kind, then Glyn says to me, Ben, your leg's cut bad and when I looked there was blood everywhere. It had gone quiet for a few seconds round us and suddenly there was a thundering of hooves and blow me more of them dammed French were coming. I was on my knees by then, trying to tie up the leg a bit I reached for my rifle, points at a Frenchie and bang. I caught him on the shoulder but he kept coming. The horse was upon me and I think a hoof clipped my head 'cos there was a terrible crack and wallop and I saw stars. Next thing I knows I'm in the field hospital, well a bit of a tent way back. Glyn and Mousey Jones had dragged me through the mud all the way.' Ben stopped to take a deep draught of ale. Everyone waited.

'You knows the rest. I've been invalided out. I managed to get on a ship and get back to England. After a few days in the soldier's hospital I used my last shillins to get back home and Robert mended my leg.'

Rupert said quietly, 'it must have been terrible.'

'Aye lad, if you know what the sound of a pig stickin's like and multiply that a thousand times, then that's the sound of the horses and the men screamin' in their death agony and over it all is the thunder and boom of the guns. And it were that close, the battle, that it could have swung either way. And then the rain started. Well it washes off the blood.'

'Ben,' Helen remonstrated, 'that's enough for one evening, you know it gives you nightmares.'

'The lad wanted to know, it's only right he hears how it was, not so much glory, as misery.'

'Did you see Lord Wellington?'

'Once, at a distance, on that great charger of his, Copenhagen he's called. He were everywhere, rallying the lads. Hold fast he said, let's show them boys. He ain't frightened, so neither were we. Helen, get us a bite to eat, I'm a bit peckish after that. Pie and pickles will do. That all right for you, boys?'

'Thank you, Uncle.' Simon thought it was time he reminded them he was there. He was watching Sukey, the way she seemed to wiggle as she came through the door carrying the tray. As she handed Rupert a plate with a slice of pigeon pie, glistening with jelly and chunks of meat she batted her lashes at him.

'Would you likes an onion?' Fat, round nut brown onions were swimming in malt vinegar in a pottery jar.

'No, thank you,' Rupert managed to stammer, his eyes mesmerised by her breasts pushing against her grey cotton gown. She was wearing a stained white apron, her hair was piled up, but the pins were loose and tendrils curled round her ears.

'Can I get you anything else?' she gave him a saucy look.

'A knife and fork and a napkin would be helpful.'

'A knife and fork coming up...sir.' She whisked around again managing to show her ankles in the process.

An hour later the boys had finished their ale and pie suppers.

'When we go out of here, in a minute,' Simon whispered, 'we'll go round to the stables near the back door. Let's see if we can get Sukey to come outside.'

'Thank you for telling us about your experiences.' Rupert said formally, going up to shake Ben's hand.

'Good night, Uncle Ben and Helen.' Simon called, ready to slip out the door.

It was very dark as they crept round the back of the inn. The sky was overcast and they stumbled on the cobbles as they giggled, whispering.

'What do we have here? Two young gentlemen is it?' Sukey had a lantern in her hand. 'And what would you be wanting?' A dark shawl draped her shoulders. Her hair tumbled down and she shook it suggestively as the boys came up to her.

'We...just want...' Rupert faltered.

'Come on, Sukey, you can give us some fun now, we've had the serious stuff in there.' Simon went to pull her arm.

'This young gentleman can come and see my kittens. In the stable they are.' She took Rupert's hand. 'Over here, Mr Honourable,' she mocked, 'and as for you, Simon Southwell, come back in a years time, or two, when you've grown up bit.'

Sukey Armitage was a terrible tease.

'How dare you, you slut.' Simon was furious. He had a good mind to go back in there and tell Sukey's father what she was up to. But if he did that Rupert wouldn't speak to him at School. He might even tell the others and he'd be branded a spoilsport.

There was a glimmer of light showing by the stable door. He crept over and peered round the crack. A male hand slammed it shut in his face. Deliberately clattering his boots he strode across the yard and went home.

Robert had washed and changed his shirt, intending to slip down the Ewe for an hour, but he sat by the fire thinking he'd just have five minutes doze. He woke to a darkened room. The candle had burnt down to a pool of guttered wax and the elm log was smouldering. He shook his head, easing his aching shoulders and stared into the fireplace willing Mary to come.

'Come to me, come, Mary.' He murmured to the empty stones. He thought of her, of that last day at the fayre and her happy, smiling face. Of her pleasure as she ate her dinner and a flake of pastry that clung to the corner of her mouth. She had dabbed at it with a dainty lace handkerchief. That was now upstairs in his chest, one of his most treasured possessions.

'Mary, Mary, come.' he implored.

She was there, as a ghostly outline and the grey gown was pale in the gloom, her face even paler under the white bonnet. She gazed at him, through him and then disappeared.

'Oh, you've gone.' He was disappointed, but elated that she had come when he called. He would try that again. He got up stiffly, went to fetch more candles and lit them. By their light he could see it was nearly eight o'clock. Too late to call down the inn, those boys should be coming back soon. He would warm some milk for them and butter a scone or two for their supper. He turned from his chores as the door opened. Simon walked in alone.

'Where's Rupert? Have you had a good evening?'

'He's yarning about the war with Ben, I'm tired, so I'll go to bed.'

'Would you like some milk and a buttered scone?'

Simon looked down his nose, 'Father, that's nursery food, we had pigeon pie and ale tonight.'

'Oh I see, well I'm pleased you enjoyed yourselves. Goodnight, son.'

Robert removed the milk from the fireplace and took it back into the scullery. He poured himself a small beaker and went into the parlour. There he added a measure of rum and carried it upstairs to his bedroom.

Simon couldn't sleep. He heard his father come up the stairs and the door close. The shutters were open and he saw the shadow of the owls' wings as it flew silently by, following the darting bats. He ached with jealousy and temper. He vowed he would get back at Sukey Armitage one day and somehow Rupert Lansing would pay for what he did tonight. He knew, girls could have two men in an evening, the older boys boasted at school. They saved money by sharing a whore.

He tensed under the bedclothes hearing the outside door close. Lansing had taken off his boots. Thank God they were in single beds and he wouldn't have to lie next to him and pretend to be asleep. Then Simon decided. He would hide his anger, he would talk, ask him what it was like and how they managed it.

The door opened silently, candlelight bobbed into the room and the candle stick was placed on the table. Lansing sat on the bed to take his socks off. Quickly he stripped off, leaving his clothes in a pile. He sniffed himself and wrinkled his nose. He stank of sweat and something else.

Mixed with the stale odour of Sukey's rosewater was another smell and he realised it was his own, the strange new smell of his body's fluid, dried on his skin. He splashed himself with dirty water left in the bowl, lathered with soap and rubbed his lower body. He wiped off with a rag and rubbed himself dry with the damp towel left from earlier. His back and chest felt itchy with sweat and he finished up washing all over. He needed to have a bath in the morning.

As he slid into bed, Simon spoke.

'You all right? What was it like?'

Lansing replied drowsily, 'She's beautiful, I didn't know it would be like that.'

'Like what?'

But Lansing was asleep. Simon lay there frustrated beyond belief. He felt like shaking Lansing,. Now it would have to wait until morning.

Robert, Tom, Caleb and Nell sat around the kitchen table. Half a crusty cottage loaf, it's top pulled off, was on the bread board. A dish of creamy, pale butter and the pottery jar of plum preserve were on the table. They were finishing up fried ham and wiping greasy plates with the bread. The large old pewter coffee pot steamed its fragrance on the inglenook. It was half past eight and the cows had been milked and put out to pasture. The cow shed was cleaned out, the milk taken to the dairy and Nell had turned all the cheeses. Still the boys weren't up.

'You're soft with them, Shipshape.' Tom got up for the coffee.

'I know, but they work hard at school, this is like a holiday for them.' Robert frowned, knowing Tom was right.

'We didn't have holidays, worked I did from ten year old.' Caleb helped himself to the jug of milk and poured it into his beaker of coffee. He took two small spoons of Demerara sugar aware of the cost of it.

'I ought to do their washing today if they're going back to school on Monday.' Nell sliced more bread and buttered it. The butter was hard and the bread new and the slice ended up with lumps of butter spaced across. 'Best I can do,' she handed one to Tom. 'as I was saying, if I wash today, iron tomorrow, air on Sunday, they'll be packing up again Sunday night. So will you tell them to bring their laundry down please, Robert.'

At that moment the door opened and Simon and Lansing walked in.

'Good morning,' Lansing spoke cheerily and hesitated, looking for a chair.

Simon had sat down. 'Is there any tea?'

'Good morning, Simon, Rupert,' said Robert mildly 'and no there's only coffee.'

'I'll make you some,' Nell sprung up.'

'No, Nell, finish your breakfast, they can have coffee and like it.'

Tom pushed back his chair scraping it on the flagstones, 'Have this one, Master Rupert, I'm out to clear that ditch up the top meadow.'

'Thank you, Tom.' Lansing felt on top of the world, refreshed in mind and body after his exploits of the evening before. Simon had been really surly, dressing without washing. One glance at the scummy water in the bowl had been enough.

'Would you like that ham and eggs?' Nell piled up plates.

'All right.'

'Please.'

'Nell will do your laundry today, straight after breakfast. So bring it all down, boys.' Robert was firm.

'Are you taking us back on Monday, Father? I'm not going with Tubbs, he's too coarse.'

'Yes, Byclere will be over here by six thirty so make sure you are both ready.'

Simon raised his eyebrows at Rupert amused at the idea of Lord Byclere's son riding in a farm cart, albeit a smart one.

'We're going up on the downs, will you put us up some food, Nell?'

'Certainly Master Simon. I'll do it whilst you bring down your laundry.'

Nell had noticed the peremptory demand and ignored it. Robert sighed, Simon was becoming so arrogant, was it due to adolescence?

'When you pick up the food you thank her, understand?'

'Yes, sir, I will.'

'And you, Simon.'

Simon was out of the door and either didn't hear or pretended not to. Robert walked into the scullery as Nell took the cheese out of the safe.

'I apologise for my son's rude behaviour, Nell.'

'I didn't notice,' she smiled sweetly, cutting off large chunks of their best cheddar. 'There, that with an apple and a slice of pork pie will keep them going.'

Half an hour later she had sorted the washing into piles. She picked up a shirt, saw it had the Lansing name embroidered in it and wrinkled her nose, sniffing it. Along with the smell of sweat was the faint scent of rosewater. She thought of the girls in the village and murmured,

'Sukey Armitage, I'll be bound, that girl will get herself into trouble.' She looked at the underdrawers of white linen and saw the stains. Shaking her head she plunged them into the soapy water, 'young Rupert you're playing with fire. Mind you, if that girl got herself pregnant she wouldn't know who the father was until it was born. Thank goodness they're going back to school.'

Rupert and Simon were sitting on a dry stone wall, two miles from Appley on the edge of the downs waiting for Byclere.

'I'm not telling it twice, I'll wait for Hugh.'

Rupert was having second thoughts about the previous evening. Sukey was so pretty, so soft, so exciting. He thought he might be in love with her, but wasn't sure what you were supposed to feel like in that condition. His sisters seemed to giggle a lot. He was starting to think that he didn't want to share all the intimate details with them. Simon wouldn't understand, being a virgin and Byclere was more experienced.

She had called him a fine young man and enthused over his private parts until he was quite embarrassed. And when she had touched him there, well, it was like starting a forest fire. His eyes unfocussed, he gazed dreamily at Byclere coming up the path.

'Hello you two, phew, what a morning I've had. I've been in with Calloway for two hours studying the accounts for three fields of barley. I didn't know there was so much involved. Oh good, food, I didn't bring any.' He grabbed a piece of pie.

'Hey! That's our lunch. Anyway, isn't that what you have a steward for, to do all the accounts and then you just spend the money.' Said Simon

'Father says I must know everything.'

'Well when you take over you can sack him and get someone else.'

Hugh was horrified. 'Oh no, he's honest, Father says that's worth half the estate to have an honest steward.'

'Well anyway,' Simon was impatient, 'we're waiting to hear all about Rupert's evening with Sukey Armitage.'

Hugh grinned and clapped an arm on Rupert's back making him cough and splutter out crumbs. 'You've done it, well done, how'd you like it?'

'It was very ...nice.'

'Nice!' The two boys were open mouthed with surprise. 'Is that all you can say?'

'Well, it was... I didn't know what to expect, not really. But the second time was better than the first, not so quick.

'Twice,' said Simon faintly, 'you did it twice. You lucky old dog, Lansing, she must be a good'un. I'd like to have a try with her.'

'Oh no, she's says she's my special girl, for when I come here.'

'Yours now, and how many others the rest of the year?' Hugh was amused, he would find out himself who this girl was.

Lansing didn't want to think of Sukey giving someone else the pleasure she had given him. He turned his back, a mulish expression on his face. Absently he bit into a hunk of cheese that made him think of Sukey's teeth and mouth on certain parts of him. He felt his body reacting and his face flushing. He stood up,

'I'm pressing on, we'll never get anywhere at this rate.'

He heard Hugh's voice, 'Whores are for lust, mistresses are for pleasure and wives are for breeding the children. That's what my father says. That's why he let me have the scullery maid, Amy, when I was just thirteen. I know whom I'm going to marry. Father says it's a good alliance so I'll have to go along with it. But I'll keep a mistress or two as well.'

Simon couldn't imagine Nell back home letting him take any liberties with her, not even a tap on the bottom. He would try and find a way of losing his virginity in Banbury. It would be difficult, prefects and masters walked about the town. If he was spotted going into a house of low repute he might be reported and there was also the question of money, of which he had little. Damn Sukey Armitage for her pert ways and damn Rupert Lansing for mooning along with that secretive smile on his face.

CHAPTER THIRTY THREE

The farm settled down again with the boys gone back to school and Robert looked forward to Violet coming home in the Spring. The Byclere family came back to the country in the early summer to avoid the heat and smells of a dusty London.

He came in from the yard one morning to find Calloway sitting at the kitchen table with a cup of coffee in front of him.

'John? This is an unexpected pleasure. I'm glad Nell's looked after you. I'll have a cup as well please.' He took the cup, their best china, decorated with roses, brought out by Nell from the parlour and sat down.

'There's a letter for you.' Calloway pushed it over. Sealed with the Byclere stamp.

'From Violet I hope.' Perhaps Violet was writing to say when she was coming home. 'Are the family at the House. Will they be they home soon?'

'They came back yesterday. Lady Byclere brought that letter for you.'

'Is Violet with her? Has something happened to her?' He looked at the letter with dread, a sick feeling making the coffee taste turn sour. He turned it over.

'I'll leave you to read it in peace,' said Calloway gruffly, draining his cup. He hadn't realised quite how fond of the seamstress Robert was. He looked quite cut up.

'Yes, thank you.'

Robert picked up the letter gingerly and went to fetch a knife, then realised he had his pocket knife in his coat. He walked into the parlour to avoid Nell's eyes. Sitting down at the table he opened the parchment and spread it out.

"Mr Robert Southwell from Mrs Violet Turner, Bates as was.

I do hope this finds you as well as it leaves me. I hope this news will please you to know that I am happy and settled up here in London. What a lot has happened. I do not know what to say first. I now have my own establishment, "Violet's Modes", in a small shop off Park lane. All the quality come in, put on to us by Lady Byclere who has been very kind to us. It was such a good chance that we had to snap it up quick."

Robert frowned, who was this "we"? He read on with the greatest misgiving.

"I have gone into business with Albert Turner who was butler in Lowndes Square, the Byclere London home. He is a dab hand with the tailoring and as we both had some money put by we decided to go into the venture together. There are rooms above the shop, nice and cosy but I told him, I wasn't living there, with him, unmarried. So we tied the knot last week and very pleasant it has turned out to be. You will be glad to know he is a real gent, kind and thoughtful and I hopes our future will be rosy. I trust this finds you in good health and all is well at Southwells. If you should ever find your way up to London we would be very pleased to see you for old times sake .

With our kindest regards.
Albert and Violet Tuner."

Robert sat on. The sun moved around and left him in a cool shadow. He thought of the happy times they shared: of the lovemaking and their chatting together in the warm bed. He should have asked her to marry him. Fool, he was a fool. He banged his fist down on the table making the letter jump. But no, Violet deserved more than this quiet backwater. She was a talented needlewoman, this was her chance and good luck to her. As for this Albert Turner, surely she was a good enough judge of men to know if he was worthy of her.

The thought that he hadn't got her homecoming to look forward to made him feel even lonelier. He took the letter upstairs to the chest and found the portrait of Mary. What a pity he hadn't had a larger one painted he suddenly thought. Then he had the notion that next time he was in Banbury he would ask if there was a portrait painter in the area who could make a larger copy of Mary's miniature. He would put it up in the parlour. That cheered him and he went back downstairs to tell Nell that she could keep Violet's cottage indefinitely, as she wouldn't be coming home.

'I had heard something to that effect, Robert.' Nell was in the dairy washing butter after she had churned it. 'I wasn't sure and didn't want to repeat gossip. Thing is, you know I'm courting? It's George, George Farthing, we get on well. I know he's older than me, and he's got a gammy arm, but he's gentle and kind and he wants to marry me. We could start off in that little cottage and then perhaps move to something better when the children come along.' She blushed, 'well that wouldn't be for a while and I always wants to work here, so perhaps it's all working out for the best.'

Everyone but me thought Robert glumly then realised that Nell deserved a decent family life.

'I hope he appreciates you, Nell.'

'He does, he's very good. He's dug over the vegetable patch at the back of the cottage and is going to plant in potatoes and beans. Isn't that kind?'

Robert repressed a smile, 'it's not very lover like, Nell, useful but unromantic.'

'We has our share, don't you fear,' she gave him her prettiest, happiest smile, 'but I'm having a white wedding and one that means it…if you know what I mean.' She nodded her head significantly.

Dear Nell, keeping her virginity when all around her were wanton. He must think of a good wedding gift for her. The Bates's wouldn't have any money for weddings and feasts afterwards. That was an idea, perhaps they could have it here, after harvest, in the barn. He would put it to her later.

Nell's wedding was set for the last Sunday in August. News that Shipshape was paying and providing the wedding feast gladdened the hearts of the villagers. With food and drink in abundance a good time was assured.

Nell went to Banbury with Robert to buy material for her wedding gown. It had to be something useful that could come out again. She brought home some pale blue sprigged cotton dimity, twenty yards of lace edging and blue velvet ribbons that George had given money for.

Her mind was not on her work the next day and Robert laughed in dismay as she threw a pot of potatoes out onto the dung heap, leaving the peelings in the bowl.

'Oh. Oh silly me…look what I've done.' She stood, hands on hips giggling and Robert was caught up in her infectious good humour.

'You're excited Nell, all this wedding talk is filling your head. I can see we'll have no sense out of you for weeks. I'd say go home, but I could do with some dinner today.'

'I'll pay attention, Shipshape, it's just that Helen, Susan, Clarrie and Fanny are coming to help with me dress.'

'Well don't let them persuade you to do anything you don't want. If Helen's involved you'll have a low neckline and no modesty.'

'It'll be fit for a Queen and my George. And it'll useful for later. I wish Aunt Violet could be here to help, she'd know all the latest designs. I should like it fashionable.'

Nell's cottage was busy that evening as the ladies crowded round a table that was piled with a delectable array of materials and trimmings. Nell had made them all wash their hands with some of Shipshape's soap and calloused, work reddened fingers caressed the soft fabric.

Susan spoke for them all, 'This'll turn out lovely, Nell, I'm pleased for you, you deserve it.'

Nell turned a beaming face to her aunt. 'We're going to have a lovely day, really special, me and George. He's buying a new jacket.'

'Well he's fortunate to come to a cottage ready made.' Helen commented a bit sourly.

'He could have a larger estate cottage but this is handy for me. George says he don't mind walking a mile or so to work. When the children come along we shall probably move.'

Clarrie thought the conversation was getting a bit heated, that Helen James always had to be the centre of attention. 'Have you got a design in mind, Nell?'

'I saw a dress on a lady in Banbury, pretty it was, I think I can copy it.'

'Draw it for us.'

Nell flattened the brown wrapping paper and a pencil stub. Frowning, she drew a shape and marked in buttons. Squiggly lines showed the lace on the collar and cuffs.

'There.' She beamed proudly and they gazed in admiration.

'Beautiful,' breathed Susan, 'beautiful. I'll be showing you up in my old clothes.'

'And me,' echoed Clarrie.

'I'll probably have something new,' said Helen casually, 'I need a new gown.'

'Well don't you try and outshine our Nell,' warned Susan..

In the following weeks through hay harvest and then into August and the barley and oats harvest Nell was at Southwell's by half past five in the morning. Robert got up to find the kettle on, the fire glowing and bread on the table. He didn't stop for food but went out to the cows with a pot of coffee in his hand. In the cool of the morning Nell was in the dairy turning cheeses and patting butter into shape.

She gave him a running commentary on her work with the dress the evening before. The women were all sewing seams but Nell wanted to trim the lace herself. Fanny, with the best eyes had been given the job of sewing the tiny buttonholes for the pearl buttons, all thirty of them. There was also a new petticoat with two layers of skirt and a new nightdress. This was to be in fine cotton lawn trimmed with some exquisite Valenciennes lace that Violet had sent down from London.

'That'll be a waste on there,' sniggered Helen who had never had any French lace, 'that'll be more off than on.'

'Don't be vulgar,' Nell replied quietly, 'I want it all to be beautiful.'

'Hold your tongue, Helen,' said Susan, 'be happy for her. That girl's worked like a slave all these years, she deserves something nice.'

Helen sniffed.

Finally the banns were called. The wedding of Eleanor Margaret Bates and George Thomas Farthing was to be Saturday August 31st, at the church of St Thomas the Martyr, Appley in the county of Oxfordshire. Nell told everyone the tea would be in Southwell's barn and when Robert heard this he realised that he really had been accepted into the village and that was what they called his farm.

He left the food preparation to the ladies and gave a guinea to Susan and told her to use it for all the food. The ladies of the village would prepare their specialities.

He had a word with Ben about the drinks and barrels of ale and cider were ordered. A light summery wine was thought of for the toasts and there would be plenty of lemonade and ginger ale for the children.

After a busy morning in the market, Robert collected lemons and oranges ordered the fortnight before. He also wanted cigars, small thin ones and every man present would get one. Simon had come in with him and had to help carry the parcels.

'Why are you wasting good tobacco on them, Father? They won't appreciate it.'

'How do you know? They never have the chance of a cigar and just for once I want them to. This wedding will be special,

Nell's been a really hard worker, she's stuck with me and you and I want to help make her day memorable.'

'They're only peasants, village yokels.'

'No, Simon, they're my friends. I don't know where you get these ideas from. That school has made you an arrogant lad who thinks he's above such things. Well if you can't enjoy the day at least don't spoilt it for Nell and George. Because if you do, with your sour little comments, I shan't forgive you.'

They sat in an uneasy silence on the way home. Simon though was thinking of Sukey Armitage. The drinking would be heavy on Saturday, he was going to make another play for her. On his home territory he would invite her up to his room and get her drunk enough to take her clothes off but not enough to be incapable and pass out. He smiled secretively. He'd make her pay for her rejection of him. No one did that to him and got away with it.

The church was decorated on the Friday evening. The estate sent over flowers, armfuls of them and there was the heavenly scent of roses and stocks in the cool, dim fourteenth century church. The pews were polished with beeswax until they shone, the precious silver candlesticks rubbed shiny bright and the windows cleaned until they sparkled.

A bouquet of white lilies lay on Nell's table with a bonnet trimmed with pink daisies. It had been far, far more than she had expected but the Bycleres and Calloway thought highly of George.

The previous day Robert told her to go home at three o'clock. She wanted to wash her hair and it took hours to dry. Susan would plait it for her and if she slept in them, her hair would curl down her back for her wedding.

With Tom and Caleb helping, the cows and dairy work was finished by ten o'clock on the Saturday morning. The wagon was taken out of the barn and the floor swept. The precious barley had been sectioned off with wood slats so there was plenty of room for the trestles. Every chair and stool in the village had been commandeered. White sheets were spread out on the trestle tops, with small pots of flowers to decorate. Helen had come up the previous evening and used the candytuft and roses that the Estate sent.

Fanny was in the kitchen overseeing the roasting of a whole pig. It had been allowed to grow on to be a big porker, enough for the feast and she had prepared it the day before, starting it off at four o'clock that morning. Robert had got up to the smell of sizzling fat with the aroma of onions and sage.

They sat at the kitchen table enjoying a companionable beaker of coffee and as they shared bread and jam at half past nine Fanny broached what was on her mind.

'I knows Nell is going to stay here, but I'd like to say, if she has time off, when the little'uns come I'd be pleased to come here. Mine are all growing up, I'd be glad to help.'

'Well thank you, Fanny, yes I'll bear that in mind. Nell's good with children, I hope her and George are blessed.'

At two o'clock the church was packed. The whole village was there plus estate workers from other villages who knew George. Mr and Mrs Calloway were present at the front, next to Robert. He was in his best blue jacket, a new white shirt and a black velvet hair ribbon tied back his clean and brushed hair. George fidgeted in his new jacket, that felt rather stiff and tight and he wished he'd broken it in, but hadn't dared to get it dirty.

Elizabeth Farthing was in her best dress, slightly dated and faded but it was a dark blue cotton, with her yellow bonnet trimmed with feathers and yellow roses. Nell had bought her new lace gloves and she refused to take them off. Tom was in his best brown jacket, steamed and brushed until it looked nearly like new. His trousers were from Robert and a little short and tight but with his boots laced up he hoped no one would notice.

Clarrie, as mother of the bride was in a dark green gown that had been the curtains from the Byclere house nursery. The material had come via a cousin and she had been so relieved that she could have something new. She didn't want to show up Nell and with clever cutting, the faded strips had been sewn as if part of a pattern. She too had pretty new cotton gloves and a bonnet trimmed with velvet ribbons and a lily from Nell's posy. She felt proud to bursting.

Joe as father of the bride was in his best and only coat, which was twenty years old and bursting at the seams. He had a new stock to go with his shirt, borrowed from Robert and breeches that had come from the second hand stall in Banbury market. Nell's precious savings had kept her family from looking a disgrace.

The morning passed in a whirl of activity with a constant stream of load bearing people into the barn. The wagon brought up the barrels with Ben supervising.

By twelve o'clock the village was quiet again as men came home from work and everyone got ready. Baths were hauled out and filled with water that had been heating all morning. Children were dumped in, scrubbed unceremoniously and hauled out to take their turn at being dried, dressed and have their hair brushed dry.

Nell was in a dream. She was too nervous to eat, but at eleven Robert sent her up some of his special Banbury biscuits, almond squares and elderflower champagne. She sat on her bed and shared a special quiet moment with her mother. Clarrie was brushing out the braids. The nut brown hair shone and rippled down her back to her waist.

Her plain daughter was beautiful. Their eyes met and they smiled.

'You're lovely girl, that George is a lucky fellow.'

'I'm the lucky one, he's good and kind and steady and we love each other, truly.'

'I hope so girl, I hope so.'

'and...he doesn't drink well, not much.

'For that we'll be thankful.'

The ribbons on the petticoats were tied, not too tightly and then the gown was slipped over her head. She stood whilst Clarrie buttoned her up.

'My, my girl,' she grumbled humorously as her fingers struggled with the tiny buttons and perfect, tiny buttonholes, 'howsoever is George going to get this off you tonight? Shall I come over?'

'Don't you dare.'

Finally, it was done. Nell twirled in a circle enjoying the way the skirt belled out over its' petticoats. She turned a shining face to her mother who handed her the lilies.

'Am I alright, really?'

'You're the most beautiful bride there has ever been.' Clarrie wiped a tear from her cheek and arranged her own bonnet, trimmed with red, sateen ribbons.

'Silly. Is it time, shall we go?'

Clarrie looked out the window. The village would walk the bride to church. The sun was shining on the assembled families as they waited. Tiny white marshmallow clouds floated along in the cerulean blue, songbirds sang in cottage gardens and Nell stood in Helen's white satin pumps in the doorway of her cottage. All of a sudden she was frightened, was she doing the right thing?

Then she saw Shipshape, smart as paint waiting up the road, good and solid. Her father, cleaner and smarter than she had ever seen him stepped forward to take her arm and her mother fussed behind. All her brothers and sisters formed up, their faces shiny with Robert's soap and their tidy clothes made good in the preceding days. All wore something new. Boots for the boys, dresses for the girls and they stared in wonder at their Nell, a beautiful creation in a blue dress with lots of flowers everywhere.

Nell heard a spontaneous burst of applause as she reached her gate, smiling faces swam before her eyes and in a panic she realised she hadn't got a handkerchief.

'Mother,' she hissed sideways, 'I don't have a hankie.'

'Here,' Clarrie handed her the tiny square of lace lovingly saved from the petticoat. Nell dabbed her eyes, straightened her back and stepped out.

Normally Mr Noble the schoolmaster played the old harpsichord in the church. For Nell's wedding he had arranged with Simon to play together. Everyone had rushed to get into church and Nell and Joe stood in the porch taking a breath. They could hear quiet music, but as they stepped through the door the harpsichord swelled out with Simon's flute playing a counter melody of an old madrigal they had chosen together.

'Oh Dad, it's beautiful,' ell sniffed.

'Hush, girl,'

Slowly they walked up the aisle and she nearly gasped out loud as she saw her Aunt Violet in the pew with a tall bearded man. Her dear George was standing, waiting near the pulpit and everything was perfect.

The hymns and service seemed to pass in a dream. All of a sudden it was time for George to kiss his bride. A slim gold ring, brand new from Mr Way was on her finger. As she stood at the top of the aisle waiting to walk out her eyes took in all the flowers. The air was heavy with the scent of roses and a bee buzzed amongst the lavender spikes set along the window ledges.

'My beautiful wife.' George took her arm and tucked it into his. They had experimented to see if he could hold his damaged left arm up for her to take it and discovered that with a little effort they could manage.

Accordingly, they walked back along the aisle, with the harpsichord playing Glory to God on High and the flute's piercingly sweet tones echoed through the church.

They stood in the doorway blinking in the bright sunshine as everyone streamed out behind them.

Robert waited to walk out with Violet. He was surprised and delighted to see her, even if she did have her husband with her. She was looking very elegant in a fawn dress, trimmed with brown ribbons. A cropped matching jacket was edged in velvet and the small hat, perched on her head seemed to have a lot of chicken feathers on it.

Nell and George stood at the lych gate, waiting for everyone to come out of church to make up the procession behind them. To avoid having a shower of rice over them, George had got in first with a shower of farthings and halfpennies, thrown for the children to scamper for. They all rushed and scrambled in the dust, with admonishments from their mothers to try and keep clean.

'I think I'm the happiest person in the whole world,' Nell turned a radiant face up at George and he smiled tenderly,

'That's me, my love, we'll share, this day and every other, till death us do part.'

'Oh, George.'

Robert cleared his throat. 'Ah, hmm, I think we're all ready, would the happy couple like to start off?'

Slowly the procession walked down the village street. Laughter, jokes and good cheer created a jolly atmosphere and Simon's flute played Greensleeves and other tunes that he thought of as he walked. It was the music that mattered, not the words and the children danced and skipped while the adult's stomachs rumbled at the thought of all that food waiting for them.

The two chairs from Nell's cottage had been brought over and placed at the centre of the table. A pretty arrangement of honeysuckle and cream roses was placed in front of their plates. Robert had even folded up two napkins and laid them by their knife and fork. Two of his best glasses waited for their wine. It had been agreed that wine would be served to the immediate family, and cider and beer to the rest. The children had to sit outside on the grass with whatever beakers and mugs they could share. Lemonade and milk was waiting for them.

Eagerly the villagers filed into the barn with oohs and aahs of delight at the feast spread out before them. Supervised by Susan Bates the children queued up for their pasty and fruit tart. The women moved around passing plates and refilling. Fanny and her husband Abel were in the kitchen slicing up the pork.

A huge platter of the golden, crispy crackling was taken out to the barn, along with two dishes of sage and onion stuffing balls. Two large trenchers from the Ewe and Lamb were piled up high with slices of steaming meat. It was so tender that it fell off the bone and Abel, perspiring heavily in the heat popped a sample into his mouth.

'This is a dam tasty pig, Fan,' he huffed a bit, having burnt his mouth.

'Well, leave some for the others,' she retorted, taking a morsel for herself.

Two large saucepans of buttered potatoes had to be carried out by Robert and Caleb. They placed them on the table for each person to help themselves and pass it on. The mothers with a baby on their lap mashed up food on the side of their plate. Two large bowls of apple sauce in Byclere china were handed round. Robert made a mental note to keep an eye on them and send a note to Cook afterwards to thank her for the Estate's contributions.

He was sitting with Nell on his right, Elizabeth Farthing on his left and Mr and Mrs Calloway next to her. Violet and her husband were opposite. It was difficult to talk over the level of noise and laughter

Ben was in charge of the drinks. He had set up a strong table to support the barrels. Sukey and two children ran round with beakers, mugs and tankards of cider and ale. There was also elderflower champagne and last years' blackberry wine for the ladies. Having poured wine for the bridal party Helen left the bottles on the table and helped herself to a glassful of the mellow blackberry. She sat down next to Simon.

He was actually enjoying himself. For once he could be himself without feeling inferior to his aristocratic friends. The merriment and coarse jokes that started to flow with the consumption of alcohol made him laugh and he ate and drank feeling quite uninhibited. Robert watched with pleasure, feeling that his old Simon was still there under the adolescent disdain.

Simon was still keeping an eye on Sukey though. He watched the way she teased and flirted, deliberately leaning over a young man, letting her breasts rise to his eye level. More than one speculative look followed her. Helen had given her an old gown. A green and white striped cotton and Sukey had trimmed it with red ribbons. She laced it up tight and her pert, young breasts were straining at their leash.

Joe, a widower for many years watched his daughter and saw her mother in her. Rosemary had been pretty and wilful, marrying Joe because as village carpenter and undertaker she thought they would have a good steady income. Even then he had been thin, with a reedy voice and bad taste in jokes. Rosemary with their second babe had died in childbirth. He knew that even at fourteen Sukey was wanton and was casting around for a husband for her. He wanted her wed before she got herself pregnant.

He turned to his neighbour, chortling with glee, 'Charlie are you enjoying yourself?'

'Course I am, this pork's done us proud. Why...?' knowing Joe of old.

'I recognise this trestle top, I had old Bertha Jackson on the very spot where your plate is now, looked a treat she did when I'd finished with her.'

Charlie looked at him calmly, for once in a shirt and neckerchief. 'And your bit of table top has been in a Bates cottage.' Charlie had his own very large tankard, taking at least a pint and a half and he drank vigorously, enjoying Joe's discomfiture. 'Course it's been well scrubbed...I hope.'

Two truckles of Robert's cheese were brought out along with dishes of butter and bowls of spiced onions. New crusty bread had been sliced to fill up any holes still remaining.

Robert cut small squares of his cheese, piled it on a dish and asked Sally Bates to hand it round the children. They were all getting very full and some would probably be sick as some stomachs were unused to so much food.

A box of sweetmeats had been kept back for later. As apple pies, gooseberry tarts and damson puddings were dished out onto plates and bowls the village of Appley started to declare itself well and truly replete. Caleb brought in the brown pottery pitchers of fresh cream from the dairy and doled out a spoonful onto each portion. Then it was discovered that there were not enough spoons and so good humouredly neighbour shared with neighbour.

Robert leaned across to ask Violet. 'How is the shop getting on?'

Her eyes lit up, 'It's going very well, isn't it, Albert? We've taken on three new sewing girls but, having seen Fanny's stitching on Nell's buttonholes I could do with her up with us. I've not seen such fine work for a long time. I'm going to recommend her to Lady Byclere. There's always room for a fine seamstress up at the House.'

Oh, thought Robert. He couldn't stand in the way of Fanny bettering herself but she had promised to come and work when Nell was unable and judging by the soft looks on George's face and her glowing eyes there would be a baby in nine months time.

Robert left the women to clear up. The tables and trestle tops were cleared away for dancing and the men were drinking and smoking pipes and cigars outside in the yard. He hadn't had a chance to speak further to Violet but he did want to have a word with her to find out how she was and if the marriage suited her.

After five he was in the dairy with Caleb starting to milk when, in his usual blunt way Caleb said,

'Violet and her new man don't seem very lover-like.'

Robert stopped in mid-strip of Belle's udder and realised that Caleb had put his finger on what was not exactly bothering him, but had made him wonder.

'She loves talking about the shop but yes, they don't act like newly weds, mind you they are in their forties. You don't bill and coo at that age.'

'True, well I just hope he's good to her, after the way Ned treated her all those years.' Caleb took a full bucket out to the calves, careful not to slop it on his best trousers.

Robert was in the dairy later, putting the milk to cool. He didn't want to do anything with it until the morning when he would start butter. It was pleasant to be on his own, quiet and reflective when he heard the tap of a shoe and saw Violet come in.

'My you're looking smart,' he told her, beaming with pleasure.

'Thank you, Robert and is that a new shirt from Banbury?'

'Yes, you weren't here to make me one. But never mind that, tell me how are you? Are you happy, content?'

'Yes, the shop is going really well. We have some of the smartest people in London coming in so I have to keep up with all the latest fashions. In fact I have been known to start a fashion.'

'I'm really pleased for you, you deserve it, both of you,' he added hastily. 'But, you haven't told me if your marriage is happy.'

Her face closed up, she looked serious.

'What is it Violet?' He asked, alarmed.

'Nothing, we're getting along well. Albert actually sews a fine, straight seam himself. He's making gentlemen's coats and trousers, he's quite a tailor.'

'Violet, what is it you're not telling me? I can see Albert is a good tailor, but what about your marriage?'

She chewed her lip anxiously and gave him a tight little smile.

'Violet?'

She made up her mind. 'Well it hasn't turned out quite like I thought, but,' at his anxious face, 'we get on well enough.'

'That doesn't sound very cosy.'

'Oh we're cosy enough in the evenings. Sometimes we have a glass of Madeira, I can afford that now. Well, I'll tell you, but you mustn't let it go any further than these four walls.'

'Good heavens Vi what is it? If he's hurt you I'll...' He stepped up to her and took her hands in his, looking down at them, so pale and delicate.

'No, it's nothing like that. It's well, we don't sleep together. Fortunately there are two bedrooms above the shop, one's a bit small but it suits him. To be honest Robert, he prefers men. You know what I mean.'

'Of course I do. Oh Violet what have you done?'

'Don't look so alarmed. I just thought he was a gentleman before we were wed, not pressing me for...you know. Just a peck on the cheek he gave me. On our wedding night he said he was sorry, but that was the way he was.

He was in the Army for five years, he's been around a bit, and it seems that that was where he found his taste for other men. He has promised and kept to it that he'll never bring one home. He goes out once or twice a week, he has a friend who lives in Chelsea and he stays there the night. But he's always home clean and tidy to open the shop. I'm not complaining.'

Robert held her hands, then pulled her into his arms. His voice muffled into her hair he whispered dolefully,

'I miss you.'

'And I miss you.'

'I wondered how you were getting on. I prayed he was kind to you. I never thought of that. He tricked you.'

'Yes, and I can't deny I was worried what the bedroom would be like. After Ned you know how wary I was, but you changed all that. You were so kind and caring. You still could be.'

'What do you mean? Do you want to stay with me, share my bed?'

Her eyes sparkled, 'Yes, Albert is going to visit a friend on the Byclere estate, he'll be away all night and I've been hoping you would let me stay.'

'What about the village, what will they say?'

'Nothing, Albert will be with me, he'll go out later, no one will see and you and I can have time to ourselves.'

'What about Simon?'

'Oh, yes, that changes things. But have you noticed him looking at the Armitage girl? She's a tease and he's smitten.'

'He's only thirteen.'

'Old enough Robert, old enough.'

Simon's several glasses of wine made him thirsty and boisterous. He palled up with some younger Bates boys and Sukey and Lucy Talbot. They were larking about in the field behind the barn throwing stones at a line of bottles set up on the wall. Broken glass was carelessly left in the grass. Clemmie Bates and Simon were having difficulty aiming and ended up falling over. As he staggered and fell Simon pulled Sukey down with him,

'Gerroff.' she squealed laughing but allowed herself to fall elegantly to the ground, with her dress blowing up to show off her shapely calves.

The boys whistled at the sight and Simon rolled over to put an arm over her.

'Now my beauty, let's be having you.' He tried to put his lips on her saucy breasts.

'Think you're a man now, do you?'

'I am a man,' he assured her, with a voice only half broken.

'Well prove it then, fellow me, lad.'

'Sukey.' Lucy was shocked.

'Lucy is a virgin, Lucy is a virgin,' Sukey chanted as she scrambled up and pulled Simon to her. 'Come on, round the back way.'

Lucy, Clemmie and Tim watched her go.

'She's a slut, that one,' she announced, her accusing voice belying her dainty face and curly black hair. 'I'm never going to be like that.'

'Pity.' Said Tim and got a slap on his cheek.

Once in the back of the house Simon and Sukey crept along the passage shushing each other. They tiptoed up the stairs as quietly as they could. Simon pointed out the creaking fourth stair and they made exaggerated steps up over it.

He opened his door for her and gave a tap on her rump to push her in.

She giggled. 'Keen aren't yer.'

'Wait, I'll get some...' he made a hand to mouth gesture and ran lightly back downstairs and into the parlour. Robert's best rum, was on the table with a small tumbler. Simon grabbed the bottle, took another glass from the corner cupboard and ran back to the door. He listened carefully, all was quiet. He had seen his father outside and hoped he would stay there talking and drinking. Suddenly there was the scrape of a fiddle and voices shouting. The dancing had started and he hoped no one would miss them.

He shut the bedroom door behind him and gasped. Sukey was lying on his bed with just her drawers on. They were white cotton sprigged with blue forget me knots and tied above the knee with lacy ribbon. Her body was smooth with a pearly sheen to her skin and her breasts were beautiful beyond his wildest dreams. He was still a virgin, but after listening to the boys in school he was sure he knew all about it.

With Violet in front of him, they left the dairy, Robert closing the door behind him. He didn't want anyone, particularly children slipping in and dipping their finger in the cream or helping themselves to cheese. They heard voices and Robert stopped, his hand on Violet's arm.

'I hope he's up to it, Sukey's a powerful hot girl when she gets going.'

'I think you're all disgusting.'

'It's natural Lucy, only what Mothers and Fathers get up to. Well, most of them.'

'Well I'm waiting until I'm married, so don't you go getting ideas, Clemmie Bates.'

'So you don't have a fancy for our snooty Simon?'

'No, anyway he wouldn't look at me. That Sukey Armitage throws herself at boys...and men.'

Their voices died away. Robert and Violet looked at each other. With one accord they hurried towards the barn.

'He's not in here. We'd better look in the house. Perhaps they've gone up to his room.'

Searching downstairs took only a minute and with his hand on the banister Robert looked at Violet. 'It's all right, I'll take over, Sukey can look after herself, Simon doesn't know it but he needs protecting from girls like her.'

'I'll wait here.' Briefly she clasped his warm hand.

Robert gave a perfunctory knock on the door and opened it. He braced himself for the scene before him. A stark naked, pale and skinny Simon was leaning over a recumbent, voluptuous Sukey.

'Father.'

'Miss Armitage, get dressed immediately. Simon get dressed and see me in the parlour in five minutes and bring the rum bottle and glasses with you.'

Robert clumped heavily back down stairs and sighed gloomily. 'We were right Violet, they're both up there, I've told Simon to see me in the parlour. I'll wait in there, Sukey can go out through the back door. He's going to be furious with me, I'll probably get sulks and tempers for days now.'

'I'll go back to the dancing and see you later.' She touched his cheek lightly with her lips and with a swirl of skirts was gone.

Dusk was setting in and the lantern light shone out across the yard. Picking her way she went back inside and was soon engulfed in the hot, smoky atmosphere of foot stamping, twirling villagers. Red faced and perspiring, the men stamped on their partners' feet, bumped into each other as they moved the wrong way and called good natured insults to each other. Dances were rare and so skill was minimal but enjoyment was paramount and everyone wanted to live the evening to its full.

Without his bottle of rum, Robert sat and waited. He heard steps trips lightly down the stairs, hesitate and then after a minute the back door was slammed. What a cheeky minx he thought. More steps, heavier and Simon came into the room. He set the bottle and glasses down hard. Robert winced as the glasses took the brunt of Simon's ill temper.

'Sit down.' He said quietly. 'Would you like a glass?' He poured a tot of rum and pushed it over

'Yes.'

'I knew what was going on because I heard your 'friends' talking about you and Sukey. I'm sorry Simon. Sorry I had to walk in on you, but you need saving from a girl like that. She's barely fifteen and already a wanton. What would you do if she got pregnant? Joe is looking for a husband for her. She's been seen in Banbury picking up men. She could have a disease already. Don't get me wrong, she's a nice enough girl but she's not for you.'

'Have you finished? Has it occurred to you I know what I'm doing? I'm old enough to know about these things, Father and you burst in to my room and humiliate me. I know she's a whore but she says there's a village remedy to stop babies. I just wanted to...' Simon was icy cool but he couldn't say how upset he'd been when Lansing had stayed and gone off with Sukey that night. He was furious with his father. Once again he'd lost the chance to lose his virginity. He drained his glass in one, gasped and spluttered as the rum hit his throat and with his eyes watering strode to the door.

'I'll go to the barn, if that's all right.'

'Of course, but try and keep a clear head.'

Robert sipped his tot, suddenly full of indecision. Had he done wrong, should he have let events take their course. Simon was growing up, he expected him to behave responsibly like a man but not to have a man's lusts. 'Dammit he's too young, he can wait until he finds a respectable young lady.' He felt confused and uncertain, how was he going to manage Simon in the years ahead. He didn't want him to go wrong, he just wanted him to have some respect for his father and their way of life.

He took the glasses to the scullery and rinsed them carefully, leaving them to drain on a soft rag. He would go out to the barn for some company.

Robert watched the dancers Violet was laughing in the arms of her husband, Nell and George were standing in a corner with their arms around each other with only a pretence of dancing. It seemed even the children had partners. He felt lonely and old. Sitting next to the fiddler was Simon, playing his flute and tapping his foot in time to the music.

He felt a hand on his arm and looked into the opaque eyes of Margie wearing her best black dress.

'With your strong arms I reckon I could have a dance.' Grinning she said, 'but no sailors hornpipes, mind.'

'Margie, I'd be proud to and I promise, it will be strictly Strip the Willow.'

Margie was wearing her best boots, second hand but better than her everyday ones. She trod on Robert's foot as he went left and she moved right. Not concentrating she commented,

'Where's that Bayley? I hasn't heard him all day, 'cept in the church. Have they left him in charge in the Ewe?'

Robert held her firmer, ignoring the perspiration odours that assailed him. 'Do you know, what with one thing and another I've forgotten about him. That's awful, he's missing all the fun. I'll go and get him after this dance. What are Ben and Helen thinking of?'

'Their profits.' She said cynically, 'they might miss a passing customer if there's no one there. Bayley can pour a pint and cut bread and cheese as good as anyone.'

The music stopped, Robert bowed over Margie's hand and she simpered at him as he thanked her. Robert strode over to where Ben was standing by the table with the barrels and flagons on it. The ex-soldier's face was flushed a dark crimson. He was mixing brandy and ale and was very drunk. Too drunk to dance with Helen who was partnered by Charley.

As long as no one crossed Ben he was an amiable bear.

Robert was drenched in fumes of alcohol but spoke reasonably, knowing Ben's temper.

'I think I'll slip down the Ewe and fetch Bayley, he's missing all the fun.'

'He's been told to stay, Helen told him to serve if anyone came in. If he couldn't manage he was to run up here.'

'Well it's after eight, no one's going to turn up now. I'll stay there if you like.'

'Up to you Shipshape, mustn't leave the inn un...t.tended, Lord Byclere wouldn't like it.'

Robert turned on his heel, that last thought had been a brainwave, he wouldn't mind an hour of peace and quiet. He stopped by Fanny,

'I'm going down to fetch Bayley, would you give him some victuals when he comes?'

'Course, I'll sort him out.'

Robert walked through the back door of the inn calling, 'Bayley, where are you.'

Dressed in his smartest, but shabby breeches and a clean shirt Bayley dashed to Robert.

'Uncle Robert, can I get you a drink?'

'No, lad, thank you, I'll stop here a bit, you get off to the barn, there's dancing now and Mrs Bewick says she'll lay you on some food.'

'But Uncle...?' The boy frowned, conscious of his orders.

'I've squared it with your father, off you go, enjoy yourself.'

Bayley flashed him a brilliant smile. He was turning into a good looking child, bright and eager, with dark blue eyes and jet black hair with no resemblance to Helen or Ben. His mother always said he was the image of her Canning grandfather whom no one could dispute as he was long dead.

Robert walked through into the kitchen and thought he'd make a cup of tea. The fire in the hearth was mostly hot ash so he tucked some logs in and swung the kettle over.

Helen's tea caddy was high up on the shelf and he stretched up and brought it down. He always brought her a quarter of tea back from Banbury after market. She often forgot to pay him so he felt he was owed a cup or two. Everywhere was clean and tidy and he knew it was Bayley's work. The table was scrubbed white and the flagstones were still damp. The lad was a good worker and completely unappreciated. Robert made his tea in the old brown teapot and then took it out to sit by the front door.

Not a soul was to be seen. He could faintly hear the sound of music, laughter and the occasional whoop as partners changed and dancers stamped and twirled. He breathed in the cooling air. Late roses glowed white in the dusk. Bats swooped overhead picking off insects and the beat of wings told him an owl was hunting. He drained his cup, went back inside and locked the door. He had better go back and see what was happening. He thought again of Mary and wondered if she had liked dancing. It would have been enjoyable to dance together and then at the end of the evening go upstairs to their bed, to share the night.

Nell and George wanted to leave the barn quietly with no fuss and ceremony but it was not to be. They arranged to leave separately but everyone was up to that trick and as George started to sidle out the back door and Nell leave at the side a shout went up.

'They're bedding.'

Nell saw Robert, holding the arm of Margie. She mouthed a comical expression of dismay at him but he called, 'Grin and bear it, Nell.'

'Come on, our Nell.' Called Clarrie, ready with a garland of flowers. Appley had its own traditions where newlyweds were concerned. George was thrust forward, a garland placed around his neck and rope was tied around their waists linking them together. Laughing and calling out ribald comments like, 'Not long now

George, is ee ready?' and 'Way up Nell, your George is a lusty fellow,' they all made their way, in a procession, down the lane. The fiddler scraped his bow across and Simon played the flute in a somewhat strange rendition of "Here we go gathering nuts in May".

They arrived at the freshly painted door of Nell and now George's cottage. It had been locked on purpose. However they had forgotten the back door and Clarrie and Susan had been in earlier with flowers from the church.

There was a small fire in the grate made with some of Robert's precious sea coal. The kettle was suspended over, gently steaming. Two mugs were placed on a tray with a teaspoon. A chocolate drink was waiting for them. Two large bowls of flowers were on either side of the stairs leading up to the small bedroom under the eaves. The beautiful nightdress had been placed on the bed next to George's new nightshirt brought in by Elizabeth. Flowers were strewn on the bed and a vase of roses was in the corner.

Nell stood in the centre of her kitchen beaming with pleasure. It was all so lovely. Even a little fire was crackling in the hearth and Robert's drinking chocolate set out in beakers for them. She looked round at all the people cramming in through the door.

'You might as well go back to dancing: My husband,' at this there were hoots and whistles, she continued with dignity, 'my husband and I shall have a drink of chocolate before retiring

'Oh we wants to see you in your nightdress, Nell.' Joe chortled, 'we're not going 'tils we've seen thee bedded.'

'Certainly not, I'll wave to you from the window. Now all of you go outside and wait.'

George handed her the cup of chocolate and whispered, 'best get it over with, lass.'

'Get what over?' asked Charley whose great bulk seemed to fill half the room.

'These shenanigans.' Said George, 'now we'll give you a wave from the window. If you don't clear this room in a minute I'll fire off my rifle and pepper your hides.'

'Come on then everybody,' yelled Charley, 'he means business.'

The tiny upstairs window was already open, in the stifling, hot room.

Nell pulled the pink brocade curtains across and saw her mother hovering in the doorway. George was standing by the bed looking uncertain.

'Thank you, mother, we'll be quite fine now, no need to stay.'

'Would you like help with your dress, Nell, they're tiny buttons, too little for George's big fingers.'

'No, mother,' said Nell firmly, 'if George can pot on a tiny seedling I'm sure he can manage my buttons. Good night.'

Clarrie gave her daughter a kiss. 'It were a lovely day, I'm sure you're both going to be very happy.' Reluctantly she edged through the door. They heard her steps down the stairs and waited for the front door to close.

'I've put the bar down on the back door, to stop intruders, shall I slip down and lock the front.' George had carefully hung his jacket on the nail in the beam.

'It might be wise, I don't trust them. Could you undo my buttons please?' Nell sat on the bed. The white linen sheets and blanket smelt clean and fragrant with lavender. The pillows were filled with new duck down and the colourful patchwork cover had been her labour of love over many lonely winter evenings. She was bursting with pride as she looked around the small room.

'Stand up, lass.' George's hands trembled a little as he carefully pulled the tiny pearl buttons through. He pushed the dress off her shoulders and brushed his fingers lightly across her skin. Underneath was the petticoat, tied with ribbons. Nell's dress pooled around her feet and she stood, mesmerised as George bent his lips to her neck.

'What's going on up there?' was a loud call from outside.

'Oh for heavens sake, snapped George with his shirt off and his best trousers half unbuttoned. 'Nell we'll put our night things on and give them a wave and then perhaps they'll go back to the dancing.'

All romance was lost, the loving mood shattered and quickly they undressed. George opened the window and looked down at the pool of pale faces gazing up at him. Nell squashed up against him in the tiny window frame.

'Satisfied?' George demanded. Now go back to the barn.'

'She be pretty as a picture,' declared Joe, 'I'll change places with you any day, lad.'

'But I won't change places. I like him as he is, big and strong, you're a scrawny old rooster, Joe.' Nell pointedly shut the window to the sound of laughter. She pulled the curtains to and looked to her husband. He had opened the door,

'This lets a bit of air in. Well after all that I think...I think I just want to look at you. Did you mean it, you like me big and strong? I have got a gammy arm and my hearing's bad.'

The candle shone bright and true on the little bedside table made from an orange box brought home from Banbury. Nell's face glowed with good health and her brown eyes were radiant.

'George, I meant every word of our vows today, I'm glad I waited for you, but you'll have to be patient with me, you knows I'm untouched.'

'Aye lass,' he carefully lay down beside her, 'I'm more full of love and pride and happiness than I can say. I'll admit I've known a few women, but they were nice girls and I've not been free with myself like some of them were. Naming no names.'

'Enough of this.' Nell put her lips to his and they relaxed into each other's arms.

The candle guttered and burnt away. The covers were pushed off in the heat of the night and Nell and George slept under a single sheet, their sweaty bodies close together as the revellers made their drunken way back home. Voices called out slurred good nights. Men hitched sleeping children up into their arms, and let the silver globe of the harvest moon light their way.

In the barn at Southwell's somnolent bodies lay stretched out, snoring on piles of straw thrown down for them. These were the families and some single men who had come from the other side of the estate and were in no fit state to walk the miles home. Robert found some threadbare old blankets that Mary had folded up with lavender sachets and left in the attic. These kept off the cool night air. No one heard the rustling of rats and mice scurrying about, feasting on the scraps.

When the church clock struck three George stirred and woke. Carefully, he pushed himself off the bed and pulling the curtain aside opened the window. The night breeze cooled his hot body and he stood enjoying the quiet air. His wedding day had been a bit of a trial for him. The noise and music was hard to bear but he would have borne much worse for his dear Nell. He looked at her, bathed in moonlight, fast asleep with her hair loose on the pillow. She felt the fresh air and stirred. Smiling sleepily she said shyly,

'George, come back to bed.'

'Would you like a drink of water, my throat's parched.'

'Please.'   She pulled herself upright and watched him disappear, stark naked. She heard the back door open as he went to relieve himself and realised that she would have to get used to all sorts of intimate happenings now.

They sat together on the bed with the sheet over their feet. Their naked bodies cooled rapidly and shivering a little Nell squirmed into the warmth of his shoulder.

'Lass you're beautiful,' George carefully put the glass down and wrapped his arms around her. Take it slow the second time was the only advice his father had ever given him.

The timbers of Southwell's farmhouse creaked and groaned as they settled in the changing temperature of the night. Mice scuttled along the wainscoting their pouches full with debris cleared up from the floor of the barn. It had been a banquet for the vermin. Children had dropped crumbs, babies had dropped crusts of bread from tired fingers and the adults became careless. After everyone was sated with food and drink the leftovers were piled onto plates and put in the scullery by Fanny. She covered it with a cloth but this was no barrier to the mice.

In Mary's large bed, in what was now the spare room, Robert and Violet slept. The windows were wide open. When the cock started crowing at half past five Robert woke from habit. Feeling the cool air he got up and shut the windows to stop a draught on Violet. Quickly he dressed, wishing he could wash himself. His throat was dry, he felt itchy from the stale sweat on his skin and his hair needed a good brushing. In his stockinged feet he crept back to his room, sat and put his boots on and combed his hair, tying it back with a ribbon. Downstairs he poked at the embers and placed logs in the middle. The kettle was swung over and coffee spooned into the pot.

Walking out through the scullery he saw the plates of food left there by Fanny. There were crumbs all over the table and two dead mice on the floor. The cat had had a busy time. Robert stood in the doorway breathing deeply. It cleared his head and he knew what he had to do.

Last night had not been an unmitigated success. He had gone to Violet feeling guilty. Guilt that she was now married, albeit in a business way, and guilt that he was going to enjoy what he had denied to Simon.

Violet had been eager, but when Robert heard Simon walk down the passage and close his bedroom door he had stilled Violet's searching fingers and waited. He hoped that Simon had had enough to drink that he would fall asleep quickly and sleep soundly. He hushed Violet when she giggled and finally to keep her quiet he put his arm around her, pulled her close and kissed her soundly. Slowly, he relaxed and tried to put his mind to their pleasure. Already he had decided that this would be the last time, even if she came home again.

Simon had gone to bed unknowing of Violet's arrangements and assumed her husband would be with her. In spite of his temper with his father he had enjoyed the evening. He liked playing the flute and little Lucy Talbot who had been his shadow when he was six, had grown into a pretty girl. She had been rather shy with him but had talked intelligently. He had suggested a walk on the downs for later and she said she would ask her father.

When Robert stepped into the kitchen for his breakfast at half past eight the Turners both turned to bid him good morning. Albert looked spruce and dapper, recently shaved and a face innocent of any nocturnal games. Violet poured him coffee and remarked how he would miss Nell.

'She'll be back tomorrow,' he cut slices off a gammon, fresh out of the cold safe. 'She's only having one day off.'

'I expect George will be anxious to get back to work.' Albert helped himself to yesterdays bread and butter.

'I thought it was a lovely day, perfect for them. Are you going to church this morning, Robert?'

'No, I've cheese to start that I should have done yesterday. I expect you want to get off soon, are you getting the coach from Byclere House?'

'Oh well, we could stay another day. We don't open the shop on a Monday.'

'But it will take us a day or more to get back,' Albert reminded her.

'Yes, yes of course. Oh hallo, Simon, did you sleep well?'

'All right, I suppose,' he said ungraciously, 'I've got a headache, does Father have any remedies?'

Robert carried fresh milk in, 'Oh hallo, Simon, how are you this morning.'

'My head's banging and throbbing, what can I have?'

Robert surveyed his son, dressed in smart breeches and a clean white shirt. His handsome face was a picture of misery. He sat at the table and Violet silently gave him a beaker of black coffee.

'I'll get you some herbal concoction that Susan Bates gives out. It doesn't taste nice though. Are you going to church?'

'No, I'm taking Lucy Talbot for a walk.'

'Does her father know?'

'She's asking him.'

'Hmm, he might not be keen. He'll probably send along the brothers and sister as chaperones.'

Simon downed the glass of brown liquid and gagged. He leapt up and rushed out to the privy where he retched. They heard him groan and the handle of the pump squeak as he pumped up some water.

He came back with his face and hair wet, looking ashen. He poured some coffee, piled in sugar and sipped it. 'Oh, that's better.'

'Is that your first thick head?' enquired Albert jovially.

Simon had been to drinking parties in school, he thought it better to pretend and nodded, making a face.

CHAPTER THIRTY FOUR

By eleven o'clock Robert had the house to himself. It was suddenly quiet after the hullabaloo of yesterday. He made himself some fresh coffee, took it into the parlour and poured brandy in. He felt at odds with himself. He had been almost glad to see Violet go and he felt sad that he should think like that. She had made a new life for herself and it didn't include him. He didn't want her to think she could come back to Appley and take up with him just whenever it pleased her.

Fancy her marrying a man like that, couldn't she tell? He could see straight away that Turner was of that persuasion but then he probably had more experience. Violet was after all, a countrywoman, not that they didn't have men preferring men in the country as well as the towns.

Simon had gone off with Lucy Talbot, followed by nine-year old Bertie and five year Will who would get tired and drag his feet. He hadn't looked pleased but the younger boys seemed to think it a lark. At least Simon couldn't try and get up to anything with two pairs of sharp eyes watching his every move.

Robert felt at a loose end, there were jobs he could do but didn't feel like and he suddenly realised that it had been a long time since he had been out on the downs. He would take bread and cheese and have a walk.

Within five minutes he was striding down the lane. A wedge of his own Cheddar made at the beginning of January and cutting up well, with a crust of bread was tied up in some cheese muslin and two rosy James Greaves apples nestled in his pocket. Feeling light of heart he took the old drovers lane out of Appley heading for Minchampton and Lasing.

It was a warm, late summer day. The air was soft with a mild southwesterly breeze and a few clouds scudded across a bright blue sky. He felt good to be alive, a bit lonely but contented himself with the thought of Simon being there in the evening. Perhaps they could have a game of cards and enjoy a glass of wine and talk. He must really make an effort to understand the boy.

Four miles and an hour and a half later, Robert was disconcerted to find himself out of breath and puffing as he climbed Whistlers hill. The view was spectacular, with miles and miles of grassy green rolling down all around him. Clusters of white sheep dotted the hillsides, there were cattle on the lower slopes and he used the excuse of watching a hawk dive on its prey to sit down.

'Oh, I'm getting old, I didn't use to huff and puff like this,' he told himself, 'my heart's not so good now. I'll have to do this more often to keep in trim.' His breathing slowed as he munched on his bread and cheese and ate one of the juicy apples.

'That was a nice bit of cheddar.' He was thirsty but there were no streams or springs nearby. He was out on the exposed hillside and looked around for a dell or dip he could sit in out of the wind and have a nap. Getting to his feet he stumbled a little. He felt some discomfort in his chest and thought perhaps the bread had been a bit stale or the apple a little sharp. He decided to press on and find a sheltered spot to sit down.

He turned the side of the hill meaning to walk round in a circle and head back to Appley The remains of an old shepherds hut was tucked into the lee and he headed down to it. It would shelter him, in the sun but out of the wind. He sweated suddenly and took his jacket off.

His chest was feeling rather strange, not like him at all. He sat down carefully, leant back against the faded timbers and closed his eyes. The wind made a soughing sound through the gaps in the planks. Quaking grass rustled around him, a distant sheep bell tinkled and his chin dropped down as he fell asleep.

He woke with a start as a sharp pain cracked across from his right shoulder down into his ribs. The muscles around his heart squeezed and he groaned, rubbing his chest, trying to get some relief.

'What's happening, am I dying?' He mopped his forehead, suddenly sweating, but clammily cold. 'Oh, oh, what can I do?' The pain stopped, but his whole chest felt bruised and he felt weak and sick. His watch said twenty past three o'clock, clouds were gathering and the air had turned chilly. He was quite alone, up on the down. No one knew where he was and he felt ill. Slowly he got to his feet, still trying to rub his chest. He pulled on his jacket and buttoned it up, needing the warmth of the old navy serge.

He looked around for a bit of a post he could use as a stick. A rather bent length of a weather bleached branch was on the ground. Carefully, feeling dizzy he picked it up and walking cautiously, like an old man, started to make his way down. He thought longingly of a hot drink. He would have a cup of tea when he got in and ask Cal to milk tonight.

He concentrated on his steps, choosing a flatter, easier path. He looked for a stream to have a drink and a wall to have a rest on. He still felt shaky and the twinges lurked in his chest sending out warnings. He watched the rain clouds building up behind him and felt the wind buffet him as he tried to hurry.

Using his stick he walked faster, ignoring the stabbing jolts. He must get down to shelter before it rained. If necessary he would stop at the first cottage he came to and ask to rest a while. They wouldn't mind. They could send a child on to Appley to give a message to Tom or Caleb. Perhaps Simon would be home. Yes he'd sure to be, he mustn't keep Lucy out all day.

Hunched into his jacket Robert made his way down the hillside. He shivered and when he caught his foot on a stone and stumbled a pain ripped through and he gasped and groaned. Trying very hard to concentrate he kept his eyes on the path, a narrow strip of beaten earth worn down by countless sheep hooves. It took him by surprise when he came out onto a track and saw with relief a small cottage tucked into the side of the lane.

A thin blue trickle of smoke plumed from the chimney and grateful to have got off the down he walked down the track. A raindrop plopped onto his head, followed by more. Gasping, he tried to hurry and grimacing at the cost of exertion he turned onto the muddy, narrow path to the front door. It was open and he reached it, holding on to the wall.

'Hallo.' He called.

A child, ragged, barefoot and grimy gazed at him with large eyes as if he was a visitor from a distant land. A young woman came over. She must have been in her twenties but hardship had aged her. Her brown hair was already fading, her face lined with discontent.

'Yes?' The place was barely more than a hovel. She was dressed in a grubby, old grey skirt and some one's long cast off white blouse. Another young child clung to her skirt, a girl with hair in rats tails, a little skirt tied up with twine and a top that looked like sacking.

'Do you think I could rest a while? I've been up on the down and taken a turn. It's raining and if I could just sit a while, I'll, I'll feel better.' He trembled.

'Come in, we've little to offer you.' The room was sparsely furnished, a small fire burnt in the fireplace, a meagre pile of sticks by it. A kettle hung over it and a rickety chair was placed in front. Two small stools were by the inglenook. An old table by the window was devoid of food, plates and crumbs. It was a labourer's cottage of the poorest sort.

'Sit down, have my man's chair. Where you from then?'

Carefully he eased himself onto the chair, aware of it's precious value.

'Appley, we had a wedding there yesterday and today I thought I'd have a walk on the downs, a nice bit of peace and quiet. But...' he rubbed his chest as a twinge flickered across.

'You overdone it probably. Would you like a cup of tea?'

'Oh yes please.'

Five minutes later he was drinking hot water. It was the weakest tea he had ever tasted. There was no milk or sugar. The rain drummed down outside and in the cottage it turned damp and steamy. At least it was warm and slowly he relaxed. He wondered how far it was to Appley and if he could walk it. Take it slow and easy. Would Tom or Caleb have a walk down to the dairy for a chat and miss him? Perhaps they'd call into the house, find him gone and start the milking. He'd left no note, told no one of his plan and he wasn't sure where he was.

'This is very good' He told the woman, sipping it gratefully. 'Could you tell me where I am, I haven't been round this way for a long time?'

'On the south side of the Byclere estate. My husband does labouring up there.'

'Oh good, you'll know George Farthing then. He married my dairy maid yesterday.'

'You'll be Southwell then, that's got the farm in Appley.'

'Yes, yes I am. I wonder, if it's possible, if you have an older child who could run to Appley for me and tell them I'll be home in a while. I'll pay you, of course, but I think I must take it slowly.'

'Reuben.' called the woman. After a few minutes a man appeared, his smock greasy and stained. He was wearing old boots tied up with twine and looked slightly simple.

'You walk to Appley and tells them Mr Southwell's been taken bad.'

'But it's raining.'

'Put a sack over your head, you'll be there in an hour or less.'

The man looked at Robert, sitting in his chair, with the chipped beaker of tea. The elderly man looked pale, his face was white with a hectic spot of colour on the cheeks. 'You looks bad. I'll go, I'll have my tea when I get back.'

He crammed a battered cap onto his head, put his head through the hole in a flour sack that hung down over his shoulders, front and back and stepped out. The rain was easing off a little and was now steady. The wind blew in and made the fire smoke. Robert coughed which made his chest spasm. Trying to calm himself he sat quietly watched by the silent children.

'I'm sorry, I don't know your name.'

'Mrs Lovett, those are Jenny and Sam. There's another who's gone up to help at the House.'

'Oh really, what's he doing?'

'She's pulling onions, ready for stringing. It's a few coppers and we're glad 'cos they don't normally work on a Sunday.'

Robert wondered how old the child would be, five or six perhaps and out working already? He watched the woman fetch a kettle from the back room. She brought back some carrots, potatoes, an onion and a small bone. She stood at the table, in the dim light of the dirty window and quickly peeled and chopped the vegetables. They were dumped into the saucepan, with the bone and water from the hot kettle. She put an old plate on top and placed it on a trivet standing in the hot ashes.

'There, they'll be done when he gets back. We eat well here.'

Robert thought of the wedding banquet, of the whole roast pig and the ham, the pies and pasties, the puddings and tarts and said nothing. His head fell onto his chest and he dozed, as his body relaxed in the warmth from the fire.

He woke with a start when he heard shouting outside. The door banged open and Tom's solid bulk filled the doorway.

'Here he is, what's up, Boss?'

Robert looked up, temporarily bewildered. He was in a strange cottage, it was getting dark and here was Tom. He moved stiffly and felt his chest again. Carefully he stood up.

'This good lady has given me shelter and a cup of tea. My chest's playing up, I'd better start the walk back.'

'No need, I've brought the cart, it was two minutes to harness the hoss and Reuben here has had a lift back. I took the liberty of a sixpence from the pot for him and a bite of cheese for the missus.'

Tom handed over a large slab of cheese, wrapped in muslin. The woman's eyes lit up and the children moved closer.

'Thank you kindly, there was no need.'

'Well the rain's less so if you take my arm, Shipshape, the path here is a bit slippery with the mud we'll get you up and home.'

Robert was ashamed of the fuss, he protested his good health but was overridden. Within five minutes he was up on the wagon, his old boat cloak tucked around him and Tom at his side clicking to Binnie to trot along smart like.

It was a relief. He hadn't relished the thought of walking home in the gathering gloom. The sky was a sullen, leaden grey and it would be dark early.

In his weakness tears trickled down his face, Tom glanced over and patted Robert's knee.

'Is...?'

'Yep, Cal is milking, it's all under control and Simon's gone over to Byclere.'

'Simon's gone to Byclere,' Robert echoed faintly feeling unreasonably disappointed.

'There was a message come, did he want to go fishing. He'd just got back from his walk with the Talbots' and he leapt at it. Went off whistling, carrying his bag he did. So I suppose he'll be gone a day or two.'

'Oh. I hoped he'd be company for me tonight.'

'Well I'll stay the night, if I'll do instead. I think someone ought to keep an eye on you. What happened, anyway?'

Robert told him of the pain and the frightening walk back down the hill.

'I'm pleased you gave the man a sixpence and the cheese, my goodness aren't they poor.'

'Reuben's all right, a bit easy like, not such a regular worker. That's Annie Truby that was. What she saw in him we don't know, it was either the baby on the way or getting away from her father that did it.'

They swung out onto the lane from Byclere to Appley and Tom clicked Binnie into an easy trot.

'Does the bumping bother you, Boss?'

'No, not much, it's a relief to be riding home. It gave me a nasty twinge just to think of walking back. It's gone cold, hasn't it?'

Tom gave him a strange look. Robert was hunched up in his cloak with his jacket underneath. It was the first day of September, hardly chilly.

'I reckon you've overdone it. You was here and there yesterday, lifting trestles, carrying chairs and stools, milking and hither and thither. And you had visitors. That's more work and this morning you insisted on milking. To cap it all you goes up Whistler down, on your own.'

'It was a lovely morning, I felt like it.'

'You know why it's called Whistler Down?'

'No.'

'Cos you can whistle all day and no one will hear you. It's lonely up there, only fit for sheep…in the summer. They do say an old shepherd died in that hut up there and no one found him for months. The sheep were looking after themselves.'

Robert sighed, thinking of his kitchen and a cup of tea. When he realised that he hadn't brought in any wood for the fire he felt a anxious spasm cross his chest. Tom would help him, he would pay him extra. He just wanted to get in the warm, take off his clammy sweaty shirt and have a rub down. A nice clean shirt, a thick wool over top and some warm breeches would soothe his shivers.

They could eat left over scraps for their supper and share a noggin of rum. He dozed as they rumbled along aware that Tom didn't know how he had spent his night and that was a secret to stay close.

'We'll get the doctor out tomorrow. And don't argue.'

'Tom.' Robert woke up and tried to speak sharply, the man was impertinent. He was also a good friend and Robert subsided back with a, 'we'll see.'

They rumbled into the farmyard and were met with a welcoming party.

'I don't want any fuss, Tom.' Robert grumbled.

'They're here to help, just for the once let them look after you.' Tom spoke sharply.

Nell was at the door, George came forward to take the horse and Caleb poked his head round the barn door and called that the milking was done.

As if made of precious porcelain Robert was helped from the wagon and escorted in.

'What's all this?' Nell, looking pink and pretty had a worried frown. She was in her Sunday dress with an apron over the top.

'Just a turn, Nell, perhaps I went too far.'

'Never mind,' she soothed, 'you're home now, the kitchen's warm and there's a kettle boiling for your tea.'

Tom took the cloak, shook the rain off it at the door and hung it on the peg. The jacket was damp and given to George to hang by the cloak. Robert lowered himself onto his chair, grateful for the support of the arms and sighed. Nell draped his woolly gherkin round his shoulders and the warmth eased his pain.

'Oh, Nell, I stopped in a little cottage, so poor it was. Such a miserable fire, but she was kind. Tom took them some cheese but do you think they ought to have a few logs as well in the winter. It was so damp and oh so dismal.'

'Don't you worry about them now, just take it quiet. We'll have a think about them later on. Did you have some dinner with you.'

'Yes, I had some bread and cheese. It was that Cheddar from the end shelf, cut nice and firm it did and tasted well, just a little bit salty.'

'Yes, well I've got some soup on and you can start with that and then a little plate of mashed potatoes and ham. How does that sound?'

'You shouldn't be here today, it's your Sunday and after your wedding day.'

'Well George needs feeding and we had an early tea and walked over to see you. What should we find but Tom saddling Binnie in a rush and Cal milking. Margie went next door to Susan, so she's alright.'

'So the whole village knows...do they?'

'Probably,' she replied with equanimity, 'but the whole village cares as well.'

'Oh.' He hunched into the woolly warmth, feeling chilled to the bone.

'Tom, could you fetch me some clothes please, so I can change.'

'Of course.' Tom disappeared upstairs.

George came in with more logs, balanced on his left arm and arranged them tidily in the hearth. The fire was blazing merrily, Nell's small cauldron with her bacon and vegetable soup was simmering on the trivet and the potatoes boiled in the saucepan. An apple pie warmed on the inglenook. The golden brown leaves

arranged carefully on top glistened with crusty Demerara sugar.
Robert wasn't sure he could manage a lot of food but he would share
it with them. A small bowl of soup would be enough.

'What's this about Simon?'

'Apparently a message came over from Byclere that
Calloway's old father would take them down to the river to teach
them fishing. He'd packed his bag and was gone in a trice. Tell
Father I'll see him in a day or two he said.'

Nell took the potatoes to drain in the scullery sink and came
back with them. Briskly she whipped them round with a large knob
of butter, set a plate on top and put it on the inglenook to keep warm.

'Now,' she turned as Caleb came in the door.

'All finished, Boss, everything's tidy and I've put the milk in
the dairy to cool. We'll sort it in the morning, me and Tom.' He
took off his old coat and stood it in the corner with the rain water
running off and puddling on the floor. 'I washed up in the dairy, so
I'll just sit a minute, see how you are and then be off.'

'Stay and have some supper, please.' Robert thought he
sounded peevish, his voice seemed a bit weak and trembly and it
would have annoyed him if he hadn't felt so tired and cold.

'We had a good dinner today and I'd best get Margie back
from next door. I'll be up in the morning first thing so there's no
need for you to get up early. You take it easy a day or two, me and
Tom'll manage. Nell can look after you in the house, if she can tear
herself away from her George.' He said with a wicked glint in his
eye.

'I can assure you, I'll be here bright and early and George'll
be back at work as usual tomorrow.' Nell replied with dignity.

There was now a large pile of logs in the fireplace, more than
enough for two days or so.

'Is there anything else I can do for you?' he asked shyly.

'No thank you, George, I'm that grateful, I can't say.'

'Tom are you having some soup?'

'I will, lass thanks.' He sat at the table.

Nell ladled out two bowlfuls. Robert was given a napkin and
tucked it into his shirt. A bowl and spoon were handed to him and
murmuring his thanks he sipped at it. It was rich in vegetables, cut
up small as Nell knew how. There was parsley and chives chopped
and tiny pieces of bacon for flavour. He felt the food going down, a
hot feeling right to his stomach and slowly his body core warmed.
He knew it was doing him good. He looked at the others. Tom was
enjoying his and Nell and George were drinking tea.

'You're not having any?' he protested.

'We had ours before we came over, a cup of tea is enough and perhaps a slice of that pie.' Nell had her hand over George's on the table. Tomorrow they would be back to work as normal and their lovely wedding weekend would be over. She was looking forward to their second night, it should be a lot quieter than the first and they planned to go to bed early.

She was up and taking Robert's empty bowl as soon as he finished.

On a plate she had placed some finely sliced ham with a spoonful of mashed potato next to it. 'Would you like mustard or some of the soup on top?'

Robert shook his head, mustard might be a bit fiery and he had almost had enough. 'Just like that please.' He put the plate on his lap and used a fork to eat with. The ham was tender and he could taste the honey it had been baked with. One of Joe Armstrong's sidelines. He cured and smoked bacon. It was said he used an old oak coffin to soak his bacon in.

After they had finished and Robert had declined apple pie and with everything washed and put away, Tom and Robert sat with their feet to the smouldering logs. Tom had dragged in a parlour chair, and they sat side by side, with the light from the fire and two candles.

'You'd best get home soon, Elisabeth will wonder where you are.'

'No need, boss, I'll stay here tonight, she'll be alright, Nell said she'd pop in.'

'Oh I can't let you do that.'

'I'll sleep in the spare room if that's alright, then I'll be here for first thing.'

Robert was silenced, thinking of the bed in the spare room. The sheets hadn't been changed since his night with Violet, if Tom knew that Albert was homosexual then would he be able to tell? Surely not. He would just get in and go to sleep. When he felt better he would change the sheets himself and save Nell doing it. They had only made love the once, so with luck Tom wouldn't notice anything on the white sheet.

Quietly they sat on in the warmth of the fire. Tom edged his chair back and volunteered to get the rum bottle. Robert declined but told Tom to help himself.

'So after everything's done in the morning I'll slip over to Doc Newton and bring him back.'

'What can he do?'

'Just check you over, perhaps a spot of physic. He must know about these heart dos.'

'Well, I'll see in the morning.'

Tom smiled to himself, Shipshape was hoping to wriggle out of it. He'd pretend he was better. It was a worry though, what if he died, they could be out of jobs just like that. He really loved it at Southwell's. The flexible hours and the close proximity suited him down to the ground. That, the pay and the milk and cheese, Robert didn't know how generous he was compared to other farmers. Tom rubbed his chin thoughtfully, sipped Robert's best rum and watched him doze in the chair.

'Tom how old are you?'

'Oh, let me see. I was twenty two when George was born and he's twenty four now, so that makes me...' Robert let him work it out for himself. 'Is that forty six? Damn me that's old.'

'Not as old as me.'

'What would you be, Boss?'

'Fifty six. Now that is old.'

'Yes,' said tactless Tom, 'but look how fit you are. Cor, look at the work you do. Mind you,' he spoke slowly, 'you've been that busy these last few days getting ready for the wedding and then going on that long tramp. It's not surprising you had a bit of a do.'

'It was such a lovely morning, I felt like a walk.'

Yes but, you did the milking...on your own, put the cows out, set the milk in the dairy. Did you have breakfast?'

'Toast and preserve with Violet.'

'There you see,' Tom exclaimed, 'no proper breakfast, no eggs or bacon. Then that long walk. And you had a late night yesterday, what was it? I bet nearer half ten before you went to bed.'

If you only knew, thought Robert. Tom was right, it had been a lot for him and now he was paying the price. Weak as a baby, but he'd soon be back to normal. A good sleep would set him right.

'I think I'll take some hot water upstairs and have a wash before I get into bed.' Robert eased himself up stiffly.

'I'll take it up for you. Come on, you go up and I'll follow.' Tom picked up the big kettle, set it by the stairs and fetched a bucket and some cold water. In his bedroom Robert stripped off and lathered his hands in the warm water. As quick as he could he washed the bits he could reach.

Tom came in. 'Would you like me to rub your back over?'

Robert sat down with a thump on the chair, the effort had weakened him again. 'Just wipe me off could you, I'll rub down and get into bed.'

Tom's hands were gentle and he handed Robert the warmed nightshirt Nell had left on the inglenook. A wine bottle, tightly stoppered and filled with hot water had been placed for his feet.

He lay back in bed, grateful for the warmth, despising himself for his weakness and feeling very old.

'Tom, if I should...go in the night, my will's made but I'd like you and Cal to run the farm until Simon's old enough. I think I want Bayley to share in it as well. This has made me realise I could go at any time, I must order things properly.'

'Me and Cal will do what is necessary, but I'm quite sure you'll live many a long day. Just have a rest, take it easy and you'll soon feel better.'

'Goodnight, thank you.'

'Night, Shipshape, I'll be next door if you want me.'

Robert lay quietly, pondering. What a difference from last night. The wedding, Simon and Sukey nearly in bed together and then him and Violet. And Albert Turner slipping off like a thief in the night to meet a man friend. Who was it at Byclere that was of the same bent? His eyelids closed and he slept, fidgeting a little as his chest muscles flexed with the lingering after shock of the heart attack.

Robert slept through until nearly seven o'clock. He opened his eyes to a bright day and thought goodness gracious, I've sadly overslept. What will the cows think? Then he heard Tom's voice calling out,

'Cleo, Clara, come on there.' There was a clink of chains, the yard pump gushing water and nailed boots. Slowly Robert lay back and relaxed. He thought he heard the door close downstairs and then he heard Nell talking to the cat. It was a strange feeling to be in bed when he should be down there, part of it all. He sat up, swinging his legs out and breathed deeper experimentally.

There was no twinge, no nasty clutch at his heart and he said, 'There, it's better, no need for doctors. I'll just take it quiet a day or two.'

He found his, thick linen shirt and woollen gherkin to keep him warm and got dressed. Tom had taken away last nights' water so he knew he'd have to put his head under the pump. Or perhaps he'd have a bowl of warm water in the scullery.

Downstairs the kitchen was laid for breakfast. Three knives and forks and four beakers were on the table. The fire blazed cheerily with the kettle swung to the side keeping hot. The frying pan was full of sliced ham to heat and bread was ready to toast. His stomach rumbled in anticipation. Nell must be in the dairy. He thought of going out then decided he could have the breakfast ready for them. First he would see how they were getting on.

A heavy dew steamed in the early sun. He put his head in the dairy door,

'Morning, Nell. How are you getting on?'

'Shipshape, we didn't expect to see you up. How are you today? Should you be in bed?' She asked anxiously, stirring a pan of curds.

'I feel a lot better. I thought I could make the breakfast for you.'

'Oh no, no, I'll be in soon enough.'

Tom walked in with two pails of milk.

'Morning Boss, can't keep a good man down I see. How do you feel this morning?'

'Good as new.' Robert replied firmly.

'Well one of us'll slip off to the doctor after breakfast.'

'There's no need for that. It would be a waste of his time and mine.'

'I knew you'd say that. You didn't look too good yesterday. That's why me and Cal's sorted it between us. He left for Hazlebury ten minutes ago. Some one said they'd heard a new doctor was coming. Old Doctor Newton retired to his daughter in Banbury. So you don't want to upset this new one when he's come over special like.'

'Oh, alright. Breakfast will be in quarter of an hour, is that too soon?'

'Fine, boss, I'm nearly finished.'

Robert busied himself with frying the ham and toasting the bread. The plates warmed on the inglenook shelf and he laid out the hot slices. He fetched butter and milk from the scullery and put them on the table. Caleb could have something when he came back.

As he sat round the table later with Tom and Nell, Robert felt strangely tired. He couldn't eat all his ham and the cat had finished it off. She now sat cleaning her paws and with a licked paw wiped her face. She was black and white, a good mouser, with no name. He put plenty of sugar in his coffee and sipped it slowly. Nell had toast, blackberry preserve and coffee. Blushing a little she told them she had had breakfast with her husband, early.

Tom smiled slyly and commented, 'I expect you was hungry.'

Nell chose to ignore the innuendo, 'George has got a busy day ahead of him, he's deputy head gardener now. It's a lot of responsibility. I've got to send him off with a good breakfast in him.'

'Aye, lass.'

As Nell started to clear the table Robert tried to stop her.

'Nell I can do that.'

'Actually, Boss could you come and have a look at Carol, she looks close to calving so I put her in the orchard paddock.'

The two men went out discussing the cow and left Nell to quietly finish clearing the kitchen. She noticed that Robert had forgotten to leave the pan in soak and she took it out and scrubbed it with her gorse brush. Shipshape was definitely not his usual self.

CHAPTER THIRTY FIVE

The sun was warmed the air nicely and by ten o'clock it was comfortable for Robert to sit in a corner of the yard. He was shooed out of the dairy and told there was nothing left to do in the barn.

A chair was placed for him and he thought he'd fetch his journal when two men on horseback appeared at the end of the lane. One he knew immediately as Caleb riding bareback on Binnie and the other he assumed to be the doctor. He watched them come, squinting into the sun.

He suddenly felt a spurt of excitement. He knew that man, this doctor coming towards him on a large grey horse. He knew that white hair, the brown face and the upright figure sitting so easily after years of walking decks and slipping in the blood and muck of the orlop deck. He got up, striding towards them.

'Well, well. If it isn't Matthew Mason. What a turn up. What a nice surprise. Caleb, this is Dr Mason from the Celeste, he's the man who took the bullet from my shoulder. Take his horse, will you?'

Smiling broadly the two men shook hands, 'Robert, good to see you. As soon as your man here said it was Robert Southwell, I knew it must be you. I've put you first on my visits today.'

'Oh I'm fine now, there's been too much fuss. Come in, we'll have coffee and you can tell me how you came to be here.'

He led the way into the kitchen, pleased to see the table was clean, the fire burning brightly and the coffee pot put to warm. There was even ground coffee in the pot so Robert poured the boiling water on and stirred it round.

'Let's leave that to brew shall we. Your man tells me you had some sort of a heart attack yesterday. You were very cold and exhausted.'

'I did too much, went for a walk up on the down. I had a good nights' sleep and feel fine now.'

'Well I have my bag with me so take your shirt off and I'll listen to your heart. How old are you now?'

Robert sighed. 'Fifty six, but I'm fit and busy.'

'Too busy apparently. Sit down.' Matthew had a wooden listening device almost like a thin trumpet which he placed on Robert's chest. He walked round the chair, 'lean forward. Take a breath.' He placed the device all over Robert's back and chest.

'Hmm.'

'What is it?' asked Robert anxiously.

'How do you feel this morning?'

'Well, a little tired, cooking the breakfast took more out of me than I thought it would. And that's nothing. I've normally milked the cows before nine o'clock.'

'Tell me what happened. Stay there, I'll pour the coffee.' Matthew was firm and Robert was alarmed, feeling he was being treated like someone who was very ill.

'Well, on Saturday we had a wedding here, so Sunday, well yesterday morning was a lovely day so I thought I'd have a walk up onto the down.' Robert went on to tell the doctor of his pain. He glossed over the slow, stumbling walk down and the wait in the cottage. 'Anyway what brings you to these parts?'

'Firstly, let's keep to the point. You had a warning. You're a fit man but there are limits. I don't think you've told me everything but we'll let that go. You always were a close cove. Your heart sounds just a little bit irregular. Take life quietly, let others do the hard work. I'll put you up some physic to soothe it down a bit. Next time there's a wedding let others do the hard work. Is there a Mrs Southwell now?'

'No, I was married briefly, she died after giving birth. I have a son Simon, he's gone over to Bycleres to go fishing. This is my home and I turned farmer. It's been hard work but we tick over comfortably and I have good men and a good lass in the dairy.'

'Your body is telling you to take it steady.'

'I will, it will be quiet, once Simon is back to school and the harvest is finished. Now tell us how you came to be in Hazlebury.'

'You remember we had a Midshipman Lansing who got to be third lieutenant. Well he wasn't a bad lad and after Trafalgar I moved ashore and was senior physician at the Naval Infirmary in Plymouth. Lansing came in with problems after losing a hand at Trafalgar. I helped him and one day his mother came in to thank me. She said then if there was ever anything she could do I was to let her know. Even in twenty years she said.

They have large estates and there was always room for a retiring doctor who wanted a quiet life. Well last year I decided to retire and wrote to them. But then Waterloo happened and I went straight to Portsmouth and offered my services. I did what I could to help the soldiers, but it was an uphill struggle. The facilities there are very poor. Mrs Lansing had asked Byclere apparently who said he was desperate for a decent doctor to come over here. I didn't mind where I went as long as the air was fresh and clean. I couldn't get the stink of gangrene and corruption out of my nostrils. So I've been here a fortnight and I'm finding my way around.'

They were sitting at the table with their coffee and a plate of Nell's buttered scones when the door opened and she put her head around. 'Is everything all right?'

'Nell come in, meet my old friend and shipmate Doctor Mason. He's come to Hazlebury, isn't it a small world?'

Nell came in and bobbed, her face beaming with pleasure. At last she thought, Shipshape has a friend, a real proper friend. 'Please to meet you, doctor. How is he, or is that an impertinence?'

Robert was secretly amused, Nell had become confident with her new married status.

'He's not so bad, as long as he takes it easy for a bit.'

'Oh we'll make sure he does, Doctor.'

Robert raised his eyebrows. Nell poured three beakers of coffee, placed them on the tray with three scones and carried it to the door. 'We'll have ours in the sun in the yard. You call if there's anything you want, sir.'

'She's rather familiar.'

Robert chuckled, 'that's what marriage does to you. She's a hard, loyal worker and I'll miss her.'

'Breeding soon?' Matthew poured more coffee. They chatted but the doctor said he must move on and they walked to the door. Robert called for the horse.

'Could you come over one evening for a bite and a drop of rum?'

'Definitely, I'll send a message, but now I must be on my way. Get someone to come over for the bottle of physic tomorrow.'

'He'll bring some money, how much will it be?'

'Nothing,' Matthew was dismissive, 'to tell you the truth, Robert, the money is immaterial. I have my pension, funds I've saved and the prize money we all shared. It's boredom I cannot stomach.'

'Thank you, Matthew, if it hadn't been for Caleb fetching you it might have been a week or two before I knew you were here.'

Matthew smiled, his open face lighting up revealing his solitary tooth left in the top gum. Caleb cupped his hands for him to swing up on the horse's back and as he cantered off he called, 'Remember, Robert.'

'Remember what, boss?' Caleb looked curiously at Robert.

'Oh I just have to take it quiet for today…or so.'

'Well that's no problem. And there's nothing bad wrong then?' Caleb was as worried about his future as Tom was.

'No, I overdid it a bit, I'll be fine now, but you have to go over to get a bottle of medicine tomorrow.'

'Certainly, I'll go after milking.'

'Well I'll be back to that.'

'Better not, just until this medicine does the trick like.'

'Well I think it's only something to calm the heart.'

'Exactly, why push yourself when there's no need. Me and Tom have it all under control, Nell's dairy is spotless and we'll keep this up until the doctor says not.'

Robert pursed his lips but kept silent, they were all being so bossy but he knew they meant kindly and to tell the truth he was glad. He had decided that he would take it quiet for a few days and then after that he'd be back to work as normal. He couldn't afford to be a gentleman of leisure. There was the market at the end of the week, he liked going in and the lifting and lugging about wasn't too heavy.

When they knew he was determined to go into Banbury Tom insisted on loading up the cart early in the morning whilst Caleb milked. Robert was not surprised when Nell expressed a wish to go with him. She said she wanted some shopping for herself. She added as an afterthought that she'd give a hand before she went off to get her bits.

It was another perfect September day as they set off at half past seven. Binnie's hooves clattered briskly and her tail swished. Robert and Nell were warm with hot coffee and beef dripping on toast. A pale lemon sun was coming up, it's feeble rays with a touch of heat glanced off the cobwebs strung across the hawthorn hedges. The diamonds of moisture sparkled and died as they dried.

A blackbird sang a piercingly sweet song. It was a reminder of winter coming. With his old cloak wrapped round him Robert held the reins lightly. He felt better. He could get through the day without so much rest and Mathew's physic seemed to be working. There had been no more pains or spasms, even with exertion. He decided to give up long walks on the downs and if Violet came home his door would stay closed. Her husband may be a homosexual but even so she was a married woman, he wouldn't sleep with her again.

And, he had thought about this, there was nothing to say that they didn't sleep together. Just because Albert was 'one of those' didn't mean he wasn't still a man. He had known of this on board ship, men liking both sexes. He couldn't see it himself but there was no accounting for taste. He kept his thoughts from Nell as they bowled along.

'So, how is married life treating you? It's nearly a week. Has George beaten you yet?' he asked lightly, but if George ever raised a hand to Nell, he, Robert Southwell would personally go over and thrash him, if he could.

'It's lovely, we're so happy. I can't believe it. He brought me home a little posy of gold chrysy...enthemums last night. It's a long word, do you know them

'Yes, I know. He's a romantic then.'

'Well people think my George is a bit slow like, quiet, you know, but he isn't, not with me. We has a lovely chat whilst we eat our supper, then a walk up the lane before bedtime.'

'It all sounds very nice, Nell, I'm really pleased for you.'

She glanced up at him and saw he was sincere. It had been a worrying week. They all watched Shipshape as he pottered about. The brisk walk, the firm orders had disappeared with the pain. She was pleased to see some colour in his cheeks.

Simon had only been home for one day after his stay with the Bycleres. He came back full of the enormous size of the fish they had caught. When Caleb asked if there was a trout waiting for their tea he told him they had all gone into the Byclere kitchens. He didn't seem to notice that Robert was quieter than usual and Nell was up to her armpits in the wash tub with all his clothes to get ready to go back to school.

Robert had asked if they could have meet at the Red Lion for their dinner on the Friday. He supplied a note requesting this to go to the Headmaster. Well he would be there at twelve o'clock anyway for his dinner and hope Simon could get away from school.

Nell helped him set out the cheese and butter on his trestle. She led Binnie and the cart away for the stable lad to look after. Somehow a stool had found it's way into the cart and he sat down, waiting for his first customer.

The housewives of Banbury and surrounding villages were quick to come. The sunny weather made for a pleasant atmosphere of relaxed banter and when Nell came back at eleven o'clock and handed him a beaker of tea he was grateful for the chance to stop and rest.

She weighed out the last of the cheese and butter whilst Robert sipped his tea. Soon all that was left was a pile of muslin clothes and crumbs of cheese. Nell swept them up and into a large dock leaf. Robert had a favourite old lady to whom an ounce or so of cheese was a special treat.

At quarter past twelve he sat in the dining room of the Red Lion waiting for his guest and their dinners. He had ordered a roast fowl, potatoes and young turnip greens. A plum pudding would follow. He sipped a tankard of ale, looked at the clock and decided to wait no longer. Simon either couldn't get away or didn't want to. Nell was back at the shops looking for wool material to make a gherkin for George, like Robert's old one. She had declined the offer of lunch, with or without Simon.

At half past twelve Robert was tucking into his dinner. There was a commotion at the door and three of the school students walked in. Robert recognised Lansing, Byclere and Simon. They walked up to the bar and shouted for the innkeeper.

'Barman, three bottles of your best claret. Look sharp now. And we'll have baked fish and the fowl.' Byclere was showing his arrogant side.

They looked round, saw Robert and walked over, pushing chairs out of the way and with disregard to the other diners.

'Father, we've come then. We'll have our dinner with you,' Simon had on what Robert called his supercilious face, 'but slip me some money can you. My treat, lads.' He said to his chums in a louder voice.

Robert handed him half a guinea, part of his butter and cheese money. It had taken months to make that cheese and it would go in minutes down the throats of these loutish youths.

Lansing turned to Robert, 'How are you, sir? My mother and my brother send compliments. She said if I was to see you I was to ask after you. Dr Mason said you had a bad turn.'

Thank you, Rupert. Very kind of you. I'm getting along fine. How is school now you're back in the new term?'

Lansing's face lit up. 'Good sir. We have a new language master. He thinks I should be able to go to university for French, German and Latin if I study hard. That's what I'd like.'

'What do you think you'd like to do after?'

'Travel sir, in the diplomatic service, go round the cities of the world.'

Robert looked kindly at Lansing, 'That's very admirable to be so certain, I hope it comes about. I could wish that Simon was as keen to study.'

'I do my share.' Simon banged his glass down on the table. 'I just haven't decided what I want to do yet.'

Precisely, thought Robert but said nothing. John Jones, the innkeeper brought their dinners. There were two bottles of a Bordeaux on the table and before anymore was ordered Robert decided to forestall it and prevent the boys getting even more rowdy.

'That will be enough thank you, John, perhaps we could have a large pot of coffee afterwards.'

Simon glared. If looks could kill Robert would be a withered branch. He ignored it. He couldn't have the boys going back to school inebriated.

'We don't want any trouble at school now, do we? They won't let you out again if you're the worse for drink.'

'We are fourteen, Southwell. Quite old enough to hold our drink.' Grumbled Byclere.

Robert ignored him. He realised that he couldn't finish his dinner and he didn't want any pudding. He would have a nice hot cup of coffee instead.

An hour later he was back on the cart with Nell by his side, loosely holding the reins and letting Binnie find her way. He was tired, he felt worn out. He wouldn't do that again.

Two evenings later Robert and Matthew Mason were sitting in Robert's parlour enjoying a tot of rum in front of a blazing apple wood fire. The day had turned damp, mist had rolled in and as he walked across the yard after watching Caleb take the cows out to their evening meadow he shivered.

Tom found him scrabbling round in the woodshed.

'What you looking for, Shipshape? There's plenty of logs by the hearth.'

'Yes I know, thank you. I want some of that apple wood we cut in the spring. Mathew's coming, I thought we'd light a fire in the parlour.'

'Let's be having you, I'll fetch it in.'

Robert watched Tom clamber over the piles of logs and lift up some smaller pieces.

'Yes, that's it. It smells nice.'

'You go in, I'll bring enough and light it.'

Nell had left their tea ready. Robert swung the kettle across. The tea leaves were in the teapot, a saucepan of mixed vegetables with a bacon hock and dumplings was on the trivet and the bowls warmed on the inglenook. Tom and Caleb often had a bit of tea with him now. Elizabeth Farthing did little cooking and lived on pies and scraps. As for Margie, Caleb gave Susan Bates a shilling a week for her to take some dinner in at five o'clock. It was also company for Margie and small feminine chores could be managed in privacy. Margie's eyes were no better.

'She be like a mole that comes blinking out in the field,' he told them, 'she says it's all fuzzy.'

Caleb was trying very hard to save some money. Coppers, the odd sixpence or shilling, all went into a box to be kept safe in case he should die first and Margie be left. She would need looking after and he didn't want her thrown on the parish. So far he had £2.18s.6d. A fortune for him.

'So, how do you feel now?' Matthew took a Banbury biscuit from the plate.

'Good, Mathew, very good '

'Robert, it's me you're talking to, you don't have to pretend, or keep up a cheerful face.'

Robert smiled ruefully. 'You're right …damm your eyes.'

'So…?'

'I get very tired, how long is that going to last? I want to be outside, working.'

'Two to three months.' said Matthew calmly.

'No!'

'Rest now and you'll be glad later, you'll come round, most do…unless they have another one.'

'How likely is that?'

Matthew shrugged, 'I can't say. I'm really a ship's doctor not a physician. But you are fit for your age so I'd say you'll come out of it, providing you give yourself a chance now.'

'Well, let's hope so.'

Matthew smiled, 'I'll drink to that.'

'To missing comrades, the Celeste and our good health.' They touched glasses, drank and gazed into the flames. A curl of fragrant blue smoke filtered up the chimney.

It was a pleasant evening. They reminisced about their shipboard days and Matthew told him what he knew of their old comrades. Neither could forget the carnage of the battles they had endured.

'I must say, I don't miss all those dreadful injuries the sailors suffered. Let's drink to the memory of Lord Nelson, bless him.'

'Lord Nelson,' they both solemnly toasted, 'and King George, God save him.'

'King George.'

'You're welcome to stay the night, we've had a tot or two, Matthew.'

He laughed, 'Yes, I feel it. That's quite a powerful spirit you have, but my old horse knows the way home and I always have an early start in the morning. I say home girl, and she gets me there.'

'A good horse is worth it's weight in gold.' Robert slurred slightly.

'So you were unlucky with your marriage then? You say the lady died.'

'Dorothy yes, in or rather just after Simon was born. A haemorrhage it was. Was there anything I could have done? We packed her with snow, but she just faded away. I think she was too old.'

'How old was she?'

'Oh, I can't remember, was it thirty eight years?'

'Well, that is quite old for childbirth, not that I'm an expert. I don't think there's much you can do when they haemorrhage like that. With an amputation a tourniquet can be put on, but that's hardly suitable for childbirth. It was unlucky, still at least you have a son. I don't even have that.'

'No, I'm sorry, your wife died suddenly?'

'Yes, I met Rosalie in Portsmouth, a widow, but young. Very pretty she was, what she saw in me I don't know, my money I suppose. We got on well and had a tidy little house. Then I suppose it was my fault, she had typhoid fever and died. That was when I decided to move away completely and thought of the Lansing offer. They spoke to Byclere and here I am. Fresh, clean air and peace and quiet. Most of my patients can't afford me, but I charge very little, as I say I have my pension and prize money invested.'

'So do I but keeping Simon in school is costly. I hope I don't live to regret it.'

'A son is a good investment, if you're getting him a good education, then he'll be set fair in life.'

'Yes, that was the idea but he doesn't seem to know what he wants to do. He's lazy and selfish, he mixes with the Byclere son, Lansing and a couple of others. Mind you that Lansing boy seems a nice lad. I don't know, have I done the right thing? At the moment he's neither fish nor fowl, a farmer's son or a landowner.' Robert sighed heavily and then brightened up. 'Well I've done my best and if he isn't interested in the farm I shall leave it to Bayley.'

'Bayley? Who's he?'

'Well, when I first came here as a lodger, Mrs James and her son Ben lived here. A few months after, she was suddenly killed on Midsummer Day, 1801. She was out on the road looking for Ben. The big lummock had taken a cow into Banbury and never came home. She went along the Banbury road and got hit by the Byclere coach. Killed instantly she was. Ben had gone and enlisted with Sir Arthur Wellesley's Rifle brigade.

I decided to stay here, but being a novice, I needed help. Mary...er..Mrs James's sister Dorothy was a widow and wanted to live here. We decided to marry and she had Simon. Ben came back from campaigns and married my housekeeper Helen. I had to have a female here to look after Simon and the house. She was a bit of a schemer but we got along.

They had Bayley and later a little girl, Marion and now baby Arthur. Ben was wounded at Waterloo. He dragged himself home. Like you say, he found the conditions in the infirmary terrible and just about got himself here. I re-stitched his leg and when he was better he bought himself into the inn here.

Bayley's a lovely boy and they work him too hard. He's a natural with the animals and I'd like him to take over.'

'I see.' Matthew scraped his chair back. He felt that something was odd in the story, with Robert calling a widow woman Mary. Was there more to that than he was telling? Perhaps it would come out later. 'I must get along. I've enjoyed this evening. When you feel better come over to me. Have you a horse?'

'I'd probably come in the little cart, but yes I'd like that. It's quiet with Nell married and gone.'

Feeling a trifle unsteady Robert carefully picked up the glasses and followed Matthew to the door.

A waning harvest moon was a golden sickle in the southern sky. The two men sniffed the air like seasoned sailors.

'It's clearing, I reckon the wind's gone round to the east nor'east,' said Matthew knowledgeably.

'Aye, well good night.'

Robert sluiced his face with cold water in the scullery, brushed out his hair and undressed, carefully laying his clothes out tidily. He felt a tiny bit light headed and thought he might have had too much rum. It was a pleasure to get between the cool sheets and lay his head on the pillow that smelt of Nell's lavender. Sleep overtook him before he could thank God for another day lived.

He hadn't written in his journal for a long time but that night he sat by his window and wrote, "*I'm so pleased Matthew Mason is close by. It's good to have a friend from our shipboard days. I feel a lot better after the heart attack the other day. Perhaps it wasn't one at all. Just a false alarm.*" a

Robert spent a quiet few days, being nurtured by his friends. On a Saturday morning he came in from the dairy to find Bayley staggering in with an armful of logs.

'Bayley, what are you doing, lad?'

'I've come to help, Uncle Robert.' He dropped his logs and quickly arranged them neatly in the fireplace.

'Well that's kind of you, but what about the inn? They'll miss you.'

'I've done my work, if I get up earlier, I can come here.'

'Oh, Bayley, it's too much for you. I like to see you, but not to work.'

'They were saying you were poorly, the doctor came, you might die.' He looked so anxious that Robert crouched down and put an arm around his shoulders.

'Look at me, back to normal and hale and hearty as ever. Come, let's have some tea and toast, like old times, eh?' He was deeply touched with the boy's concern and sorry that he had been frightened.

They sat at the table with their beakers and Robert let Bayley chatter on about school and what was happening in the village. He wished the boy could come and live with him but Ben and Helen wouldn't let him go, he was too useful.

'Can I come and sleep here?' Bayley set down his beaker, there was a milky line above his mouth and he wiped it with his sleeve.

'Sleep here?'

'Yes, 'cos you've been poorly. What if you were taken bad in the night, there's no one here. I could run and get Father, or Tom.'

'What do they say to this?'

'Well, as long as my work is done, I can come up at bed time and if I get up at six o'clock and run home, I'll be able to clear the pots before school.'

'Bayley it's too much for you.'

'It's what I do now.'

Robert felt a fury at the abuse of this child. What was Helen thinking of? They had Sukey to do the kitchen work, he would speak to them. But oh, he would dearly love to have the boy here.

'I'll walk down later and have a word with your parents. Now, come and see the calves and the piglets, they're growing nicely.'

CHAPTER THIRTY SIX

'It's very beautiful, I bet they'd like this up at the House.'
George gently touched the lace collar, laid out on the table. The
scalloped edges were exquisite and the pattern was beautifully
complicated. His hands were too rough and calloused to pick it up.

Nell had befriended an elderly lady, Miss Smith who lived in
The Rows in Banbury. Robert noticed that she only bought a tiny
piece of cheese the previous Friday and was obviously very poor.
Nell followed her home and discovered that Eveline Smith had been
buying cough syrup for the neighbours' children who had the croup.
'I felt sorry for her, she's obviously gentry, come down in the
world and she didn't like taking the charity. Her dress and jacket
were good quality but old and faded, perhaps she was a governess or
a lady's maid. Anyway, Robert made sure she had a better
Christmas. A few logs and a bacon hock don't cost much he said.
Now look, I've bought a small toy each for my younger
brothers and sisters, wooden ones so they last a while and a penknife
for Kenny. That was thruppence on a stall and a tin whistle for
Jackie, as he likes a tune. Mother has a new shawl, it were on the
second hand for five pence, a nice thick wool one and father has a
new pipe and an ounce of baccy.'
'We'll give them half the beef joint that the Estate will give
me, shall we? Your father, being casual cannot really expect much.'
George knew the Estate had a low opinion of the Bates's families.
'That would be kind and we cannot eat it all. We'll have our
Christmas dinner on our own shall we? Perhaps go in with your
parents after. Oh no we can't, they're going to Southwell's for their
dinner. I expect they'll stay there for the day. Well, we'll go in with
my family for a bit, shall we? That way we don't have to stay too
long. '
George got up and kissed her tenderly, 'You're a good, kind
wife and daughter, Mrs Farthing, we're going to have a grand
Christmas holiday.
Let's have our dinner, I've cut you some nice thin bacon
slices to fry with the cold potatoes from last night.' Nell turned to
the stairs to hide her grimace at the thought of frying.

George had his own secret. He bought his wife a soft wool
shawl in a misty blue that she could wrap the babe in later and some

fine cotton lawn that would make baby clothes. He knew she would like that and had been pleased when the pedlar came to the back door of the House selling Christmas gifts and novelties. Mrs Greaves had suggested he also purchase some of the little pearl buttons and a large reel of fine cotton for sewing. At Mr Way's shop he bought a silver thimble, engraved with roses. It was very pretty and he was looking forward to her pleasure.

'You'll never guess what Robert has bought Bayley. Father is going to make a hen coop and there will be four Buff Orpingtons for the lad, all his own, plus a cockerel.' Said George, laying the table.

'More useful than something he doesn't want and he does love the hens. It's a bit of a funny present for a four year old but Bayley's old for his years. Even so, I've got him some wooden animals, a cow, a horse and two sheep. I bought Janey a comb and some ribbons. Her hair is that wild sometimes and I don't suppose she'll get anything from the James's.

'She is a servant, Nell.'

'I know, but she's a lot better than that Sukey. I'll call in to see that Miss Smith again and see if she has any more of her lace. Not for me, but I'm wondering if they wouldn't like some of it up at the House. Perhaps she could make them some. I don't know why she don't make it to sell.'

'Don't tire yourself out running around after other people.'

Nell didn't mind that, she just couldn't tell George the frying smells made her feel so sick every morning, all day in fact.

Christmas Day dawned bright and clear. Quite mild but with a fresh south westerly wind and as Robert stepped out the door he smelt rain in the air. It was just after seven, dark but with the sky lightening in the east. A rattle of a chain and a glimmer of light in the milking parlour told him Caleb was out there. Tom had also been busy on another mission. Bayley was still fast asleep. He had gone to bed late after sitting in the parlour on his own secret task. Robert had gone in for some rum and found him sitting bent over some paper with just the one candle.

'Go away.' Bayley cried in alarm.

'Yes, yes I will but can you see? Are you cold?'

'It's a bit dark.' He admitted.

'I won't look but I'll bring you in candles and light the fire. Nell's left the hearth ready and it is Christmas. I'll be back in a minute.'

Five minutes later there were three more candles, giving a good light and the fire burned brightly giving its own soft glow to the room. Gigantic shadows on the wall could have frightened a child but Bayley was oblivious, although he felt better for the warmth. He was making his Uncle's special Christmas present. Presents for his mother and father and little sister had been made in school. Nell's present was hidden in the scullery.

'Morning, Boss, Merry Christmas.' greeted Caleb.

'Yes, greetings to you and Margie. I've just put the goose on the spit, I'll have to look at it in a bit, won't I. Actually Cal, I'm going to need some advice. I've not done this before, cooked a dinner like this. I think I should have asked the baker to put it in his oven yesterday. To tell the truth I forgot.'

'Oh we'll manage. Margie can't see to do anything but she can tell us what to do. Me and Tom, we'll give a hand. We're looking forward to it.'

'We'll just do the basics this morning. The cows can go out in the lower paddock for the day and then they'll be close to get in tonight in case it's raining. I'll just go and see how Tom's getting on.'

Tom was over in the far corner of the orchard. 'What do you think, Boss?'

'Tom, it's a grand coop, he'll be pleased as punch. What a lovely job.'

'Aye, the foreman in the Estate forests found me some small planks. He's my cousin you know. I borrowed the joiner's tools to make holes and he let me have some nails. The hens are snug on some straw and...' he laughed, 'there's even an egg in the nest box.'

Robert smiled. 'Grand, Tom, it's grand. We'll show him after breakfast. Come in when you're ready.'

When Robert went back in a sleepy Bayley was sitting on the inglenook stroking the cat. He was in his nightshirt with his bare feet and legs dangling. Robert felt a lurch in his chest and a bubble of happiness, he loved the little boy so much.

'Well, sleepyhead, Christmas greetings.'

'Happy Christmas, Uncle, when's the gifts, 'cos I've got one for you and Nell.'

'After breakfast. Go and put your head under the pump, put a clean shirt on and get dressed.'

Robert busied himself with the huge gammon that had been boiled yesterday and this morning they would have a thick slice with some baked eggs.

The goose was spitting fat and the grease was starting to run into the tin placed underneath. Robert turned it again and brought the saucepans of vegetables in to stand by the hearth. He would have to juggle things around a bit. The Christmas fruit dumpling was tied up in muslin and Robert wondered if he couldn't put the potatoes in the boiling water. He would ask Margie later. Tom was bringing Elizabeth but she was not much use. By the time she'd fluttered her hands and hesitated and put a pinny on it was easier to do it yourself.

It was a merry kitchen as they all sat down to breakfast. Without Nell, they all helped themselves and Robert poured coffee.

'All men together.' remarked Tom winking at Bayley. He could see the child was glowing with excitement. He had had a small plate of ham and one egg, as if the less he ate, the quicker would come the gifts. He had made Tom and Caleb pictures and was dying to pass them out.

It seemed to take forever for the men to finish and then clear the table. Tom took the kettle out to the sink to sluice the plates with hot water. Robert wiped the table over and watched Bayley brimming over with impatience.

Bayley was disappointed to see them all put coats on to go outside.

'Oh,' his voice quivered, 'I've...I've got gifts for you. Can I give them to you now?'

'That's kind of you, but we're just popping out for a minute, do you want to come? Put a coat on.'

Bayley followed them. Robert felt a hand steal into his.

There in the orchard, in the corner, tucked under the wall, out of the wind was a brand new hen coop. Hen noises were heard, clucking and chattering and Bayley stopped.

'Merry Christmas, Bayley, this is yours, your coop, your hens and...your eggs.'

'Oh, oh.' He ran over the grass and pulled up the pop hole. A reddish brown head popped out and pecked his fingers. There was a plank set in for them to run down and Tom walked over and demonstrated how he could lift one side of the of the roof to pick up the eggs. They had already made nests. There were two medium size speckled eggs, resting in the straw in a nest box.

'Uncle, thank you, thank you. I shall give them names and look after them, every day.'

'There's a cockerel in there as well, so you'll have chicks in the Spring.'

Bayley had scooped up a chicken and was stroking it.

'This one's Janey.' he announced.

'You'll be calling them after people you know then, I suppose that's an honour.' Chuckled Tom.

'Yes, Janey, Nell, Bella and Emmie and Tom for the cockerel.'

'Cheeky lad,' laughed Caleb. 'Well, I'll just go home and change into my best and fetch Margie. We'll be back within the hour, Boss to help with the dinner.'

'I've got gifts for you,' cried Bayley, 'I've got gifts.'

'We'll look forward to them when we come back, lad.'

Robert left Bayley with his hens, even the cockerel had been stroked and petted and quickly finished off in the dairy. He left the pail of milk ready for the village people to come and help themselves plus some cubes of cheese to go with it.

His customers had been generous as usual, as much as they could be. A current cake had been left one day, another time a stone jar of blackberry wine. Someone else had knitted him socks and there had even been a small clay pipe. They didn't need to speak their thanks to him or he to them, it was an accepted way of life.

The dinner plates were warming on the inglenook. The goose had turned a golden brown and there was a huge panful of fat. At Margie's suggestion the potatoes had been par-boiled and then roasted in a sprinkling of fat. The cabbage and carrots were tucked by the hearth, gently simmering. All was in order and everyone was ravenous. They sat round the table with a glass of Robert's special wine, a very pleasant Rhenish suggested by the wine merchant.

'Now, Bayley, if you look in the parlour, you'll see a green bag. Bring it in.'

Whilst the child ran into the other room Caleb and Tom both reached down and produced parcels from the bags by their chair. Onto the table went the interesting shapes. Robert fetched his from the dresser.

When Bayley came back into the room a minute later there were so many exciting looking gifts on the table. Proudly he laid his out, then he realised, sadly that he hadn't wrapped them in anything. Never mind.

'I've got a picture for you, Caleb and Mrs Pound, though I'm sorry she can't see it so I's made her a peg bag.' A cloth bag with a handle made of a willow stick was put into Margie's hands. She felt it and held it up to the light. The material was from one of Nell's old skirts, faded but still strong and the stitches were rather large and cobbled but she was delighted.

'Thank you, Bayley, thank you very much,' she said, 'It's just what I need.'

Bayley beamed. 'Tom, here's yours and a little mat for Mrs Farthing to put her things on.'

'How kind.' Exclaimed Lizzie.

'This is very well done.' Tom took the picture to the door for a better light. 'You do good drawing, Bayley. Does the teacher say so.'

'Not much. I did that at home.'

'Uncle Robert, here's yours,' proudly Bayley placed the drawing on the table in front of Robert, 'it's a map of the farm, the whole farm.' H added unnecessarily.

Stunned, Robert gazed at it. It was very well done for such a young child.

'Here's the house and the dairy, there's the cow barn and the yard where the ricks are. I've only done two ricks, 'cos it's winter and they've eaten the hay. That's Clare and Cathy, just come from milking,' he pointed at two rather thin stick like creatures, 'and the others are in the shed with Cal and Tom. I'm at school and you and Nell are in the dairy. Shall I draw in the new hens, my hens and the coop in the orchard? And I've put in the pasture and there's the sheep.'

'Bayley this is excellent, you couldn't have given me a better gift.' Robert pulled the child towards him and gave him a hug. Everyone admired the map. 'I think I'll have this framed and we'll put it on the wall, what say you, Tom?'

'Yes, I should, and I think I'll do the same with mine. It's a right pretty picture.

Perhaps Joe could make us some dainty frames.'

Robert handed out his gifts. Bayley had a book and he looked at it trying to say the words, 'R..?'

'It's "Robinson Crusoe" by Daniel Defoe, I'll read you some later, it's a real adventure.'

'Thank you, Uncle, thank you.'

Robert marvelled at the lad, at his manners and speech, he certainly hadn't learned them at the inn with his parents, but then of course, Ben was not his father.

After everything had been exclaimed over and admired Robert declared he thought the dinner to be ready and what did he have to do.

'If you take the goose down and put it on that large trencher and Tom takes the fat outside to a bowl, I'll make the gravy.' Lizzie tied Nell's apron round her best skirt. 'Leave all the onion bits and bring the tin back, Tom and then I'll stir in some flour. Where is it?'

Bayley fetched the cutlery and Caleb laid out glasses and a jug of ale, with cider for the ladies. Chairs were fetched from the parlour and the goose was placed on the table as Robert sharpened his knife with a steel. Lizzie was stirring the gravy, Tom took the saucepan of vegetables out to drain and Bayley helped Margie to her chair.

The goose was done to a turn, the skin was a crisp, dark gold and the flesh underneath cut into thick, succulent slices. A large jug of gravy was set on the table by the dish of carrots and cabbage. The roasted potatoes were a mite dark brown but within minutes they were served out and they had platefuls of steaming food in front of them. Robert put the trencher with the goose back on the inglenook to keep hot for second helpings.

He stayed standing, 'I'd just like to say a thank you to you all for working so hard in the year, for our good health and for next year to be as good, or better.'

'Aye, good health to you, boss and a thank you from us.' Tom raised his glass.

'Good, now tuck in everyone, we have Nell's current and spice pudding as well, specially made for today.'

Bayley, with his own smaller plate in front of him, heaped with goose meat and vegetables and his legs swinging from the chair felt he had never been happier.

Everything was perfect, everyone he loved except Nell and Janey were there, but she was coming over later. He was supposed to go and see his parents but he didn't expect any gift from them. His mother would tell him to bring in some wood or make himself useful and his father would probably ignore him. He prayed every night that he would be able to stay with his Uncle Robert.

Caleb helped Margie with her food, cutting it up so that she could eat with a spoon and fork. He put the beaker of cider in her hand so she would not fumble for it and knock it over. He knew she still missed her daughter but Rissie would probably have been at her work over Christmas and they would not have seen her. Coming here to the farmhouse had made it one of the best days of the year for her.

Every morsel was eaten, plates were cleaned off and Robert and Tom between them carried the dumpling to the scullery to place on a dish. The muslin wrapping was untied and it emerged, a pale honey brown and steaming fragrantly.

'My, that's a beautiful sight,' said Tom in a reverent voice, 'Nell makes a tidy pudding.'

It was carried to the table. They all watched as Robert cut slices. It smelt of nutmeg and cinnamon, allspice and Demerara sugar. It had been rolled up and the currents were plumply sprinkled through. It was a grand sight.

Bayley had a small piece, which he struggled to finish. The others had thick slices, glad that they had eaten so little that morning. Cream was generously lavished on top. No one could ever call Robert anything less than the most generous of hosts.

'My, what a feast.' Tom pushed his chair back, drained his glass and sighed happily. 'I wonder how our George and Nell are getting on?'

'This time next year you'll be a grandfather.'

'We're looking forward to it, George is proud as punch.'

Nell and George were sitting in their chairs, on either side of the cast iron box stove.

'That was a real tasty dinner, Nell, I'll wash the dishes for you later. I'm glad you ate up, you're looking peaky, love. So you like the shawl?'

'It's all lovely, thank you, my dear. I think I might go upstairs for a rest, if it's not too cold up there, then we'd better go in next door.'

'Shall I come with you?'

'You are coming with me.' She teased.

'Upstairs I mean.'

Nell turned at the bottom step and gave her husband a mischievous smile, she beckoned with her finger and he grinned. Quickly he locked the front door, dropped a log into the stove and leaving the door open so that the heat would rise upstairs he tiptoed upstairs in his stockinged feet with a broad smile on his face.

Bayley was at the inn, with the two eggs he took as presents. He was thrilled to receive a rush basket that Margie, with Cal's help had woven for him. Just what he needed to collect his eggs in. They had made peg dollys in school and he had made one for Marion. He walked in the back way through the kitchen and saw Janey with her hands in hot water. A pile of washed dishes was on the table.

'Merry Greetings, Janey, I've a gift for you but it's up at the farm and you're coming back with me, are you?' He said in a rush.

'Yes, straight when I've done this.' Her face was as red as her hair. 'Non stop, I've been, all to do, so I'm leaving them to it now.' Tiredly, she pushed the hair out of her eyes.. She had had no help with the dinner, a goose to cook and all the veggies. And they hadn't even asked her to share it with them. On her own she'd been in the kitchen. She knew, Helen had been a maid of all work at Southwell's but she was no better than anyone else. She spent the morning titivating herself and dressing Marion in a new fancy frock all smothered in lace and bows. And Marion had gone and got gravy down it. Well Sukey would have to try and wash it off, she was having nothing to do with it.

Janey Kerridge had come to The Ewe and Lamb from The Red Lion in Banbury. John Jones was her uncle, she was an orphan and had worked there for four years. At fifteen with her untameable red hair, temper nearly to match and a cast in one eye she was a character.

Sukey was well enough with the customers but a useless cook and when Helen heard that Janey was a dab hand with the pastry she asked Robert to bring her over.

Janey saw instantly the situation with Bayley, of how he was used and readily shouldered some of his burden so that he could sleep with Mr Southwell. Her cooking was a huge success and the inn started to profit from its' enhanced reputation.

Her plum pudding with raisins and spices had turned out well. A milk custard had been baked and even Ben had complimented her. She sat at the kitchen table eating her dinner, letting them wait. Helen had insisted on eating in the parlour so Ben had lit a fire in there. There had been no giving and receiving of gifts apart from Marion who had a new ball and a rag book. Normally. the baby, Arthur was left upstairs with Sukey to look after him but she was with Joe for the day so he was getting minimal attention from his mother.

Now Bayley presented his father with his gift, a drawing of the inn, done after school one day before it got dark. It was in pencil, and Ben was standing at the door with a tankard in his hand. He stared at it, amazed that the child had done it. No one in his family could read and write much, let alone draw. He still couldn't write very much and his father had made chalk strokes on the barn door to count sacks of barley. It only hardened his heart further, the child was a real cuckoo in the nest and was nothing to do with him.

'Look, Helen, the boy is a clever artist, I wonder where he gets that from?'

'I'm sure I don't know,' she said peevishly. She wanted a cup of tea and Janey had ignored her.

'Look, Mother,' Bayley had made her a small mat sewn round with careful, large stitches in white thread, 'this is for your table upstairs, to put your bowls and bottles on.'

'Thank you, it's very...nice.' She had the grace to give him a smile.

'Marion, here's yours.' He gave her the peg doll, in a funny skirt and shawl made from the same material.

'Oh, a dolly.' Marion clutched it to herself, with glee.

'And,' triumphantly he produced the basket with the eggs, 'special eggs, Marion, my special eggs from my very own special hens.'

Marion saw two ordinary brown eggs. Their significance meant nothing so she ignored Bayley and ran to the kitchen to show Janey her dolly.

'You've done well then, boy, you've got your own hens now I hear.'

'Yes father, four and a cockerel.'

'Well with all that you won't be wanting the silver sixpence I was going to give you.'

'No, sir.' Bayley knew better than to answer back and he slipped out the room.

'That was mean.' Helen admonished.

'Look at him, like a pig in muck he is now with Robert doting on him. Spoilt he is.'

Helen shook her head as she went out to the kitchen to make her own tea. It was deserted but two brown eggs were sitting in a dish.

CHAPTER THIRTY SEVEN

Whilst the men milked the cows and piled up hay for the night, Margie and Elizabeth went back to their cottages. Lizzie had been shocked to see how much help Margie needed. She felt ashamed that the woman had been living close by and she had rarely been in to offer help.

It was as if a veil had been lifted from her eyes and she suddenly realised how lazy and stupid she had become. The simple action of Robert asking her to make the gravy had pleased her and made her feel like she belonged. She knew the others thought her silly and empty headed. She wasn't really she told herself as she held Margie's arm and they walked down the track. She had offered to go back and top up the fires so that they would keep in for later and the cottage was warm to go home to.

'I'll do yours as well, Caleb,' she promised as she saw his raised eyebrows, 'Margie would like to go home for a bit, we'll be back by six.'

They went into the Pounds' cottage first. It was small and dark in the gloom of the winter afternoon.

'I'll light a candle first, Margie, do you want to use the privy?' But Margie, holding on to the twine that Caleb had strung along the fence was already slowly walking down the path. Lizzie placed two large logs on the fire, swept the ash tidily and placed the fire screen in front. This had been made by Charley to stop Margie burning herself. The blaze flared up and brightened the room. Lizzie checked the kettle was full and stood uncertainly waiting for Margie.

A brisk knock and the door opened. Susan Bates put her head round. 'Oh hallo, Lizzie, I've just popped in to top up the fire and you've done it. Where's Margie?'

'She's in the privy. Is there anything I can do?'

Shocked, Susan stared at her. Lazy Lizzie volunteering? 'No, Cal will do all the usual when he brings her back later.'

What was 'the usual, Lizzie wondered. 'I realise how thoughtless I've been, not doing more for Margie,' she said slowly, 'and you're always so busy, so I'd like to help if I can. I'm ashamed to say I didn't realise how Margie was, so blind like.'

Susan stared at the faded woman, in the shadows of the room she seemed to almost disappear. 'Well,' she blew out the breath from her cheeks as she thought, 'you could get her breakfast in the morning. Sometimes she has to wait until I've got all the children sorted and Cal's up at the farm. She only has some tea and Cal leaves porridge in the pan but he don't like her being too close to the fire.'

Elizabeth nodded, 'I'll come in at eight o'clock, if that's all right with you and Margie.'

Margie was standing by the door, holding on. 'What's going on? I haven't lost my voice, or my ears. What are you planning?'

'Well Lizzie here has offered to come in and get your breakfast in the morning. It's not that I don't mind doing it, you know that but I could get on that much quicker and be round later to do the washing. I'm sorry Marge, we should have asked you first.'

'It's all right, I don't want to be a burden to anyone.'

'You're not Margie, I'm the one that's been, well thoughtless. Now shall we walk back to Southwell's? We're going to have some supper and the children can have a game. Tom's got a bottle of port for us, as a treat like.' She took Margie's arm and closed the door behind her. The fire was well banked up with the screen in front, the room was cosy and leaving the curtains open helped a pleasant light shine out.

The farm had not seen so many people since Nell's wedding. Janey and Bayley were busy in the corner of the parlour with the toy animals, making a farm Bayley had gathered sticks and grass and was busy making plaited fences. Janey was trying to make him a barn out of paper. They were so engrossed they didn't see Dr Mason at the door.

'Mathew, come in, come in.' Robert exclaimed delighted. It had been his idea that his friend spend Christmas night with them. The doctor had only his housekeeper for company and she had gone to a cousin.

'Evening everybody, here Robert, that's some spiced pork Mrs Lee made for us, and a bottle or two of Malmsey. An old gentleman out Hathercott way gave me it in lieu of payment. It's reckoned to be very old, so I hope it's all right.'

'We'll try it, shall we? Right,' he looked round, 'we'll go in the parlour. Cal can you sit Margie comfortable by the fire, everyone else go on in. We'll have a drink before supper.'

Some of the chairs were hard, but they were used to that. The pleasure was in the company, a good blazing fire crackling up the chimney and a glass in your hand.

'Well I hope Nell's had a good day,' Tom commented as they all sipped their wine reflectively, 'her first Christmas wed.   By George, Doctor, this is a beautiful drop of wine, it's going to spoil us for the port I bought in.'

'Did you get your Christmas dinner, Janey?' asked Robert.

'Yes, sir, we had a goose, it turned out nice and the plum pudding was good.'

'Did you eat with them?'

'They had it in the parlour.'

'And you had yours in the kitchen I suppose?' grunted Tom.

'I don't mind, you know how Marion plays up.'

'Well, Janey come here, there's a gift for you on the table.'

Janey looked at Bayley who grinned at her.

'Me?' she was shocked, she had had no gifts given to her since her parents died when she was a child and she couldn't remember that time.   She saw some parcels on the table. 'Oh.' Hesitating she touched one.

'Go on, have a look.' Encouraged Caleb.

Janey unwrapped the paper carefully. The parcel had been sealed with a blob of wax. She was breathless, excited and almost crying. She thought it was the happiest moment of her life. Being here with all these friendly people, having Bayley to play with and a warm room with a beaker of milk and rum had been enough for her. She took out a book.

'A, e,' she said slowly.

'Let's see? S o p.' helped Bayley.

'Aesop's fables,' said the doctor, 'shall we have one after supper?'

'I like a story.' Ventured Lizzie.

'Janey's learning to read so I thought that would help her.' Robert smiled at the flame haired girl whose face was red with pleasure.

'And this.' Bayley gave her his gift.

'Oh Bayl, I ain't got you anythink, I didn't know about this.' Her mercurial temperament changed in a flash.

'That's all right,' said Bayley stoutly, 'I've had lots of things today. I'll share them with you. You can see my hens tomorrow. They are all shut up tight now, I don't want the fox to get them.'

Janey had unwrapped a handkerchief, with her initial on it. Bought by Robert in Banbury to be from Bayley.   She was speechless. There was another package tied with string. A label said *"To Janey from Nell and George."* Inside was a hairbrush, with all new bristles and two satin ribbons, green and blue. Janey started crying.

'Don't upset yourself, lass,' said Robert kindly.

'I'm going to run and thank them.'

'Leave it til the morning gal, Nell will see you then.'

Janey's hair was a wild bird's nest. She had a comb, purloined from a guest at the inn but half the teeth were missing.

Margie called her over, 'Here, let me brush your hair, I used to do my daughter's, she had such beautiful long hair.'

They all watched as Janey knelt in front of the sad woman. Margie lightly felt the girl's head, then gently started teasing out the tangles. 'You come in to me, Janey, I'll dress your hair up lovely, you hear me?'

'Yes Mrs.' Janey vigorously nodded enjoying the sensation of a firm brush across her scalp and the female attention.

As seven struck on the old clock Robert clapped his hands together. 'Is anyone feeling hungry, shall we get the food and then we can have a game or two.'

'I'll help.' Lizzie placed Robert's best glass on the table.

'And me.' Janey sprung up, knocking the brush out of Margie's hand.

'Wait a minute girl, let's put a ribbon in it.'

'My this is nice for a change, doctor.' They were back in the parlour, with their chairs round the table. Robert could never see it without remembering Mary in her coffin. The rest of that memory, of him lifting her out and taking her upstairs was something he tried not to think about.

'Call me Mathew, I'm off duty tonight and too far away for anyone to call me out.'

'Right you are.' Caleb piled up his plate and transferred food to Margie's. Carefully he cut it up and gave her a fork. Bread was cut up into smaller pieces. She sat next to him and ate with a fork and her fingers.

The candle light was kind to them. Robert's face had aged since his chest pain, sometimes he looked tired and drawn but now, relaxed and content he felt tranquil, happy in the knowledge that Bayley would be with him to see out his days.

Mathew was enjoying himself. Robert's farm workers had proved to be genial company, with a fund of amusing stories. He was relaxed and the malmsey had been a nectar from paradise. He decided to obtain some more before the old boy died.

Tom was pleased to see Elizabeth so animated. She was more like the girl he had married and as their eyes met across the table he was amazed to see a smile lighting up her pale face. Hope flared, perhaps tonight, when they got to bed they could have a bit of a cuddle, it had been a long time. He watched her helping Margie and saw a change in her.

Caleb was pleased to see Lizzie actually doing something. He felt the pressure of caring for his wife increasingly and it was wearing him down. He wasn't getting any younger, he needed to work and with Robert doing a bit less he had his hands full with the extra hours at the farm and Margie. He would see how it went. Perhaps Lizzie would like to earn some coppers tending Marge. He knew Susan was stretched so it could work out well for all of them.

Janey and Bayley sat side by side, their small plates had a helping of pork and pickle and a slice of buttered bread. She watched carefully. Everyone except the blind lady was using a knife and fork for their meat. She did the same, copying Bayley. It was slower, but you didn't get such greasy fingers and they didn't wipe their hands on their clothes either.

She sipped her wine and water and touched her new green hair ribbon. Everyone had said she looked a picture, even with her squinty eye and she wanted to believe it.

Margie was enjoying herself. The wine was the most delicious taste she had ever had and she looked round the table at the faces. They were pale shapes and the candles were bright golden lights in the fog. She heard their voices, with all the hidden nuance of meanings. It was lovely to hear everyone so happy and the girl Janey sounded almost, a bit like their Rissie, with that same accent. She hoped she would come in to see her again, it had been good brushing her hair, woken up the happy memories..

Robert sat by the diminishing plate of meat. He ate less than he used to. He found nowadays he didn't seem to be so hungry and two glasses of malmsey had been quite enough. It was good to have a change from rum. He would write in his journal before he went to bed. The year was ending on a better note than he had dared to think about after that terrible chest pain. Mathew was a good friend, he was keeping an eye on him and with Bayley hovering at his elbow he felt almost cherished. A very unfamiliar sensation.

'Right then, we'll clear the dishes and then have a game for the children, shall we?' Robert stood and within seconds the table was clear.

'What are we playing, Uncle?'

As Robert stroked his chin, Janey watched, with bright, expectant eyes. She had never played games, although she had seen plenty of card games at the inn.

'Something with pennies? Shall we roll them and if you can catch them off the table you can keep them. Get a beaker each and take it in turns and we'll see how we go.'

The adults moved back to watch. Mathew sat at the head of the table and rolled a penny down the length of it. Bayley watched intently and held his beaker ready. He caught it easily.

'I've got one.' He yelled.

'Right, I'll make it harder.' The penny was rolled and spun, it whizzed down the table, veered slightly and the boy dived for it. He laughed and Janey, watching intently clapped her hands.

'My turn?' she got ready. She had an easy one.

'Yes, well done. Now...are you ready?' Mathew sent it off at speed, it caught a knot in the wood and spun over the edge on the side and she missed it.

'Oh.' She was crestfallen.

'My turn again.'

'One more and then we make it difficult.'

They all laughed. 'It's not so easy now, said Bayley seriously.

He watched his penny coming and caught it. 'Three pennies,' he crowed, 'I've got three pennies.

'My turn please?' Janey was anxious to catch up.

With longer legs and arms she was able to catch it as it rolled off.

Mathew looked at Robert, 'Shall we make it harder?' Robert nodded, producing a kerchief.

'Here, Bayley, now you do it blindfold. So you have to listen for it coming.'

Bayley's hand gripped the edge of the table with the room silent apart from the odd crackle as a burning log settled. They all watched as the penny rolled slowly down the table. It was angled away from his right hand and he had to move a little if he wanted to catch it.

Bayley listened. He heard the breathing sounds and then the slight hiss of the coin coming towards him. He concentrated, it was coming to his right, he held himself taut, moved the beaker along and heard a ting as it fell in.

'Well done.' Everyone clapped and Robert removed the blindfold. Bayley's face was split into the biggest grin they had ever seen. He jumped up and down in excitement and childishly shouted,

'Again, again.'

'My turn now, you wait, Bayley.'

'All right Janey, Robert...tie her up.' Matthew was smiling as he stood at the end of the table, the penny balanced on the tip of his finger. The girl stood tense, trying to listen as Bayley had done. She heard a quiet rattle as it rolled towards her. She held the beaker ready under the table lip, ready to catch it, feeling with her hand to steady herself. Suddenly it was there, she caught it in the beaker and jingled it round and round.

'Yes, yes, I've got it.'

Everyone clapped and cheered. Janey was so proud of herself. Never had she had such a lovely time in her life.

'Well, shall we quiet down a little? Anyone for a top up?'

They busied themselves with draining glasses ready for a refill and whilst Tom fetched the bottle over Robert said to Janey.

'Would you like to read from your book?'

'Aw no, I couldn't do that, will you read to us?'

'All right, you children get yourselves some milk from the scullery and we'll sit and have a story. Janey's learning to read,' he explained, 'and I found this Æsop's Fables in the bookshop.

Robert sat at the table with a candle either side of the book. He didn't want to admit that his eyes were not as good as they had been. Mathew had declined to read, saying it was very pleasant just to sit and do nothing.

Janey and Bayley sat by the fire on the old cloak. The cat crept in and was curled up next to Bayley who she loved. He sipped his milk and dribbled a little on the warm stone for her. She lapped it clean with a pink tongue.

Robert turned the pages looking for a short one. 'Right.' He said looking round. There was a look of expectant pleasure on all their faces, Matthew tamped down his pipe tobacco and Bayley wriggled happily.

'"The Farmer and the Snake. A farmer found in the winter time a Snake stiff and frozen with cold. He had compassion on it and taking it up placed it in his bosom. The Snake on being thawed by the warmth quickly revived, when, resuming its natural instincts, he bit his benefactor, inflicting on him a mortal wound. The Farmer

said with his last breath, I am rightly served for pitying a scoundrel.
The moral is, the greatest benefits will not bind the ungrateful. "

He looked up. Tom nodded, true, very true.'

Bayley piped up, 'What's a bosom?'

Janey pointed to her rather flat chest, 'This, silly.'

'Oh.'

Elizabeth said, 'What sensible person would pick up a snake anyway, I hope you wouldn't, Tom. Nasty, dangerous things. Don't you go picking up any snakes Bayley, they're poisonous.'

'Not all of them, Mrs Farthing, the grass snake is safe, but I've seen adders up on the downs.'

'There you are.' She looked meaningfully at Bayley's small shape caught in the fire glow.

'Another please, Uncle.'

'Well, here's one. *"The Mole and his Mother. A mole, a creature blind from it's birth, once said to his mother. I am sure that I can see, mother. In the desire to prove to him his mistake, his mother placed before him a few grains of frankincense and asked, What is it? The young Mole said, It is a pebble. His Mother exclaimed: My son, I am afraid that you are not only blind, but that you have lost your sense of smell.'"*

'There's no moral with that one.' Robert looked round at them.

Margie said slowly, 'I reckon, since my eyes have gone, I do smell better and my hearing's sharper. Is that possible?'

'Yes, Mrs Pound, the other senses do improve. I noticed it on board ship with the sailors. But, sadly it still doesn't compensate for losing your sight.' Said Dr Mason helpfully.

'Well I manages, don't I, Cal?'

Caleb looked at his wife, she was almost pretty in the candle light, her face was flushed with heat and wine and he was pleased to see her enjoying herself.

'We gets by, my dear.'

The clock chimed and Robert looked up. 'Young man, it's nine of the clock, long past your bedtime. Hurry along now. Say goodnight and thank you to everyone. Janey, let the lad settle and then you go up. She's bunking down with him tonight, it's too late for her to be going back to the inn.'

'Right, lads.' Tom produced a pack of cards. 'Shall us have a game or two?'

'I'll sit by Margie.' Elizabeth walked over and pulled a chair up next to her, near the fire. 'What a lovely evening it's been.'

Margie smiled, 'Yes, that boy's a lovely child and so clever, I can hear it in his voice.'

Elizabeth lowered her voice, 'They do say as how it isn't Ben's child. He don't look nothing like a James. Did you see him when he was a babe?'

'Yes, he has dark hair, I couldn't say now but his voice...it's sort of, well almost like the gentry sometimes, even though he lives here.'

'Exactly,' Lizzie was triumphant, 'well, he's happy here, that Helen treated him like a slave and Ben was too tough with him. I'm glad he's got Shipshape.'

In the background the men's voices rose and fell as they called cards and slapped down pennies. The candles flared and one guttered.

Elizabeth got up, 'If you tell me where, I'll go and get another.'

Just as the old clock prepared to wheeze out another hour they heard the outside door bang shut as if slammed. Footsteps sounded.

'What the devil?' Robert exclaimed.

The parlour door swung open wide and Simon stood, staring at them. 'What's this? A party for the workers? My horse needs stabling.' He strode in, leaving wet footprints across Nell's clean flagstones. His long coat glistened with raindrops and his fair hair was plastered slickly to his head. He let his coat drop to the floor by the fire and held out his hands to the warmth.

Robert sat, outwardly calm. Mathew's eyes flicked from one to the other.

Knowing that there must be trouble involved for him to come home like this caused Robert's heart to beat faster. He felt the twinge and a slow beat.

Pleasantly he asked, 'What brings you home now? It's good to see you anyway.'

'Oh, I'd had enough of it over there.' Simon replied carelessly, knowing the full truth would probably come out when his father next spoke to Calloway. 'Is there any food? Is Nell here?'

'Yes, there's food in the scullery, a nice piece of pork Matthew brought over. Help yourself. Oh, you haven't met Dr Mason before, have you?'

'Pleased to meet you, Simon.'

Simon stared at a middle aged man with sharp blue eyes. He remembered his manners. 'How do you do, sir? Now who's going to put the horse away?'

Tom got up, 'It's time we were going, I'll do it on my way out.'

'No, Tom, thank you, Simon is already wet, he's perfectly capable. Simon, light a lantern and go and do what's necessary. Pick up that coat. Now.'

The boy glared at his father, mutiny in his face but Robert calmly stared him down.

Simon backed off. He needed his father's goodwill too much to annoy him further. With a disgruntled mutter about what were servants for he picked up his coat, trailing it along the floor and went out, leaving the door open and a draught coming in.

Matthew looked in concern at Robert's pale face. 'Are you feeling unwell?'

Robert summoned a smile, 'No I'm alright, I'm sorry the evening's had to end like this.'

The guests were moving to the door, Caleb had hold of Margie's arm but she turned to Robert and thanked him for a very pleasant evening.

Matthew waited until they had gone and then said, 'Look it makes it awkward for me to stay, I can be on my way now.'

'No, no need, you have Simon's room as we arranged. He can sleep with me. You never know, we might get to the bottom of this visit in the morning, although I'm not sure I want to hear. Now let's sort out candles. Would you like a nightcap? A tot of rum?'

Mathew laughed, 'I've had quite enough for tonight thank you, there's too many drunken doctors as it is.'

Robert walked through checking all was tidy. The doors were never locked. He left a large log on the fire in the hope that it would keep in for the morning and the door to the stairs open so that the warmth would rise and take the chill off the landing. In his bedroom he saw that Simon was just stripping off, leaving his clothes in a pile on the floor.

'Would you put your things tidily on the chair for now, you can wash in the bowl there.'

'I can't be bothered, I'm tired now.'

'Just do it, Simon.'

His son stared at him. He had never heard that tone of voice before, it was almost a mixture of wearisome defeat. Silently he grabbed his clothes, folded them quickly and stacked them on the chair.

'Shall I do yours, father?'

'They're done, let's get into bed. You blow out the candle.'

Robert relaxed into his bed, waiting for the bedclothes to warm through. It had been a happy day, but he was tired, very tired and now Simon was home, obnoxious as usual. He loved him, he always would, but oh dear...perhaps he was too old for all this.

There was a rustle in the bed and Simon said quietly, 'Good night, father, thank you for the money.'

CHAPTER THIRTY EIGHT

Robert rode over to Byclere two days later to offer Calloway greetings for the New Year. He found him in his office, sitting by a glowing coal fire with a mug of spiced wine.

'Come in, come in, here have a glass of this to warm you.'

Robert placed the bottle of Bergundy on the table that he had brought as a peace offering and accepted the glass tankard.

'Thank you, John, I wasn't sure of my welcome.'

'Hmm, that lad of yours…'

'What did he do?'

'He made a proposal to Lady Sophia, she laughed at him, told Verena who told her mother. Lady Marigold told her husband and Simon, by this time had turned sulky. He was rather impertinent and that was why he was turned out of the house on Christmas night. Have you brought the horse back?'

'Yes and a letter of apology for his Lordship. I'm at my wit's end with the boy. We've got him working hard today, he doesn't like it but I've warned him to mend his manners or he'll be out of school and working on the farm. If I have to stand over him with a whip. Shall I go up to the house and see his Lordship or give it to you to give him?'

'I'll keep it for him, he's gone back to London. It's all blown over. That Sophia is a tease, I think marriage is on the cards for that young lady. I'm afraid Simon won't be invited here for a while.'

'Good, perhaps that will make him think about his conduct. Now tell me did you have an enjoyable Christmas?'

They warmed their legs in front of the fire and sipped their drinks. Robert told him about Bayley's hens and how they were reading Robinson Crusoe at night. It was a pleasant way to end their day.

'He's a clever little artist, John. For his age he draws well. He's making drawings of the story as we go along.

'I've decided to get rid of the Jersey Bull. Much as he's good for the butterfat content of milk, he's no good as a beef cow. And he's dangerous, he nearly had the cowman yesterday.' Calloway topped up his hot wine.

'I know Jerseys are dangerous, I'm always impressed with the way Michael handles him.'

'Yes, well we're going to get a Red Poll and see how he turns out.'

'I haven't got a cow due until the spring, so you can tell me then how he's getting on.'

On the Friday after the New Year of 1816, Robert, Nell and Bayley sat close up on the dog cart and rattled along the road to Banbury market. They were using this because it had been decided that the Robert's cart would be too bumpy for Nell, in her delicate condition. The groom in charge of the carriages at Byclere house had willingly agreed to lend the cart to George Farthing and he had taken Binnie over the day before, riding her bareback, and brought her back with the cart. It was smaller and had a nicely sprung body with smartly painted red wheels.

Bayley was thrilled to be going. As luck would have it for him, Mr Noble was poorly with an ague so school was out. Now dressed warmly in Simon's old woollen coat, a flannel shirt that was warm but itchy, brown corduroy breeches and his new second hand boots, he sat between his Uncle and Nell. A blue woolly scarf tied round, kept his ears warm and small leather mittens lined with rabbit skin for toasty hands.

It was only just past seven o'clock and getting light enough to see the road. The riding lantern had been lit and they made a steady speed with Binnie knowing the way. The air was cold, with a fresh north westerly blowing and Robert had his old cloak tucked around him. Nell had on smart brown boots, a grey flannel skirt and warm, cream thick cotton blouse. Wrapped round her was a wool cloak Violet had brought down from London. It had the neatest soft brown fur collar that blended with the russet colour. She had given Violet a whole guinea for it having fallen instantly in love with it. Helen was smitten with jealousy and that pleased all the Bates women immensely. The hood was drawn up round her face and she felt cosy and so proud to have the dog cart arranged specially for her.

Caleb arrived early and harnessed Binnie to the cart left ready in the barn, loaded with butter and cheese.

Now, with the sky lightening rapidly they reached the out lying villages.

With the three of them working the stall was soon set out and serving early customers. Comments were made of the likelihood of snow with the wind from that quarter and everyone said they hoped it would hold off until the evening.

Just before twelve Nell went off to see Miss Smith, the lace maker. She took with her a rabbit and bacon pie, baked yesterday that would keep the old lady going for two or three days. She also had an order for lace from Byclere house with two shillings up front to purchase the necessary silks and cottons. She hoped the elderly lady would be pleased.

Bayley was in his element on the stall. Robert allowed him to serve the customers with small orders. Yesterday they had spent time before tea with the scales, cheese board and wire. Robert had shown Bayley how to weigh out two ounces of cheese and butter and the lad had then insisted on weighing out three portions of the best cheddar for their tea.

'I don't eat two ounces do I, Uncle?'

'No, try to cut an ounce.'

With his tongue between his teeth, concentrating hard Bayley looked at the cut pieces and worked out how much half would be. Carefully he pulled the wire and laid it on the scale pan.

'Oh, a bit over, shall I take it off?'

'No, you can eat that but if you do that tomorrow you have to ask the customer if they mind. Not only that you'll have to work out how much it would cost. We'll sit down now and write out prices.'

Robert fetched a sheet of paper and pencil. Only places like inns and shops purchased a whole cheese and not many families could buy more than a half pound of cheese in a week at a cost of one shilling and with butter to buy as well. Robert was again impressed at how quickly Bayley grasped the sums. Neatly he wrote out the prices: Butter: ¼lb = 3d. ½lb= 6d. 1 lb = 1s. Cheese was more expensive: ¼lb= 4½p. ½lb= 9d. 1lb = 1s.6d.

He had quickly got into the rhythm of it and on the stall he gave each customer such a bright and charming smile that small discrepancies were overlooked. His dark eyes in his open, cheery face won the hearts of the housewives and one or two even allowed him to keep the halfpenny change. They were also told of the forthcoming sale of his own hens' eggs. Robert watched with amusement as the good and sober ladies of Banbury succumbed to Bayley's charm.

As they were clearing up he became aware of a man on a large, black horse watching them, although he seemed to be looking carefully at Bayley. The man's hat was pulled down but Robert could see some long dark hair and that the clothes were of good quality with well polished riding boots. He thought vaguely that the man was familiar but dismissed it in the bustle of packing up. Bayley trotted off with Nell to have dinner with Miss Smith and Robert walked into the Red Lion.

Within five minutes he had a plate of roast beef dinner on the table. His stomach rumbled and he settled back in his chair feeling somewhat tired. John, the landlord brought him over a hot toddy and he sipped it, enjoying the spices.

Later, as he sat with a beaker of coffee, he had refused a plum pie pudding, the man he had noticed earlier watching them, came across the crowded room. Without his hat Robert could see him clearly and with a shiver of apprehension realised that he was looking at Bayley's father. He must be, but how or why he couldn't think. Bayley was the image of this man.

'Excuse me, Mr Southwell I believe.' The man bowed courteously.

'You have the advantage of me, sir.' Robert was cool.

'May I?' The stranger indicated a chair.

Robert nodded, waiting.

'My name is John Chadewick of Filstone Manor, three miles north of here. You I understand live on the south side two miles hence.'

'You know a lot about us, for strangers.'

'Yes, I have asked, there were plenty, free with their knowledge.'

'And why, sir?' Although Robert had a feeling he knew.

'The boy with you this morning, I was surprised, startled even to see someone who looks so close to my family.'

'He has parents, Mr Chadewick.'

'Of course, naturally. Might I be so bold as to ask in what...?'

'You would like to know who I am? Yes?'

'It's just that he is the image of us.'

'Yes I can see.' Robert couldn't deny that.

'What is his name, please?'

'Bayley James. His father was a rifleman with Lord Wellington, Bayley was another soldier he admired. His mother is Helen James, they have the Ewe and Lamb in Appley, but Bayley lives mostly with me, I have Appley Glebe farm, well, it's called Southwell's now. He should be in school today.' Robert felt he had told him quite enough. But it was what he had suspected for a long time, Ben was not the father and neither was Mark Calloway.

On a trip into Banbury Helen had gone with this man, close enough to pass him off at first as Ben's child. Now though, Ben and Helen had acknowledged that he was a cuckoo in their nest and had almost thrown him out, to live with Robert. He would tell Chadewick none of this.

'And you sir, I take it you did not suspect a lovechild's existence.'

Chadewick scowled, 'I think it was an hour's pleasure, bought with a half-guinea from a beautiful girl with silver hair. I can hardly remember it.'

'And do you have a family?'

'Three daughters, my wife died at the last childbirth and I seek no other, although plenty chase me.'

'My wife died after birthing our son.'

'You have a son, as well?'

'Simon is in school, here in Banbury.'

'You are fortunate, Mr Southwell.'

Robert eyed him narrowly. Surely the man would not be after Bayley, a bastard born of a quick tumble in a back room.

'I was impressed with his character this morning.'

'He is a quick, intelligent child. He loves the farm and the animals and we all love him dearly.' he added firmly.

'Of course, yes of course.' He saw Robert's cup was empty. 'May I order more coffee?'

'No, thank you, we must get home in the light, the weather could close in.'

Nell appeared in the doorway, waving to him. Bayley was at her side holding a roll of paper.

'Excuse me,' Robert stood, 'good day, Mr Chadewick.'

'Good day, Mr Southwell.'

Robert walked steadily to the door, aware of the man's eyes on him and the lad. Nell had taken in the situation at a glance. She put a hand on his arm.

'Not now, Nell,' he murmured, 'I'll tell you later.'

Bayley was chattering as they walked round to the mews to find Binnie and the dog cart. 'Look, Uncle, Miss Smith gave me this roll of wallpaper to draw on and Nell has bought me a brush and two colours. Blue and yellow, and do you know, I can mix them and then I get green. So I've really got three colours and I'm going to save my egg money and buy a red colour soon.'

Robert admired the elegant brush, wrapped in a twist of paper. He smiled at Bayley who chattered, oblivious to the tall, dark man who watched and listened from the corner of the mews.

'I must pay you for the paints, Nell.'

'It's nothing, Shipshape, Bayley's going to draw our cottage...aren't you?'

'Yes,' he piped up, 'and if I'm allowed, I'm going to paint Uncle George's greenhouse.'

Robert raised his eyebrows. 'That's very ambitious.'

'What's that?' said Bayley suspiciously.

'It might be difficult.'

'Well, it won't be until I've got more colours anyway, 'cos Uncle George has lots of flowers in there and I've only got these.'

'Are you set, Nell, we must get home, the sky looks a bit like snow to me.'

CHAPTER THIRTY NINE

In the short days of January, George came home early and both looked forward to a cosy evening together.

A fortnight later Nell had finished all her work by three. She hurried home to get their meal ready so that she could get on with sewing for the baby. The room was still warm as she took off her cloak. The log in the stove had burnt to ashes but she thrust in some kindling and flames caught the dry wood and flared up.

She placed the kettle on the top and once again blessed George for the stove's invention. Her saucepan of mutton shank, potatoes, carrots and an onion was cooked from the night before and she placed it on the heat. Within ten minutes it was simmering with some fragrant steam puffing out of the ill fitting lid. She laid the table and made a pot of tea. George came home to a very happy domestic scene.

'You look better, lass.' he commented as he sat opposite, blowing on his tea.

'I've seen the doctor.'

'Oh, who do you mean? That Mason chap, a friend of Shipshape's'.

'Yes, he called by this morning and Robert asked if he'd see me, because of this sickness you know. Anyway, he, no, well we went in the parlour...in case anyone came in the kitchen. I pulled down my skirt, modest like and he felt the bump with his fingers, ever so gentle and then he listened with that thing like a bit of a trumpet. Anyway he says I'm fine, the baby's well and I could try having a ginger cake in the morning and a pinch of ginger in some warm water, first thing like. That's supposed to help the sickness. It doesn't usually last this long.'

'That's good news that all's well and we'll try the ginger. I'll see Cook at the House if she could spare an ounce. I don't like seeing you so pale.'

'And he wouldn't charge, he is nice, quite old, but calm...and gentle.'

'I'll ask in the morning about the ginger and then perhaps Robert would buy some ginger cakes or spice in Banbury. Now, I'm famished in this cold weather, is that stew ready yet?'

January progressed into February and although bitterly cold there had been little snow. The fields were bleached by frost and the cows stood outside in the shelter of the barn, their breath huffing in misty spirals. Robert constructed a hay rack for them out of wood and sisal twine. It had been his idea after seeing all the waste when the hay was thrown on the ground.

He thought of all the hanging racks on board ship and with Tom's help made a frame. They then wove sisal twine across from side to side and end to end pulling it taut around nails. Placed on a low frame it was movable and Bayley enjoyed staggering out with bundles of hay to fill it up. He had filled his arms so full the night before that he had tripped and gone smack on the hard ground. The hay had saved his fall, cushioning his chin and face from damage. He shrieked with laughter but Robert paled at the sight, he could have broken a limb.

No word or sign had been seen of Chadewick but Robert couldn't stop fretting. It made him quiet and a little short tempered. Finally, after a particularly desultory conversation one breakfast time Caleb asked what was the matter.

'Is your chest bothering you, Boss?'

Nell was upstairs polishing, singing and lah lahing when she couldn't remember the words.

'What? No, that's been all right lately, the cold's in my shoulder a bit, but nothing to bother with.'

'My leg's giving me gyp, where I broke it, that Dr Mason says the rheumatics have gone in it. Clarrie's putting me some salve up to rub in. Oh sorry, Boss, what was you saying?' Tom interrupted slurping his tea.

'Well, it's not me I'm bothered about, it's Bayley.'

'The lad's happy as a sandboy, especially after this morning. He's tickled pink that hen of his is sitting on a clutch of eggs. Let's hope the weather is a bit warmer when they hatch in a few weeks time.' Caleb drained his tea. He thought he should be getting on but there was something in the air, they had all felt it.

'Well, it's like this, but keep it just with us. Nell knows 'cos she was there.'

Tom and Caleb shifted their chairs closer, as if to keep the words in the room.

'You know we've thought for a long time that Ben is not Bayley's father.'

They nodded, 'Yes.'

'We met a man in Banbury a few weeks ago, his name is Chadewick, he's the spitting image of Bayley. He introduced himself in the inn. I knew straight away. He said he just about remembered a quick tumble in a back room at the inn some years before, with a pretty silver haired girl. For a half guinea it was, it sounds like Helen, doesn't it. She does love the gew gaws and bits and bobs she buys. I think he wants to see him again, but I haven't heard anything.'

Caleb looked at him. They all loved Bayley but he knew how much the lad meant to Shipshape. For him, with his only daughter dead, there was no hope of grandchildren but with Bayley around it was like having an extra light on. The smiles and laughter, even the odd spit of temper seemed to bring the old farmhouse alive. Children made a big difference to your life, even if you only had a small share in them.

Tom harrumphed. 'Well, let's wait and see, shall we. Do you want him to have anything to do with Bayley?'

'No. But, he only has daughters, his wife is dead, and he has money. I've got a fear he'll want Bayley, even if he is a bastard.'

'The child's too young to leave his home. Perhaps when he's older, a lot older, something could be arranged. You can't be telling a five year old that his father isn't his father…can you?' Tom stood up, 'I mean, he thinks Ben is his father doesn't he, even though he lives here. Now, I must get those stalls cleaned out.'

'I'll be out with you in a minute.' Caleb put his hand on Robert's shoulder. 'Whatever you want, we'll be with you, we'll protect the lad, never fear.'

Robert looked troubled. 'Thank you, Cal.' but he stared glumly at the letter on the table.

He was in a quandary. Simon had written to say that his friends were arranging a walking holiday in North Wales at Easter and he wanted to go. He would need at least five guineas. Please let me know as soon as possible, he had written.

That was why they were drinking tea instead of coffee. Robert's first instinct was to say yes, he would take the money in to school next market day.

But he was having second thoughts. Why couldn't Simon save some money himself? He was having a good allowance every term. Robert thought of the two or three years of school left. Could he afford it? He hadn't known it would cost so much. There would have to be a compromise, he would give him two guineas and tell him to put the rest to it himself. No doubt there would be sulking and petulant temper. Well he would walk away from that. Robert had Bayley to think of now as well.

The meeting with Simon the following Friday took place in the Red Lion at lunch time. Robert told him to come alone, they would have their dinner and perhaps have a pleasant chat. He ordered a ham and egg pie for them both. A tankard of small ale for Simon was ready on the table as he came in. He was now a good looking young man, his school wear of black trousers and bottle green tail coat suited him and he turned heads.

They greeted each other carefully, 'Hello, Father, how are you?'

'We've all had colds and the cough but I'm over it.'

They tucked in to their dinner. 'How's the farm?'

'Pretty steady, thank you, we're looking forward to Spring.' Robert got his purse out. 'I'm sorry, Simon but I don't have more than two guineas for your holiday.' He placed them on the table and waited for the expected roar of outrage.

'I'll have to manage then, won't I. It won't be easy.' He pocketed the money knowing that he had got what he needed. Hugh Byclere had told him to always ask for more than you need, that way you got some, or all if you were lucky.

'You'll have to use some of your allowance. I can't spare anymore.'

They finished their meal in silence, Robert paid the bill and Simon hurried back to lessons.

As he walked to the stable he was accosted by a familiar voice.

He turned and saw John Chadewick walking towards him, a smile on his face.

'Mr Southwell, what a pleasure, how do you do?'

'Fine thank you, and you?'

'Oh good, very good. Did I see a young man with you? A very fine looking lad indeed.'

'Yes, my son, Simon, he's just gone back to school.'

'Would you share a pot of coffee with me?'

Robert hesitated, Chadewick saw it and said, 'It's a bit draughty here to talk, this March wind is straight from Siberia.'

Robert was wearing his old woollen gherkin under his coat, he hadn't felt the cold before but Chadewick's words did what the wind had failed to do.

'Yes, all right, but just briefly, I like to get home early.'

'Naturally. After me.' He gracefully waved an elegant arm to a small table with two chairs, placed by the fireplace that had miraculously, become vacant.

John Jones brought over a silver coffee pot with two cups of his best china, Demerara sugar and cream.

'How is Bayley? I must confess I've thought a lot about him.'

'He's fine, one of his hens has just had chicks so he's very pleased.'

They sipped the steaming coffee. Robert poured cream in to cool it down. He stirred in two spoons of sugar in defiance of Mathew's instructions to cut down.

'I should like to see him again.'

'He has a father in Appley, what can you tell him? He's too young to be upset by tittle-tattle about his parentage.'

'I know, I don't want that. Perhaps he could come in with you at Easter time, we could have luncheon here, I would say I was a friend of yours.'

'He goes to an old lady we know for his dinner. She dotes on him.'

'Well, invite her as well.' Chadewick responded waspishly.

Robert stood abruptly. 'I must get home. Good Friday market day, he'll want to come and help me. We'll be here at half past twelve for our dinners.'

Chadewick nodded, 'Thank you.'

Robert stalked out. The stable boy had Binnie and was standing at her head, the cart behind, all ready. Was that Chadewick's doing too?

Later that evening, when the house was quiet, Robert lit two candles and took out his journal. It had been a happy evening.

After their supper of muffins and preserve he read Robinson Crusoe to Bayley and Janey. They were at the exciting part where pirates had captured Robinson and taken him to the port of Sallee. They heard how he was looking after his master's garden and going out in a fishing boat with the slave Xury. The teenage girl and the young boy listened with rapt attention.

For Janey's benefit Robert showed them how 'Xury' was spelt. Using the paper he had had from Miss Smith, Bayley was drawing the story.

He started with a rather stick-like figure leaving home, with a pack on his back, then the terrible storms on the way to London and the shipwreck. Now they were at the port of Sallee on the coast of Africa and had to guess what the Moors looked like. This kept them entertained and Robert had to shoo Bayley up to bed and Janey back to the inn. He decided to try and buy a map of the Mediterranean and the Africas to teach the children some geography. He would ask in the bookshop in Banbury or perhaps Simon might have a spare one in school.

"I have seen Chadwick again today. We have arranged to meet on Good Friday after the market. I shall ask Miss Smith to have dinner with us. She is a pleasant woman and her presence will lighten the atmosphere. I spoke to a man at law about adopting Bayley. He said there should be no problem but it must have the consent of both parents. I think Ben and Helen will agree but it will cost me. I think they would sell to the highest bidder and I am sure Chadewick would pay more than me. I shall have to sell some of my London bonds."

He put his journal back and hid the key in a different place.

Printed in the United Kingdom by
Lightning Source UK Ltd., Milton Keynes
139785UK00002B/24/P